FIRST ENCOUNTER

Briana realized that he was very, very handsome. He was at least six feet tall, and sheathed in light buckskin; his long, muscular limbs and powerful chest magnificently revealed. His luxuriant hair was black as a raven's wing, his skin a smooth copper color. And there was a surprising gentleness in the depths of his dark, proud eyes.

"I am Night Hawk," he said, as his gaze roamed over Briana, her body slight and slender as a sapling, her features perfect, her delicate cheekbones blooming with color, her eyes blue as the sky. Her honey gold hair flowed from beneath her straw bonnet in soft swirls around her shoulders, and he ached to run his fingers through it, knowing that nothing could feel as fine.

D0829040

Cassie Edwards

Savage Touch

LEISURE BOOKS 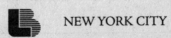 NEW YORK CITY

A LEISURE BOOK®

November 2007

Published by

Dorchester Publishing Co., Inc.
200 Madison Avenue
New York, NY 10016

ISBN 10: 0-8439-5887-1
ISBN 13: 978-0-8439-5887-4

Printed in the United States of America.

10 9 8 7 6 5 4 3 2 1

Visit us on the web at www.dorchesterpub.com.

A Warrior's Heart

White woman,
Can you not hear the faintness of heart crying in the wind?
Do you not see my eyes cascading upon your beauty?
You are the princess in the vision of all tomorrows.
Do you not know that I am without completion
If you do not become as one within my life circle?
The stars are naught but reflections of you.
How can this man in me endure, without the woman in you?
Do you not taste my tears?
Do you not feel this emptiness that divides us?
White woman,
I am truly haunted.
Can you not understand that it is only I who can love you?

—NICOLE R. JOHN

Savage Touch

1

I will be the gladdest thing under the sun,
I will touch a hundred flowers and not pick one.
I will look at cliffs and clouds
With quiet eyes.
—MILLAY

O-day-ee-min-ee-gee-zis, Strawberry Moon
Minnesota Territory, June 1857

The flames spread over the cabin like waves on an ocean, the fire coughing black belches of smoke into the sky, hiding the sun behind its death pall. Whooping and hollering, several Indians rode away on horseback into the early morning light, heavily laden with stolen firearms and ammunition.

A hawk hovered low over two bodies sprawled scalpless at the edge of the forest. Not so far from where they lay, the first shoots of corn sprouted from the rich black earth of an abandoned garden. . . .

At peace with herself and the world, having just finished what could be her favorite painting for her upcoming art showing at the St. Paul Art Museum, Briana Collins guided her horse and buggy carefully along the narrow forest path

Although the sun's rays shone like a tongue of flame among the stately Norway pines, the air was cool beneath the arch of trees. Briana's blue-and-white-striped floor-length sundress, worn over white cotton eyelet pantaloons and camisole, did little to ward off the chill. The straw bonnet perched upon her flowing honey gold hair gave her some comfort, as did her net gloves and cotton knit stockings.

9

The pure, sweet smell of the cedar and pine trees filled Briana with pleasure, and all around her the activities and songs of nuthatches, sparrows, wrens, and chickadees thrilled her with the wonderful sounds of nature.

Smiling, she thought of her productive day. She had found the perfect, serene spot for her latest painting. Ethereal blooms limned in muted watercolors were her secret pleasure, painted on her most restless evenings in the privacy of her bedroom. But on her outings, she chose to paint in oils, to recreate the soft, clear light of Minnesota. Through extensive study and practice, Briana had developed the subtle palette and delicate brushwork that had made her reputation as one of America's most promising young painters.

Snapping her horse's reins, Briana urged him into a gallop as they broke from the trees into open land. The buggy carried her across a meadow of softly blowing grasses and wildflowers that turned their colorful faces toward the warmth of the afternoon sun. She held her chin high and her blue eyes sparkled as she considered her chosen profession, and what a commotion her work had already caused. Most American painters celebrated the beauty of European cities and landscapes. Most Americans saw little subject matter of artistic merit in their own country, and didn't care to depart from traditional themes.

Briana considered her decision to paint her homeland a worthy and patriotic gesture, but it was seen as an act of artistic rebellion, a challenge to the artistic establishment of America. She was devoted to promoting greater appreciation of American art in her own country, trying to overcome the prevailing preference for all things European.

Briana had studied in New York, and when her

parents moved to Paris to establish their permanent residence, she spent two years studying in Paris's finest art academies. But she had missed her homeland, its grandeur . . . its wonders!

When her Uncle Arden invited her to live with him, she grabbed the chance, even though she knew that his reasons for having her there were selfish ones. Surely having a niece of Briana's talent to brag about and to show off at his political rallies would draw more attention to himself and his aspiring political career.

"Blackie," she whispered, her eyes dancing. "Governor Blackie Collins."

She laughed aloud, throwing her head back so that her laughter wafted across the land like a melody.

In the far distance, the dome of the capitol building rose grandly and statuesquely over the frontier city of St. Paul.

"No," she murmured to herself, "my uncle would not want to be known as Blackie by his constituents." The name Blackie had a less than sterling reputation, but she had known him for so long as Blackie, she found it hard to think of him as Uncle Arden.

Yet she must. He now insisted that she address him only by the name Arden while in public.

Briana's thoughts were jolted from her uncle as she was thrown violently sideways and her buggy came to a sudden, pitching halt.

Caring more for her paint paraphernalia and the treasured painting that was still drying on canvas than her own well-being, Briana looked quickly over her shoulder. Upon discovering that she had secured everything well enough, and that her painting had not been smeared in the mishap, she sighed with relief and turned back to the problem at hand.

Letting the reins go slack against the seat of her

buggy, Briana slid to the ground and walked slowly around the buggy until she found the cause for the delay.

"Oh, no," she groaned, bending over the wheel that had fallen into what appeared to be a gopher hole.

She spread the knee-high grasses to get a better look, to see just how locked the wheel was in the dreadful hole. She quickly realized that she was helpless in the dilemma. The depth of the hole covered half the wheel. She did not have the muscle required to lift it back to level ground.

The sun was beating down on Briana, making her wish that she was back beneath the cool umbrella of trees in the forest. Turning, momentarily resting her back against the buggy, she wiped a bead of perspiration from her brow.

Suddenly her heart stood still, her throat went dry. A lone rider was approaching her from the distance. Alarm filled her as she realized how foolish she had been for leaving home without the protection of a firearm. She had been so anxious to be on her way, to enjoy her day of painting in the wilds of the forest, she had simply forgotten.

"White Wolf . . ." she whispered aloud, dread creeping over her. She now realized by the color of the approaching man's skin, and the clothes he wore, that the lone rider was an Indian. Her uncle had spoken of the renegade Sioux, White Wolf, and how, after many years in hiding, he was on the warpath once again. There had been several raids on settlers these past months. The first man to be suspected was White Wolf, for the soldiers at Fort Snelling were all familiar with this Indian's ruthless reputation. Never in the history of the Minnesota Territory had there been an Indian as elusive and as deadly as White Wolf.

Oh, Lord, Briana wondered with despair. How can I have been such a fool?

Having no choice but to stand her ground, she watched the Indian with unwavering eyes of courage as he came closer on a beautiful white-faced bay with white hind legs.

When the brave got close enough for her to see his face, she exhaled a quivering sigh of relief. This was not White Wolf. The renegade Sioux that everyone dreaded was an Indian well along in years. The Indian brave approaching her was much younger, perhaps somewhere in his mid- or late twenties.

As he came to a halt beside her, she realized, with her heart skipping a beat, that he was strikingly handsome. He was at least six feet tall and sheathed in a light buckskin garment which revealed the shape of his lean, muscular limbs and powerful chest. He had long, luxurious hair as black as a raven's wing, and wore a fillet of beads at his brow to keep his hair in place. His skin was a smooth copper, and there was a surprising gentleness in his dark, proud eyes.

It was this that Briana's heart answered to, making her trust him immediately.

"Hello," she said, extending a polite gloved hand to the brave. "My name is Briana. And you are?"

Amazed to find a white woman unescorted and so far from St. Paul, Night Hawk was almost too in awe of her to speak.

Then he recalled his father's tales by the evening fires about Night Hawk's pale-skinned mother, Mariah, having been daring in her youth—as carefree and courageous, it seemed, as this woman.

And, he thought, as his eyes roamed over Briana,

she is so *mee-kah-wah-diz-ee*, so beautiful! Her voice was like the cooing of a dove, her body as slight and slender as a sapling. She had perfect features, delicate cheekbones blooming with color, thick golden lashes, and sky blue eyes as big, round, and soft as a doe's.

His gaze drifted to her honey gold hair that flowed from beneath her straw bonnet in soft swirls around her shoulders. He wanted to reach out and run his fingers through it, knowing that surely nothing could feel as fine to the touch.

"*Boo-shoo*, hello," he blurted, accepting her offer of friendship, eagerly wrapping his fingers around her small hand. "Night Hawk. I am called Night Hawk, the son of Chief Echohawk."

His solid grip and piercing eyes warmed Briana inside and caused a strange sort of weakness in the pit of her stomach that she had never before experienced in the presence of a man. Despite her various escorts both in Paris and St. Paul, it was not until she had touched Night Hawk that her pulse raced with such alarming speed.

She knew this handsome Indian brave was of Chippewa descent. Chief Echohawk was known for his gentle ways and considerate leadership. Surely the son must be the same, made in his father's image.

And she was not at all surprised that he spoke the English language so fluently. Everyone who knew of Echohawk also knew of his white wife, Mariah—Night Hawk's mother.

"It is very nice to make your acquaintance," Briana finally managed, blushing, keenly aware of the admiration in Night Hawk's eyes as they swept over her again.

She slipped her hand from his and nervously twined her fingers together behind her. Suddenly the woman who spoke her mind at any cost was at a loss for words.

Night Hawk slid easily from his saddle and stood towering over Briana. "It is *mah-nah-dud* to be alone away from the city," he observed, his eyes narrowing down into hers. "Your parents? Your husband? They allow this?"

She puzzled over the Indian word that he had used, but she was certain it was a word meant for scolding, as his tone implied.

"I am not married and my parents do not know my every move," she said in defense, her upper lip stiffening. "In fact, they only know my activities by way of letters. They live in Paris. I am living temporarily with my uncle in St. Paul."

"It is your uncle who is the foolish one, then," Night Hawk again chided, walking away from her to bend beside the lodged wheel. He ran his hands over the wheel as he studied it, then stood to his full height and turned to her.

"You can soon be on your way," he said, their eyes locking, stirring his heart to a strange sort of throbbing. This was not usual for him when he was in the presence of a woman—any woman. He had never allowed himself to feel many emotions toward any one woman; his life was too full to want such interferences.

"Think twice before heading out alone again," he continued. "There are those along the trail who will not be as kind as I. Remember that, and live longer for it."

"I was foolish only in that I forgot to bring a firearm for protection," Briana answered, whipping the skirt of her dress around her and going to stand beside Night Hawk as he bent to lift the wheel from the hole. She could not help but admire the muscles of his shoulders and upper arms that were flexing powerfully as he managed quite easily to get the wheel back on level ground.

Night Hawk rose to his full height and wiped the dirt from his hands on his fringed buckskin breeches. "Let me escort you on to St. Paul," he said, his gaze rediscovering the sweetness of her lips, the softness in her eyes, and creaminess of her flesh. He could hardly repress the desire to take her in his arms and kiss her, with her lips only a heartbeat away, so tempting, so alluring.

It seemed to Night Hawk that he had been taken as quickly by a white woman as his father had those many years ago. He did not see any wrong in such feelings, perhaps only a bit *gee-wah-neh-dis*, foolish! It was apparent that this was a woman of purpose, and that she would not have time for a Chippewa brave. She surely would only allow one passion in her life. He had seen the painting in the back of the buggy and could tell by the feelings transferred to canvas that this painting was that passion. Seeing this had made him realize that no matter how many times he scolded her for being away from the city, she would not be able to resist the beauty of the forest which supplied her heart and soul with ideas for her art.

Somewhere in that knowing there was a reason for being pleased—for was he not a man of the forest? Somehow, whenever possible, he would try to protect her from the likes of White Wolf.

"I appreciate your kind offer," Briana said, becoming unnerved by Night Hawk and the way he continued to look at her, as though his eyes were branding her. She could not deny that this made her feel sweet inside, and she could not help but greedily absorb the sight of him also. In all of her fantasies she had never felt as alive as now. And even as he bent slowly over her, his hands softly clasping her waist to draw her near, she could not speak against it.

She melted against his broad chest when his tongue brushed her lips lightly, and he pressed his mouth softly against hers.

His touch was scorching!

Her heart threatened to beat out of control!

She began to push herself away, but not because of being kissed by this extraordinary man, but because she heard the thundering of an approaching horse.

Easing away from Night Hawk, her lips parted and eyes wide, Briana stared up at him momentarily, her knees scarcely holding her up.

When she turned away from him at last, a sudden panic rose within her when she recognized the bulky shape of her Uncle Blackie riding toward her like all hell and brimstone had been set free on this earth.

She covered her tingling lips with her hand, wondering if Blackie had seen her in the gentle embrace of Night Hawk. If so, she knew what to expect. He did not hide the fact that he hated Indians. He had spoken openly against Chief Echohawk, when everyone else had nothing but praise for the gentle chief. If her uncle knew this was Echohawk's son, all the freedoms she enjoyed would be put to a stop. He might even place guards at her door, all hours of the night and day! She knew that he felt responsible for her welfare, but sometimes he carried his guardianship just a mite too far.

Trying to put Night Hawk momentarily out of her mind, Briana lifted her chin stubbornly and faced her uncle as his black stallion wheeled to a halt before her. She shuddered when she saw that her Uncle Blackie's attention was fixed fiercely on Night Hawk.

At first glance it seemed that they knew each other,

as both men exchanged looks that were filled with a fiery hatred. Sadness surged through Briana. She feared that her uncle would create problems for her and this handsome Indian brave whom she felt certain was meant to be a part of her life.

2

I'll tell you how the sun rose—
A ribbon at a time.
—DICKINSON

Briana looked guardedly from her uncle to Night
Hawk, and back again to her Uncle Blackie. Having
never truly seen the dark side of her uncle, only having heard from close friends that he had not always
maintained the cool composure he displayed in public,
a shiver raced across her flesh. His eyes were filled
with silent rage as he slipped down from his saddle to
place a possessive arm around her waist, never taking
his eyes off Night Hawk.

Attired in fawn-colored trousers, a black coat, black
satin vest, and a black cravat on his high shirt collar,
and with his black hair slicked down, except for his
bushy, broad side whiskers, Blackie looked like the
man of prominence he had become after marrying a
woman of wealth and standing in the community many
years ago. His marriage seemed to have transformed
him overnight from a riverboat gambler and man of
ill repute, having once aligned himself with renegades
and highwaymen, to a man with aspirations in politics.

Since the death of his pretty Agnes five years ago,
he had become driven even more energetically than
before to his work, his ambitions taking the place of
his lovely wife.

Briana wanted so badly to look past the dark side
of her uncle, and admire the part of him that had
become respectable. His heart was set on winning the
governorship of Minnesota one day, but he was happy

enough now with the prospect of becoming a congressman for this territory that soon would be a state.

"Briana, after making my rounds of campaigning
today, I found you gone when I returned home. I've
been looking for you for hours," Blackie said, his
voice steady, his eyes still locked with Night Hawk's.
"And I find you here. With an injun. What do you
have to say for yourself?"

"This is Night Hawk," Briana said, smiling weakly
at the handsome Chippewa brave as he gave her a
quick glance and focused his attention on Blackie
again. She had not missed the gleam of a pistol beneath the flap of her uncle's coat as the wind momentarily whipped at its corner.

"I have been on an outing, painting," she said cautiously. "I was on my way home when . . ."

She paused, exasperated that her uncle only seemed
to hear half of what she said, his gaze still intent on
Night Hawk.

"Uncle Arden, Night Hawk came to my rescue,"
she persisted more loudly, trying to keep from showing her anger at her uncle's attitude toward the kind
Chippewa brave. "Uncle Arden, the buggy wheel became lodged in a hole. If not for Night Hawk—"

"Night Hawk?" Blackie said, interrupting her as he
glared even more heatedly at the Indian, recognizing
the name, knowing who his father was. He could not
help but recall with much bitterness the humiliation
Echohawk had caused him on a riverboat many years
ago.

Blackie remembered quite clearly that first time he
had encountered Chief Echohawk on an excursion to
Saint Louis. Blackie had not been able to stop himself
from taunting the Chippewa chief over wearing eyeglasses—a strange sight, to say the least.

And Blackie had also taken great delight in tor-

menting Mariah, a white woman, for being Echohawk's traveling companion, having gone so far as to
call her a whore.

Echohawk had reached the limits of his endurance
then and wrestled Blackie to the floor. When Blackie
drew his knife in defense, Mariah hit him over the
head with a whiskey bottle, rendering him unconscious.

On the return journey to Minnesota, Blackie had
tried to avenge his earlier humiliation by cornering
Echohawk, but he was too quick and was soon holding
Blackie by his heels over the ship's railing, threatening
to drop him into the cold, muddy water.

The incident ended when Blackie was incarcerated
on the riverboat like a common criminal. Eventually,
he had managed to escape.

It was many years later, but the humiliation Blackie
had suffered then had not diminished.

He had not pursued his revenge only because he
had met his beloved Agnes shortly after that incident
on the riverboat. She had become his life—and then
politics. Echohawk had been the last thing on his
mind, until now.

"Night Hawk?" he said again, this time through
clenched teeth. "The half-breed who mingles with the
whites in town, as though he's one of them? Once I'm
congressman for this proud land, I'll do something
about that. An Indian has no place among whites!"

Briana stepped back from her uncle, dislodging his
arm from around her waist. She paled as she stared
disbelievingly at him. She had heard his bigoted re-
marks against the Indians in conversations with other
politicians, but never had she seen him act this way
before her very own eyes.

It was embarrassing!

So much so that she could hardly stand there with
him, claiming to be his kin.

She finally found the composure to speak again. "Uncle Arden, I believe you owe Night Hawk an apology," she said, her eyes squinting angrily into her uncle's. "He—he does not deserve such unkindness!"

Blackie's cruel mouth twisted into a grin. "Just because his mother is white makes him no better than the rest of the Injuns who beg for handouts day in and day out at Fort Snelling," he said, slipping his hand beneath his coat, resting it on the pistol thrust into the waistband of his trousers. "An Injun is an Injun. They are all liars, beggars, and scalp takers."

Briana gasped and looked guardedly over at Night Hawk, seeing a seething hatred in the depths of his dark eyes. She was amazed at how he could possess the restraint to just stand there and let this man talk down to him.

Yet she was proud of Night Hawk for having the willpower not to lash out at her uncle. The Chippewa brave knew the dangers in speaking out against a white man of Arden Collins's standing in the community. He did not want his careless actions to cause his people harm.

The word of a man as politically powerful as her uncle would always be believed over an Indian's, even if the Indian was the son of the most respected chief in the region.

Briana felt helpless. She could not offer more assistance to this handsome Indian whose lips had stirred passion deeply within her. Her heart cried out to him. Her body longed for his touch in ways she did not understand.

Night Hawk doubled his hands into tight fists at his sides and had to restrain himself from wrapping his fingers around the smug politician's throat. He wanted to show him exactly what this Chippewa brave was capable of doing to such an arrogant and merciless man who was driven by ambition and who would let nothing stand in his way of becoming a congressman.

Night Hawk had found many friends among the white community, and he tried to understand men like Arden Collins. He knew Arden was called Blackie among those who frequented the back rooms of saloons and gambling halls. They laughed at the pompous man who had been no better than a snake in his younger years.

The hardships and perils of the raw frontier seemed to repel men of culture and sensitivity, Night Hawk thought bitterly. For the most part, the territories attracted misfits. The ignorant and the bigoted, like Arden Collins, were the ones who flocked to this land of sky blue waters to steal from the original people— the Indians!

This man standing before Night Hawk was like so many others, the brave continued to ponder. Arden Collins had more ambition than ability *or* sense. It was his type who were most frequently elevated by necessity to offices of responsibility that they were totally unfit to hold.

They were the men most frequently responsible for the shameful massacres and inhumane treatment of the red man.

Night Hawk, for the first time in his life, felt the savage instinct to murder a man, and this troubled him more than the man and his ugly words. He gave Briana a troubled gaze, pitying her for being kin to such a black-hearted man, then spun around on a heel and mounted his horse in one leap, riding away in a hard gallop.

Night Hawk's heart pounded. He wondered how he could ever find a way to see this woman again, whose fiery spirit and big, soft eyes had stirred passions deeply within him.

He knew that her uncle would try to keep them apart.

He smiled to himself, sensing that nothing would keep Briana from the delights of the forest.

Gah-ween-geh-goo, nothing!

"Or from my beckoning arms," he said, shouting to the heavens. "She will be my *ee-quay*, woman. She will be mine!"

Then he frowned, knowing that some day something would have to be done about Blackie. The Chippewa had been tolerant of him and his kind for much too long already.

He flicked his reins and sank his moccasin heels into the flanks of his horse and turned him away from the direction of the city, no longer in the mood to seek out friends in St. Paul.

He needed to be alone.

He needed time to think.

Briana stomped to her buggy and pulled herself up onto the seat. "What you did today is unpardonable, Uncle Arden," she said, glaring at his unwavering eyes as he came and stood beside the buggy. "How could you? Night Hawk did you no harm. And he was quite a gentleman to me. If not for him, I could have been stuck here all night! What then, Uncle Arden? Would you rather I be food for wolves or bears? Or— or even be left to the mercy of that renegade Sioux, White Wolf?"

"You wouldn't have been stuck anywhere," Blackie said, trying to take her hand, flinching when she jerked it away. "I came for you. I would have gotten the wheel out of the hole. You didn't need that Injun."

Briana's eyes filled with rage. "There!" she cried. "You did it again. Did you hear what you said? You do not even have the decency to call Night Hawk an Indian. You have to refer to him as an Injun. That's disgusting. Do you hear? Disgusting. Next you'll call him a savage, and, Uncle Arden, he is anything but a savage."

Blackie arched a thick black eyebrow. "Oh?" he said, clasping his hands tightly behind him. "You were with him long enough to know that much about him?"

Her face flooded with color, recalling the kiss shared with Night Hawk. Still not sure if her uncle had witnessed it, Briana looked away from him. She picked up her reins and rested them on her lap, afraid to speak, fearing that she would reveal too many feelings that were washing through her. Already her knees grew weak and her heart began a strange sort of thudding just remembering his lips on hers.

Her uncle could never know that Night Hawk had that sort of effect on her. She was afraid of what her uncle was capable of doing.

She looked warily at him, wondering just how safe she was living with him. Little by little she was witnessing the side of him that made her afraid.

"Briana, I think it's time to get a few things straight between us," Blackie declared, sensing her hesitation in answering him. "This is not Paris. You are not with your doting parents who spoiled you outrageously. You are my responsibility now, at least as long as I am your appointed guardian so you must do as I say"

He paused and took a step closer, leaning into her face so that she could not help but look him squarely in the eye. "Do I make myself clear?" he growled. "Do you understand?"

Briana stiffened. She had no intention of being trapped. If she wished, she could flee back to Paris tomorrow.

But now, in addition to her love of painting this

beautiful land, she had another reason for wanting to stay.

She had to see Night Hawk again!

Yet how could she tolerate living under her uncle's strict regimen? How could she stand living with this man who had proven to her that he was little more than an ignorant bigot? How could this man be her wonderful father's brother?

Yet they were brothers, and respect for her uncle was expected of her, for this was what her father would want. And she did appreciate her uncle having taken her in.

"I understand, Uncle." She paused, then leaned farther into his face and said, "Blackie."

She flicked her reins and sent her buggy racing across the flower-spotted meadow. Smiling, she realized that she could not help but call her uncle the name that fitted him best.

Respect her uncle?

Perhaps.

Sometimes.

She would pretend.

Sometimes.

Briana stiffened when she heard her uncle's horse fast approaching her from the rear. When he began shouting at her, his words pierced her heart.

"I forbid you ever to leave St. Paul again to do your damnable paintings!" he shouted. "I forbid you ever to see that damn injun again. Do you hear? Forbid!"

Briana bit her lower lip with frustration and her eyes burned with tears. Never in her life had anyone refused her anything, for she had never been selfish.

Nor was she now.

She would not let her uncle rule her life!

When he rode up beside her, she ignored him. But she could feel his cold, steely gaze on her, sending currents of dread and foreboding throughout her body.

The sun was casting its last rays of light through the leaves of the birch trees. Night Hawk was following the Mississippi River through the forest, having learned long ago this was the quickest route to his village. He was troubled, but was distracted by another object of concern when he spied Chief Strong Branch and a number of Chippewa braves just up ahead, also following the course of the river toward their home.

Before letting Strong Branch and his braves discover his presence, Night Hawk fell back and urged his horse into a soft canter. He watched Strong Branch from a fair distance, having only recently begun to suspect him of dirty dealings, but not knowing with whom. Except in the presence of his friend, Gray Moon, Strong Branch's attitude had become haughty, self-assured, and cold, while in the past he had been humble and a kind leader of his people.

Of late, it seemed to Night Hawk that Chief Strong Branch wanted more: he wanted leadership of all the Chippewa. If he succeeded, Echohawk would no longer be chief. Strong Branch, the son of the dearly departed Nee-kah and Chief Silver Wing, was now the chief of his people. Before reaching adulthood, he had relinquished his claim on this leadership to Echohawk, who had, upon the request of Chief Silver Wing on his deathbed, accepted the duties of leading both Chief Silver Wing's people and his own. But that had been many years ago, when Strong Branch was just a child. Now he was a man.

Until recently Strong Branch had even been Night Hawk's closest friend and ally, and Night Hawk had given him the right hand of his heart.

But envy and greed had changed that. Strong Branch no longer wanted to share this leadership with Echohawk, who remained the main voice of both their peoples. And he certainly did not wish to share leadership of two bands of Chippewa with young Night Hawk upon the death of Echohawk.

Strong Branch's plans were to take over all of this leadership, Night Hawk realized, but he did not know how or when, which made him uneasy in the company of this Chippewa whom he no longer considered a friend.

Worried, Night Hawk wanted to get to his village, to be at peace with himself in the privacy of his wigwam. He needed to devise a way to see Briana again—without having to shoot her uncle first. Night Hawk thrust his heels into the flanks of his horse and rode ahead, drawing the reins when he reached Strong Branch. They exchanged fierce glances. Night Hawk was the first to speak.

"So, Strong Branch, where have you been with Gray Moon and so many other braves?" Night Hawk asked, his voice taut with suspicion he hoped he had not revealed. He looked warily at Gray Moon, who rode at Strong Branch's right side, then glanced over his shoulder at the braves who followed, most of them friends who were slowly turning into his enemies, thanks to Strong Branch.

"My *bay-bay-shee-go-gah-shee*, horse, is not lathered too much, would you say?" Strong Branch said, glowering at Night Hawk.

"That does not mean you have not ridden far today," Night Hawk said, glowering back at him. "What, but the *gee-wee-sayn*, hunt, takes you from your people for days at a time, Strong Branch? You are their *chee-o-gee-mah*. A chief does not go wandering all over the countryside, unless there is a good reason. What is your reason, Strong Branch? Or do you dare tell me?"

Strong Branch's dark eyes matched the midnight dark of Night Hawk's, and his features were as genuinely Chippewa as Night Hawk's. Yet Strong Branch was leaner, even taller in stature, and less muscular. He had a sour, pinched look which revealed his less generous nature.

The small scars on Strong Branch's body proved that he was also more warring than Night Hawk, always ready to skirmish with anyone, for any reason.

"You are not my *gah-nah-wayn-dun*," Strong Branch said, bitterly. "Nor are you anyone's keeper. You are not even chief of your people yet."

Strong Branch chuckled, his eyes flashing fire as he looked even more intensely at Night Hawk. "Your father is an old man, yet he still does not die," he taunted. "You will never be chief, Night Hawk. You will always only be a *nin-gwis*, son, answering to a *gee-bah-bah*, father. Do you not feel just a little bit *wah-yay-szhim*, cheated, Night Hawk?"

"Strong Branch, you are a young man, a youthful leader of your people, yet you speak with the tongue of one who is old and *mah-shee-po-gwud*, bitter, with life," Night Hawk said, holding back the words that he truly wanted to say yet would surely regret. "Why is that, Strong Branch? Once you and I were inseparable. We enjoyed the hunt. We enjoyed the secrets of *nee-gees*, friends. There are no more hunts. But there are many secrets, and none are shared between us. What do you hide within your heart that you cannot tell me?"

"What do you hide in *your gee-day*?" Strong Branch challenged. "You are friends with too many white people. That is *mah-nah-dud*, bad, for the Chippewa!"

"You speak of false friendship with white people,

yet you have confessed to loving my sister, Lily, whose skin is as white as alabaster," Night Hawk chided.

"Her skin is white, but her heart, her very soul, is Chippewa!" Strong Branch hissed between tight lips. "Her white mother is the only reason her skin is white."

"You say you look past my sister's white skin, yet you have yet to marry Lily," Night Hawk pressed.

"When I marry Lily is of no concern of yours," Strong Branch said sourly. He flicked his reins and rode on ahead of Night Hawk, who soon caught up and rode beside him again.

"Leave me in peace," Strong Branch said flatly. "If I wanted your company, I would request it."

"You have it without the request," Night Hawk said, laughing lightly. "Old friend, soften your mood. Let us talk as we once did. Tell me, what has taken you from your village today?"

Strong Branch challenged him with a set stare. "What has taken you from yours?" he questioned, his lips curling into a sly grin. "From a distance, I believe I saw you with a white woman. You were giving her assistance. You even kissed her. Do you not realize that one day the white people will send the Chippewa from Minnesota, as they did the Sioux? Then will you defend them? Where is your loyalty to your people, Night Hawk? As I see it, there is none."

"The 'enemy people,' the Sioux, were chased from this land by the white pony soldiers *and* the Chippewa because they were snakes in the grass who killed innocent people, both red- and white-skinned alike," Night Hawk defended. "The Chippewa can never be accused of such unjust actions. They will be a part of Minnesota's history until the end of time. *Ah-pah-nay*, forever!"

Strong Branch frowned, but said no more. He and

Night Hawk had not seen eye to eye on many things for a long time now, and Strong Branch felt superior enough not to care. He was the chief of his band of Chippewa. Night Hawk was only the son of a chief.

Strong Branch smiled to himself, knowing that one day both Night Hawk and Echohawk would no longer be in the way of his idea of progress.

Feeling uneasy, Night Hawk rode away, realizing that his friend was no longer someone he knew.

Strong Branch needed to be watched. How shameful for the son of the late, peace-loving chief, Silver Wing, who had sought friendship with everyone, using the word *enemy* only when referring to the Sioux.

Gray Moon rode up to take his place at Strong Branch's side. They exchanged troubled looks.

"Gray Moon, do you think Night Hawk knows more about our activities than he says aloud?" Strong Branch asked, his dark eyes searching Gray Moon's.

"My friend, only time will tell," Gray Moon said solemnly. "Night Hawk was never someone to be taken lightly."

Strong Branch nodded. "*Ay-uh*, that is so," he mumbled. "That is so."

3

Now summon the red current to thine heart—
Old man, thy mightiest woe remains to tell.
—ANONYMOUS

Sitting tall on his mighty steed, Night Hawk rode into his village. It had been constructed in the image of the other Chippewa village near the outskirts of his own. Many moons ago, two chiefs had brought their people together as one heart, mind, and soul. Chief Silver Wing and Chief Echohawk had been brought together by Chief Echohawk's chieftain father, Gray Elk, when his people had fallen on hard times and sought help from his old friend, Silver Wing.

From that time on, the two bands of Chippewa had shared everything—laughter as well as pain.

Night Hawk's village sat serenely beside the Mississippi River, shaded by many tall oak, elm, and cottonwood trees with their leaves rustling in the breeze. He was proud to be a part of this land, and of these people. He surveyed his village, made up of a number of wigwams which were built on a framework of poles and saplings covered with the most suitable material the Chippewa could find in this beautiful land of sky blue waters.

Horses grazed at the far edges of each village. Gardens prospered. The people were content—the women moving to and fro, performing their daily chores, while the elderly braves sat amongst themselves beside the large, communal outdoor fire, sharing their long-stemmed calumet pipes and tales of long ago.

Night Hawk reined up beside his parents' wigwam and dismounted. A young brave dressed in only a breechclout scampered over to him, eager to help, to please. Night Hawk handed his reins to the lad. He smiled at the boy.

Ay-uh, to Night Hawk it was the best of times. All that was lacking in his life, it seemed, was a woman to warm his bed at night. Until now he had not thought much about it. He had busied his mind and hands while walking in his father's shadow, readying himself for the day when he would become the chief of their people.

Night Hawk's future *was* his people.

Yet he could not be expected to deny himself the pleasures of a wife. Had not his father reigned proud and sure with a woman at his side?

He could even remember times when his mother had helped his father with crucial decisions.

Night Hawk lifted the entrance flap to his parents' wigwam. The first person he saw was his mother, and a deep sadness engulfed him. Though she had been a strong force in the Chippewa village in the past, this was no longer so. Called No-din by his father, which meant "Woman of the Wind," and Mariah by the white community, his mother's skin was no longer the beautiful white of her youth. Now it was gray from a long, lingering illness.

Before going to the fire to sit among his loved ones, Night Hawk studied his mother a moment longer. Although she was busying herself close beside the fire, sewing beads onto a moccasin, he could tell by the trembling of her fingers that even this small chore had become almost too much effort for her.

His pitying gaze swept over her, seeing how her red hair no longer had a lustrous glow but hung limply over her frail shoulders. And having lost so much weight, her buckskin dress almost seemed to swallow her whole.

Her skin was drawn tautly across her face—a face that at one time had been so beautiful that Night Hawk had loved just watching her, so proud to boast of his *gee-mah-mah*.

He was as proud now. Yet he was troubled by how she continued to waste away from recurring bouts of malaria. The fevers sapped her strength, and sometimes even her will to live.

Standing in the shadows, still unnoticed by his family, Night Hawk's gaze moved to his *gee-bah-bah*, father.

The powerful, cherished, peace-loving Chief Echohawk.

Night Hawk's anxieties mellowed, as always, at the sight of his beloved father. He had been the best of teachers, as well as a friend *and* father. A man who knew how to guide with gentle words and his own example, Echohawk stood tall among his people as well as his family.

Night Hawk smiled, so very proud of his father of sixty winters who was still muscular and virile. Only a trace of wrinkles on his brow and around his eyes betrayed his age. Only a thread or two of gray wove through his thick, shoulder-length black hair.

Night Hawk's smile faded as he saw his father's glance settle sadly on his mother. There was something in the depths of his father's eyes that revealed a lonesomeness that Night Hawk understood, although it had never been spoken aloud between father and son. Night Hawk knew that his mother no longer warmed his father's bed at night. Being ill for so long had caused her to lose her desire of the flesh, it seemed.

Night Hawk had expected his father to take another

wife long ago, yet Echohawk had remained faithful to his No-din.

Night Hawk noticed how his father's attention had turned to his daughter, Lily. His pride was quite evident as he watched her beading a doeskin robe.

"Night Hawk!" Mariah said, suddenly noticing him standing in the shadows. She lay her beadwork aside and rose unsteadily to her feet. She began walking slowly and shakily toward Night Hawk. "*Nin-gwis*, son, how long have you been standing there in the shadows?"

When she reached him, she stood on tiptoe and kissed him softly on the cheek, then ran her thin fingers over his smooth copper face, always relishing her son's extraordinary handsomeness. She did not know how much longer she would be alive for such enjoyments. Every time she became ill with the fever, more and more of her strength was drained away. Even now it took much effort to stand, her knees almost buckling beneath her as she tried to look strong in her son's eyes.

"I only just arrived, *gee-mah-mah*," Night Hawk answered, folding his arms around his mother, hugging her gently to him.

Mariah enjoyed the warmth of the hug, then stepped away from Night Hawk and looked up into his midnight dark eyes. "Surely you have not been to Fort Snelling and back so soon," she questioned. "I expected you to spend the night away from the village. What caused you to return so soon? Did you run into difficulties? There are many rumors about White Wolf being in the area, stirring up problems with the settlers. You know how he would love to bring grief to our Chippewa people."

Echohawk looked up quickly at the mention of the Sioux. "White Wolf?" he said, laying his calumet pipe aside. "What about him? *Nin-gwis*, did you come across White Wolf while on your journey to Fort Snelling?"

Night Hawk walked arm in arm with his mother to the fire, then helped her down onto a pallet of pelts, seating himself between his mother and father. "*Gah-ween*, no," he said, staring into the fire. Seeing his white mother had stirred thoughts of another woman with white skin. It was hard not to think about Briana. Her body had been slight and slender, her eyes so big, full, and soft. Her voice had touched his very soul.

"I did not see White Wolf, or even speak of him with anyone," he finally said, feeling not only two sets of eyes on him now but three, as his sister too had begun to look to him for answers.

"Then why have you returned to the village so soon?" Echohawk prodded, leaning closer to Night Hawk. "In your eyes, my son, I see something I have never seen before. What happened today? Who did you meet while traveling to Fort Snelling?"

Night Hawk's shoulder muscles stiffened, and his jaw became tight. He did not want to talk about his feelings for this white woman whom even he did not yet understand.

And then there was also this politician, Blackie. Echohawk would not like the fact that his son had come face to face with an enemy of his past.

"It was not so much who I met on my journey that made me turn back, but perhaps the awkwardness I now feel when I am there," he said, in a sense telling the truth. He looked from his mother to his father. "Of late, there has been much tension among the soldiers at the fort. I believe it is caused by the tales of White Wolf and his renegades being in the area, stirring up trouble for the white community again. In some soldiers' eyes, an Indian is an Indian, even if he is from a peaceful Chippewa village. Even if he is the son of Chief Echohawk." He glared into the fire again. "My people are best served with me here, not there."

Echohawk nodded, he too staring into the fire. "*Ay-uh*, this I understand," he said somberly. "It is sad that the soldiers still see us as the enemy. For many years now there has been no reason to call us that wicked name. And now it is because of the aging renegade Sioux White Wolf! Why has he chosen to come out of hiding again?"

"Let us not talk of White Wolf or the soldiers at Fort Snelling," Mariah said, always saddened at the mere mention of Snelling. Her true father, Colonel Josiah Snelling, had never known that she was his daughter. Even her brother, William Joseph, had never known her true identity.

And now both were dead.

The name Snelling cut into her heart, always, as though an arrow were lodged there.

"So we shall talk of my darling sister, Lily, and how she so dutifully sews beads onto her doeskin robe which is meant to be worn on her wedding night," Night Hawk said, looking at his sister, loving her so much sometimes it hurt. "Lily, when will you and Strong Branch marry?"

Even the thought of his sister marrying Strong Branch made Night Hawk's insides knot. Since Strong Branch's personality had changed he did not deserve anyone as kind and sweet as Lily. She was a slight little maiden of sixteen summers, with sleek black waist-length hair, the facial features of the Chippewa, and the darkest eyes of all midnights, yet her skin was lily white, like her mother's.

Lily was a blessed one, the daughter that had filled the aching vacancy after Night Hawk's parents lost a son during childbirth. Night Hawk had been so young, he could not even recall his mother being swollen with child.

Because of her rare charm, Lily had not only become the darling of his family, but also of the tribe.

She had been the last child born to Night Hawk's mother, and her dream of having many children stopped with this daughter.

"Do not fret so much over your sister's welfare," Lily scolded, laying her sewing aside. "Strong Branch and I will be married soon." She gave her father a sweet smile, one that always got her way with him. "May I be excused, *gee-bah-bah*? I would like to take my evening walk."

Echohawk did not reply immediately. Instead he sat thinking about his daughter, and the reasons for her evening strolls. Though she was not aware that her father knew it, Echohawk did realize that she met with Strong Branch every night. And, without complaint, Echohawk allowed his daughter to go to him. He had once been a young lover, with young, fresh desires of the heart. And he had wanted a brave who could prove himself worthy of his daughter. He had wanted him to be strong in the swim and race, and courageous in the hunt. All these things Echohawk had seen in Strong Branch.

Before Echohawk had begun to suspect that not everything was right with Strong Branch, he had even encouraged his daughter to marry him. Only recently had Echohawk wavered in such encouragements.

But tonight, when everything seemed at peace within the world of his village, Echohawk chose not to voice doubts about Strong Branch to his daughter.

He had to have proof. Once he had evidence of any wrongdoing on Strong Branch's part, then Echohawk would say his piece—even forbid his daughter ever to see Strong Branch again.

"*Ay-uh*, you can go for your walk," Echohawk finally said. "But do not wander far."

Lily scurried to her feet. With one long braid hanging down her back to her waist, dressed in a colorfully beaded buckskin dress, she was a vision of lovely innocence. She hugged her mother and father.

After embracing them, she turned to Night Hawk and hesitated. Of late, she had become aware of tension growing between them. This was something she could not understand, and regretted with every beat of her heart.

"Night Hawk, my brother, will you hug your sister tonight?" she asked softly.

Night Hawk looked down at her silently for a moment, realizing that she was aware of his misgivings about Strong Branch and that she did not understand. He could not find the courage to say the word *betrayal* to her, so he said nothing at all.

He quickly embraced her and held her tightly, as though this mere gesture could protect her from all harm, then gave her up to her world of fantasies. He watched as she left the wigwam with haste.

Night Hawk glanced at his father, whose eyes were trained on him, and they seemed to exchange the same doubts about Strong Branch.

Then Night Hawk turned and left, and went to his own wigwam at the far edge of the village. The fire in his firepit had burned down to low embers, casting weaving shadows on the walls of his dwelling.

After placing several logs on the fire, Night Hawk stretched out beside it and let himself get caught up in remembrances of Briana. How might he arrange to meet her again? It was obvious that it would not be an easy task. Because of the damnable politician there just might not be a way to get to know her better.

"Perhaps that is best," Night Hawk sighed, turning to lie on his back and stare at the curved ceiling of his wigwam. "She is from a different world. And she has her love of painting to fill her days and nights."

He tossed himself back on his stomach, holding his chin in his hands as he once again stared into the dancing flames of the fire. His jaw became tight with determination. Nothing would keep him and Briana apart.

He even welcomed a reason to go up against Blackie. No Indian ever dared to speak up against him. It was time that someone of the Chippewa community did.

"And that will be Night Hawk!" he whispered harshly to himself. "Somehow I will find a way to show that politician's true colors to the people of Minnesota Territory."

He smiled to himself, thinking that through Briana Collins, many things were possible—even achieving the long sought-for revenge against Blackie Collins for his father.

Using a high white bluff as a trysting place with Strong Branch, Lily melted into his arms as he lowered her to the ground. In a wild embrace, they made passionate love. Lily writhed beneath him, never getting enough of Strong Branch's lovemaking. Her dress was hiked up above her waist, and Strong Branch's fingers were tight around her buttocks, lifting her so that she could meet his every hungry thrust. She groaned in whispers against his neck.

"My darling," she said, feverish with the intense, building passion, "say that you will marry me soon. Please say it!"

Strong Branch placed a finger to her chin and lifted her lips to his, silencing her words with a fiery kiss.

She clung to him, but was aware that again he was ignoring her questions.

Yet at that moment she did not care. The ecstasy was all that mattered, the wondrous wild rapture that being with him evoked.

She cried out against his lips as he buried himself even more deeply inside her, his strokes becoming maddeningly faster until her head was swimming, and the flood of bliss washed through her in wild torrents of pleasure.

And then they lay there, panting and clinging to each other. Darkness had fallen and the moon was a sliver overhead, taking on the appearance of a canoe in the sky. Lily knew that she could not stay much longer. She did not want her father coming to search for her and finding her in the midst of such questionable behavior.

"Strong Branch," she said, easing from his arms, "I do not think I can continue meeting with you in such a way much longer." She pulled her dress down, to hide her nakedness beneath it, while Strong Branch repositioned his breechclout around his hips. "Even now I suspect my father knows about us meeting."

She badly wanted to tell him that she had missed her monthly weeps, but she wanted the mood to be right when she told him that she was with child—their child. She wanted him to be less moody, less subdued. Yet this was something that she could not keep secret from her beloved for much longer.

Strong Branch framed Lily's pale face between his copper hands and drew her lips to his, and gave her a gentle, soft kiss.

Then he held her away from him at arm's length, his fingers clasped to her shoulders. "My woman, you know that I am now practicing chief of my people," he said thickly. "My decisions are many. When we will marry is not as important at present as other things that concern my people. But soon, Lily, I shall concentrate on you and our marriage only. Be patient. Things must be right in my village before I bring a wife to them to accept."

"Your people and my father's people have lived as one entity for as long as you and I have had breath in our lungs," Lily argued softly. "They would not resent having me as your wife. They see me as one of them already. You know that, Strong Branch. Your argument is not enough!"

"But it is the one I give you tonight," Strong Branch said firmly. "Let us talk no more about it. I am the man. I am chief! My word is final!"

Lily stared disbelievingly at him, fighting back tears. She stiffened as she leaned her face into his. "You are not my chief yet," she said sourly. "So do not tell me that your word is final with me. Strong Branch, you marry me soon or not at all!"

She turned and fled from him, holding her tears back until she was out of his sight, then let them rush down her cheeks in torrents. She placed her hand to her abdomen, thinking of the child that was growing there.

Would the child have to be raised without a father? Would she be forced to have the child in shame?

She stopped and turned, looking back at Strong Branch's silhouette against the dark sky, thinking that perhaps she had spoken in haste to the man she loved. He was the only answer to the dilemma in which she now found herself.

She bit her lower lip and began running blindly again toward the village, never before having felt so terribly confused.

Fort Snelling

There was a commotion in the courtyard as several soldiers arrived on horseback and quickly dismounted.

His saber clanking at his side, Lieutenant Braddock hurried to the commandant's office and stood over a huge oak desk, saluting Colonel Hawthorne.

"What is it?" Colonel Hawthorne asked, forking a shaggy gray eyebrow as he stared up at Lieutenant Braddock through thick-lensed eyeglasses. "Why the flurry in the courtyard? My God, man, your eyes are wild. Your clothes are filthy."

"It's another massacre, sir," Lieutenant Braddock announced, stopping to catch his breath. "An Indian attack on another settlement. As in the other attacks before, there were no survivors."

"Good Lord," Colonel Hawthorne declared, sinking lower in his leather chair. "What's the Minnesota Territory coming to? And what's the cause of this sudden unrest among the Indians?"

"I think it's for guns and ammunition," Lieutenant Braddock offered, wiping a bead of perspiration from his brow. "Those items are always taken."

"Of course that would be part of the stolen loot, you dimwit," Colonel Hawthorne growled. He placed an unlit, half-smoked cigar between his thick lips. "But you can't say that's the only reason for the raids on the settlers." He chewed on the cigar for a moment, staring into space, then lifted his gaze back to Lieutenant Braddock's. "By damn, we've got to find out who and why."

"White Wolf," Lieutenant Braddock said, narrowing his blue-gray eyes. "You know damn well it's

probably White Wolf. That renegade has eluded us
for too many years to count."

"Yes, as before, I strongly suspect it is White Wolf
back to his old tricks," Colonel Hawthorne mumbled.
He placed his fingertips together before him and
rocked his desk chair slowly back and forth. "Yet it
could be any Indian." He glared up at Lieutenant
Braddock. "Tell the men to keep an alert eye at all
times. Bring in any Indian that stirs up problems of
any sort."

"Yes, sir," Lieutenant Braddock said. He saluted
the colonel, then spun around on his heels and left
the office.

Colonel Hawthorne rose to his feet and went to
look at a large portrait that hung in a gilt frame above
the mantel of the fireplace. "I wonder what you'd do
about the uprisings," he said, staring at the portrait
of Colonel Josiah Snelling, Fort Snelling's founder.
"What was your magic formula for keeping peace with
the Indians? Josiah, seems I need some advice about
now."

He turned and gazed slowly around the room, always feeling a presence there other than himself. He
felt it now, even though the room was quiet, except
for the popping and crackling of the fire.

The shelves were lined with books that had been
Colonel Snelling's. The desk had been custom made
for him, as well as the large desk chair. The maps
that hung from the walls still held Colonel Snelling's
markings, as did the hardwood floor—streaked with
the wear and tear of Colonel Snelling's relentless
pacing.

"You're here now, aren't you, you restless sonofabitch?" Colonel Hawthorne chuckled. He nodded and
smiled. "Josiah, it's good to have your company. But

damn it, I'd sure like to have the honor of you talking
back to me sometime!"

The flame of the kerosene lamp on the desk flick-
ered low momentarily, then burned again in a steady
blaze. Colonel Hawthorne bowed and kindly saluted
the flame.

4

Under a sky of blue with a leafwove
awning of green,
We placed our basket of fruit and wine
By the runlet's rim,
Where we sat to dine.
—HARDY

The hills in the distance were mantled in mist. The morning dew glistened on blades of grass like shimmering teardrops. A great bell in the distance clanged the morning hour of six from the slender tower of the church steeple, then quivered into silence.

Briana's uncle's stately mansion on Snelling Avenue was behind her. It was a grand Victorian home, rectangular with a wide porch, stained glass windows, and a mansard roof. Snuggled beneath a warm shawl in her buggy, Briana snapped the reins, sending her horse into a steady trot along the cobblestone street. She smiled victoriously as she glanced behind her at what lay at the back of her buggy—her painting equipment, plus a wicker picnic basket brimming with delicacies and plates as pretty as the flowers that bordered the walkways of the city.

Sighing leisurely, Briana looked straight ahead at the forest that was unfolding before her. She had managed to elude the men that had been ordered to stand guard outside her uncle's house so that she could not venture again into the forest. The men had stood watch for several days, but they finally grew lax in their assigned duties, perhaps thinking that her Uncle

Blackie had been wrong to suspect his niece of having an adventurous nature. They had slipped away earlier last night and she suspected they were asleep in the arms of women, or sitting at a poker table in the dark back room of a saloon.

It was a beautiful, clear morning. The sky was blue with little white clouds floating about, the sun just peeping over the hilltops in the east. As Briana drove her buggy into the shadows of the forest, the birds were waking and chirping their morning songs, filling her with the anticipation of surrounding herself with nature again, painting.

Briana peered ahead into the darker depths of the forest, where in its thick underbrush the gentle deer reared their young, the great bear stalked about in search of food, and wolves stealthily crept about, endeavoring to surprise their prey. Briana hoped that the wild beasts of the night had entered their dens. She did not want to have to use the pearl-handled pistol that she had brought for protection this time to shoot anything two- or four-legged that might endanger her. She was not practiced in firearms, yet her uncle had insisted that she have one since he was a celebrity of sorts, which drew all sorts of questionable people to their doorstep.

Her heart grew cold at the thought of the true reason why her uncle had given her the firearm.

To keep her safe from Indians.

And he had warned her not only of White Wolf, but also of being friendly with any men with red skin, which regrettably included the wonderfully handsome Night Hawk.

As she rode alongside the waters of a lake that were clear and calm and reflected the blue of the sky, Briana's thoughts were catapulted back to the last time she had ventured from the city to paint. She could

even now feel Night Hawk's lips pressed against hers,
and his powerful hands at her waist, drawing her body
against his. Although it had been just a brief kiss and
embrace, never had she experienced such rapture,
such bliss.

She glanced down at what she was wearing today
for this outing, knowing that she had purposely
dressed for the handsome Chippewa brave should they
meet again, yet feeling foolish to even think that they
might. Beneath her warm shawl she wore a fully gathered soft cotton dress resplendent with lace, and lavender iris designs embroidered on a white backdrop.
The bodice was low, revealing the upper, gentle
curves of her breasts, where a cameo necklace lay
against her pale white skin.

Her golden hair was drawn back from her face and
tied with a lavender satin ribbon, so that it hung in
long, lustrous waves down her straight back.

Her blue eyes sparkled and her cheeks were tinged
pink from both the chill of the morning and the excitement of being free from her uncle to paint—and possibly to see Night Hawk again.

Briana rode for a good portion of the morning, then
chose to stop at an attractive spot with shade and cool
breezes off the water. As she stepped down from her
buggy, she feasted on the serenity beneath the grand
trees spreading their leafy boughs to curtain the day.
The water in the lake was clear and teeming with fish.
The great forest trees seemed to reach almost to the
clouds which were mirrored in the water.

Briana eagerly unloaded her supplies from the
buggy, not taking long at all, for when she painted
out of doors she always put herself in as light
"marching order" as possible.

After setting up her easel and folding seat close to
the lake, she noticed the abundance of wildflowers in

a variety of shapes and colors that grew along the ground for as far as she could see. Always anticipating finding wildflowers on her outings, she carried a lace bag with her, as light as a dandelion seed, in which to collect the flowers. She had a scrapbook already half filled with flowers she had found in France, England, and all corners of America.

Yet her fondness for her wildflower collection always came second to her love of painting.

As the noon sunlight shone down through the high canopy of elm leaves, dappling the shaded ground with shimmering light, Briana plucked several small dogtooth violets, pale blue bird's foot, and delicate moccasin flowers, placing them in her bag.

Sensing motion behind her, she stopped. Her heart thudding from fear, unsure of who the intruder might be, she bent gingerly to one knee and placed her bag of wildflowers on the ground. Slowly she slipped her trembling fingers inside her dress pocket and circled them around the handle of the small pearl-handled pistol.

She slipped the pistol from her pocket, her finger quickly poised on the trigger as she rose to her full height and spun to see if this was all in her imagination, or if someone was truly there.

Night Hawk stepped out of the shadows, his piercingly dark eyes locking quickly with hers. Briana's heart did a quick leap, then her lips quivered into a relieved smile.

"You frightened me to death," she said, breathing out a heavy sigh as she lowered her pistol to her side. "My mind conjured up all sorts of things that might be ready to jump out and devour me," she laughed.

"And seeing that it is an Indian does not frighten you?" Night Hawk tested, already having seen in her eyes that he was welcome. "Did I not warn you about being so far from home alone? There are renegade Sioux who are not as friendly as I. White Wolf is stalking the forests again, earning his name, the vicious wolf!"

"I would never be afraid of you, and as for White Wolf and others like him, I brought a firearm along with me for protection this time," Briana defended, showing him the pistol that lay in the palm of her hand. "If I were threatened, I would not hesitate shooting it."

"Your uncle. He is the one who gave you this firearm?" Night Hawk asked, taking the pistol and gazing down at it mockingly. He thrust it back into Briana's hand. "He knows nothing about firearms if he thinks you can defend yourself with this thing that does not even have the capacity to fell a frog!"

Briana's eyes wavered and her lips parted in a gasp as she also gazed down at the almost weightless pistol in her hand. Then she looked up at Night Hawk. "I imagine my uncle did not think that I would truly ever have a need to use it," she said softly. "He did not know that I would be this far from home again unescorted. I came on my own while he slept. Perhaps I should have brought his rifle instead?"

"*Ay-uh*, that would have been the wisest thing to do," Night Hawk said, his gaze now moving over Briana. As when he had seen her before, his insides warmed at the sight of her slender body, but this time an even fiercer heat was enveloping him, tightening his loins.

She was so perfectly feminine in her lacy dress with the curves of her well-formed breasts revealed at the low bodice, and with her honey gold hair drawn back with a satin ribbon. Again he was swept into waves of desire when her round, soft eyes locked with his, her delicate cheekbones blooming with color.

"I will be sure to do that the next time," Briana said, almost breathless beneath his steady stare. He stirred many strange yet delicious feelings within her. Although there was a gentleness in his large, bright eyes, there was something else there that she felt was reserved only for her.

She could not help but feel that again he wished to kiss her. She could not deny that she wished he would.

Yet how foolish this was! she silently scolded herself. The fact that he was there again was pure coincidence, and it was just the chivalrous side of him that had made him stop, to be sure that she was all right.

She looked past him. She could see his white-faced bay with white hind legs grazing lazily, tethered close by to a low limb of a tree. She had not heard the approach of a horse. He must have been there before her and she had not realized it.

Fate seemed to have drawn them together a second time.

Night Hawk bent to his knee and picked up Briana's lace bag of flowers, then rose to his full height over her again and handed it to her. "I did not mean to frighten or disturb you," he said huskily. "I was just beyond the trees resting my horse, before traveling on into St. Paul, when I saw you arrive. I watched you unload your painting equipment, and then collect the wildflowers."

Briana accepted her small bag from him, the scent of the flowers wafting between them, sweet and spicy. "You then chose to let your presence be known," she said, turning to walk slowly toward her buggy. She cocked her head toward him as he fell into step beside her. "Why did you?"

In one sweep of the eye she was again in awe of his solidly built body, sheathed in fringed buckskin leggings. His limbs were long and muscular, his chest and shoulders powerful. Again she was overpowered by the sensation of having been held in those arms, so strong, so protective.

"Had it been you, would you have been content just to watch?" Night Hawk asked, following her to the buggy, his eyes gleaming into hers. "Would you have had no desire to speak to me? To become more acquainted? As I recall, our other meeting was cut short by the arrival of your uncle."

"Yes, it was," Briana said, feeling suddenly shy beneath his steady gaze and the sensual way he disturbed her. "And no, I would not have been content just to watch you silently. I too would have come to you and introduced myself again."

Night Hawk smiled, and as Briana placed her wildflowers in her buggy, he went back to her easel and stood over it, noticing that it was blank. She had come to the haunts of the forest again to begin a new painting. Knowing that, he expected her to stay quite awhile longer and he was glad.

"I haven't yet started to paint today," Briana said, going to stand beside Night Hawk. "First I wanted to collect the flowers—I guess, in a sense, to get the feel of the setting that I am going to paint."

"And do you feel that you are now ready to place your brush to the canvas?" Night Hawk asked, arching an eyebrow toward her. "It would please me to watch you, to see how you capture the sky and the trees. It is a talent known by my people for generations, yet we do not use canvas. We use the hides of buffalo and elk and other such animals. And we do not paint just to be painting. There are meanings behind each symbol painted on our dwellings and clothing."

"You truly wish to watch me paint?" Briana asked, clasping her hands behind her as she stared up at him, her knees growing weak as he gazed warmly at her from his great height.

"Some," Night Hawk said, nodding.

Briana unclasped her hands and eased down onto her folding seat, lifting the brush from her easel. She had to force her hand not to tremble as she dipped the brush into a tiny vial of color and began painting beneath his watchful eyes. He saw her create a whisper of sky blue, a blush of rose, the white touch of a butterfly wing after her eyes had followed an adventure-bound butterfly, and again the summer's softest and gentlest blues.

"My paintings are small in scale and usually completed in a half day's time," she explained, finding it hard not only to paint under his close scrutiny, but also to think. "I feel that the best paintings are those candid views which are executed on the spot. It is my opinion that this is the only way to rightly interpret nature as it truly is."

"It is most beautiful," Night Hawk said, admiring how the different colors seemed to rush against one another like the competing reds, golds and purples in a shifting wall of flame.

"I like everything I paint to fight for space on my canvases," Briana further explained. "It is impossible to exaggerate the abundance of nature."

Thoughts of her upcoming art show suddenly came to her. She paused and turned anxious eyes up to Night Hawk. "Very soon my work will be displayed at the art museum in St. Paul," she said, laying her brush aside on the easel. "Do you think that you could come? It would please me so much if you would."

Night Hawk frowned at the suggestion, having never been welcome at the social functions of the white people. Nor had he ever wanted to attend such gatherings.

Not until now.

"Perhaps Night Hawk will come," he replied, his jaw tight.

"Oh, how wonderful it would be to have you there!" Briana exclaimed, her stool toppling over as she rushed to her feet. She laughed nervously and bent to right it, then turned her eyes up to Night Hawk again. "It will be two weeks from today. Please don't forget."

He smiled at her exuberance, yet did not offer any more encouragement, for he truly doubted that he would go. His presence would most likely disrupt the showing. All eyes would be on him, wishing him away.

"Strange how I am so suddenly exhausted," Briana said, laughing lightly. "And hungry. Would you share a picnic lunch with me, Night Hawk? Are you hungry? Perhaps thirsty?"

"Picnic lunch?" Night Hawk said, painfully remembering times with his mother long past. "My mother made many picnic lunches before she became ill. *Ayuh*, I would enjoy sharing with you."

Briana was thrilled by his acceptance. She felt strangely giddy and lightheaded as she went to the buggy and got the basket, then walked beside him until they reached the edge of the lake.

"Your mother," she murmured. "You said that she made picnic lunches for you until she became ill." She bent to her knees to spread the lace-trimmed table-cloth on the ground. "I hope that she is well again."

"My *gee-mah-mah* will never be totally well again," Night Hawk said, marveling over how Briana had prepared her picnic, which she had most surely thought she would be eating alone. "She has been weakened over and over again by malaria. Each time she is gripped with a fever, I think it might be the last moments of her life."

"I'm so very sorry," Briana said, giving him a tender glance, then busying herself again setting out the food.

She plucked a handful of wildflowers and placed them in a small vase and set it in the middle of the tablecloth.

She placed two peaches along with bread and cheese on delicate china plates, then offered Night Hawk pink, shimmering lemonade in a cut-crystal, long-stemmed glass.

Night Hawk took the glass and eased down on the ground opposite Briana. "You are a woman of wonder," he said, chuckling. "Even lemonade? My mother first drank this special drink many moons ago while living for a short while with Colonel Josiah Snelling and his wife, Abigail, at Fort Snelling. She treated me to lemonade when I was very small. I have craved it ever since."

"It is also one of my weaknesses," Briana said. She eyed him over the rim of her glass as she slowly sipped her drink.

"Have you many?" Night Hawk mused, setting his empty glass aside.

"Many what?" Briana asked, also setting down her empty glass.

"Weaknesses," Night Hawk replied, drawing his knees to his chest, clasping his arms around his legs.

"I am not sure what you mean by weakness," Briana said, picking up a small knife, slicing first her peach, then his.

"Your love of painting?" he said, smiling at her. "Would you call that a weakness?"

"No," Briana said softly. She lay the knife aside. "I see that as one of my strengths."

"That is good," Night Hawk said, grabbing her hand before she could reach for a slice of peach. He urged her to her feet as he rose to his, moving around the tablecloth until they were in a sweet embrace.

"Would you say my wanting to kiss you is a weakness?" Night Hawk asked huskily, lifting her chin with a finger so that their lips were only a heartbeat away.

"I don't think so," Briana whispered, her heart pounding.

"Would you consider it a weakness on your part should you want to kiss me?" Night Hawk further teased, brushing her lips with a slight kiss, his tongue flickering against them.

Briana almost swooned from the sweet currents coursing through her. "No, never," she breathed, twining her arms around his neck.

Their lips met, bodies straining together hungrily.

Then Night Hawk wrenched himself away, and for a moment he gazed with a strange foreboding into her eyes. He then turned and fled.

Briana covered her mouth with one hand, her eyes wide, as she watched him mount and ride away on his beautiful horse, shaken and stunned by his quick escape, but even more overcome with how he had affected her again.

She realized that she was falling in love with him.

And he surely felt the same—it was clear in the way he had kissed her. It had been there in his eyes.

But she was confused by why he had kissed and then left her so suddenly.

It must be because of the differences in their cultures, she concluded. She was from an affluent family. Perhaps because of this, he was afraid that she could never live the life of an Indian's wife.

Yet the thrill of being with him forever gave her cause to believe that she could live anywhere, and endure any hardships. It would surely be paradise with Night Hawk.

And isn't his mother white? she suddenly remembered. Hadn't his mother adapted?

Smiling, she went back and sat down on her folding seat to resume painting, but she could not keep her mind on what she was doing. It kept drifting to Night Hawk, and how she felt about him—and he most surely about her. Immersed so deeply in such thoughts, she found it impossible to paint anymore today. She gathered up her things, returned to her buggy, and was soon heading back toward St. Paul.

"My art show," she whispered. "Will he truly come?"

She would anxiously be watching for him, for something told her that he would be there, if only outside, awaiting her departure from the museum after everyone else had left.

From somewhere north a loon laughed hysterically, startling Briana. The tall pine forest around the lake bounced the eerie cry back across the water, where it echoed until it died in a soft quaver.

Then she heard another sound which sent spirals of fear through her. She yanked her reins, drawing her horse to an immediate halt, her face paling as she heard the thundering of hoofbeats drawing closer and closer across the nearby meadow, the trees around her blocking her view.

She searched around her desperately, needing better cover, for she did not want to be at the mercy of a gang of men—recalling the highwaymen and Indians that were ravaging the countryside with their hideous raids!

Seeing a cluster of lilac and forsythia bushes that were not only thick but also tall, she snapped her reins and led her horse behind them. With wide, frightened eyes she watched the men come into sight and go past her, then suddenly they stopped. "Indians," she whispered harshly to herself. "My Lord, there are so many!"

She held her breath as she watched them enter a cave not far from where she was hiding. Everything became still—except for her whirling thoughts, wondering what these Indians were doing in a cave.

A sudden thought gripped her insides like clutching, squeezing fingers.

Night Hawk!

Had he left her so quickly so that he could come to this cave to meet with his braves? Were they in some sort of council? It had looked innocent enough.

She wanted to go closer, to see if she could hear them talking, yet thought better of it. These Indians could be renegades. They could even be participating in the raids. They could be led by White Wolf! If so, surely Night Hawk was not a part of this. He obviously hated White Wolf. He had said so often enough.

For more than one reason Briana couldn't confide in her uncle about what she had seen. She would be confessing to having left the house, and the city, without his permission. And her uncle hated all Indians, especially Night Hawk. This would give him the perfect opportunity to seek him out and kill him, convincing the authorities that he was the leader of the marauding renegades, without Night Hawk having the chance to defend himself. Then his people would certainly suffer.

No, she could not tell anyone what she had seen. Not until she knew that Night Hawk was innocent of belonging to any renegade band of Indians.

She couldn't even tell Night Hawk what she had seen. If he was not one of the renegades, she did not want to see him getting involved in the dangers of fighting them. She would protect Night Hawk at all costs.

She eased her horse and buggy from the bushes and snapped the reins, soon finding herself far away from the cave. She kept looking over her shoulder, not feeling at all safe until she finally entered the outskirts of St. Paul.

She inhaled a quavering breath of relief, yet she was still troubled over whether or not Night Hawk was involved in the tragic crimes against the white settlers of Minnesota.

5

And I will make thee beds of roses,
And a thousand fragrant posies.
—MARLOWE

Two Weeks Later

Briana had placed the incident at the cave at the furthest recesses of her mind. She was all aflutter about her art showing, an elegant selection of her rich oil paintings in carved gilt frames spaced evenly along the walls of the St. Paul Art Museum.

Having wished upon a star the previous night that Night Hawk would attend the exhibition, Briana had tried to make herself as beautiful as possible tonight. She had chosen a pale blue gown of rich satin, her breasts curving just slightly above the plunging neckline, the bodice coming to a point in front, emphasizing the smallness of her corseted waist. The little puffed sleeves of her dress were trimmed with a lace ruffle that draped to the elbows, and her glorious hair cascaded from a topknot of flowers and ribbons.

Around her neck she wore her cameo necklace, a treasured gift from her mother at their last parting in Paris.

Briana glanced over at her Uncle Blackie and sighed heavily. She could not keep from being somewhat embarrassed over his antics tonight. He was forever mingling with the people at the museum, trying to win favors for votes on election day, his tuxedo and his forced manners making him appear to be a man of distinction. But Briana had to wonder just how many people knew the real man behind the false toothy smile. It was apparent from some sly glances that his clever schemes to get votes might not be working.

Not wanting to think further about her uncle using her popularity as an artist for his own personal gains, Briana turned her eyes from him. She sipped on a long-stemmed glass of wine and stared at the closed double doors at the far end of the room with dwindling hopes that Night Hawk was going to arrive.

Yet she could understand why he would not come, and felt foolish for having harbored even the smallest hope that he would. She did not allow herself to have any suspicions about Night Hawk being a part of what might have been renegades at the cave. She was going to force this from her mind. She was going to trust him. One could not build a relationship on mistrust— and she badly wanted a relationship with him.

When people came to her, complimenting her on her paintings, she smiled politely and thanked them, yet could not help but look past them, again staring at the doors. Every time one would open, her heart stood still for a moment, then, disappointed, she would nod more thank-yous and accept more warm, affectionate hugs from those who truly did care about what she had achieved in the art world.

She painted a false picture of warmth for her uncle when he came to her and gave her a hearty hug, almost causing her to spill her wine down the front of her dress in his eagerness to display his affection for his niece. Briana set her glass on a table and forced a smile as Blackie moved to her side and placed a possessive arm around her waist. Her face became splashed pink with blush as he began complimenting her in a loud voice. Everyone turned to stare at the man whose thunderous voice drowned out everyone else's.

"Now, who among you would not agree with me that my niece's paintings are veritable little jewels?" he proclaimed, his dark eyes gleaming. "They are marvelous little masterpieces. They are brilliant, strong, and joyous works!"

He bent and gave Briana a wet kiss on her cheek. She was suddenly aware of a change in his mood as his arm stiffened around her waist and he gazed past her with intense hatred toward the doors that had just opened at the far end of the long gallery.

There was a sudden hush in the room as everyone turned to see the cause for her uncle's silence.

Briana's knees grew weak and her heart leapt with joy when her eyes locked with Night Hawk's. He entered the room proud and square-shouldered, and so very handsome in his porcupine-quilled embroidered shirt, fringed leggings and moccasins, and beaded headband.

She also noticed that he was wearing bands of fur around his wrists and ankles, the ends hanging and decorated with beads. And his long black hair was glossy and arranged in two plaits, with otter skins braided into them.

Briana's insides grew warm knowing that just for her Night Hawk was defying many people by appearing at a social function normally frequented by white people. Plus, he had gone to a great deal of trouble to make himself more acceptable in the eyes of the people who were now staring at him.

She saw him as courageous. They were aghast that he was brazen enough to mingle with them.

Again she forced herself to forget what she had seen at the cave, although she knew he must be innocent of all wrongdoing. A man with the compassion he had showed could not perform heinous acts against humanity!

"What is *he* doing here?" Blackie growled, his eyes filled with rage. He glanced down at Briana. "Did you know he was planning to come?"

"No," Briana lied, her eyes never leaving Night Hawk as he moved in a slow, dignified manner toward her. "How could I have, Uncle Arden? You made sure that I couldn't by posting men around the house, as though I were your prisoner."

"Do you think I don't know that you managed to elude them?" Blackie hissed, leaning closer to her face so that no one else could hear their conversation. "But since it was only that one time, I didn't bother scolding you. Now I see that I should have! Surely you met with the Injun again. Tell me the truth. Have you seen him since the day you broke the wheel? Have you?"

Briana didn't have the chance to respond. Night Hawk was there, standing over her, making her forget everything but him.

"You came," she said, her heart fluttering with a wild rapture within her chest.

"Did you think that I would not?" Night Hawk said, looking into Briana's soft eyes, ignoring Blackie's cold stare. "I hope it is not an embarrassment that I have come to celebrate your success with you."

"An embarrassment?" Briana said, smiling up at him. "I think it is an honor that you have taken the time from your many duties to share this special event with me."

She stepped away from her enraged uncle, ignoring his gasp as she locked her arm through Night Hawk's and walked away. The silence in the spacious room was strained as the gawking crowd stepped aside, making room for Briana and Night Hawk to go to the broad wall of paintings.

Blackie was so incensed by Briana's outrageous behavior, he could hardly get his breath. His face was beet red with embarrassment as everyone's attention slowly turned back to him, a strange sort of questioning in their eyes.

"That you came tonight is such a wonderful surprise," Briana said as she slowly walked with Night Hawk beside the paintings, still ignoring the stares and the disfavor in her uncle's eyes. "I had hoped that you would, yet I did not believe it. There are many bigoted people in this room who would just as soon shoot you as look at you. You are brave to come up against such odds as this."

"It has nothing to do with being brave. Perhaps I'm a bit careless," Night Hawk said, chuckling. "I owed it to a certain lady whose eyes are the color of the sky and precious lakes of Minnesota."

"Oh?" Briana said. "And why is that?"

"Did you not share your picnic lunch with me?" Night Hawk said, his eyes dancing. "Did you not share your lemonade?"

"Yes, and it was my pleasure to do so," Briana said, tingling inside when she thought back to something else that they had shared—a sensual kiss and embrace!

"I did not yet thank you for those special moments," Night Hawk said softly. "And I must apologize for later—when I kissed, then left you without an explanation."

"Why *did* you leave so quickly?" Briana whispered so that only Night Hawk could hear. She did not want to hear the truth if it had anything to do with the cave. No! She would not allow herself to continue thinking about it. To do so was perhaps dangerous, for herself and Night Hawk.

"It was so sudden," she quickly added. "I could not

help but think that I—that I had done something wrong. Did I, Night Hawk? Was it because of me that you left?"

"It was because of you, *ay-uh*," Night Hawk returned in a whisper. "Twice now I have rushed into kissing you. I felt that perhaps that was not best. I did not want to frighten you."

In truth, he thought to himself, he had left her so suddenly because he had begun to feel somewhat guilty. *Ay-uh*, in his heart he truly wanted her, yet a part of him wanted to use her, to achieve a revenge so long sought for by his chieftain father.

Ay-uh, that was what had troubled him while kissing her.

But after days of deep thought and sweet remembrance, he had overcome that guilt, knowing that he had kissed her only because it was Briana that he wanted, not how she could help in achieving vengeance.

It was his duty to show her this truth. But not now. Not among a crowd of white people.

Later, when they would be alone, he could tell her many things that were meant to be spoken in private.

"You were right to think that I was frightened," Briana whispered back. "But not because of you having kissed me. But because of my response to the kiss. I thought that perhaps you saw me as—as a loose lady for responding so passionately to you when, in truth, we scarcely knew each other. Please never think that I do this with every man that chances along in the forest!"

"Do not fret so," Night Hawk said, his insides tightening when, out of the corner of his eye, he saw Blackie deliberately pushing his way through the crowd toward him and Briana. "I see you as a genuine lady, nothing less."

Briana also caught sight of her uncle coming. She cleared her throat nervously and changed the conversation to something less intimate. "How is your mother?" she blurted, looking away from her uncle and up into Night Hawk's eyes again. "I hope she is better. I would love to meet her someday. I have heard so much about her—that she is a special lady."

"The bouts of malaria have weakened her. She is scarcely at all what she used to be," Night Hawk said, his voice filled with sudden emotion. "She rarely has the strength to do anything but sit and sew. It saddens me to see this. I can recall when she joined in the hunt with my father and me. She was quite spirited. I can safely say that before her illness she could shoot a firearm as well as any man and ride a horse even better. Now—"

Blackie grabbed Briana by the arm and jerked her away from Night Hawk. He took her aside and glowered down at her. "Briana, I can't stand any more of your insulting behavior," he said, his teeth clenched. "Get rid of that Injun. Quick! Do you hear?"

She leaned up into his face, her nostrils flaring angrily. "I will do no such thing," she said, placing her hands on her hips.

"Then you are forcing me to see to it myself," Blackie said, doubling his hands into fists at his sides to keep himself from striking Briana. Her sudden bouts of insolence were something he could not understand, or tolerate.

Briana's eyes wavered as she backed away from Blackie. "Uncle Arden, please don't embarrass me or Night Hawk by ordering him to leave," she begged.

"Tonight you are the embarrassment," Blackie said, then turned and stomped away.

Briana stood by herself long enough to regain composure and to swallow back the bitterness that had risen in her throat over her uncle's crude behavior toward Night Hawk and even herself.

She was glad when Night Hawk came to her, and even happier when her uncle was no longer in sight, surely having decided not to create a scene by forcing Night Hawk to leave.

Briana lifted her chin and, with Night Hawk at her side, began saying her good-byes to everyone that had been kind enough to come and view her paintings. Her heart was not in it, and having to force a smile, she began mingling with the crowd, shaking hands and receiving warm hugs. She ignored the icy stares and forced handshakes from those who did not approve of her choice of friends, and was glad when the room was cleared of everyone except for herself and Night Hawk.

He clasped her shoulders with his hands. "I have a sad heart that my being here has made your special night an awkward one," he said thickly. "It would have been best had I not come. Perhaps my place, always, is with my people, in the forest. Never are the Chippewa welcomed at functions such as these. But my heart grows tired of giving into the wishes of white people. And my heart was anxious to see you again, no matter how or where."

Briana placed a hand to his smooth copper cheek. She smiled sweetly up at him. "And I was anxious to see you," she murmured. "Although awkward at times tonight for both you and me, I am glad that you came." She giggled. "You showed them, didn't you, Night Hawk? The damn bigots!"

"Perhaps so, but I hope it does not cause you to

lose face in the community because of your association with me," Night Hawk said, taking her hand from his face and holding it endearingly over his heart. "Although I am part white, I am at heart a full-blooded Chippewa."

"And such a kind and generous Chippewa," Briana said, sighing. "And so very, very handsome."

"I want to kiss you," Night Hawk said, framing her face between his hands.

Briana stood on tiptoe and slowly twined her arms around his neck. Their lips met in a tender kiss, and then Night Hawk drew his lips away and placed an arm around her waist and walked her outside. His horse was tethered to a low-hanging branch of a maple tree, and he started walking her toward it.

Suddenly Blackie gripped Briana's arm firmly and jerked her away from Night Hawk. "Get outta here, Injun," he snarled. "Haven't you done enough harm for one night?"

Night Hawk and Blackie exchanged looks of hate for a long moment that seemed an eternity to Briana. Then Night Hawk walked away like a noble prince—tall, stately, and proud.

Briana placed her hands to her throat, stifling a sob in its depths, as she watched Night Hawk grab his horse's reins, mount his steed in one leap, and ride away.

She turned and glared at her uncle. "How could you be so cruel?" she said, her lips trembling.

"I warned you about such loose behavior," Blackie said hotly. "I forbid you to see the Indian. Why can't you understand why? No one will vote for me if they know my niece is an Injun lover!"

"Of all the bigots in this city, you are the worst!" Briana said, sobbing. Tears splashing from her eyes, she ran to her buggy, and in a flurry she was soon heading for home.

"I'm so sorry, Night Hawk," she whispered, wishing that he were there to hear her.

6

Quick!
I wait!
And who can tell what tomorrow may befall—
Love me more, or not at all!
—SILL

As Briana wished that Night Hawk were there to hear her apologies, he suddenly appeared on his horse in the shadows at the side of the road, and came to ride beside her buggy.

"It seems I am always leaving you too suddenly," Night Hawk mused, his gaze meeting hers in the soft glow of the moon. "I should not have left you with your uncle. I should have swept you away in my arms and defended you against that tyrant."

"I appreciate the thought, am even thrilled by it, but that wouldn't have been wise," Briana said, startled at the thought of him whisking her away into the night in full view of her uncle. "You would have been the loser, Night Hawk. My uncle is a powerful man. No Indian dares go against him in public. Not even you, Night Hawk, the son of the beloved Echohawk."

"Does that not remain to be seen?" Night Hawk said, his lips lifting into a slow, confident smile.

"Please don't do anything foolish on my account," Briana said softly. "I would never want to be the cause of you getting in trouble with the white community. As it is now, you are somewhat accepted. As you saw tonight, only a few people gave you frowns.

In some ways, Night Hawk, you have already won against my uncle."

"Your home," Night Hawk said, turning from her to look ahead at the streets lined with houses on both sides. "Is it near?"

"Very," Briana said, dreading to have to go there, especially so soon after the confrontation with her uncle.

A sudden thought came to her. She jerked on her reins and led her horse in another direction, on a road toward the forest.

Night Hawk nudged his horse's sides with his knees and rode up next to her again. "You are no longer going toward the houses," he said, questioning her with his dark eyes. "You will soon be in the forest."

Briana straightened her back and heaved a heavy sigh. "It is too beautiful a night to go directly home," she said, giving him a quick glance. "It is so deliciously warm tonight, I do not even need a shawl. And look at the winking fireflies: don't they look like the eyes of ghosts? Before going on to my uncle's home, I would love to spend a few moments in the forest among the fireflies. Would you come with me? Would you sit with me and talk? It is the only way we will ever achieve privacy from the probing eyes of my uncle."

"*Ay-uh*, I will go with you. There is no need for me to get back home quickly," Night Hawk said, his pulse racing at the thought of being alone with her again. While with her at the art museum, it had been hard not to wrap her in his arms and hold her to him, never to let her go.

She was quickly stealing his heart, as well as his soul.

He found it hard to envision a future without her.

Yet achieving this goal could mean much heartache

for her. Except for her uncle, she seemed quite content with her life. If she hungered for the attention of people to view her paintings, how could he ever expect her to be content living away from the city, in the haunts of the forest with the few people of his village?

Ay-uh, having her forever seemed an impossible dream. But it was a dream worth fighting for.

And he would do it. She *would* be his!

An awkward silence ensued in which they rode together into the darker shadows of the forest. When the moon's reflection could be seen in a body of water only a short distance away, Briana steered her horse toward it. She arrived at the small lake surrounded by low-hanging branches of willows and drew her horse to a halt.

As Night Hawk reined in his horse beside Briana's buggy, she gazed up at him, her heartbeats like crashes of thunder within her. She felt wicked for having invited him to come into the forest with her, yet it had been as though an unseen force had compelled her to do it.

As she watched Night Hawk dismount and tether his horse to a low branch of a tree, she had the urge to flee. Yet the promise of another kiss from this adorable man made her stay.

When he came to her and placed his strong hands on her waist and lifted her from the buggy, she felt the beginnings of the same sort of warm feelings soaring through her that his presence always evoked. She hardly felt her feet meet the ground, for his hands were now framing her face, drawing her lips to his mouth.

His kiss caused a tingling sensation to engulf her. And when he lowered her body to the ground, she did not even feel its hardness against her back. A blissful ecstasy overwhelmed her as one of his hands touched her breast, kneading it through her dress, while the other hand inched along one of her legs beneath her skirt. When his hand cupped her mound at the juncture of her thighs, she became aware of intense feelings that she had never experienced before, frightening her.

She pushed him away and rose to a sitting position, breathing hard.

"Night Hawk, please . . . don't . . ." she murmured. "I was wrong to encourage this." Her hands went to her hair, discovering that her ribbons and flowers were no longer there. Her hair had fallen from its bun and was now hanging loosely around her shoulders.

She began to push herself up from the ground. "I . . . really . . . must go." She faltered, her words untrue to how she felt and what she wanted to do.

He gently took one of her hands and helped her up from the ground. "Night Hawk's feelings are too strong for you," he said thickly. "I regret that I have frightened you. But please do not leave just yet. If you leave in this state of mind, I fear we will never see each other again."

Briana was aware of the hurt in his voice and felt guilty for having caused it. She turned to him and placed a gentle hand on his cheek. "It was not you I was frightened of," she murmured. "It was myself. Never before has a man caused me to feel foreign to myself. That frightened me, Night Hawk. Only that. Although we are from different cultures, and although I live in a community which sees the love between a white woman and a red man as forbidden, I must confess that neither matters to me. But my feelings do. I want to love you without feeling . . . shame for giving myself to you so easily."

"This shame you say you do not want to feel," Night Hawk said, taking her hand and placing it on his chest, over his heart. "If you love someone, truly love him, there should never be feelings of shame while with your beloved. As now, only moments ago, what I did to make you feel ashamed is a natural thing shared between two that are in love. Did you truly not enjoy the sensations caused by my lips and hands?"

A blush colored Briana's face a soft pink. Her eyes wavered as she gazed up at Night Hawk, disbelieving that she was with a man, talking so openly about such things!

But as time went on with him, it seemed only natural to say what she pleased, and perhaps even do what she so badly wanted.

"I enjoy everything you do," she finally said, her heart thumping wildly within her chest, knowing that to continue with this conversation was to continue with that which she had just denied him.

"Did you feel shame while confessing your feelings to me?" Night Hawk asked, drawing her against his hard body. "Do you feel shame while being held within my arms? Would you feel shame should I decide to kiss you again?"

"No, not shame, Night Hawk, just an intense yearning for you," Briana admitted, her knees weakening as he lowered his mouth to her lips and consumed them in a long, fiery kiss.

Sculpted against him, she could feel the hardness of his manhood through her clothes. She knew that this should frighten her, but it only excited her.

And she did not fight him off when he eased her to the ground again.

She even allowed it when he began to busy his fingers disrobing her.

Her pulse racing, allowing everything as though she

had never breathed a denial across her fevered lips, Briana reached her arms out to him as she now lay nude on the ground, an offering to him.

Night Hawk stood over her and slowly removed his clothes, his eyes locked with hers, so as to hold her there with the sheer force of his will.

Never had he wanted a woman as fiercely!

And he knew that her need for him was just as intense, and that they would be linked together forevermore, as though one heartbeat.

Briana's breathing was shallow as she watched him lower his fringed breeches, revealing this part of a man that was only somewhat new to her. During her studies in Paris, many men had posed nude for the aspiring artists during class. At first she had been embarrassed by seeing the most private part of a man's anatomy, but eventually it had become commonplace.

But this time—this man—was different. Seeing his satin hardness made her want him even more. And as he moved his hand over himself for the moment it took for him to kneel down over her, Briana was mystified by how even this made her feel. A spinning sensation flooded her entire body, feeling oh, so close to going over the edge into total ecstasy.

"Say that you want me," Night Hawk said, nudging her legs apart with a knee. "We have not gone so far that it cannot be stopped. If you wish to leave, leave now. If you wish to stay, I will take you to paradise with me."

"I feel like I am already there," Briana whispered, twining her arms around his neck as he lay down over her, his hardness resting against her thigh.

His lips close, she ran her tongue slowly over them, then gasped with pleasure when he again kissed her.

His hands at her hips, she could feel him lifting her from the ground. She tightened her hold about his neck and cried out with pain against his lips as he entered her with one hard thrust.

Night Hawk smoothed his lips over to her ear. "The pain was brief, was it not?" he whispered, concerned. "The enjoyment I shall bring to you will be forever."

He held her close and started his rhythmic strokes within her. His mouth lay against her cheek, where he could breathe in her sweetness as he felt pleasure mounting deeply within his loins. He smiled to himself when he felt her relaxing more and more in his arms and beginning to move her body with his, opening herself to him so that he had full access to loving her. Surges of tingling heat flowed through him. He was not sure how long he could hold back the pleasure, yet he knew that he must. This time, the first for her, had to be unforgettable. That she was a virgin, having never been with a man before in this sensual way, made him know that from now on she would be his, a woman he wished to give the world to.

And he would not let himself think about the fact that she already had so much in her life—so much that she just might not want to turn her back on it all once he asked her to be his *ee-quay*, woman.

But, he had decided, he would turn heaven and earth to have her with him. He would make her want him, not the rich life of white people.

The air heavy with the inevitability of rapture in Night Hawk's wild embrace, Briana let herself enjoy these wondrous moments with the man she adored.

Who was to say they would ever get the chance to be together again? If her uncle had his way, she would be tied to her bedpost, the key to her locked bedroom door thrown away—until he wanted to show her off to his constituents! That was all that her uncle wanted her for—to use her.

Yes, tonight was hers and Night Hawk's. She would

take from this night all that she desired, and never look back. Shame no longer filled her. Rapture was carrying her away on silver wings into the night. She so badly wanted it to continue.

Her body reacted even more wildly to Night Hawk now. Ecstasy spilled over within her and was spreading, deliciously spreading . . .

She cried out and clung to Night Hawk as that most wondrous instant of pleasure overwhelmed her, drenching her with a lazy, unforgettable warmth.

Night Hawk felt her release and let himself go now. He moaned throatily against her cheek as his thrusts within her became fast and deliberate. His body stiffened momentarily, and then he clung to her as his body convulsed into hers.

She rocked with him until he lay still above her, their bodies slick with perspiration glistening like dew beneath the silvery beams of the moon.

"I have a hold on your heart," Night Hawk whispered against her lips. "In Chippewa, that means 'I love you.'"

Tears of happiness came to Briana's eyes. She looked up into his dark depths and touched his lips. "I also have a hold on your heart," she whispered back.

They gazed into each other's eyes for a moment longer, and then kissed again, this time more softly, more sweetly, more devotedly.

7

She could feel as if she were out for the day,
As she had not done since she was a little girl.
—JAMES

Her painting paraphernalia left in the downstairs
study, Briana almost floated up the spiral staircase,
the ecstasy within her was so intense.

She could still taste Night Hawk's kiss.

She could still feel the crush of his hard body against
hers.

As she took the last step to the second-story landing, she stopped and inhaled a quavering breath and
placed a hand over her pounding heart, closing her
eyes as she allowed herself to recall that very instant
that she had found total paradise within Night Hawk's
passionate embrace.

It had been no less than a wild rapture that had
overwhelmed her, and there was no shame, no remorse at all that she had allowed the handsome, wonderful Chippewa brave to teach her how it truly felt
to be a woman.

The distinct sound of someone clearing his throat
caused Briana's eyes to open in a nervous flutter, her
thoughts flooding back to the present. When she
peered toward her bedroom door, she saw that it was
open, lamplight pouring out onto the floor of the
corridor.

"Uncle Blackie," she whispered, alarm setting in at
the thought of him waiting for her, afraid to wonder
why.

She knew the answer already. She should have been home hours ago! Her uncle was keenly aware of when she had left the art museum.

She touched her trembling fingers to her hair, checking to see if it was in place and not too mussed from the rapturous moments with Night Hawk in the forest, and then smoothed her hands over the skirt of her dress to make sure it lay in place over her crinoline slip. She moved slowly toward her bedroom.

Just outside the door she inhaled a nervous breath and squared her shoulders, then with a lifted, proud chin, went in. The room would have pleased a queen in its decoration of lacy curtains, bed skirt and spread, velveteen chairs, and a gilded mirror that hung over her dressing table, which was crowded with assortments of fancy bottles filled with even fancier perfumes, most of which were French.

"And so my wandering niece is finally home," Blackie said, folding his arms angrily across his chest. He peered at Briana with his dark, glaring eyes, slowly assessing her. His look became one of utter contempt as his eyes locked with hers.

"Uncle Arden, I-I . . ." Briana said in an attempt to explain, but the words wouldn't come.

She had not thought to think up an excuse for her late arrival. She had not expected that her uncle would be there waiting for her. Then again, she had never given him cause before. She had always come right home after her outings, which had never lasted this long into the night.

"I'm not going to waste my time questioning you as to where you've been, or with whom," Blackie said, taking two angry strides toward her.

He raised a hand and slapped her hard across her face, causing her head to jerk sideways with the blow. "The flush of your cheeks and the glow in your eyes give me all the answers I need," he growled, his voice filled with disgust. "You are a disappointment. A trollop."

Stunned, her cheek burning from the blow, Briana turned and watched her uncle leave in a huff, disbelieving that he had actually hit her!

That he had called her a trollop made a rush of tears flood her eyes. She ran across the room and threw herself onto her bed, sobbing. She was so confused.

She had never been wanton before. No man had ever stirred such uncontrollable passion within her before. Her passion had always been her painting, but she realized now that painting did not feed certain hungers.

Nor had her uncle treated her cruelly before.

Not until she had met Night Hawk.

Firming her lower lip, Briana wiped the tears from her cheeks, realizing that she could not please everyone. She would have to turn her back on either her uncle or Night Hawk.

She wished that such a choice had not been forced upon her, but now that passion for something besides painting had been unleashed within her, she did not want to deny herself of it, or the man who had awakened her into loving.

She did love Night Hawk, and would chance anything to be with him.

Rising from the bed, Briana went to the window and drew the sheer curtain aside. Peering toward the moon-drenched forest, she wondered what Night Hawk was thinking, if he was still feeling the afterglow of the ecstacy they had shared. Now that she had been able to sort through her feelings and realize that nothing her uncle said or did would stop her from seeing

Night Hawk again, she was reliving the delicious rapture all over again.

Oh, but if only he was feeling the same about her, and would not allow anything to stand in his way of feeling free to love her.

Her uncle. If he dared interfere again . . .

She shook her head desperately, not wanting to think ahead to what her uncle might do to keep her from the handsome Chippewa brave—her love, her desire.

Her hand went to her cheek, still feeling the imprint of her uncle's hand and the heat from the blow. A shiver coursed through her. She knew that if her uncle had the nerve to slap her, he was capable of doing anything. Yet surely he wouldn't, for he knew that if his brother ever found out, he would live to regret ever having loosed his rage on his niece.

That thought made Briana smile.

Deep in thought, Night Hawk rode in a slow trot through the forest. His mind was filled with the shared moments with Briana, still in awe of her. She had made him forget all of the women he had ever had in his lifetime, and the fact that she was white.

It had been hard for him to leave Briana after having found such wondrous bliss within her arms. He had wanted to ask her to go with him to his village, to stay with him forever.

Yet he had not spoken.

He never wanted to give her cause to say no to him again. And she would not have had a choice this time but to say no, for he knew that she had to set things right with her uncle before ever embarking on something with Night Hawk which would be for eternity.

"In time," he whispered to himself. "Until then I

shall take what I can, when I can, and give back twofold."

Although a half-breed himself, he had always thought that he would not allow his eyes to stray to a woman other than that of his own skin coloring, as his father had all those long years ago.

Ay-uh, he argued to himself, his mother was beautiful! She was special. Yet so were the Chippewa maidens.

But there was no more arguing with his heart. None of the Chippewa maidens had stirred his insides into wanting them for a lifetime.

Only Briana, whose skin was lily-white.

The first time he had laid eyes on her, he had known. Oh, how he had known!

He frowned darkly at the thought of her uncle, who was called Blackie in the back rooms of the saloons, where cards were dealt over felt-covered tables and cigar smoke hung like thunder clouds low and thick in the room.

This man pretended to be something to the people that he in truth was not. His reputation had been an unsavory one even before settling down in St. Paul. This uncle, whose heart was cold toward all Indians, would be an obstacle that Night Hawk would have to deal with.

This man who Night Hawk's very own father despised would not be allowed to stand in the way of Night Hawk's happiness. Somehow he would find a way to deal with him.

Riding out into an open meadow, Night Hawk sank his heels into the flanks of his horse and sent it into a hard gallop, then slowed it back down to a lope when the moonlight allowed him to recognize several soldiers advancing on him from the front.

Having no cause for alarm, since almost all of the

soldiers at Fort Snelling knew of his peaceful nature, Night Hawk rode onward and drew the reins as the soldiers stopped, only one coming to Night Hawk's side. His jaw tightened when he saw the soldier reach for his pistol, and by instinct, his own right hand started to reach for his firearm in the gunsling at the side of his horse.

"I wouldn't do that," Lieutenant Braddock warned, yanking his pistol from its holster and aiming it at Night Hawk. With his free hand he leaned over and eased Night Hawk's rifle from the gunsling, then rested it on his lap. "Come along with us to Fort Snelling. And I'd advise you to go with us without complaint. Several of the soldiers have an itch to shoot an Injun. I might be obliged to allow it should you try to run."

"I guess I can't ask you to have the courtesy to explain what this is about," Night Hawk said, his voice void of emotion. "Lieutenant Braddock, isn't it? I know of you. I have seen you many times at the fort. You have seen me. You know that I am a peace-loving Chippewa. You know that my father is Chief Echohawk, and that my mother is Mariah, who was close friends to the Snellings."

"I know all of these things," Lieutenant Braddock said, slipping Night Hawk's rifle into the gunsling with his own. "And, yes, I am Lieutenant Braddock. But none of this changes the fact that Colonel Hawthorne has asked all of the regiments of Fort Snelling to round up any Indian that looks suspicious. So get along with you, Night Hawk. Being the son of a chief makes no difference to me. None at all."

"What have I done that is suspicious to you?" Night Hawk said, arching an eyebrow.

"It's not so much that you look suspicious," Lieutenant Braddock said, motioning with the barrel of his pistol for Night Hawk to move ahead of him. "Word has spread of the commotion you caused at the art museum earlier this evening. What are you turning into? A rebellious renegade? We can't have that, now, can we? We can't have you bursting into all functions of the St. Paul elite, now can we?"

"No, we would not want the dark skin of an Indian brushing against the snow white skin of the St. Paul elite," Night Hawk said in a feral snarl. He moved on ahead of Lieutenant Braddock, his head held high, yet his feelings severely injured by the bigotry of the world. He had to wonder just how far this would go against an Indian who was guilty only of loving a white woman.

As he rode along with the regiment of soldiers in the direction of Fort Snelling, he once again became lost in thoughts of Briana, and the fact that she was very much a part of that elite group of socialites in St. Paul.

Yet she had proven to be different. She did not see him as anything but the man whose heart had been lent to her. While with her, it was easy to forget the bigots—the prejudices against his people as a whole.

And he was also reminded of his mother—how she had turned her back to such prejudices and become as one with the Chippewa culture without a glance backward at how the white community lived so differently in houses, with furniture, curtains, and stoves for cooking and heating. She had accepted, and learned to love, the simple life of the Chippewa.

But he was not sure if Briana could ever go that far. She was from a different sort of world. She had been across the large body of water, where she had attended the finest of schools in a land they called France. How could living simply in the forest ever be enough for her?

How could she accept the fact that her Chippewa lover could not ride through the forest without being accosted and accused unjustly by the white pony soldiers as though he were no better than the "enemy-people," the Sioux that had once roamed the land in droves, killing and maiming all of the white settlers, putting fear in their eyes and hearts at the mere thought of stepping outside their cabins on a dark winter's night.

But even though Night Hawk had only known Briana for a short while, it was enough time to know that she would let nothing shadow her feelings about him. She knew that his heart was peaceful toward whites, and that he would do nothing to stir up bad feelings between his people and the soldiers at Fort Snelling.

Night Hawk just had to convince the person in charge, and it would only be a matter of moments before he was standing face to face with Colonel Hawthorne. Night Hawk rode beneath the tall shadows of the stone walls that surrounded the fort, then through the open gate. Except for one, there was hardly any lamplight in the windows of the establishments within the fort's walls, which meant that most of the soldiers were in bed.

Night Hawk dismounted and, flanked on both sides by soldiers, went into the central headquarters building. He soon found himself standing before a huge oak desk piled high with papers and journals. Lamplight glowed brightly on the bald head of a man in a chair behind the desk, bent low over his ledgers, inking figures onto the pages.

"Sir, we've brought you a suspect," Lieutenant Braddock said, standing at attention beside Night Hawk and clearing his throat nervously when the colonel did not look immediately from his journal. "Sir, we found Night Hawk. We brought him to you for questioning."

Colonel Hawthorne finally responded. He slowly lay his journal aside, then turned his ocean blue eyes up at Night Hawk. He frowned for a moment, then began speaking in a succinct manner, his voice deep and mannerly. "What's this I hear about the commotion you caused at the art museum tonight?" he asked, stretching the fingers of one hand out atop the journal, as though not wanting to part with it for even one second.

Night Hawk folded his arms across his chest, his midnight black eyes flashing at Colonel Hawthorne's. "It is not written into law that a Chippewa brave cannot go and view paintings," he said, obviously trying to keep his anger at bay. "It is hard for me to understand why you would have your soldiers search for me because of my interest in art, when it is known by many that even you sometimes dabble in painting. Why were you not among those attending the art show tonight? Was it because it was a lady whose paintings were being celebrated instead of yours? Did you have to find someone to punish, to help alleviate some of the anger within your heart because your artistic abilities have been ignored by the white community?"

Colonel Hawthorne rose slowly from his seat. He leaned over toward Night Hawk. He splayed his fingers against the top of his desk and leaned on them. "You'd better watch your tongue," he grumbled. "I am the authority here. I say who is arrested and who is not. I would think twice before humiliating me in front of my soldiers."

"The humiliation is well earned," Night Hawk said, not wavering in his determination to put the colonel in his place. "You see, it is a widespread fact that there are many raids being carried out in Minnesota.

Should your White Father in Washington hear that you are wasting your soldiers' time bringing in an Indian because he is interested in art instead of searching for those responsible for the killings of innocent settlers, I believe your position would soon be filled by somebody more deserving."

"I could easily accuse you of those ghastly deeds and order my men to stand you before a firing squad tonight," Colonel Hawthorne said, his lips tugging into a smug smile.

"That would work for only a short while," Night Hawk said, returning the half smile. "When the raids continued after my death, then who would be blamed?"

Colonel Hawthorne's smile faded. He eased back down in his chair. He picked up some papers and began absently stacking them, all the while looking up at Night Hawk. "Perhaps you have an idea who is behind these raids?" he asked, his voice shallow. "Of course I have never blamed you. It is known that you walk in the shadow of your father, who is a man of peace, and that your mother is white, another reason why you would not turn to murdering white settlers in cold blood."

Colonel Hawthorne cleared his throat absently. "Also, the rumors spread quickly to me about your, ahem, interest in Arden Collins's niece," he said smoothly. "You wouldn't be making eyes at one white woman while with your next breath you were killing others, would you? So, Night Hawk, who is responsible? We are never there in time to catch the sonofabitches red-handed. They are as elusive as the wind!"

"I do not know why I would offer you any assistance after being treated as though a renegade myself," Night Hawk said stubbornly.

"The part of you that is white would lead you into

assisting me," Colonel Hawthorne grumbled. "Now, Night Hawk, who do you think it is? Who hates so much that they must kill over and over again?"

Night Hawk paused for a moment, searching through his heart for answers as to whether or not he should help or even trust the white colonel. Then knowing that he would like to see the killings stopped, he decided to give the only clues that he knew.

"It is my belief, as I am sure it is yours, that your search should end when you find the renegade Sioux, White Wolf," Night Hawk said solemnly. "He is a crafty, cruel, and bitter old man with unflinching endurance. He is surely at the root of most of the trouble in the Minnesota Territory today. Find White Wolf, and the massacres will stop."

He turned and started walking away. Lieutenant Braddock drew his pistol, but Colonel Hawthorne rose from his chair and went quickly to Braddock, taking his pistol. "Let him go," he said, politely placing the lieutenant's pistol back into his holster.

Night Hawk walked out into the splash of moonlight, and without looking back, mounted his horse. With a jerk of the reins and a nudge of his heels into the flanks of his steed, he quickly rode away from the fort, a cold, mean bitterness eating away at his heart.

Lily lay on her pallet of furs in the far recesses of her parents' wigwam, watching in the dim glow of the fire for her parents to go to sleep. As soon as she was sure they were, she drew a blanket around her shoulders, crept toward the entrance flap, and hurried outside.

The moonlight lay a silver path across the ground as she fled from the village and into the darker recesses of the forest. Her heart pounded out her anxiousness to be with Strong Branch again, loving him so much she felt possessed by such a love.

And tonight. She would tell him tonight. Now that she had made up her mind, she could hardly wait.

Yet a part of her feared telling him this sweet truth. He had turned his back already too often when she had spoken of marriage. What if he saw the child as interference with his plans to better his life as chieftain?

"Perhaps I should not tell him," she whispered to herself. Tears pooled in her eyes as she found him waiting for her at the foot of the bluff, his hand extending to her.

She ran to him and took his hand, and her breath was taken away when he swept her fully into his arms and gave her a long, passionate kiss. She felt his anxious hands on her, and she allowed it. His need for her seemed greater tonight, for he did not lead her up to their usual trysting place. Tonight he eased her to the ground beneath the giant sycamores and oaks, one hand lifting the skirt of her dress above her knees, his other lowering his breechclout.

He began kneading her throbbing center with his skilled fingers, then knelt down over her and curled his tongue around it, so warm, wet, and soft. All her thoughts of truths tonight melted away into the wonders of how he was sending her heart into a sensuous spinning.

Tonight was meant for loving. Only loving.

Perhaps tomorrow night she would tell him, she found herself thinking amid the joyous bliss of building pleasure.

Or perhaps the next?

At this moment, like the other times with him, all she wanted was the passion. The wild rapture!

She did not want to do anything to spoil these times

with him. She had plenty of time to tell him about the baby before she began showing.

Repositioning himself, Strong Branch nudged Lily's legs apart with his knee, then entered her with a deep, thick trust. She lifted her hips, welcoming how he so magnificently filled her. She closed her eyes and tossed her head back and forth with ecstacy, her whole body quivering as he pressed endlessly deeper within her.

At this moment they were the only two people in the universe.

There wasn't even a child to consider.

8

My conscience hath a thousand several tongues
And every tongue brings in a several late,
And every late condemns me for a villain.
—RICHARD III

Clouds were floating across the moon like great puffs of gray cotton. The wind had picked up and was howling through the pines as a lone traveler rode his horse to higher ground, where the river wound like a narrow ribbon below, in the shadows of a great cliff.

Dressed in black riding gear and dark, heavy boots, Blackie blended well into the darkness of night. A pistol was thrust into a holster at his waist, and a rifle rested in the gunsling at the side of his black stallion.

A wide-brimmed black hat pulled low over his brow, his dark eyes peering through the night, Blackie left the higher ground again and began watching for a cave. He had been there more than once. Lately, in fact, he had been there quite frequently with White Wolf, the two of them inciting the terrorism that was being spread across the land.

There was a part of him that would not let go of his past—that which lived for the excitement of not only gambling but of seeing people bend to his will.

By entering politics, he had felt the power that came with the reputation of being a politician—bending people's will in that more genteel way. And by joining forces with White Wolf, he was able to bend other people's wills with force—a thrill no woman ever gave him!

But he had not been able to actually participate in the raids as much as he would have liked. It was too risky. His face had become too well known to take a chance at being recognized. He had helped the cause mainly by backing it with his money. He had even encouraged White Wolf to set up camp elsewhere, in a fortress, where he and his men could live more comfortably, even though White Wolf had not wanted this sort of life. He was happier living off the land, in a cave.

Blackie's eyes narrowed as his thoughts drifted to Briana and her obvious feelings for Night Hawk. He was not upset that Briana had fallen in love with an Indian. But the whole affair brought Night Hawk too close to Blackie and his illegal activities with White Wolf.

Night Hawk was a threat, a threat that had to be eliminated.

The clouds had slipped past the moon, leaving it bright and round in the sky. It sent down enough light for Blackie to make out the shape of the entrance of a cave only a short distance away. He rode onward until he came to a thick stand of cottonwood trees. Reining in his horse, he slipped out of the saddle and walked his stallion the rest of the way.

Just inside the mouth of the cave, Blackie tethered his horse with several others. Squinting, he began feeling his way along the wall of the cave, and as it made a bend, he finally got his first sight of a campfire up ahead.

Blackie walked onward, farther and farther into the cave, the rocks crunching beneath his boots, the musty aroma of the damp walls curling his nose. Every once in a while he would hear the squeak and flap of a wing as a bat became frightened and scrambled from its dark hiding place.

In the far distance, Blackie heard the sound of splashing water, and he knew that at the very far end of the cave was a stream that had cut its way through the heavy rock, giving White Wolf and all of his renegades a good supply of fresh water every day.

Overhead, he saw occasional winks of moonlight through the cracks in the cave ceiling. Those cracks made it possible for White Wolf to build a camp fire, so that the smoke would have an escape.

Blackie listened to the hum of voices as he grew closer to the campsite, recognizing many of the men that were sitting around the evening fire, chatting and planning the next strike of terror against humanity. He recognized White Wolf's voice, and several of his renegade warriors, none of which had ever fit into any way of life.

"Misfits, all of them damn misfits," he snickered to himself. "Especially that damn White Wolf."

Blackie went on into the cave and arrived at a torch-lit area. He stopped and looked slowly around him at the stacks of firearms piled high at each side of the cave, the flames from the torches glistening on the barrels of the rifles. Boxes of ammunition were spread about, along with some sticks of dynamite, which gave him cause to be unnerved.

As he approached, White Wolf embraced him, then stepped back, folding his arms across his chest. "Why have you come tonight?" he said, his voice deep and resonant. "Do you carry with you bad tidings?"

Blackie tossed his hat onto a pile of bearskins. He laughed gruffly as he went with White Wolf to the campfire and the circle of Indian renegades lounging beside it, some smoking their long-stemmed pipes, some eating.

"Well, in a way, I guess you might say that," Blackie said, settling down onto a thick layer of blankets beside White Wolf, the fire warm against his face. He reached inside his coat pocket and pulled out a leather pouch of tobacco, handing this over to White Wolf.

"Tell me about it," White Wolf said, lifting a long-stemmed pipe and resting it on his lap. He opened the drawstrings of the buckskin pouch and sprinkled some of its tobacco into the bowl of the pipe.

The pouch laid aside, White Wolf placed the stem of the pipe to his lips. Bending close to the fire, he lifted a burning twig from its periphery and placed its glowing tip to the tobacco, inhaling deeply as it became lighted.

"Of course, since we have both allied ourselves with Strong Branch and Gray Moon, you are familiar with Chief Echohawk," Blackie said in a low growl.

"Who is not familiar with the Chippewa chief?" White Wolf said, his voice filled with annoyance. He looked over at Blackie and handed him the lit pipe. "He is my same age. We are bitter enemies, he and I. But we have not come face to face for years. There was no need to. He went his way—I went mine." He narrowed his eyes as he leaned closer to Blackie, who puffed slowly from the pipe. "Tell me, why do you mention his name to me now? Has he become an irritation to you?"

Blackie gazed over at White Wolf as he leisurely enjoyed the pipe, seeing him as surely sixty years of age, yet still virile and muscular. He wore his graying hair long and past his waist, secured by a fur headband. His attire, no matter whether it was winter or summer, was only a breechclout. He had explained to Blackie that his body had been trained to tolerate the extremes of both heat and cold.

The soft sound of a baby crying a short distance away, where lamplight flooded the low, damp ceiling of the cave with its golden light, made Blackie turn his attention from White Wolf. "Your squaw and child?" he asked, resting the bowl of the pipe on his knee. "They are well?"

"Both are well," White Wolf said, nodding.

Blackie caught sight of Gentle Fawn as she rose to her feet, strolling back and forth with her baby. The child nursed from a breast where Gentle Fawn had lowered her buckskin dress only low enough so that the child could have benefit of her sweet milk.

Blackie saw Gentle Fawn as young and beautiful, knowing that she could hardly be more than twenty years old. He knew that she was not there of her own free will, yet he had done nothing about it. He never interfered in anything that White Wolf felt strongly about.

And what did it matter to him? he thought, shrugging. She was no concern of his. He had his hands full enough keeping his niece at bay.

Anyway, he concluded to himself, once the squaw's child had been born, it seemed Gentle Fawn had settled in and accepted her fate, never trying to escape from her "keeper" any longer. The child had made her afraid to leave. She was frightened that White Wolf would seek her out and kill the child for spite should she ever manage to flee from him.

But he would kill both her and the child, Blackie thought to himself, having heard White Wolf lay this threat on her many times.

Blackie turned his eyes back to White Wolf and gave his pipe to him. He raised his legs before him and, hugging them, scowled at White Wolf. "I need your help," he said, his voice low and threatening. "It seems my niece has become a nuisance, to say the least."

White Wolf forked an eyebrow, again sucking on

the stem of the pipe, inhaling a deep whiff of smoke, then exhaling it slowly. He placed the pipe aside and leaned back on an elbow. "You want me to kill your niece?" he said casually. "Is that why you have come to me tonight?"

Blackie felt the sudden silence on all sides of him and looked slowly around, seeing that everyone had begun listening alertly to the exchange. Blackie cleared his throat nervously, then looked into White Wolf's midnight dark eyes again. "That isn't what I want at all," he said thickly.

"Then what?" White Wolf said, straightening his back and folding his arms across his chest. "You speak in circles tonight."

Nervously, Blackie ran his fingers through his dark hair, then placed his hands on his knees as he leaned closer. "My niece has fallen in love with an Indian," he said dryly. "I want you to make sure he's no longer a problem." He leaned his face into White Wolf's. "I want him killed, White Wolf. I want you to do the killing."

"You spoke of Echohawk earlier," White Wolf said blandly. "Is he the Indian your niece is infatuated with?"

"No, it isn't Echohawk," Blackie mumbled. Yet deep inside his heart he knew that Echohawk would be a problem for him as long as he was alive, although the threat seemed to have lightened through the years. Now the son was his main concern.

"Oh?" White Wolf said, obviously confused.

"It's his son," Blackie said in a snarl. "Night Hawk. He's made his way into my niece's heart. Soon he will be trying to squirm into her life totally. He's a half-breed, you know. Perhaps he's tired of living with his Indian half, and wants to make a life with the whites. How better to worm his way into my life and try to take advantage of my money? I can't allow that. Nor can I allow him to get closer to me and discover how I spend my time when I am away from St. Paul. If it was ever discovered that I was associated with you and your men, I'd be finished. Do you hear? Finished!"

"I know of Night Hawk," White Wolf hissed. "He sees all Sioux as snakes in the grass. He is my enemy as well as his chieftain father. Tell me what to do. I shall do it."

"It's plain and simple," Blackie said, shrugging. "Kill him."

A slow smile tugged at White Wolf's thick lips. "That will be a pleasure," he said smoothly. "As long as I can do it at my leisure, and in my own way."

"However it is done does not concern me," Blackie said, rising slowly to his feet. He glared down at White Wolf. "But just be sure to take him out of commission soon. Get him away from my niece."

White Wolf rose to his feet and placed a hand on Blackie's shoulder. "Why not let me also kill your niece and get her out of your way?" he said thickly.

"You don't get the point, do you?" Blackie said, brushing White Wolf's hand from his shoulder. "She's important to me. Having a devoted niece at my side makes me look legitimate."

"I see," White Wolf said, kneading his chin thoughtfully.

"Can I trust you to do this for me?" Blackie asked, picking up his hat and placing it on his head.

"It is as good as done," White Wolf said, walking Blackie away from the camp fire and into the dungeon darkness of the outer part of the cave.

"You owe me, White Wolf," Blackie said in a growl. "Damn it, you owe me good for what I've done for you and your renegades. On those lean weeks when you didn't net enough loot from the raids, who was it that gave you food to eat and tobacco for your damn pipes? Damn it, White Wolf. Never forget that you owe me."

There was a strained silence when White Wolf didn't offer any response to this different sort of threat.

Blackie spoke again. "I hear you have another raid planned soon," he said, taking his horse's reins, leading him out into the moonlight.

"That is so," White Wolf said, following beside Blackie.

"Are Strong Branch and Gray Moon planning to go on this raid with you?" Blackie asked, peering intently at White Wolf.

"As far as I know, yes, they are planning to ride with me and my men," White Wolf said, his gaze locking with Blackie's. "And what does that matter?"

"Do not reveal our plans for Night Hawk to either of them," Blackie flatly ordered. "I've never trusted them."

"They feel the same about you," White Wolf said in a low grumble. Then he nodded. "Nothing will be said to them about our plans to kill Night Hawk. But it is not necessary to keep it from them. They both would benefit from the death." His lips lifted into a smug smile. "And also, if anything should happen to Echohawk, it would make the life of those two young braves much more comfortable. Perhaps after I see to Night Hawk's death, I will also see to Echohawk's."

"Whatever. That sounds fine to me," Blackie said, mounting his horse. "But one thing—one person at a time. Take care of Night Hawk. Do you understand? Soon!"

Blackie did not wait for a response. He nudged his horse's sides with his knees and rode off into the darkness, feeling as though he had just signed a pact with the devil tonight, and feeling comfortable with it.

His laughter rolled into the hills and treetops as he sent his stallion into a hard gallop across the meadow.

9

So teasing!
So pleasing!
Capricious!
Delicious!
—IRVING

It was a June night, scorching and breathless. As twilight fell on the small city park, drummers, tuba players, and saxophonists in black uniforms with bow ties and gold braid took their seats beneath the gingerbread of a bandstand. At the conductor's cue, they struck up a venerable American traditional song, setting hands clapping.

Among those who were enjoying the concert were small children sitting in the front rows of seats that had been placed close to the outdoor platform, picnic parties at tables along the sides of the park, and others sitting comfortably on blankets beneath the deepening shadows of the trees.

Briana was standing away from the crowd beneath a tree, trying not to be noticed and hating every minute of being there, acting out the role of the dutiful niece for her uncle's political rally. She gazed with contempt at Blackie sitting smugly on the platform in his dark suit and tie. He was tapping his foot in time with the music, papers clutched in his left hand—his speech carefully prepared for tonight, with hopes that he might pull more voters into his political arena.

Briana knew that as soon as the band ceased playing her uncle's favorite patriotic tunes, he would stand up behind the podium and pretend to be the people's savior, pretend to be something that he was not.

Shaking her head with disgust at the thought of her uncle's pretenses and his forced smile and aloof smugness, Briana leaned her back against the rough bark of the tree, then eased away from it again, not wanting to muss her dress. Today she wore a floor-length, soft silk dress dappled with tiny petals, the floating tiers of lace on her dropped sash designed to waft as she walked, creating a floral whirl. She also wore a big hat with a brow full of bows, and was clutching a beaded purse in her gloved hand.

Yes, she had dressed the part of a niece who should want to look uncommonly pretty for her politically aspiring uncle, but as she dressed, she had felt anything but glad to help him in his aspirations. She knew that he did not deserve to be involved in the formation of Minnesota as a state, or anything else that might decide the good of the land or the people.

Her gloved hand went to her cheek, recalling how her uncle had slapped her, realizing then that he was a vicious, unpredictable man. She was only pretending to be a dutiful niece now because she needed time to chart out a future that would not include him. If she wrote her parents of her unhappiness, they would send her the money required to return to Paris.

But she did not want to leave St. Paul. Her heart was there. She could never leave Night Hawk.

As the band ceased playing and her uncle rose to the podium to begin his speech, Briana tried to focus her mind elsewhere so that she would not have to listen to his lies. She centered her thoughts on her paintings, for even while not painting she always carried with her the memories of a certain golden light, the delicious hues of rivers and the sky, of fields and flowers.

She could not concentrate long on her painting, because something about her uncle's speech tonight puzzled her. For some reason he appeared to be more fired up, more priggish, and more self-assured.

She looked up at the platform, seeing that lanterns were now lit on both sides, darkness having fallen like a velvet cloak draped across the heavens. A chill coursed through her as her uncle's eyes searched for her, and then singled her out in the crowd, making eye contact with her.

She blinked nervously when she saw an even stranger sort of smugness in the way he gazed intensely at her as he talked about why he would be the best man for Congress for this land that was moving quickly into statehood. He spoke of the railroad that was being planned that would stretch from coast to coast, saying that the people of Minnesota knew that the chances of the railroad passing through their wonderful land were much better if Minnesota was a state and had a vote in Congress.

He spoke more loudly when he declared that he would be the best man for that vote.

Trumpets blared and people shouted, his approval quite pronounced tonight by the attitude of the citizens who were there rooting for him!

And then there was silence again, enough for him to resume his speech.

Briana cringed when he raised a hand and pointed at her, causing heads to turn when he introduced her to the crowd, saying that she was a renowned artist who had studied abroad, someone he was proud to call his niece, and who was herself bringing attention to their proud land—her reputation as an artist was spreading far and wide across the vastness of the United States.

Briana saw his smugness fade and a dark frown

crease his brow when she smiled awkwardly at the crowd and began slipping back farther into the shadows, no longer able to play the game with her uncle. She knew that her dodging the gawking crowd would infuriate him, and that he would accuse her of trying to spoil everything for him.

But at this moment it did not matter. Tonight she just could not stand any more of his lies.

Turning to leave the park and the drone of her uncle's voice as he continued speaking behind her, Briana gasped when she found Night Hawk on his horse, reined in at the roadside.

"Night Hawk, you frightened me," Briana said, holding her hat as she tipped her head to look up at him. Fear crept quickly into her heart. "You shouldn't be here. If my uncle knew that you were, there would be hell to pay."

"For him perhaps, but not for Night Hawk," the brave said stiffly.

"How long have you been here?" Briana asked, his mere presence stirring her insides passionately. "Why are you here?"

"I followed you here and have been waiting," he said thickly. "I could not stay away. I have thought of you day and night. Come with me, Briana. Let us be together again. Let us talk."

Briana glanced over her shoulder toward the lamp-lit platform, able to see that her uncle was occupied, his audience staring raptly up at him as he spoke fluently and moved his hands in the air like a preacher to keep their attention.

She turned back to Night Hawk. "I really shouldn't," she murmured, recalling her uncle's fury and his threats over her feelings toward Night Hawk.

"You should," Night Hawk teased, reaching a hand

to her. "Come. Let us go and sit by the Father of Waters. We will not stay long if you wish not to."

"It's only because of my uncle," Briana said, casting her eyes downward. Suddenly she felt a strong arm around her waist. She inhaled a quivering breath as she felt herself being lifted onto Night Hawk's lap. She did not fight his decision to do this as he held onto her and began riding away.

They rode for a while, then Night Hawk reined in his horse at a secluded spot overlooking the river. He eased Briana to the ground and quickly dismounted.

After securing his horse's reins to a low-hanging tree limb, he took Briana's gloved hand and led her beneath the trees toward the shine of the Mississippi River. They made their way down the winding path to the river's edge, and once there they stood side-by-side, content to just be there together.

"Tonight the stars are so soft, the river so quiet," Briana whispered, the first to break their silence. She removed her hat and dropped it to the ground, dropping her purse beside it.

"Tonight you are all that is truly beautiful," Night Hawk said, releasing her hand to place his hands at her waist to turn her to face him. Yet he did not kiss her. He urged her to sit on the ground, where he then drew her to his side and held her next to him.

"I love being here with you," Briana said, gently leaning against him.

"But first you fought this decision to be with me," Night Hawk said, peering down at her. She seemed so delicate in her dress of lace and frills.

"I know," Briana said, turning her eyes up to him. "But I was wrong." She laughed softly. "No matter what, I will never again let my uncle, or my fear of him, stand in the way of our being together." She removed her gloves and cuddled closer. "Night Hawk, I've missed you so much."

The brave turned to her and placed his hands on her shoulders, easing her onto her back on the ground. When his lips came to hers in a fiery kiss, she no longer worried about mussing her dress, or what her uncle might do when she came home with grass stains on its skirt, or perhaps a piece or two of dried leaves in her hair.

This was her life. Her uncle would not control it!

Night Hawk was her life, her very breath, it seemed.

A noise behind them startled them to their feet. Breathless, her heart pounding in fear that perhaps her uncle had followed them there, Briana watched as Night Hawk drew his pistol and began stalking around the high bushes and trees, searching for the intruder.

Briana raised an eyebrow and her heart slowed when she heard Night Hawk utter a sudden, deep laugh, then came into view carrying a raccoon with its bandit eyes peering through the darkness at her.

"It was only a raccoon?" Briana said, her shoulders relaxing with her relief.

She did not dare go any closer to Night Hawk as long as he held the wild animal in his arms. "They are known to bite," she murmured.

"The forest animals are as one with me," Night Hawk said, bending to a knee and releasing the raccoon. "None has ever bit me."

After placing his pistol on the ground beside Briana's hat, Night Hawk went to her and began taunting her. "You are afraid of a mere raccoon?" he mocked, lifting her up in his arms. He held her over the water and began swinging her back and forth teasingly. "Are you also afraid of the Father of Waters and the fish with their large teeth and mouths?"

Briana turned her eyes to the river, knowing its reputation of being muddy. That was what she truly feared—not the innocent fish. "Night Hawk, let me down," she said, laughing softly and clinging to him with all of her might. "You might drop me. Please . . . let—"

Night Hawk teasingly took another step closer, but suddenly he tripped over a rock and found himself toppling over the edge, carrying Briana with him into the water.

Briana didn't have time to scream from alarm. She was already in the depths of the water. She loosened herself from Night Hawk and swam to the surface. Coughing and gasping for air, she stood on the muddy bottom of the river, her hands smoothing her hair back from her face.

Night Hawk came to the surface beside her, his long black hair floating around his shoulders as he placed his feet on the bottom.

"You!" Briana cried, seeing the lace of her dress floating ugly and wet in the water. "Night Hawk, why did you do that? How am I to be expected to go home? My dress is ruined. I-I look like a drowned rat!"

Night Hawk chuckled. "I do not think the comparison is accurate," he said, reaching for her wrist, bringing her close, anchoring her against his hard body. "You are much lovelier."

He held her in his embrace with the strength of one arm, while his free hand roamed over her, feeling the suppleness of her curves through her wet dress, and the tempting triangle at the juncture of her thighs. "And you do not need to go to your uncle's home," he said huskily. "Return to my home with me. Be my woman. Stay with me *ah-pah-nay*, forever."

Briana was only half hearing what he was saying. His fingers were awakening her to the wild rapture that she always found while with him. As he caressed her through her dress, his mouth so temptingly close, she closed her eyes and let the euphoria claim her.

When he brought his lips to hers in a frenzied kiss, she clung to him and wrapped her legs around him at his waist. Night Hawk somehow released his throbbing need from his fringed breeches, and tore her undergarment away. He found her open and ready for him, his thick, hard manliness moving within her with powerful, rhythmic strokes.

His lips moved away from her mouth, down her neck, and to her breast, stopping to suck on the nipple through the soft, textured silk of her dress. Briana held her head back and sighed with bliss. Her hair swirled around her in the water, her shoulders swaying in her passion. Her gasps became soft whimpers as she felt the pleasure growing.

And when she felt a great shuddering in Night Hawk's loins, she strained her hips to accept his seed inside her, crying out at her own fulfillment the same moment he groaned out his own wild ecstasy.

Afterward, her heart still beating soundly, Briana clung to Night Hawk, savoring his closeness. As he slipped himself from inside her, she placed her feet on the bottom of the river, steadied herself, then reached and found his limpness and began caressing it with her fingers. She felt the first stirrings as it began to grow within her hand. She could feel him groan and she looked up at him, at his eyes hazy with renewed passion.

She was not at all surprised when he moved her hand away from his newly aroused pulsing need of her and swept her into his arms and carried her to dry land.

He lay her down, his fingers quickly disrobing her. He began disrobing himself. She watched, loving it.

He tossed all of his clothes aside and knelt down over her, worshiping her body. It seemed his tongue left no dip or crevice untouched. She breathed hard, closing her eyes, enjoying it.

As his tongue stopped at her throbbing mound, she parted her legs and twined her fingers through his thick, dark hair and led him on to what he sought. She became lost in the sensual pleasure that swam through her like soft waves on an ocean, needing it.

She was soon overcome with the shocking sensations of sheer bliss.

And then she reciprocated. As he rolled onto the ground, she moved toward him, the flesh of her thighs rippling in sinuous hollows. Her hands moved over his body, until they cupped his buttocks. They were smooth and hard as she clung to him, her mouth giving him pleasure that seemed to make him mindless.

His groans filled the night air.

And when it seemed that he could no longer stand this sort of loving, he turned her beneath him and plunged his throbbing shaft deeply within her.

Their naked flesh became one as they rocked and swayed in a gentle pressure of bodies. It did not take long for them both to go over the edge into total ecstasy again, leaving them breathing hard, laughing softly as they clung to each other.

"It was maddeningly beautiful," Briana said as Night Hawk rolled away from her and onto his back. "Always with you I am awakened to so many feelings that until now I could never, in my wildest dreams, fathom." She turned to him and smoothed a hand across his flat, tight stomach. "Was it as wonderful for you, darling? Will you love me forever?"

"Did I not ask you to return with me to my village and be my woman?" Night Hawk said, smoothing some of the wet strands of her hair from her face. "I would want you there with me, *ay-uh*, *ah-pah-nay*. Marry me. Be the flower of my wigwam."

"Marry you?" Briana gasped incredulously. "Be the flower of your wigwam?"

The clouds shifted and rays of the moon fell upon the two. Night Hawk looked heavenward, smiling. "See?" he said. "The Great Spirit is pleased with our togetherness and is smiling upon us."

He turned to her and grasped her shoulders, drawing her atop him so that her legs straddled him. "We are good together, you and I," he said huskily, shifting his body so that his arousal was probing for entrance inside her again. He clung to her rounded hips, smiling as Briana gasped with pleasure as he thrust himself inside her, finding her tight and willing. He lifted himself more deeply into her with steady thrusts.

"Tell me that you do not wish to be mine, to live with me until I am old," Night Hawk said, his heart pounding as his own pleasure mounted. He did not slow his strokes within her. He kept them steady and demanding. "Tell me that you would not desire awakening to these sorts of pleasures every morning, when my body aches to be touched and kissed. Is it not the same for you?"

"My body never felt much of anything until you awakened it to these sensual pleasures," Briana said, sucking in a wild breath when his hands moved to her breasts, cupping and kneading them.

"And now?" he urged huskily.

"Now all of my soul cries out day and night for what we are now sharing again," Briana said, choking back a sob as the passion began to peak. She covered his hands with hers, causing his fingers to press more tightly into her breasts. "Oh, how it would delight me to live with you—to be your woman. I love you so much! Oh, so much!"

"You will tell your uncle tonight?" Night Hawk said, slipping himself from inside her, turning her so that she was now beneath him. He spread himself atop her and plunged inside her again, his whole body stiffening as he found himself so close to that brink of joyous bliss, so much so that he scarcely heard what she said, her words seeming to come from deep within a tunnel as his body spasmed, for a moment blotting out everything but the sheer pleasure.

Briana responded in kind, everything within her warming from the ecstasy anew within her.

And then she lay with him, side by side, her head cradled between his arm and chest. "Didn't you hear me?" she whispered. "I'll marry you. But first I must write my parents. I-I mustn't rush into anything as serious as this without first sharing the news with my parents. Do you understand?"

Stunned that she had actually agreed to marry him, Night Hawk leaned away from her, his eyes wide, his lips parted. And then he shouted to the wind, the stars, the heavens, and the moon as he picked her up and began dancing around in a circle, she in his arms, clinging and laughing.

When he finally placed her on the ground, the grass cold beneath her bare feet, she sobered, knowing what lay ahead of her.

She gazed down at her wet, ruined dress, then up at Night Hawk.

"How on earth am I going to get past my uncle without him seeing me in such disarray?" she said, her voice breaking at the thought of how he might react. He had given her a slap only on his *suspicions* of her and Night Hawk having been together. Seeing her like this, he might react even more violently. Yet she had no choice but to return to his house.

But it thrilled her heart to realize that soon she would never have to face him again. Night Hawk was giving her a place to go—a haven—in his arms forever.

"You do not have to face him ever again," Night Hawk said, stooping to pick up her dress, then handing it to her.

"Yes, I must," she murmured. "If I didn't go home tonight, Uncle Blackie would come looking for me, and I do not want to give him any excuse to bring a rifle and use it on you."

Even though the night was still deliciously warm, she shivered as she slipped into the wet garments. Soon, riding on Night Hawk's lap on his horse, her uncle's house came within view.

"You'd better let me go the rest of the way alone," she insisted, turning wistful eyes up at Night Hawk. "Please, I'd best face my uncle alone."

He drew a tight rein and stopped his horse. He eased Briana to her feet and slipped out of the saddle, standing beneath low-hanging branches of an elm tree. He circled his arms around her waist and drew her against his hard body.

"Go with care, my beloved," he whispered. He gave her a long and feverish kiss before releasing her.

Her heart fluttering wildy within her chest, Briana broke free and began running toward her uncle's great mansion, dying a slow death inside when she heard Night Hawk riding away in the opposite direction. She ran her hands down the front of her wet dress and then through her hair, knowing what a sight she was. She dreaded what awaited her, but she rushed onward.

When she reached the house, she tiptoed as softly as she could up the steep front stairs, gently opened the heavy oak door, and crept into the dimly lighted foyer.

Before climbing the spiral staircase, she stopped to get her breath. She looked up the stairs, toward the second-floor landing, and noticed that hardly any lights were on, except for the candles glowing softly in the sconces along the corridor walls.

Sucking in a breath of air, she crept up the stairs. Then, just as she reached the landing, she almost toppled backward when she found her uncle suddenly standing there, holding a razor strop in his right hand, smacking it threateningly against the palm of his left hand.

"Uncle Arden, what are you doing there, with—with that thing?" Briana said, inching around him, wanting to get to the safety of her bedroom. Yet she knew that while she was in this house, there was never anything akin to safety. It was as though she had just entered the pits of hell—and the devil was there awaiting her, glaring.

"Go to your room at once," Blackie snarled, continuing to slap the razor strop against his hand.

Frightened nearly to death, Briana walked backward, inching her way to her room. When she reached it she rushed inside and slammed the door.

But she did not get it bolt-locked quickly enough. Her uncle burst the door open with one shove of his shoulder.

Blackie pushed Briana, which made her lose her balance and fall across the bed on her stomach. When the razor strop fell across her back, the pain almost made her black out. She screamed and clawed her fingers into the bedspread.

Then her pain changed to anger.

She flew from the bed and, surprising her uncle, jerked the razor strop from his hand before he had a chance to stop her. Raising it, she brought it down across his face, instantly drawing blood.

Realizing what she had done, Briana gasped, dropped the razor strop, and tried to run.

But a tight hand on her wrist swung her around and her whole body shuddered as Blackie hit her across the face.

Briana's body doubled over with pain, and she

crumpled to the floor. She lay there sobbing as Blackie stood over her.

"You bitch," he grumbled, then walked away.

Briana lay there for a while, then rose slowly to her feet. She wiped a trickle of blood from the corner of her mouth and stumbled to the door, bolt-locking it. She rested her back against the door for a moment longer, then went to the desk and sat down shakily at it.

Opening the drawer, she found a pen, ink, and paper. Sobbing, she began penning a letter to her parents. She first explained about her uncle's behavior toward her, and then told them that she soon would be married, and to whom.

Once the letter was sealed and ready to take to the post office on the morrow, she went to the window and drew back a sheer curtain, thinking that perhaps she should escape into the forest tonight, away from her demon uncle.

Yet another thought came to her that made her smile. She was going to wait at least another twenty-four hours before mailing the letter, or leaving this house of horrors. That was the date of her uncle's next political rally. She was going to be at his side, but this time when she was introduced, she was going to step boldly up to that podium and make an announcement that would ruin her uncle's political career forever!

She would tell all of the ugly truths about this man who most did not know as Blackie.

"Yes, my dear uncle, I'm going to make you pay for what you've done to me," she whispered to herself. "Pay dearly."

10

There are loyal hearts, there are spirits brave,
There are souls that are pure and true.
—BRIDGES

After leaving Briana, Night Hawk rode hard to get to his village by midnight, the designated time for the council meeting of the elders of not only his village but also Chief Strong Branch's village, whose people were as one with Chief Echohawk's.

Night Hawk swung himself out of his saddle and gave his horse's reins to a young brave who took his steed swiftly away to the corral. Night Hawk walked somberly toward the great outdoor fire that was reaching its flames toward the sky, lighting the heavens as though it were midday instead of midnight.

Night Hawk's troubled mood was caused by what he expected from Strong Branch tonight. Echohawk had given his son the duties to preside over the council meeting, having told him proudly that he soon would take over the full duties of chief of their people. Echohawk had taught him well, and his preparations for stepping down to let his son become chief were almost completed now.

Echohawk wanted more time with his ailing wife, a luxury that being chief did not allow him.

Night Hawk knew that Echohawk's announcement at the last council meeting—that his son would soon be chief—also had stirred jealousy within Strong Branch's heart, for it was known by everyone that Strong Branch was not happy with being chief of just his band of Chippewa.

Suddenly, it seemed, Strong Branch had become obsessed with power, and he would not be pleased at all when he had to sit by and watch Night Hawk preside over this meeting tonight, when Strong Branch had never been allowed to.

Until tonight, Echohawk had been in control of such meetings. He was the elder of these two chiefs of the adjoining bands of Chippewa, and respect for his age gave him more authority than Strong Branch was comfortable with.

Needing time to collect his thoughts, Briana still sweet on his breath and in his heart, Night Hawk stepped into the shadows of a wigwam and inhaled a shaky breath. Tonight it was important to show his father that he was worthy of soon becoming chief. He must run the meeting with a calm reserve, and should Strong Branch or Wise Owl, an elderly spokesman of Strong Branch's band who spoke his mind more often than not, stir up resentment tonight, he knew that he must be prepared to meet this challenge head-on.

It was sad that this was even a worry to him. In their youth, Strong Branch and Night Hawk had been the best of friends. Strong Branch had been the chief of his people even then, with Echohawk having full control of Strong Branch's people, until Strong Branch had grown old enough to realize what the title of chief meant, and what powers were needed to take over the role that was meant to be his upon the death of his father, Chief Silver Wing. Chief Silver Wing's last dying words had been to Echohawk—asking him to assume the powers of chief over his people until his infant son grew into them.

Bitter and old, and having never agreed with Chief Silver Wing's decision to allow Echohawk to reign as chief over Strong Branch's band of Chippewa, Wise Owl had pressed Strong Branch into the decision to try to oust Echohawk from power. This had changed the younger chief's life. He was no longer a carefree person who laughed a lot. He had turned into a suspicious, greedy young man that frowned now more than he laughed.

Now it was only Lily, Night Hawk's sister, who seemed to find any goodness left inside Strong Branch's heart.

"Perhaps that is for the best," Night Hawk grumbled to himself. "Perhaps this marriage between Strong Branch and Lily could bring our people together again with much love, compassion—and respect." Yet he doubted that and wished that his sister would look elsewhere for a husband—for a man that would treat her like the jewel that she was instead of just something to use.

"Big brother Night Hawk?" Lily said suddenly from behind him.

Night Hawk turned with a start, yet he knew that he should not be all that surprised to find his sister standing there, and that she was not in bed, as was usual for girls her age at this time of night. "Lily, do you plan to sit in council with the men of the two adjoining villages?" he said, chuckling low as he placed a gentle hand on her lily-white face.

"You know that I would not do that," Lily said. "It was just as usual . . . I am too restless to sleep. I plan to take my nightly stroll through the forest." She lifted the fringed hem of her dress, displaying a knife that was sheathed at the calf. "And, yes, big brother, I am weaponed in case I find myself face to face with danger during these hauntingly late hours."

Night Hawk drew her to him and gave her a gentle hug. "Then you have listened well to your brother's worries about you," he said. "But if you would listen even more attentively, you would not leave your dwelling at all after the moon replaces the sun in the sky. You would sit beside the fire and do your beadwork with *gee-mah-mah*."

"There is more on my mind than mere beadwork."
Lily sighed heavily. She leaned away from Night
Hawk. "As there is more on your mind than your
sister and the council meeting tonight." She touched
his cheek with her fingers as she peered into his eyes.
"My brother, I see something about you tonight that
is different. It is in your eyes. It is in your voice. My
brother, you are courting a woman? Who is she, Night
Hawk? Is she beautiful?"

Night Hawk took her hand from his cheek and
pressed his lips against the palm, kissing it, then held
it as he smiled down at her. "Baby sister, you think
you see and hear all," he said softly.

He glanced over his shoulder, at the men in council
awaiting his arrival, knowing that he was delaying the
meeting much too long. In preparation for this meeting, a great outdoor fire had been built and lighted at
noon when the sun was high so that by midnight there
would be many red coals. The Chippewa believed that
great wisdom was to be found in the embers of a fire.

The village was brightly lit by these burning embers,
and all of the braves were sitting with their knees
drawn up against their chests, held in that position by
wrapping their robes tightly around their loins and
knees. This fixed them somewhat in the fashion of a
rocking chair during this meeting of neighboring bands
of Chippewa, sharing plans for the summer activities.

"I must go," Night Hawk said, releasing his sister's
hand. He frowned down at her. "Go home. Go to
bed. Forget this foolishness about marrying Strong
Branch. Do you not know that I realize this is why
you are not able to go to sleep peacefully? He is the
cause. You deserve better, Lily. Do you not see that
he has changed into someone neither you nor I know?
He would not be a good husband, Lily. Choose some-

one else from another band of Chippewa. Will you consider this, for your brother?"

Lily's hand moved to her abdomen. She swallowed hard, thinking that if her brother knew about this child growing within her womb, he would not be asking her to seek another man to marry! She must marry the child's father, for the child's sake. And for hers—for she loved Strong Branch with every beat of her heart—and also her baby's!

But she could not share her secret with anyone except Strong Branch. She would be shamed in the eyes of her people if they knew that she was with child before her wedding vows were shared with the Great Spirit's blessings.

And she had lied to Night Hawk. She was not planning to venture into the forest tonight for her nightly walk. She was going to stand in the shadows until the council meeting was over, and then follow Strong Branch to his dwelling and demand that he hear her out—and this time before he was able to kiss her senses away!

"You do not answer me," Night Hawk said, placing his hands on her shoulders. "Will you, Lily, consider searching for another man to be your husband? Will you?"

"I cannot make you such a promise," Lily said, her voice breaking. She flinched when he jerked his hands away, within his eyes a deep, angry hurt.

Night Hawk glared down at her for a moment longer, then turned on his heel and went to the circle of men and made his way to the place assigned him, beside his chieftain father, and sat down.

Lily moved into the shadows of the wigwams, her heart anxious, her eyes intently on Strong Branch. Her insides froze when she saw his utter contempt as he glared at Night Hawk. Her brother accepted the lighted, long-stemmed calumet pipe that a young brave brought to him. She watched Strong Branch as he accepted the pipe as it was passed around to him, his eyes never leaving Night Hawk, the hatred increasing, it seemed, as each minute passed.

Lily placed a hand to her mouth, stifling a sob of remorse, knowing that her brother was right about Strong Branch, yet knowing there was nothing she could do about it now. She moved farther into the shadows, tears flowing down her cheeks.

The pipe was passed around the complete circle of men, each brave taking a puff, or if a particular brave did not care to smoke, he touched the tip with his lips or laid his hands gently and respectfully on the stem. Another way of conducting devotion was to blow the smoke in the mouth into cupped hands, then rub the hands over his head and arms, as if pouring water over his body.

Then the pipe was laid aside.

"Summer is upon us, my friends," Night Hawk said, smiling at those in council. "Let this summer be a festive one. Let us share many dances, feasts, and songs! The crops are planted. The hunt has been good. The maple trees gave us much sugar last autumn which will last until the next sugaring season. There is much to be thankful for. It is a time of prosperity for both our bands of Chippewa."

He wanted to speak even more loudly and say that perhaps even a wedding would be celebrated—his and Briana's. But that would wait. *Ay-uh*, that would come later, at a different sort of council.

Wise Owl, bent and haggard, who had sat close-mouthed and narrow-eyed while waiting for Night Hawk's arrival, pushed himself up from the ground, clinging to his robe, which was draped over his lean shoulders. "I wish to be heard," he announced, his voice a low rumble.

Night Hawk peered up at him, trying to show consideration for the old man, since respect was always shown to the Chippewa elders, and because at one time he had been Chief Silver Wing's best friend and most devoted brave. But it was difficult.

Wise Owl had become a nuisance, a troublemaker, not only for Night Hawk's tribe of Chippewa but Wise Owl's own. Until his interferences, for the most part these two bands of Chippewa had lived side by side for more than twenty-five winters in peaceful coexistence.

Night Hawk glanced over at Strong Branch, seeing his smug sneer, knowing that he was behind coaxing the elder Chippewa into interfering, for only Strong Branch would benefit from it.

Knowing that he must give Wise Owl his time to speak his mind, Night Hawk turned his gaze back to him and nodded.

Wise Owl's eyes moved around the circle of braves as he began talking in a low drone. "It is time that our two neighboring villages become truly one entity," he said. "One chief should be named to rule over all, and that chief should be a younger man, with younger ideas and ideals." He raised a shaky hand and pointed toward Strong Branch. "This young chief should be Strong Branch! He is dependable! He has proved his abilities as chief!"

He lowered his hand to his side and narrowed his eyes on Echohawk, and then Night Hawk. "It is known that Echohawk will soon hand over his title of chief to his son, saying he is worthy of it, but I say that he is not. He is half white. Most have labeled him a half-breed! Do you wish to be led by a half-breed who is mocked behind his back?"

Again he looked at Strong Branch. "Strong Branch is Chippewa through and through. His father was the great Chief Silver Wing. His mother was Nee-Kah!" he said more loudly. "He deserves to be chief! Only he!"

Night Hawk was stunned by Wise Owl's obvious dislike of him and lack of respect for Echohawk. He was speechless that Wise Owl seemed willing to do anything to keep Night Hawk from becoming chief at all.

He sat there for a moment longer, then turned his head slightly when he felt eyes on him. His heart ached when he saw his father staring at him, within his eyes a strange sort of embarrassment that Night Hawk had never seen before. At this moment he almost felt hatred toward Wise Owl for what he was trying to encourage both bands of Chippewa to do. It was a moment of humiliation for both Night Hawk and Echohawk.

Strong Branch squirmed uneasily on his pallet of furs, his sneer erased from his face almost as soon as Wise Owl began speaking. Strong Branch gave Gray Moon a fleeting, troubled glance, knowing that if their secret was ever disclosed, Strong Branch would not even be chief for his own people, much less both bands of Chippewa. Not unless their plans were first carried out to the fullest.

And they had only just begun to sketch out the future for both bands of Chippewa. They had to have time. And now Wise Owl was interfering.

Strong Branch ducked his head. Wise Owl was his elder and had to be shown respect by not telling him the wrong he was doing the tribe as a whole. Strong Branch just sat there, stiff and silent.

Echohawk was shattered by Wise Owl's declarations tonight, yet he did not respond to his comments, realizing that he himself was growing old and might one day say things that he might just as quickly regret. He hoped Wise Owl was regretting his words even as he eased back down on his thick cushion of furs.

These past years Echohawk had spent much time sitting by his lodge fire, smoking his pipe, and watching his tall, stalwart son grow into manhood. He had felt great satisfaction that his son was even now efficiently managing the affairs of their band of Chippewa, though not yet bearing the title of chief. The day would soon come when Night Hawk would be proclaimed chieftain, and no one would rob his son of this honor!

Not even Strong Branch, the Chippewa who would one day be the husband of Echohawk's beloved daughter, Lily.

This thought brought Echohawk to his feet. He nodded at Night Hawk for him to rise and stand beside him. Proudly he placed an arm around his son's shoulders and faced the others.

Then he glared at Wise Owl. "Old man, you have interfered in my people's affairs one time too many!" he grumbled. "Through the years, since Chief Silver Wing's death, I have tolerated these interferences only to keep peace between two bands of Chippewa that have joined together as one, yet were ruled by two separate chiefs. The younger chief, Strong Branch, has too often been guided by your suggestions. But, Wise Owl, you have overstepped your challenges of power this time. Any more interference and I will see to it that you are banished from the Chippewa tribe as the troublemaker that you have become!"

There were rumblings and gasps of shock among those being witness tonight to the battle for power. Yet no one offered any argument. They became silent again, just in time for Echohawk to say one more thing to Wise Owl before returning to his pallet of furs.

"Wise Owl," Echohawk said in a low, measured voice, "You ought to follow the example of the wolf. Even when the wolf is surprised and runs for his life, he will pause to take one more look at you before he enters his final retreat. So should Wise Owl take a second look at everything he sees, and even more important, have a second thought about everything he speaks."

Night Hawk smiled at his father as they both eased down onto their comfortable cushions. Wise Owl humbly lowered his head in a pretense of humility, but to himself vowed revenge.

The rest of the meeting concerned ordinary matters which did not stir up confrontations. The meeting came to a close and everyone began disbanding. Echohawk walked Night Hawk to his wigwam.

"My heart is heavy that this happened tonight between myself and Wise Owl," he said, more in apology than a statement of fact.

"It was not just between you and Wise Owl, *geebah-bah*," Night Hawk said, stopping at his wigwam. He turned and faced his father, placing a hand on his shoulder. "You spoke for us all. Wise Owl spoke for only himself and Strong Branch. His heart is not good toward those who look to him as a man that can be trusted. He surely knows that Strong Branch is no longer the caring, kind person that he was when he first became chief. Wise Owl has to know that Strong Branch is no longer fit even to be chief of his own people, let alone be chief of ours." He lowered his eyes, then looked slowly back up at his father again. "I believe it is time that you forbade Lily to see Strong Branch," he said thickly. "It is no longer in her best interest, or that of our people."

Echohawk kneaded his chin, then nodded. "Perhaps I shall tell her tomorrow," he mumbled. With his head somewhat bowed, he walked away, dreading having to deny his Lily anything. Perhaps he would give it awhile longer, this relationship between his daughter and Strong Branch. Surely the young chief would come around to the ideas that would truly be better for these two bands of Chippewa as a whole.

Perhaps Lily in her sweet kindness could persuade him.

Lily shied into the darker shadows of the wigwams, waiting for Strong Branch to go past so that she could reach out for him and draw him into the shadows with her. She had to speak to him tonight. These delays were driving her wild! Surely once he heard about the child, everything would be changed back to how it was before. She wanted to be the one to bring him back to his senses so that her brother could step up into the status of chief without further interference from Wise Owl or Strong Branch.

She sorted through the disbanding figures that moved from the outdoor fire in groups, searching for Strong Branch. When she finally found him, she frowned.

Again he was with Gray Moon! The brave seemed to mean more to Strong Branch now than Lily, and she could not help but resent him with a passion.

She watched as they made a quick escape from the others into the corral, quickly loosening their reins and mounting their horses that were already saddled.

She started running after them, but too quickly winded, stopped, sobbing when she realized that she could not catch up with them. They were already lost to her in the dark depths of the forest. Another night, it seemed, they were taking flight to do whatever consumed them away from their people.

This mystery she was not sure she wanted to unravel, afraid of what she might discover.

Sullenly she headed back toward her wigwam. She wiped the tears from her face before going inside, not wanting her family to question her about why she was crying.

In truth, they would not really want to know.

11

Give me a mind that is not bound,
That does not whimper, whine or sigh.
—WEBB

Having seen his father's distress during the council meeting, and torn with feelings himself about life in general, Night Hawk did not go directly into his wigwam. He needed to go and commune with Wenebojo, the Great Spirit, in the aloneness of the forest, where he would be as one with the night, stars, and sky.

On foot, he broke into a soft run away from his village, the night noises soft and filled with melancholia. A renewed rage filled his soul when he thought back to Wise Owl's insistence on challenging Night Hawk and Echohawk's right to be chief! Night Hawk realized that his father had humored Wise Owl through the years, having allowed him to believe that he had been in more control of things than he actually was, thinking there was no harm in it, especially if he was always in agreement with Echohawk's suggestions to the young Chief Strong Branch.

But Night Hawk now realized that the humoring had been wrong. Wise Owl had become too prominent a figure in the Chippewa community, taking away some of the powers of Echohawk. Night Hawk's jaw tightened, knowing that Wise Owl had to be stopped, but how? Strong Branch was the chief of Wise Owl's band of Chippewa. If Wise Owl was banished, it should, in truth, be Strong Branch's decision.

But now that both Night Hawk and Echohawk had begun to have uneasy feelings about Strong Branch, should not they make sure Strong Branch no longer made decisions that might affect Echohawk's people? Strong Branch had changed, and these secret meetings in which he was involved were a great, troubling puzzle to Night Hawk.

"I will follow him soon, to see where he goes and who he meets," he whispered to himself. "Also, Gray Moon. He is involved in the same mysterious secrets as Strong Branch. They have become inseparable."

His eyes became two points of fire, knowing that secret meetings could involve many ugly things, perhaps even the renegade Sioux, White Wolf!

He shook such a thought from his mind. Strong Branch could never be that deceitful—the Sioux had always been arch enemies of the Chippewa, especially White Wolf. Night Hawk ran onward. He came to a path that led upward, taking him to a high limestone bluff.

He stood there, tall and square-shouldered, his chin lifted proudly, his senses alive and alert to the myriad forms of life about him. Much depended upon the senses of hearing, seeing, and smelling. Half-dormant senses meant to be only half alive.

As before, he drank in the marvelous beauty of the night, the river winding like a silver ribbon toward the horizon, again finding peace, as he had so often found peace along the shores of the broad, silent river.

He loved the river, its flow music to his ears. Ah, but was it not a beautiful sight tonight as the water shimmered with moonlight? How he loved this valley filled with towering trees and clear, cool running springs.

And it was all there because Wenebojo allowed it. Wenebojo, the maker of all things of earth, sky, and water, had breathed life and motion into all things, both visible and invisible. He was over all, through all, and in all. Wenebojo's greatness and goodness could not be surpassed. All of the mysteries of birth, life, and death, all the wonders of lightning, thunder, wind, and rain were but evidence of his everlasting and encompassing power.

Ay-uh, all that he gazed upon tonight was a blessing from the Great Spirit, he thought to himself, feeling most grateful.

Yet did his people not deserve such blessings? They had been a peaceful and home-loving group, not seeking fame in war. And now there were those who were trying to spoil the peace, even take away the chief that had guaranteed it.

The leaves of several white birch trees trembled in the breeze behind him as he knelt down on a soft bed of grass and reached for a small buckskin pouch that was tucked inside the waistband of his fringed breeches. He took the pouch and loosened the drawstring. He shook some tobacco out onto the ground, his offering to Wenebojo, then lay the tobacco pouch aside.

His hair streaming down his back, he raised his face and voice to the sky and began a soft prayer, asking for guidance.

"Oh, thou Father of Waters, thou who has been such a friend to me and my father's people, stay with the Chippewa forever and ever," he whispered.

"Oh, thou beautiful valley, thou who has been such a joy to me and my father's people, be a home to the Chippewa forever and ever."

"Oh, thou great and mighty Great Spirit, thou who has led me and my father's people wisely and lovingly for many years, stay with the Chippewa forever and ever—"

His prayer was brought to an abrupt halt when a blow across his head rendered him quickly unconscious.

When he awakened, he found himself gagged, blindfolded, and his wrists and ankles bound tightly. The first thing he was aware of was the throbbing of his head, and then the gurgling of water from somewhere close by, a musty smell, and a dank sort of coldness enveloping his face.

Otherwise, there was a strained quiet that surrounded him. He heard the crunch of rocks and sensed a presence, realizing that he was not alone.

When his gag was roughly removed, he heard someone chuckling beneath his breath. He tensed, then spoke. "Who is there?" he asked, wrestling with the bonds at his wrists, trying to loosen them. "Where have you brought me?"

When there was no response, Night Hawk's thoughts went quickly to Wise Owl and how the old Chippewa had been humiliated in front of the others at the meeting when Night Hawk's father had threatened to banish him. Wise Owl could have abducted Night Hawk for revenge, yet he was too old to see to such an abduction alone.

Night Hawk could not believe that Strong Branch had helped Wise Owl, yet it was true that Night Hawk hardly knew Strong Branch anymore, and that, *ay-uh*, perhaps he could stoop this low to fulfill his aspirations.

Yet there was always White Wolf. And there was Briana's Uncle Blackie!

Night Hawk was suddenly aware of having many enemies, when he had tried so hard not to have any.

He stiffened and listened intently to the sound of voices and laughter in the distance, and then only footsteps as they came closer. His ears picked up the sound of not only one person but many.

His head snapped to one side as someone slapped him across the face.

"And so we have us a prisoner, eh?" an unfamiliar voice said. "White Wolf, is he of blood kin to you?"

"He is Chippewa, not Sioux," White Wolf growled. "Were he Sioux, he would not be here to be tortured, then sentenced to death. He would be treated as though he were my brother."

Night Hawk turned his head slowly, now realizing who had abducted him.

White Wolf.

Night Hawk was not sure exactly why White Wolf had done this now, when he could have done the dirty deed many winters ago!

Night Hawk had rode, prayed, and hunted in the forest alone many times. It was his second home. There had to be a reason why White Wolf would act upon his hatred for him now.

And to speak of torture and then a death sentence? Why would White Wolf hate him this much, unless his hatred was being transferred from someone else, for him to do the dirty deeds for them? He had to wonder if it was Wise Owl, or his childhood friend, Strong Branch, or perhaps Blackie.

If it was Strong Branch, it stung his heart to realize that the love that he had shared with Strong Branch could have turned to such hate.

He lifted his chin proudly, fear foreign to him, for he had been taught that it was not honorable to be afraid even when faced with possible death.

"And so it is you, White Wolf," Night Hawk said, his voice slow and emotionless. "And who else stands beside you tonight, just as guilty of kidnapping as you?"

"It is enough that you know that White Wolf has finally achieved a measure of vengeance," White Wolf said, bending to a knee, grabbing Night Hawk's hair at the back, yanking it hard. "The torture I spoke of? It will not begin just yet. I will give you time to wonder what sort of Sioux torture I will choose for you. Tonight White Wolf has better things to do."

Night Hawk straightened his back when White Wolf released his hair. "And so you leave me to go raid innocent white settlers?" he said, his voice drawn. "It is you, is it not, White Wolf? *You* are responsible for the raids and killings."

"This is not confession time," White Wolf said with a feral snarl.

"You do not need to admit to these unspeakable actions for me to know that you are responsible for them," Night Hawk said smoothly. "My father told me many moons ago about you. He also warned me never to believe that you had cowered away into the hills, a beaten man. It seems that he was right. But this time your days are numbered, White Wolf. Once my father hears of my abduction, and searches and finds you, your life will be ended as quickly as my father can plunge a knife into your dark heart!"

White Wolf laughed boisterously, then walked away. Night Hawk listened and realized that everyone had left along with White Wolf. And as he listened more closely, he could define the sound of many horses' hooves in the distance, strangely muffled by something.

And then he heard a sound that made his heart jump with surprise—the sound of a baby crying from somewhere close by.

He turned his head in the direction of the sound, wondering why a woman was there with a child—and if she was also a captive. He could not envision any woman loving a man like White Wolf or any of his renegades that rode with him.

Soon the baby's cries became muffled, making Night Hawk feel alone again. His shoulders slumped as he leaned up against the cold wall behind him, at least glad that neither Strong Branch nor Wise Owl had anything to do with his abduction, feeling guilty for having silently accused them of it.

Now he had no choice but to wait and see what fate awaited him, wondering if Briana would ever know why he never came to her again, filling his arms with her, smothering her lips with his kisses.

Echohawk awakened with a start, as though someone were there, pressing a heavy hand on his shoulder. He leaned up on an elbow and looked at Mariah, finding her sleeping soundly on the platform next to his, the low embers of the fire casting faint golden shadows on her frail face.

He looked over at Lily, who lay beautifully asleep, her thick lashes closed over her lily white skin, her hair having tumbled down, to hang in a black sheen on the floor.

He looked slowly around him, finding no one else there, yet he still felt the presence that had awakened him. It had to be for a reason.

His thoughts went to Night Hawk, almost numbing him in the sudden fear that perhaps something had happened to him!

He bolted from his sleeping platform, jerked on his fringed breeches and shirt, and stepped into his moccasins. He took a lingering look at Mariah, hurting deeply inside when he saw how she had changed so much in appearance since having been ravaged by her lingering illness. It was as though he were looking at

someone else; not a trace of her loveliness remained
from the debilitating malaria.

Turning away, the pain too great to gaze for any
length of time at his beloved wife, Echohawk grabbed
his rifle and left the wigwam in long, even strides. He
hurried to Night Hawk's wigwam. He wasn't there.
He sighed heavily, fear building inside his heart with
each footstep as he then went to the corral and found
his son's horse there. This was not normal if Night
Hawk had not left the village.

He left the corral and walked determinedly into the
darkness of the forest, knowing where Night Hawk
went to commune with the Great Spirit. Surely that
was where he had gone on foot this time of night.
Echohawk prayed silently to Wenebojo that he was
right, and that he would soon feel foolish for having
left his warm bed tonight to follow his fears.

Onward he trudged, the rifle clasped in his hand,
his heart heavy. When he reached the path that led
up to the butte, he inhaled an unsteady breath, then
went onward. Daybreak was just lighting the world
in its violet glow when he reached the top, revealing
nothing.

His heart pounding as his fears for his son mounted,
Echohawk went to the edge of the butte, where he
could look down upon the beauty of the land, knowing
that was where even he had paid homage to Wenebojo
with offerings of tobacco.

His heart stopped dead cold when he found something lying at his feet.

He knelt quickly to a knee and picked up the empty
buckskin pouch. He recognized it, now knowing for
certain that his son had been there. His offerings of
tobacco was still there on the ground, slight wisps of
wind stirring it around, spreading it farther and farther
into the tall grasses. Echohawk held the pouch to his

heart and let out a loud cry to the heavens, flooded with emotions that made him suddenly weak all over.

His son. His beloved son! Surely he had been abducted!

"*Ah-neen-dush*, why? Who would do this thing?" he cried, unashamed of the tears that rushed from his eyes.

Anger soon replaced fear and hurt as he recalled the council meeting the night before and Wise Owl's bitterness. Yet although Wise Owl was filled with resentment and jealousy, Echohawk could not envision the elder Chippewa being capable of anything as horrendous as this.

And Strong Branch? he wondered, arching an eyebrow.

Gah-ween, no. Strong Branch did not *hate* Night Hawk. He just wanted to steal what was his so that he would be the most powerful of the two in the eyes of the Chippewa.

"White Wolf," Echohawk said, the words bitter even as they crossed his lips, as though having bitten into a sour grape. "Could it be White Wolf? Has he waited until my son got to his prime and then taken him away? Would he not know that this would hurt me more than if he had stuck a knife into my heart?"

Frustration set in and a dull ache knotted within his chest. Even though he truly believed that White Wolf could be responsible for his son's abduction, no one knew where White Wolf was. He had been elusive for years. And even though White Wolf was suspected of being responsible for the raids on the white settlers, the white pony soldiers had not been able to find his hideout.

Echohawk's eyes widened and a small ray of hope flashed within his troubled mind. He knew of a man whose reputation had been joined with White Wolf's many years ago.

Blackie. Blackie Collins! The gambler and highwayman turned politician.

"Blackie, after all these years, it is time for us to meet again," he said, recalling the last time they had come face to face, clashing. It had been many, many moons ago, yet it seemed as though only yesterday.

Rushing down the path that led him from the butte, Echohawk realized that perhaps Blackie, who no longer went by that name, was an upstanding man, yet Echohawk did not think so. Once a lying, cheating crook, always a crook. And back then, no man could have been more crooked or dirty-dealing as Blackie Collins.

With the sky splashed crimson in the morning sunrise, Echohawk went on through the forest. He would tell his wife that he would be traveling into St. Paul, yet he would not tell her the reason why. As far as she would know, Night Hawk was safe, doing his daily chores that often kept him from his mother's wigwam now that he was an adult with his own life to lead.

She would never know that her son was in *nah-nee-zah-ni-zee*, danger.

Hopefully, there would never be a need to tell her, Echohawk worried to himself.

12

Be strong!
Say not; The days are evil,
Who's to blame?
—BABCOCK

Her paintbrush steady in her hand, her fingers deftly adding the final touches of color to a painting that she was completing, Briana sniffed the tantalizing aromas wafting from the kitchen and up the staircase outside her room, realizing that it would soon be time for lunch. She planned to take it alone in her bedroom, as she had her breakfast. She not only lacked the stomach to take meals with her uncle after last night and his fit of violence, she did not want to show off her black eye more than was necessary.

One maid was enough.

Briana had recruited Maria, her personal maid, to see to her needs.

But soon, no matter how embarrassed Briana would be to stand before the people of St. Paul with a blackened eye, she was going to walk determinedly to the podium and allow everyone to see exactly what her uncle was capable of. Surely they would decide that a man of violence had no place representing them in Washington.

This gave her cause to smile, knowing that this chance to ruin her uncle would come tonight. There was to be another political rally close to the capitol building. It had been highly advertised in the city's two newspapers.

A sudden commotion below in her uncle's study caused Briana's eyes to widen and her paintbrush to drag out the color of orange on a sunset into a wavering smear, disgruntling her. She sighed heavily, knowing that no amount of effort could repair this blunder—it was ruined! Absolutely ruined!

She slammed her paintbrush onto her palette and started to remove the painting from her easel, but stopped, alarmed, when the commotion became louder beneath her, the voices in a heated debate. And when the name Night Hawk could be distinguished from the rest of the words being shouted, Briana paled, and for the moment stood frozen to the spot.

With an anxious heartbeat she rushed to the door and opened it. She stepped gingerly out into the corridor, hoping that this would enable her to hear what was being said more clearly.

Why was her uncle discussing Night Hawk? Who was so angrily discussing Night Hawk with her uncle?

The thought frightened her. She knew that her uncle was capable of anything, especially if it had to do with Night Hawk. He surely would go to any lengths to see him dead—and that thought sent spirals of terror through her, knowing that he had the means and the money to pay someone to see the deed done.

Stepping lightly, she went to the head of the staircase and leaned against the banister, peering down at the closed door to the study. Her eyes widened and her pulse raced listening to the angry debate, now realizing that the man with her uncle was Night Hawk's father—Echohawk!

She was stunned, having never before seen any Indians at her uncle's mansion, knowing that the bigot would never allow it. This had to mean that Echohawk had arrived unannounced, and that her uncle had been forced to listen to what the Chippewa chief had to say.

She grew numb and covered her mouth with a hand, gasping when she heard Echohawk demanding to know where White Wolf's hideout was, for he was surely responsible for Night Hawk's disappearance!

"Night Hawk has been abducted?" Briana whispered, paling, her knees weakening. Hardly able to stand there just listening, wanting to demand answers from her uncle herself, almost certain that he was responsible for her loved one's disappearance, she held herself back and listened.

Echohawk leaned his face into Blackie's. "Many years ago you were in alliance with White Wolf," he said, his voice steady yet threatening at the same time. "Although you now hide behind the mask of a politician, Echohawk knows that you still mingle with renegades. Now tell me, Blackie, where can I find White Wolf? There I will find my son!"

Blackie went to his desk, lifted a cigar that he had left resting on an ashtray, and placed it between his lips. Smoke spiraled upward, his eyes squinting behind it. "Your son and White Wolf may have become friends, working for a common cause—to scare the hell out of the settlers, stealing from them," he said out of the corner of his mouth, the cigar fat and obtrusive in the other corner. "Who is to say that maybe they got caught while raiding and were lynched on the spot?"

Blackie gestured with a hand, as though drawing a picture before Echohawk's eyes. "I can see it now," he taunted. "The rope tight around Night Hawk's broken neck, his tongue hanging out with flies buzzing around it. His raven black hair is blowing in the breeze, his body swinging back and forth, his bare toes pointing down to the ground. . . ."

Hearing such a horrible description of Night Hawk's possible demise, Briana felt faint. She grabbed the banister and steadied herself, tears flooding her eyes. Then she jumped with alarm when she heard Echohawk's explosive reaction below.

Echohawk moved as quickly as a panther across the room and reached across the desk. Grabbing Blackie by the throat, he lifted him from the floor. "You go too far, *chee-mo-ko-man*, white man!" he growled, tightening his fingers around Blackie's throat, causing the cigar to pop from his mouth and his eyes to bulge.

"Let . . . me . . . down!" Blackie gasped, grabbing at Echohawk's fingers. "I'll . . . call . . . the law on you! I should've the minute you stepped inside my house!"

"But you did not," Echohawk said, jerking his hands away, letting Blackie fall back to his feet. "You wanted to have some fun first with an *ah-nee-shee-nah-bay*, Indian. Is that not true?"

"No time spent with an Injun is fun," Blackie said, rubbing his raw throat. He walked quickly to the door and flung it open. "Leave now, or by God, you'll be the one hanging with a noose around your neck. I'll see to it, Echohawk. Do you hear? Now get out!"

"Echohawk leaves, but only because it is my duty to think of my people first, myself last," he grumbled, walking slowly toward the door. "Without me, and now my son, they would be lost." He stepped up to the door and glared at Blackie. "You know my son would never ride with White Wolf in raids. His heart is peaceful. If he is with White Wolf, it is because White Wolf forced him!" He took a threatening step closer. "If anything happens to my son, I will be back. And your death will not be quick. I shall take you far away and take my time killing you!"

Blackie swallowed hard as he watched Echohawk

stroll in a dignified manner from the room and down the narrow corridor. He inhaled a heavy breath of relief as Echohawk then left the house, yet he was already weaving a plan that would finally rid the land of the cocky Chippewa chief.

He smiled, knowing that Echohawk would never have the chance to enter this mansion again. Soon, Echohawk would be walking among his ancestors in his "Land of the Hereafter," hopefully with Night Hawk walking along beside him.

Briana stood like a stone as she watched her uncle finally return to his study, slamming the door behind him. She sighed deeply, her mind spinning with how she might be able to help Night Hawk, knowing that nothing could keep her in her bedroom, safe, while the man she loved was out there somewhere in danger.

She went to her bedroom and closed the door softly behind her, then began pacing back and forth. Her heart pounded out the seconds that she was not with Night Hawk, knowing that time was wasting while she stayed there in her room.

"Perhaps he's even dead!" she worried aloud, stopping to peer out the window toward the beckoning forest. "I can hardly bear not knowing!"

She turned and glowered at the closed door, so badly wanting to go to her uncle and force answers from him, but she knew that was impossible. He would never tell her anything that might help her find Night Hawk.

Yet she knew almost for certain that he was behind Night Hawk's disappearance. As far as she knew, her uncle was the only one to truly gain from Night Hawk's absence.

"I can't go to Uncle Blackie and ask him," she kept reminding herself. "I must stay calm and collected so

that I can think of what to do, how, and when. I must
try and find Night Hawk. I must!"

She had a flash of insight. She stopped in mid-step.
"The cave!" she whispered harshly. "The cave where
I saw all of the Indians go. Perhaps that is where he's
being held prisoner. It did seem a likely place for
hiding something or someone."

She went to the window and drew the sheer curtain
aside again, looking toward the forest in the distance.
"I must go and see," she whispered. "And if he's not
there, I will look elsewhere. I won't give up my search
until I find him."

Cold fear gripped her at the prospect of what she
was planning for herself. She had never been the adventurous sort, having only lived the serene life of an
artist.

Yes, that had taken her beyond the city, yet it had
not been the adventure she had been seeking. It had
been that perfect setting—that perfect sunset, that
perfect sky, that perfect flower.

Again she started pacing, wringing her hands as she
continued to work out a plan. She had to wait until
she could leave the house without her uncle knowing
it. He now seemed to be aware of her every move.
She suspected that even now he was in his study, listening to her footsteps overhead as she paced, wondering about her sudden restlessness.

"Unless he knows that I heard the confrontation
between him and Echohawk, and wonders now what
I plan to do about it," she whispered, stopping dead
in her tracks, not wanting to get her uncle's suspicions
aroused. She wanted him to forget that she was even
there. Then she would sneak out of the house, take
her uncle's beloved stallion, and ride free of him and
his wicked ways.

Once she was gone, even having to leave her beloved painting paraphernalia behind, she knew that she could not return.

She reached a hand to her black eye, feeling the soreness as she pressed her fingers into the bruise beneath it. "No, I can't return, ever," she murmured to herself. "Who is to say what he might do to me next?"

Tiptoeing around the room, avoiding the sections of flooring that she knew creaked when stepped upon, she started gathering clothes from her drawers and chifforobe, placing what she could into a paisley-embroidered satchel.

She eyed her canvases and paints hungrily, yet knew for certain they had to be left behind. Sacrifices had to be made if she were to go searching for Night Hawk. And she was willing to make them.

She eyed the letter that she had penned to her parents, but had not yet mailed. It was too late for such a letter, it seemed, but hopefully not for her and Night Hawk to have a life together.

Her jaw set, her eyes flashing angrily, she tore the letter to shreds, then changed into a heavy riding skirt and long-sleeved blouse, and tied her hair back with a ribbon. She slipped into boots her uncle had recently bought for her riding outings with him, glad for at least this one generous gesture. Unknowingly he had prepared her for leaving him. The riding clothes and boots, and even the wide-brimmed felt hat, were perfect for her escape into the forest.

"And these gloves," she whispered, slipping butter-soft leather gloves onto her hands.

Sighing resolutely, she went to the full-length mirror at the end of the room, grabbed up her hat and plopped it onto her head, and then eyed her reflection in the mirror, smiling.

"Yes, that'll do just fine," she whispered to herself. She grew tense when she heard the sound of a single horse's hoofbeats leaving the estate grounds. She twirled on a booted heel and rushed to the window. Her eyes widened when she discovered that it was her uncle leaving, goading his beautiful black stallion into a hard gallop.

"He's making it easy for me," Briana said, smiling smugly. "There's more than that stallion in the stable. I'll get the beautiful brown mare that was bought just for my use."

She turned and eyed the drawer in the nightstand. Her heart thundered as she went to it and opened it, eyeing the pistol that lay there. "Uncle Blackie bought it for my protection, so that's exactly how it shall be used," she said, yanking it up, slipping it and several spare bullets into the depths of her deep pocket at the right side of her skirt. "If I'm forced to, I shall even use it to protect myself from my uncle!"

Then a thought came to her that made her heart skip a beat. "Where else could Uncle Blackie be going but to where Night Hawk is being held?" she whispered, a shiver coursing across her flesh to think that she might not get to Night Hawk in time.

She hoped that the route she had taken that day of her outing was closer than the one her uncle was taking. She crept down the stairs, thinking that her uncle might have ordered someone to stand guard. When she found no one, and even saw that she was free to go to the stable without being stopped, she had to believe that it was because her uncle felt that he had the upper hand with her—that he had frightened her into obedience.

"He couldn't be more wrong," Briana laughed, running now, the satchel heavy in her hand, the gun bouncing in her pocket.

Night Hawk could not tell whether or not a day and night had passed. He had not allowed himself to fall into the trap of sleeping. To survive, he knew that he had to stay alert and find a way of possible escape. Thus far he was helpless, in that each time he tried to work the ropes loose at his wrists, this only caused them to become tighter.

And as he had tried to get to his knees to crawl away he fell back down clumsily to the rock floor of his prison.

Night Hawk's stomach growled almost unmercifully as his nose picked up the scent of food wafting from somewhere close by. His ears picked up the sound of men talking and laughing boisterously, surely around a campfire, eating.

And when his abductors got into a more serious discussion, their laughter fading, he did not have to strain his ears too much to pick up the voice of White Wolf. He spoke more often, and Night Hawk heard him handing out orders about a raid that was to take place tonight.

Then there was silence, except for the crunch of rock as someone came and stood over Night Hawk. Still blindfolded, he could not see who was there, but soon knew why. He felt the heat of a burning stick on the back of his hand, causing the smell of burnt flesh to rise into his nostrils. He winced, yet held back the cry of pain that had risen from his gut to the tip of his tongue.

"What is it you would like to say to White Wolf?" the renegade Sioux said, chuckling low as he continued holding the flaming stick to Night Hawk's hand. "Do you beg White Wolf to stop? Does not your hand pain you? Would you prefer it to be your neck instead?"

Sweat was pearling on Night Hawk's brow as the pain worsened, yet he clenched his teeth together, proving to White Wolf that he would never allow a

Sioux to hear this Chippewa show his pain, for this would be humiliating. The pain was much easier to bear than humiliation.

Night Hawk was relieved when White Wolf took the stick away. When he heard the crunch of rock, he realized that White Wolf had decided not to play with him any more this time.

Then, willing himself to bear the pain, Night Hawk tensed and leaned his ear toward the sound of White Wolf's voice as he made a low threat to someone other than his men. He was talking to a woman, ordering her to stay hidden in the depths of the cave with her baby until he returned. He threatened her, telling her that should she do anything to help Night Hawk escape, he would search and find her and cut out her tongue, kill her slowly and unmercifully, and then he would kill the child.

The woman's low sobs tore at Night Hawk's heart, making him forget his own pain. It was obvious that the woman was a prisoner, and more than likely, one forced to share many things sexual with White Wolf, and even perhaps all of the low-down renegades!

The thought of this filled him with intense rage. He vowed to somehow get loose and not only set himself free but also the woman.

And he had to wonder who the father of the child was. If it was White Wolf, it was apparent that he had no feelings for it.

Night Hawk sucked in his breath and held it for a moment when he heard the other men approaching, their feet crunching loudly in the rocks, their voices low.

When they had passed and everything was silent again, he listened to see if he could hear the woman or the child, but sighed heavily when he heard neither.

It was obvious that White Wolf had frightened the woman into total obedience.

"Set me free and I'll take you out of here," Night Hawk began shouting. "Wherever you are, come out of hiding. I will take you and your child with me. You will be safe. No harm will come to you. I would not allow it."

The ensuing silence disheartened Night Hawk. He again worked with the ropes at his wrist, scooting along the rock floor until he found one sharp enough that he felt might cut the ropes in half. He tightened his jaw as he began to saw the rope back and forth across the jagged rock, hope rising within him.

Blackie rode hard across the flat stretch of meadow, now seeing Echohawk up ahead. Smiling, he turned his horse in another direction, knowing how he could cut off Echohawk, then take him prisoner.

Echohawk would sit beside his son and they would die together!

Finally, Blackie would get his revenge for those many years ago when Echohawk had humiliated him on the riverboat. He could still feel it now—Echohawk's hands on his ankles, the damn Indian holding Blackie over the sides of the boat while everyone on the riverboat watched, surely feeling Blackie's humiliation.

Blackie had carried this hatred inside him for too long. If it hadn't been for getting so involved in politics, his main goal in life would have been to go after Echohawk and make his life miserable.

Now riding through the protective covering of the forest, Blackie could see a short distance ahead through a break in the trees where Echohawk had just entered the forest himself. Riding hard, Blackie went onward, then snatched his pistol from its holster at his waist and lifted it, aimed, and fired.

He laughed into the wind and slipped the pistol back inside its holster when he saw that the bullet had hit Echohawk, even if only grazing his right arm. It had been enough to cause Echohawk to fall from his horse. He clutched hard at the wound, blood seeping between his fingers.

Blackie rode up to where Echohawk lay on the ground and reined in his horse. Leaning on the pommel of his saddle, he smiled crookedly down at Echohawk. "Seems we meet again," he said, chuckling.

Echohawk glared up at him, his dark eyes narrowing in hate. *"Geen-gee-wah-nah-dis chee-mo-ko-man,"* he hissed throatily.

The hair rose at the nape of Blackie's neck, not so much because of what Echohawk had said to him but the manner in which it had been spoken. His smugness quickly waned.

13

Who walks with beauty has no need of fear;
The sun and moon and stars keep pace with him.
—MORTON

The brown mare was lathered into a sweat. Briana snapped the reins more determinedly and rode hard across the land, first across a stretch of meadow, and then in a slow trot through the denseness of the forest, now almost certain that she was near the cave. She was seeing the setting around her as she had painted it on the canvas, recognizing a certain tree, a certain outcropping of rocks, the silver stream winding across the land beneath the low-hanging branches of elm trees.

Her heart was pounding, her anxiousness to find Night Hawk and save him outweighing any fear that kept trying to edge into her heart at the thought of being caught by either Blackie, or White Wolf!

But the risks were worth it if she was right in her assumption, that those who had abducted Night Hawk were the same Indians that she had seen enter the cave. Or, she despaired to herself, she could be wrong on all counts, and then where would she go? Where would she search? And where would she go when it became dark?

She had left her uncle's home knowing that she could never return. This time he could be waiting for her with a rifle clutched in his hands, a bullet with her name on it waiting for her in its dark chamber.

Briana's heart skipped a beat when she heard hoof-beats of many horses approaching her. Frantically she drew a tight rein on her mare, bringing it to a shuddering halt. She dug the heels of her boots into the flanks of her horse and raced into a thick stand of trees.

Breathless from fear, she quickly slipped out of the saddle. Taking the horse's reins, she led it behind the denseness of some brush and hunkered down, waiting for the riders to pass.

She held her breath as they came closer and closer, then uttered a heavy sigh when they were finally past, the hoofbeats soon fading into the distance.

When she turned around, she was surprised, and grateful in the same heartbeat, when she found that she was within walking distance of the cave. With her pulse racing, she tethered her horse to a low limb of a tree, took the pistol from her pocket, then moved stealthily and breathlessly onward. She constantly surveyed the land around her, watching for any sudden movement, or the signs of someone hiding, guarding the cave.

When she saw that no one was near, she rushed to the cave's entrance and stopped short as she peered inside. Its dankness made her clasp her fingers more tightly around the pistol and swallow back the building fear. The one other time she had discovered the cave, she had not entered it, having viewed the Indians as too dangerous to do anything but flee.

It was the same now as then. She knew too well the risks of being discovered. But she would do anything to find Night Hawk.

Her pulse racing, her knees somewhat weak, Briana tiptoed lightly into the cave, suddenly blind in the darkness. Yet that would not stop her. She would travel the full length of the cave if necessary. She would not give up until she knew that she had searched every inch of it. Even if she had to do it in pitch darkness!

Reaching around until she found a side wall, she began inching her way along, grimacing when the mossy dampness of the wall caused her fingers to become cold and stiff. Listening, she could hear water dripping somewhere in the distance. Her eyes widened when she caught the distinct smell of food cooking over an open fire.

As she made a turn, still letting the wall guide her, her heart fluttered wildly within her chest when she saw the first signs of a fire up ahead.

She lifted her eyes and stopped to give a soft prayer that she was not entering her own death trap, and that she would find Night Hawk alive and well.

Pursing her lips tightly, she moved cautiously ahead, again watching for any signs of movement, relieved when she still saw none.

Determinedly she moved onward. The fire was still quite a distance away, yet its dancing gold light had spread to where Briana was now walking. She gasped as she peered on both sides of the cave passage up ahead, seeing stacks and stacks of firearms. Her heart tightened within her chest when she discovered stacks of dynamite lying around also.

Her legs almost buckled beneath her when she first caught sight of Night Hawk. He sat slumped against the wall, his ankles and wrists bound, his eyes covered with a blindfold.

"Night Hawk!" Briana screamed, throwing all caution to the wind as she began running toward him. "Oh, dear God, Night Hawk, I've found you. Darling, I've found you!"

Night Hawk's head jerked up and he looked sightlessly around him. "Briana?" he gasped, his heart thudding like drums being beaten within his chest. "You are there? How did you know where to find me? Briana, it is not safe! Go! Go now!"

His words of warning were falling on deaf ears. Briana dropped her pistol into her pocket and fell to her knees before Night Hawk. She so badly wanted to hug him, yet knew that she had to hurry. Her uncle could arrive at any moment! He would not hesitate to shoot her as well as Night Hawk. She was more of a threat to her uncle now than an asset he could flaunt before his constituents.

At this moment she realized that by taking flight, she would never get the opportunity to go on the podium with her uncle at his next political rally and expose him for what he truly was.

But there were other ways to do that. Hopefully she would be given the opportunity. If she got out of this cave with Night Hawk in one piece!

Briana's fingers trembled as she untied the blindfold, letting it drop to reveal his midnight dark eyes that had mesmerized her the very first moment she had lain eyes on him. Her eyes locked with his for a moment, and then she bent over him and began untying his wrists. She paled when the light of the fire revealed his tortured hand to her.

"Oh, Lord," she cried, lifting the hand, examining the wound. It was red and raw. "They tortured you!"

She wanted to take the time to doctor his wound, but knew that time was running out for them.

Her uncle. He could arrive anytime!

Somehow the villain would pay for what he had done to Night Hawk. She knew that he had to be responsible. Who else would gain so much by Night Hawk's absence . . . or death?

Tears near, she quickly untied Night Hawk's ankles. His powerful hands were suddenly at her shoulders, drawing her directly before him. She could see in his eyes that he had discovered the black eye that proved her uncle's abuse.

"Who did this to you?" he growled.

"Perhaps the same person that did that to your hand," Briana said, holding back a sob.

"Your uncle did not burn my hand," Night Hawk said, loosening his grip on her shoulders. He framed her face between his hands and drew her lips close to his. "My beautiful Briana. You came in the face of danger to rescue me. How did you know about the cave? It belongs to White Wolf and his renegades. He is the one who abducted me. Of course, I do not hold your uncle blameless. He is in cohoots with White Wolf. He is as guilty!"

"I'll tell you later," Briana said, slipping away from him. She rose to her feet, taking him by the hand, urging him up. "My uncle left before me. He could be arriving soon. We must be gone!" She looked down at his hand again. "We must doctor that wound. It— it could become infected. You—you could lose the hand."

Frowning, Night Hawk looked past her, at the cache of firearms and ammunition. "My concerns are not for my own welfare," he said, taking her by the elbow, hurrying her away into the outer darkness of the cave. "If your uncle can hit an innocent woman, there is no telling what he would do if he found you here, obviously where the loot from the raids is being stored. We will leave now and I will tend to him later. He will regret the day he was born—especially the day he laid a hand on you!"

Then Night Hawk abruptly came to a halt. He turned and stared at the distant soft light of the flames from a campfire, where the woman had surely prepared the food for the renegades—where she had probably sat while nursing her infant.

She was White Wolf's prisoner. Night Hawk had to save her and the child.

He turned to Briana. "You stay here," he flatly ordered. "I've something to do. Someone to get. *O-wahbum-ow-way-nayn-yah-ow*, I must go look for her."

Briana's eyes became wild and wide, fearing that they had already taken too much time. "No," she cried, grabbing him by the arm and trying to pull him onward. "We can't. My uncle could arrive at any moment. Please, Night Hawk. So far we've been lucky. Let's get out of here. Now!"

Night Hawk brushed her hand aside. He started walking away from her toward the light of the fire. "You go on outside," he said over his shoulder. "I will follow soon. *Wi-yee-bah*, soon! Leave now. Who can say why no guard was watching the entrance of the cave when you arrived here? Perhaps he will return at any moment. Go to safety while you can!"

Frustrated, Briana chewed on her lower lip, then broke into a run and moved up beside him. She walked with him, pleading with him. "Who are you going after?" she asked. "I saw no one but you."

"There is a woman," Night Hawk said thickly. "There is a child. I cannot leave them behind. They are *gee-tay-bee-bee-nah*, captives, also. I must release them from their captivity."

"A woman?" Briana said softly, lifting an eyebrow. "A child?"

Night Hawk said no more. He hastened his steps and moved through the part of the cave where he had been imprisoned, stunned anew by the number of firearms there, and then moved past them, finally arriving at the campfire. He stood with his hands on his hips and looked around, seeing the bedding, the clothes, and the cooking utensils. He gazed at the pot of stew cooking over the fire, then past this into the deeper depths of the cave.

"I know you are there!" he shouted. "*Mah-bee-szhon*, come. I am free now. I can take you to safety!"

When there was no response, Night Hawk cupped a hand over his mouth and shouted again. "There is not much time!" he said. "Come now, or I will be forced to leave you and the child. You will be again at the mercy of White Wolf and his renegades. Surely you wish for a better life than this!"

Again there was silence. Briana moved to Night Hawk's side. "She's too afraid to come out of hiding," she murmured.

"She has good reason to be," Night Hawk grumbled, moving quickly around the fire.

He began looking for them, but soon discovered that the cave separated into different avenues at this point, giving the woman and child many opportunities for hiding. He was losing hope of ever finding them.

Sighing, he returned to Briana. "She does not want to be found," he said, shaking his head slowly. "Her future and the child's is bleak. And that is *gee-mah-szhan-dum*, sad. There is no need for it. I could take her to my village. She would be welcomed. Whether she is red-skinned or white, she could stay there forever, her child being raised among the best of people."

Briana was getting edgy. "Let's go," she pleaded. "You did all that you could. Now let us try to save ourselves." She glanced down at his injured hand. "And I've got to find a way to medicate your hand as soon as possible."

Looking back over his shoulder a last time, Night Hawk hurried alongside Briana through the cave.

When he saw the weapons again, his jaw tightened. "My hand is *way-way-nee-ee-shee-ah-yah-mah-gud*, fine," he grumbled. "What we must do now is go to my village, get many armed braves, then come back to the cave and get these weapons. We will also search the cave from end to end and find the woman and child. Once they and the firearms are taken to my village, many Chippewa braves will go after White Wolf."

He paused and added, "And soon, your *gee-szhee-shay*, uncle," he growled. "If he thinks he is going to escape the wrath of Night Hawk, he is mistaken!"

Together they stepped out into the twilight of evening. Briana took Night Hawk to her horse. Together they rode away, Briana snuggled on the saddle behind him, her arms wrapped solidly around his waist, so glad that she had been given the opportunity to be with him again. Through the traumas of this night, she had discovered that Night Hawk was most definitely not involved with renegades. For this she was most grateful.

Blackie gave Echohawk a shove into the cave. "Just keep walking," he snarled. He stepped up behind Echohawk and pushed the barrel of his rifle into his back. "Move slowly ahead of me. If you try anything, you will have more to worry about than a mere flesh wound in the arm."

Echohawk said nothing, his heartbeat anxious. Blackie had said that he was going to join Night Hawk. That had to mean that his son was being held in this cave. Echohawk was allowing Blackie to feel smug in his abduction, biding his time until he was with his son. Together they could take flight—with Blackie finally dead!

"White Wolf isn't here to greet you," Blackie said,

laughing softly. "Nor are any of his renegades. Their horses are usually corralled just inside the entrance of the cave." He chuckled. "It seems they're out having some fun at the expense of some of my constituents. I guess losing a couple more voters won't interfere in my being elected."

"You will not live long enough to see election day," Echohawk threatened. "In fact, I would say that you are taking the final breaths of your life. You have to know that you cannot get away with abducting two powerful Chippewa. If I do not kill you first, my braves will tear the countryside apart until they find you."

"Who says I abducted two Injuns?" Blackie said, giving Echohawk a nudge with the rifle barrel as they walked farther into the dank darkness of the cave. "As I see it, I have only one damn Injun on my hands, either to hang or shoot."

"You spoke of my son earlier," Echohawk said, his jaw tightening.

"Yes, I think I did," Blackie said, his voice filled with amusement. "But I only ordered the abduction. I didn't actually do it."

"White Wolf did the deed for you," Echohawk said, his gaze picking up a slight wavering of light from a fire on the cave ceiling a short distance away. His trained ears picked up the sound of trickling water of a spring, and his nose, the aroma of food cooking.

"Let's just say that it's done and soon you'll both be dead," Blackie said. "Now just shut up and move on. I don't like debating anything with you, a dumb Injun. I leave that for my cohorts in St. Paul."

Echohawk walked softly in his moccasins, looking anxiously ahead. When he turned a corner and got his first sight of the firearms, his insides tensed. It was apparent now that White Wolf and his renegades *were*

responsible for the raids that were terrorizing the
countryside. And it was obvious why they raided—to
build their supply of firearms!

But why? he wondered.

"And so you see the firearms?" Blackie said, shov-
ing Echohawk into the main chamber of the cave.
"Does it make fear grab your guts? I guess you have
to know that I agree with White Wolf about how he
plans to use them. He's going to rid the land of a few
Injuns for me!"

Echohawk turned and glared at White Wolf. "You
are an *gah-gay-go-gee-kan-deh-zeen-ee-mee-nee*, ignorant man," he said, his teeth clenched. "You think
White Wolf will stop at just killing innocent Chippewa? He will also kill as many whites as he has ammunition for. That means he will probably take over
Fort Snelling and the city of St. Paul." He laughed
softly. "He will probably make your house his *en-dah-
yen*, lodge!"

Blackie paled and he took an uneasy step backward,
his eyes flashing as he thrust the rifle barrel into Echohawk's chest. "Just shut up with your Chippewa
mumbo-jumbo," he growled. "Do you hear? I don't
want to hear any more of that nonsense. White Wolf
is my partner."

Blackie glanced away from Echohawk, slowly
around the cave, feeling a sudden absence. Where the
hell was Night Hawk? he wondered, panic rising
within him.

Keeping a steady aim on Echohawk, Blackie began
slowly walking around, thinking that perhaps White
Wolf had hidden Night Hawk behind some of the
stacks of ammunition.

"Night Hawk, where are you, you sonofabitch?" he
finally shouted, knowing that Night Hawk could not
answer, having been gagged.

Echohawk was beginning to fear that something was wrong. It was obvious that Blackie had expected to find Night Hawk there. The thought that White Wolf had possibly gone ahead and killed him caused his knees to grow unsteady and a bitterness to rise into his throat.

When Blackie shouted another name, a woman's name, Echohawk's eyebrows rose in surprise.

"Gentle Fawn, damn it, get out here," Blackie shouted. "It's me, Blackie. Now get out here this minute, or by God, I'll come shooting. Both you and your kid will be killed. White Wolf can always find himself another broad to keep his bed warm at night. One that doesn't have a brat sucking on a tit morning till night."

Echohawk scarcely breathed as he watched a beautiful woman step into view a short distance away. A child wrapped in soft doeskin was held protectively within her arms. He was taken quickly by her loveliness, her innocence.

A slow ache crept into his heart as he continued gazing at Gentle Fawn. He felt as though he was being catapulted back into time, as though his beloved first wife, Fawn, were there. This young woman who bore half of his dearly departed wife's name was almost a mirror image of Fawn.

That she carried a child in her arms made the comparison twice as painful—it was as though this child was the unborn child that had died at the exact moment his wife had been slain, but was now miraculously alive.

He ached to rush to her, to hold her, to say endearing things to her.

And then shame engulfed him, for while he had been transported back in time almost forty winters, he had forgotten his present, beloved wife, Mariah.

Gentle Fawn walked slowly toward Blackie, her heart pounding out of fear of what he had threatened to do. She had learned to live in fear, yet had no choice but to stay. White Wolf's threats were never idle.

"What do you want with Gentle Fawn?" she asked meekly. She held her daughter more tightly to her bosom when Blackie gave an ugly snarl as he looked at the bundle with utter disgust.

Gentle Fawn turned her sad, wondering eyes on Echohawk, seeing the kindness in his eyes, mingled with a strange sort of anxiety. She gazed slowly down at his injured arm, knowing that it needed attention, then back at Blackie, thinking that the evil white man had different plans than offering any sort of medical assistance. He more than likely planned to kill this handsome Indian, as he had planned to kill the Chippewa called Night Hawk.

She smiled to herself, glad that at least he had been able to escape.

"Where's Night Hawk?" Blackie said, holding a steady aim on Echohawk.

"Gone," Gentle Fawn said thinly, flinching when Blackie's face turned grotesque in his anger.

"You removed the ropes that bound him?" he said darkly. "You let him go?"

Tears flooded Gentle Fawn's eyes, fear revealed in their depths. "No!" she cried. "I did not do that. Someone else. A lady. She came and set him free. I could not stop them. Please. Please do not blame me!"

"A lady?" Blackie said, arching a thick, dark eyebrow. "What lady?"

"She was called Briana by the captive," Gentle Fawn said, swallowing hard.

"Briana?" Blackie gasped, paling. "My niece?"

Blackie was stunned at first; how had Briana known to come to the cave and rescue Night Hawk? Then anger quickly seized him at the thought of her going this far over her love for the Indian, no matter how she had discovered him or where he had been held hostage.

How could she have done this? She was risking her whole future as an artist over an Indian.

Then another thought came to him that seized him with panic. Surely she would discover his role in this abduction, if she hadn't already. He had to wonder what she would do about the information. Would she use it against him? Or would she keep quiet for the sake of the family name?

He glared down at Gentle Fawn. "You dumb broad," he said. "If my future is ruined because of what happened here today, you will pay. Do you hear?"

He inhaled a desperate breath as he looked around the cave at the supply of firearms, ammunition, and dynamite. His fingers began to tremble, realizing that if Night Hawk was free, he would be returning with his Chippewa braves to take the firearms and to finish off White Wolf and whoever was in the cave. And also to point an accusing finger at Blackie!

"How long has White Wolf been gone?" Blackie asked, his eyes narrowing as he looked over at Gentle Fawn.

"A short while," Gentle Fawn said faintly.

"Enough time for me to catch up with them, I hope," Blackie said, giving Echohawk another nudge with his rifle barrel. "Go over there. Sit down against the wall."

He gazed angrily down at the ropes that had held Night Hawk captive, then glanced over at Gentle Fawn. "Put the brat down and tie up the chief," he ordered. "Tie his wrists and ankles. And do a good job. If he escapes, by God, you'll be sorry."

Trembling from fear, Gentle Fawn carefully laid her child on the ground, then went to Echohawk and knelt down before him. She quickly tied his wrists together and then his ankles, then stopped and gazed into his eyes.

"*Gee-mah-szhan-dum*, I am sorry," she murmured. "Truly I am."

Echohawk realized by the language she spoke that she was of Chippewa descent. Remembrances of his first wife again pierced his heart. She had been Chippewa! She had been as sweet and innocent!

He was deeply touched by this young woman, and what she must have suffered at the hands of White Wolf and his renegades. Somehow he would find a way to release her from her misery.

And if the day came, he would take her back to his village with him and try to make all wrongs right for her.

"If I don't get back here soon enough with White Wolf, and I'm forced to go into hiding with him because your son escaped today, I'll be back. I won't stop, Echohawk, until I see both you and your son dead," Blackie growled.

With that statement he spun on a heel and ran from the cave.

Gentle Fawn reached a hand to Echohawk's wounded arm. "I will make it *nah-wudge-o-nee-shee-shin*, better," she said, smiling warmly at Echohawk— a smile that touched his soul with a remembrance of what it was to be young again.

He returned the smile and nodded.

14

Serene I fold my arms and wait.
—BURROUGHS

Night Hawk rode into his village and passed the outdoor fire that was lifting its light into the dark heavens. He drew his reins before his wigwam. He slid easily from his saddle, and Briana dismounted before he could offer his assistance. It was obvious to her that his hand was paining him more than he would admit.

She moved to his side, wanting to take another close look at the hand, but was stopped when several braves approached Night Hawk with questions, everyone speaking at once.

"My friends, we have no time for discussing where I have been, or why I have returned with a white woman," Night Hawk said, interrupting them, causing a strained silence. "Saddle your horses. We have much to do, and there is little time in which to do it!"

He turned and saw his mother step into view at the entrance of her wigwam. She was so thin and frail in her cotton nightgown, she looked no more than something the wind might grab up and send floating away in the breeze.

Mariah moved slowly toward her son, each step obviously an effort. When she reached him, she placed a trembling, weak hand to his cheek. "My *nin-gwis,* son," she murmured. "Where have you been?" She looked slowly around her, her gaze stopping momentarily on Briana, then peered up at Night Hawk again. "Your father? He is not with you? I missed you both all day. I thought you may have decided to join in a hunt."

"*Gee-mah-mah*, I have not been with Father," Night Hawk said, fear suddenly gripping his insides. "He has been gone long? Did he not tell you where he was going? Mother, this is not like *gee-bah-bah*. He never leaves without first telling you about it."

"Sometimes he does not tell me everything," Mariah said, swallowing hard. "You see, Night Hawk, he doesn't want to worry me." She looked slowly over at Briana again. "Who is this woman? Why is she here?"

Night Hawk reached for Briana's hand and drew her close to his side. "She saved my life," he said. "Her name is Briana Collins." He frowned down at her. "She has yet to tell me how she knew I was in the cave, being held prisoner. But that she did is all that is important now."

Mariah swayed and placed a hand on her throat, alarmed that her son had been held captive. Night Hawk caught her and drew her into his arms. "It is all right, *gee-mah-mah*," he reassured her. "I am safe now. Father will be also. I promise you that."

He held her for a moment longer, then eased her out of his arms and turned to face his braves, who had brought their saddled horses and were standing beside them, awaiting Night Hawk's orders.

"My friends, it seems we have another reason for riding tonight," he growled. "My father is missing. We must search and find him!"

A warm hand in his made Night Hawk turn wondering eyes down to Briana.

"Night Hawk, the reason I came searching for you was because your father came to my Uncle Blackie. He demanded that my uncle tell him where you

were," she said. "I heard your father saying that he
knew that my uncle had been in cohoots with White
Wolf many years ago, and suspected that he was now.
I heard him threaten my uncle, and in return, my
uncle threatened him. Your father left when he could
not get the answers he sought." She paused and swallowed hard. "My uncle left shortly after your father
left. Perhaps he was going after Chief Echohawk?
Could he be the reason your father hasn't returned?"

Night Hawk's jaw tightened and his eyes narrowed
angrily. "The cave," he said. "He has probably taken
my father to the cave, thinking that I would still be
there. What a triumph for him if he could abduct and
kill both Chief Echohawk and his son."

He turned to a young brave. "Go to my dwelling
quickly!" he shouted. "Get my rifle and gunsling.
Bring them to me. *Wee-weeb*, quickly!"

Without further thought, even forgetting the pain in
his hand, Night Hawk swung himself into the saddle
of Briana's horse, not taking the time to go and get
his own trusted steed.

Time was of the essence. And although he was
weary from lack of sleep, and hungry from lack of
food, nothing was important to him now—only his
father!

He knew the importance of arriving at the cave before his absence was discovered. Once it was, and if
his father was a prisoner of the same gang of renegades, Chief Echohawk might not live this night out.

The young brave brought Night Hawk his rifle and
gunsling. He then slipped Briana's satchel from the
side of the saddle, where she had placed it, and
handed it down to her. He then secured his gunsling
to the horn of the saddle and thrust his rifle into it.

"You will be all right here with my people," he said
softly to Briana. He smiled over at his mother. "Go

with Mother. She will welcome you as though she has known you forever. She is that sort of woman, compassionate and caring."

Mariah stepped to Briana's side and placed a frail arm around her waist, proof that Night Hawk knew his mother well. Briana smiled at her, then, clutching the handle of her satchel, she nodded her head and smiled through a haze of tears up at Night Hawk.

Yet she knew that at the first opportunity she would flee into the night herself, knowing that she would never be able to wait to see if her beloved came out of this ordeal without further wounds. She wanted to help him in his fight.

"God speed," she said, sniffling as tears crept down her cheeks. She mouthed the words "I love you" in a whisper that she saw pleased him.

Reaching her free hand inside her skirt pocket, she circled her fingers around the small pistol. She held onto it tightly as she watched Night Hawk and his braves ride away. Mariah gently placed a hand under her elbow and guided her to the warmth of her wigwam, settling her down beside the fire on a pallet of pelts.

Briana gazed at a sleeping platform in the dark shadows of the wigwam. Someone was asleep on it. She had to believe that was Lily, Night Hawk's sister. She then looked back at Mariah as the older woman leaned down and whispered to her.

"I wish I felt like talking," Mariah said, wheezing, the exertion of having gone outside to see Night Hawk having taken its toll. "But I must go on to bed. Please understand. I-I'm not at all well."

"Please don't worry on my account," Briana said, sad to see this lady who had traces of once having been beautiful, now so thin, almost to the point of death. "I'll sit here for a while beside the fire, and then I'll stretch out and go to sleep myself."

"Tomorrow when I am rested, I would like to talk to you at length about what has happened, and about how you happen to know my son," Mariah said, getting more breathless by the moment. She placed a hand on her throat, gasping for air. "I-I must lie down."

Pityingly, Briana watched Mariah go to a sleeping platform piled high with comfortable blankets and pelts. She saw the effort it took for the woman to get onto the platform and position the blankets comfortably over herself.

Briana then watched and listened, hardly able to wait until she knew that Night Hawk's mother was asleep. She wanted to be able to find Night Hawk before he reached the cave.

She wanted to be with him, no matter what transpired between the renegades and the Chippewa braves. She wanted to be there for him if he needed her.

Laying her satchel aside when she realized that Mariah was finally asleep, Briana crept to her feet. She looked guardedly from Mariah to Lily, then lifted the entrance flap and stepped outside into the stillness of night.

Somewhat disoriented, she stood there for a moment. Then the neighing of horses drew her in the right direction.

Soon she was riding away from the village on a horse, the night air cold against her face. But she continued onward, hoping that she was going in the right direction. While on the horse with Night Hawk, he had been the one leading the way. She had not thought to see exactly which route he took.

She continued riding for a while through the forest,

across meadows, and then suddenly she felt herself being thrown across the horse's head, realizing that it had tripped in a gopher hole.

When she hit the ground, her head cracked hard against it, knocking her unconscious.

Blackie drew his reins as he saw White Wolf approach in the splash of moonlight. When the Sioux reined in beside him, Blackie explained why he was there, and the urgency in returning to the cave.

"You found Night Hawk gone?" White Wolf hissed, reaching over to grab Blackie by the throat. "Do you think I will believe that you are not responsible? You are a coward! You went and set him free because you thought over what you had ordered me to do and feared his father's wrath, then pretended he escaped!"

"You damn Injun, let go of my throat," Blackie said, coughing. "Let me tell you the rest. I abducted Echohawk. I only went to the cave to take him there, to let him join his son! I was handing him over to you, White Wolf, to do with him as you pleased. He's still there, damn it! At least you still have him to toy with."

White Wolf dropped his hand from Blackie's throat. His eyes gleamed. "You abducted Chief Echohawk?" he said, laughing. "He is in the cave?"

"That's what I said, isn't it?" Blackie grumbled, frowning. He rubbed his raw throat, his hate for White Wolf swelling, not sure how much longer he would tolerate him. He put up with him only to get him to do his dirty work. But when White Wolf became more of a threat than a help, Blackie would kill him.

"That is good," White Wolf said, rubbing his chin. "We will soon have Night Hawk again as prisoner. He will come for his father. We will be ready!"

Blackie edged his horse closer to White Wolf's.

"You damn idiot, the first thing we've got to do is move the ammunition," he growled. "We can worry about Night Hawk and Echohawk later."

Anger flared in White Wolf's eyes. "How did Night Hawk escape?" he hissed. "Is Gentle Fawn responsible? She was the only one there to help with the escape."

Blackie swallowed hard, not wanting to disclose that his niece was responsible. Yet he could not cast the blame on Gentle Fawn, either, for once White Wolf discovered the truth, Blackie would be the one to pay, and he did not want to imagine the ways in which he would. He had seen White Wolf's ways of torturing those from whom he wanted obedience.

"I questioned Gentle Fawn," Blackie said guardedly. "She said that she didn't release Night Hawk. God, White Wolf, you know she wouldn't. Your threats lie heavy on her heart. She's scared to death of you!"

"Then how?" White Wolf cried.

"Night Hawk is a crafty sonofabitch," Blackie said hoarsely. "He could probably escape from a pit of rattlesnakes." He chuckled. "As for Echohawk, it won't be that easy. I wounded him."

"That is good," White Wolf said, also chuckling. "That is very good." He raised a fist in the air. "Let us ride! Let us go to the cave and move the firearms to our next best hideout—to the other cave that we have used from time to time. No one will ever find it." He smiled over at Blackie. "As for Echohawk, we will take him with us. We will keep him alive awhile longer, at least long enough to see his son die. Night Hawk *will* be our prisoner again! Soon!"

Blackie smiled, yet could not help but worry about Night Hawk being free, and about his niece possibly knowing about his secret alliance with White Wolf. Both could ruin his political career.

As he slapped his reins, sending his horse into a

gallop beside White Wolf's, he became calmer. Who
would believe an Indian over him? As for his niece,
he doubted if anyone would listen to her once they
saw that she had joined up with an Indian, for in the
eyes of most white people, it was forbidden for a white
woman to love an Indian. They would look down their
noses at her and pity her uncle.

He smiled broadly, feeling confident that everything
would work out after all. Somehow, for him, it always
seemed to. He shrugged, thinking that now was no
different.

And what did they know, anyhow? Only Echohawk
knew the truth, and he was being held prisoner. Yes,
besides Echohawk, there was no actual proof. And
Blackie knew the art of playing the role of an innocent
man to the hilt.

When they arrived at the cave, much haste was
made to load the firearms onto the horses, leaving the
dynamite and some of the ammunition scattered along
the floor of the cave.

After everyone was safely out of the cave, Echohawk was tied onto a horse on his stomach. Gentle
Fawn walked beside his horse, clutching her child to
her bosom. Finally, a torch was pitched into the cave.

As they rode away, they soon heard the explosion,
felt the ground shake with the force of it, and saw the
sky light up with the crimson flash of the fire.

Blackie slapped White Wolf on the back, laughing,
then they fled into the depths of the forest.

Night Hawk heard the explosion and saw the sky light
up. A gnawing agony swept through him, knowing that
anything that exploded with such force had to be caused
by dynamite. And that meant that the cave had just
exploded. In that cave could have been his father!

He hung his head, hoping that he was wrong, then

more determinedly rode through the forest until they came close enough to see the fire that had spread to the banks of the river, twisting cool and serene just below the cave entrance.

He jumped from his horse and searched as close as he could to the hot debris of the cave, yet saw nothing akin to the remains of a body. He wondered about the woman and child, and whether or not they had been out of the cave at the time of the explosion. Had it gone off by accident? Or had someone purposely set it?

He then quickly remounted his horse and rode away with his braves, back in the direction of his village. Hopefully he had been wrong to think his father had been abducted. Hopefully, it had just taken him longer to get home today, perhaps having been sidetracked by something more innocent than White Wolf or Blackie.

His heart pounded with a dull throbbing as each mile was traveled. Finally, he was back at his village. He slid quickly out of his saddle and went to his parents' wigwam. He grew frantic when he discovered that not only was his father gone, but so was Briana!

He went to his mother and gave her a gentle shake. "Where is Briana?" he asked, his voice hollow. "Mother, where is she?"

Mariah leaned up on an elbow and looked around her. "She was here when I fell asleep," she said, wiping her eyes sleepily. She looked with alarm up at Night Hawk. "Your father? Did you find him?"

Night Hawk shook his head, despair filling him.

He left again, this time alone, and searched the forest until he almost dropped from hunger and lack of sleep.

Downcast, and shaken to the core by his losses, Night Hawk returned home. He went to his wigwam and fell into a restless sleep.

15

The aroma of rabbit stew awakened Night Hawk from his troubled sleep. His stomach responded to the smell with a low, rumbling growl, and he leaned up on an elbow. By the dim glow of his lodge fire, he made out a figure sitting beside the fire pit, hanging a pot over the flames, and then adding more wood to the fire. Night Hawk's first thoughts were of Briana.

Through the golden haze of his wigwam he saw the petiteness of her straight back as she leaned over closer to the fire on her bent knees. He saw the swirl of hair across her shoulders, then her delicate fingers.

But when she turned and faced him, he was quickly awakened from the illusion, a wish so deep that even now it seemed lodged in his heart. He realized that the young and beautiful thing looking after his interests this morning was not Briana at all, but his sister, Lily.

She crawled to his bedside and placed a gentle hand on his cheek. "You are awake," she said, smiling sweetly at him. "Did you sleep well, my brother?"

"Well enough," Night Hawk said, not wanting to tell her that he tossed most of the night, dreams of various things haunting him—especially of his beloved father and woman being somewhere out there in the forest in danger.

"I have brought you food," Lily said. "I have built

170

you a fire." She glanced over her shoulder, then back at Night Hawk. "I have gone to the river and brought you fresh water for bathing. I have also brought new moccasins that I beaded for you."

"You are too kind to your brother," Night Hawk said, brushing his blankets aside. "Is there a reason for you being this attentive to Night Hawk?"

Lily cast her eyes downward, guilt washing through her, yet she knew she could not reveal to her brother what troubled her day and night.

She was concerned about her unborn child and ached to confide in Night Hawk about it, yet she could not. He no longer approved of Strong Branch. He would shame her for allowing herself to get so intimate with him.

No, she could not share this secret with her brother. She could not share it with anyone, except the father of her child.

She would have to tell Strong Branch soon. Or it would be too late. She would soon be showing.

"Lily?" Night Hawk said, placing a finger under her chin, lifting it so that their eyes met. "What are you not telling your brother?" His gaze swept over her face. "You are pale this morning. Why is that, Lily?"

"There are many reasons," she murmured, her throat tight. "Most of which trouble you also my brother. Yes, my heart lies heavily within my chest today, as I am sure it does in yours."

"Yes, very," Night Hawk said, swinging his legs over the sides of the sleeping platform.

He held his face in his hands a moment, trying to sort out exactly what his first move would be today.

He had to search for Briana and his father. He would send braves in different directions. Surely someone would find his woman and father.

He looked anxiously up at Lily. "Father?" he said.

"Tell me that he arrived home safely last night. Tell me, Lily, that Briana has found her way back to our village. I cannot believe that she returned to St. Paul. It is not a logical thing for her to do, and she is quite a logical person."

Lily lowered her eyes. "Neither have returned," she said softly.

Night Hawk emitted a low moan of regret, then stormed to his feet. With his fringed breeches that he had worn the past few days still on, having been too tired to remove them the evening before, he went and knelt on his haunches beside the fire and lifted a bowl, ready to dip stew in it. He needed stamina to do what was necessary today.

He must find his loved ones.

Lily came to him quickly and dipped the stew into his bowl, handed him a wooden spoon, and sat down beside him as he ate ravenously.

It was then that she saw the wound on his left hand. "My brother, what happened to your hand?" she gasped. She reached for it, but he pulled it away from her.

He frowned as he placed the bowl aside. "During my abduction I was tortured," he said, seeing the sudden alarm in her eyes. "These men who ride with White Wolf are less than human, my sister. But soon, if the Great Spirit lends a hand, all of the renegades will be found and dealt with. Never will they be able to ravage the land again, killing and maiming."

Thinking of her brother being tortured made a sudden bitterness rise into Lily's throat. And as she had these past few days, she felt the urge to retch. She rushed to her feet and stumbled from the wigwam. Going behind it, she vomited until her stomach ached from its emptiness.

When she felt a warm hand on her arm, she turned,

startled, and saw Strong Branch. But she did not have a chance to say anything to him, for Night Hawk was suddenly there, concern in his eyes as he moved past Strong Branch and framed her face between his hands.

"You are not well," he said. "I knew it by your paleness." He glanced over his shoulder at Strong Branch and glowered at him, then swept an arm around his sister's waist and led her away, toward their parents' dwelling. "Tell me, little sister, what is ailing you?"

"It is *gah-ween-geh-goo*, nothing," Lily murmured, her knees trembling and weak. She glanced back at Strong Branch as he stepped into view, her heart crying out to him, so badly wanting to him to be happy about their child yet fearing that he would perhaps even think that she was tricking him into marriage by having allowed herself to get pregnant.

Oh, how she still loved him—but she feared that he would turn his back on her forever once he knew of this burden she was carrying in her womb.

Trying to behave as though there was nothing wrong, Lily went inside her parents' wigwam with Night Hawk. She knelt beside the fire and added some wood as her brother went and knelt beside his mother's sleeping platform.

"Gee-mah-mah?" Night Hawk said, smoothing his hand across her cool brow. "How are you today?"

Mariah did not want to worry her son. She reached a hand to his cheek and gently caressed it. "I am *nay-mi-no-mun-gi*, fine," she murmured. "Just somewhat tired." She swallowed hard. 'Go and find your father, Night Hawk. He has never been gone this long unless he told me where he would be. Please, Night Hawk? Go and find him for me."

Night Hawk took her hand and kissed its soft palm. "This I will do for you," he said, his voice breaking.

"Thank you, my sweet one," Mariah said, soft tears rolling down her cheeks.

Night Hawk rose to his feet and took one last, lingering look at his mother, then turned and gave Lily an appraising look, knowing that she was hiding something from him. He then left the wigwam and began rounding up his braves.

Today he would ride until he dropped from the saddle, if need be! He would not rest until both his father and woman were safely with him again.

Her hair tangled, her dress torn, Briana awakened from a restless night of sleep beneath a covering of leaves that she had swept over herself to keep her body warm as best she could through the long and dreary night in the forest. Shivering, she rose on an elbow and looked around her, seeing the gleam of the river, hearing the rustling of cottonwood leaves above her, like softly falling rain.

She had wandered until she almost dropped from exhaustion late the night before. Since her fall from the horse, and its ensuing escape from her, it seemed to her that she had been going in circles, everything looking the same to her one minute to the next.

She was lost. She doubted if she would ever find her way to civilization again. And to survive, she had to find food.

Scraping the leaves aside, she groaned and placed her hands at the small of her back as she rose slowly to her feet. Except for the aching of her body, she had survived the fall without mishap.

As she began walking aimlessly beside the river, allowing this to be her guide today, her thoughts went to Night Hawk and his father. Had Night Hawk found him? Had Night Hawk returned to his village unharmed himself?

Was he even now searching for her?

She raised her eyes to the sky that peeked through the dense foliage overhead. "Please, God," she prayed. "Let him be searching. Let him find me! I-I don't want to spend another night alone in the forest!"

She hooked her fingers around the pistol in the pocket of her skirt, having not used it—for protection or for food. She feared that she would have to soon. But the thought of killing an animal or bird sickened her. She would not do this unless absolutely forced to.

A cool fog began rising from the river as Briana stumbled onward through a maze of thickets, briars and thorns, and great mats of vines. She was about to give up ever finding anything to eat when up ahead, in the mauve light of dawn, she saw huge vines hung with cluster after cluster of grapes!

"Thank the Lord," Briana said, tears spiraling down her cheeks as she broke into a run.

She fell to her knees before the grapevines and began picking the delicate clusters of grapes from the vine tendrils. She ate ravenously, unaware of horse hooves stopping a short distance away, or of someone approaching her from behind.

When strong arms snaked around her waist and drew her to her feet, she turned and found herself looking up into Night Hawk's dark eyes. She flung herself into his arms, sobbing.

"Night Hawk, I didn't think I'd ever see you again," she cried, clinging to him. "Thank you, darling, for finding me."

He held her close, his heart pounding with hers, then held her away from him, frowning. "Why was it necessary for me to search for you?" he grumbled. "Why did you leave the security of my village? Did you not know the dangers?"

He looked her over, seeing her total disarray, then gazed into her eyes again. "What happened?" he said more softly. "Why are you here without a horse? Are you all right?"

"Yes, I'm all right," Briana murmured. "Now that you are here, I am. I'm just a bit weary from wandering in the forest, and eager to have a substantial meal to fill my stomach."

She glanced down at herself, cringing, then smiled up at him. "I am a sight, aren't I?"

"You still did not say why you are here instead of my village," Night Hawk said. "Were you on your way to St. Paul? Had you decided that you wished to live under the tyranny of your uncle instead of living with Night Hawk and accepting the love he offers you?"

"No," Briana said, her voice breaking. She crept into his arms again, relishing his closeness. "My darling, I never want to even see my uncle again, unless it is behind bars, much less live with him."

She leaned away and gazed up at him. "Night Hawk, I left on horseback shortly after you left your village to follow you to the cave, searching for the firearms and your father," she murmured. "But—but my horse threw me, and here I am, a mess."

She frowned up at him. "Your father?" she murmured. "Did you find him? Were you able to transfer the firearms from the cave to your village?"

Night Hawk cast his eyes downward, recalling the instant of the explosion and the fear that had swept through him for his father.

Then he looked at Briana again. "There was a great explosion," he murmured. "The cave was destroyed, and most surely the firearms that were inside it." He swallowed hard. "I am not sure if my father was in the cave. My heart tells me that he was not. Many

GET UP TO 4 FREE BOOKS!

You can have the best romance delivered to your door for less than what you'd pay in a bookstore or online. Sign up for one of our book clubs today, and we'll send you **FREE* BOOKS** just for trying it out...**with no obligation to buy, ever!**

HISTORICAL ROMANCE BOOK CLUB

Travel from the Scottish Highlands to the American West, the decadent ballrooms of Regency England to Viking ships. Your shipments will include authors such as CONNIE MASON, CASSIE EDWARDS, LYNSAY SANDS, LEIGH GREENWOOD, and many, many more.

LOVE SPELL BOOK CLUB

Bring a little magic into your life with the romances of Love Spell—fun contemporaries, paranormals, time-travels, futuristics, and more. Your shipments will include authors such as KATIE MACALISTER, SUSAN GRANT, NINA BANGS, SANDRA HILL, and more.

As a book club member you also receive the following special benefits:

- **30% OFF all orders through our website & telecenter!**
  (Plus, you still get 1 book FREE for every 5 books you buy!)
- **Exclusive access to special discounts!**
- **Convenient home delivery and 10 days to return any books you don't want to keep.**

There is no minimum number of books to buy, and you may cancel membership at any time. See back to sign up!

*Please include $2.00 for shipping and handling.

YES! ☐

Sign me up for the **Historical Romance Book Club** and send my TWO FREE BOOKS! If I choose to stay in the club, I will pay only $8.50* each month, a savings of $5.48!

YES! ☐

Sign me up for the **Love Spell Book Club** and send my TWO FREE BOOKS! If I choose to stay in the club, I will pay only $8.50* each month, a savings of $5.48!

NAME: _____

ADDRESS: _____

_____

TELEPHONE: _____

E-MAIL: _____

☐ **I WANT TO PAY BY CREDIT CARD.**

☐ VISA   ☐ MasterCard   ☐ DISCOVER

ACCOUNT #: _____

EXPIRATION DATE: _____

SIGNATURE: _____

Send this card along with $2.00 shipping & handling for each club you wish to join, to:

Romance Book Clubs
1 Mechanic Street
Norwalk, CT 06850-3431

Or fax (must include credit card information!) to: 610.995.9274. You can also sign up online at www.dorchesterpub.com.

*Plus $2.00 for shipping. Offer open to residents of the U.S. and Canada only. Canadian residents please call 1.800.481.9191 for pricing information.
If under 18, a parent or guardian must sign. Terms, prices and conditions subject to change. Subscription subject to acceptance. Dorchester Publishing reserves the right to reject any order or cancel any subscription.

JOIN NOW!

braves are searching for him now. I was among them until I saw you kneeling here, eating. I told them to keep searching and I came for you."

Briana lowered her eyes. "I am sorry to be such a bother," she said. "If not for me, you could still be searching for your father."

Night Hawk placed a finger under her chin and lifted her eyes to him. "You know your importance to me," he said. "It is good that I found you. Now, together, if you are able, we will resume the search for my father. If he is not found by this evening, we will return to my village. There we will eat and rest, and I will resume the search again the next day."

Her stomach and thirst both quenched by the grapes that she had stuffed into her mouth, Briana eagerly nodded. "Yes, let's go," she said anxiously. "I want to help you. Thank you for allowing it."

When he started to lift his left hand to her cheek, she saw the redness of the burn on the back of his hand. She gasped and looked quickly up at him. "Night Hawk, I believe it's infected!" she said.

She took his good hand and began half dragging him to the river. "Before we go anywhere, you are going to let me cleanse and wrap the wound," she said stubbornly.

He smiled and went with her.

After she had bathed the wound for him, he left her and went beneath the trees and began gathering different herbs. Taking them back to Briana, he showed her how they worked as medication. After crushing them between the palms of both of his hands, he spread the crushed leaves atop his wound, pressing the mixture into it, then smiled again as she ripped away a portion of her petticoat and wrapped it.

"Now, isn't that better?" Briana said, sighing as she looked into his dark eyes.

Night Hawk said nothing. He drew her into his arms, his mouth meeting hers as he kissed her long and hard, feeling the press of her breasts into his chest, wanting her yet knowing that this want must be delayed until later.

Thanks to the Great Spirit he had found his woman.

Now he hoped to be as blessed a second time—and find his father.

The long procession of horses heavy-laden with firearms, and the renegades riding alongside, keeping close watch for any approaching horsemen, wove its way through the forest.

Echohawk, whose wound pained him little and who was now riding tall and square-shouldered on his assigned horse, kept watch himself, trying to memorize every detail of the forest they were traveling through. He was also glancing over his shoulder, checking often on the welfare of the beautiful woman and child traveling on foot beside the horse.

A father's affection for Gentle Fawn made Echohawk want to offer her his horse. A lover's affection made him want to have her on the horse with him so that he could hold her tender body against his. Then he turned away, again ashamed for allowing himself to become caught up in feelings for another woman when his sweet No-din was surely weeping over him even at this moment. But she did not mourn the loss of him as her husband. She only treated him in a motherly fashion now, all the while his body was crying out, was burning to be caressed—to be loved!

A soft, tiny hand was suddenly in Echohawk's, making his heart leap. He turned his gaze back down to Gentle Fawn. When she smiled up him so endearingly, he knew that loving her was not impossible. Had not his very own father loved two women at once? One white-skinned, the other red? Was he not his father's son, borne to him of his Chippewa wife?

He circled his fingers around Gentle Fawn's hand, no longer hesitating to return her affection. When he asked her to get on the horse with him, a warning shot rang out over his head and Gentle Fawn resumed walking beside his horse, fear deep in her wide eyes.

Again, Echohawk tried to work the ropes loose at his wrists, at least glad that his ankles had been untied to let him ride the horse, instead of being forced to lie across the horse's back, as though something worthless. But no matter how hard he tried, he could not loosen the bonds at his wrists, and his flesh was now raw from having tried so often.

Suddenly looming before him was another massive cave that he was not familiar with. He had hoped the journey would take longer, for being out in the open heightened his chances of being found.

Echohawk's jaw tightened and his eyes narrowed with hate when Blackie rode up next to him.

"Now that I've seen you've arrived without mishap to your next dark prison, it's time to bid you adieu, Chief," Blackie said, laughing loudly. "My constituents await me."

He leaned closer. "Don't ask me what awaits you," he taunted. "I'm leaving it all up to White Wolf. He has much more interesting ways of dealing with people like you!"

White Wolf came to the other side of Echohawk's horse and glared at him, then rode on away, leading the procession into the cave.

Echohawk had no choice but to follow.

16

To nestle once more in that haven of rest—
Your lips upon mine, my head on your breast.
            —HUNT

Briana's head nodded, only half awake when she entered Night Hawk's village on his horse with him. She was only vaguely aware of being lifted from the horse and carried into Night Hawk's wigwam, lit by the flickering glow of a cedar fire.

When he lay her down on a thick pallet of furs beside the low-burning embers, she was barely aware of him gently drawing a blanket over her. Though every bone in her body seemed to be aching from the lengthy time spent on Night Hawk's horse, searching for his father in vain, she felt content in the fact that she was with Night Hawk again.

And it felt so good to be safe!

While she had been lost, wandering aimlessly about, she had begun to think that she would die out in the midst of the wilderness, alone. She had doubted she would ever see Night Hawk again, much less be with him.

Her eyelashes fluttered partially open, and she smiled drunkenly at Night Hawk as he slipped beneath the blankets beside her, allowing her to snuggle into his embrace. "I love you," she whispered, twining an arm around his neck. "I adore you."

He swept her against him, their bodies straining together. He kissed her passionately, then drew away.

He turned his back to Briana as he stared into the dying embers of his lodge fire, unable to make love to her—his disappointment of not finding his father haunted him.

Sensing his pain, Briana fitted her body against his from behind, her hand reaching over to gently touch his face. "I'm sorry you didn't find your father," she murmured. "But, Night Hawk, no one could have been so persistent in his search as you. It seems that White Wolf has more than one hideout. Surely the firearms and your father have been transferred there. Can you think of a section of the forest that you are not familiar with—where White Wolf could go, realizing that you do not know of the place?"

"Minnesota is a vast land, with many lakes and forests," Night Hawk grumbled. "It would be impossible to know every secret place. But perhaps I know someone who might know of this one."

He turned to her. "Tomorrow I will ride to St. Paul," he said, smoothing a fallen lock of hair from her brow. "I will question your uncle."

Panic seized Briana. She sat up quickly, her eyes wild. "Please don't," she said, her voice filled with fear. "You could be walking into a trap, Night Hawk. Surely there are other ways of finding answers. Please try anything but going to my uncle. He could have you seized and jailed. He could say you are responsible for my disappearance! He would say anything to anybody if it would bring harm to you. And what will you say about me should he ask if you've seen me? I don't want him to know where I am now—or ever!"

Then she lowered her eyes. "My one regret is that I was forced to leave my painting equipment and my paintings behind," she said sullenly. "Without them, I-I feel so empty."

Night Hawk turned and pulled her into his arms. "I

would hope that my love for you would banish all of your emptiness," he said, his gaze locked with hers. "But if that is not enough, I promise you that I will manage to get anything that you ask." He kissed her eyes closed. "I want you to be happy. Totally, unconditionally happy."

"Darling, never think that my love for you comes second to anything else in my life," Briana whispered, feeling secure in the warmth of his arms. "You are everything to me. Everything."

"I saw your passion for your painting," Night Hawk said, his hands caressing her back. "Such a passion must be fed. I shall see that it is."

Briana leaned back and smiled. "My passion for you is greater, my love," she murmured. She laughed softly. "But tonight I am too tired to prove it to you." She sighed heavily and snuggled against him again, pressing her cheek against his chest, feeling his strong, rapid heartbeat through the buckskin fabric of his shirt.

"No proof is needed tonight, or any other night," Night Hawk said, easing her down on her back, stretching out beside her. "You have already proved it to me, in many ways. Remembrances of sweet times with you are locked within my heart, to draw from at times like these. I will go to sleep and you will be there in my dreams, kissing me, holding me, making love to me."

When she didn't respond, he leaned over and pressed a soft kiss to her cheek, thinking that it was hard to tell when she was the lovelier. Now, when she slept so beautifully beside him? Or when she was awake, laughing, her eyes twinkling into his?

"You are always lovely," he said, snuggling down beside her, his eyes heavy with sleep himself.

When, in her sleep, her hand sought his and held

it, he brought it to his lips and kissed it, then held it above his heart, finding at least this moment of peace while the rest of the world beyond his wigwam seemed to be crashing down.

The moon was high in the sky, and the treetops were silvered with its glow as Lily stood on her secret limestone bluff that overlooked the river way down below.

Falling to her knees, she looked heavenward, tears burning the corners of her eyes. Sorrowful over her father's absence, her mother's health, and Strong Branch's desire for the company of Gray Moon over hers, she began to sing to the nightly spirits, hoping to find some sort of peace within herself.

Lily was unaware that Strong Branch stood apart, watching and listening.

He stepped closer, clasping his hand on the handle of his knife, thrust in a buckskin sheath at his side. A lump grew in his throat, for he was a lover of songs, and each pretty song that Lily sang thrilled him with delight, then shame. He knew what Lily expected of him, and it was not yet his to give. He had plans that did not include a wife at this time. He wanted to better himself before taking a wife—especially not one whose father was the chief of the opposing band of Chippewa!

"He is not chief for long," Strong Branch whispered to himself. "He is now a captive, and soon a corpse."

He shifted his feet nervously in the loose rocks, frowning at the fact that Echohawk was still a captive at all. He would have slit Echohawk's throat the moment he arrived at the cave. But White Wolf had forbade it, as well as forbidding Strong Branch and Gray Moon to enter the cave lest Echohawk see them.

That was a part of White Wolf's devious plan—just

before Echohawk died, he would see at last who was
going to kill him—who had betrayed him! As he took
his last breaths he would realize that Strong Branch
had won the battle of chiefs. As the knife lowered to
Echohawk's heart, he would be told that Night
Hawk's death was next.

Strong Branch would finally be chief of both bands
of Chippewa. There would be no one else to question
it. The two villages would finally become as one under
one leadership—Strong Branch's!

White Wolf would benefit by having a Chippewa
chief as an ally. As far as Strong Branch knew, it
would be the first alliance between the Sioux and
Chippewa of Minnesota in the history of these two
warring tribes.

Strong Branch refocused his attention on Lily as she
sang to the rippling waters, the dancing stars, and the
shifting winds. He hated disturbing her. He too loved
the moon, the night noises, the call of the birds as
they sought their mates, the calming waters, and the
swish of the night breeze in the tree tops. Yet he knew
that time was wasting. He must go to Lily and hope
that she would understand when he told her that tonight they could not be together. Gray Moon was
waiting. They were going to ride into the night again.

His moccasin-padded footsteps as soft as a panther's, Strong Branch went to Lily and bent down beside her. He took her hand. "Lily?" he said softly.
"My love?"

Lily's heart leapt into her throat, having not heard
his approach. She turned startled eyes to him, then
laughed softly as she crept into his arms. "Strong
Branch," she whispered, clinging tightly. "I am so
glad that you came. I was beginning to think that you
had forgotten, or—or just had not wanted to."

"I have come, but I cannot stay as long as usual,"

Strong Branch said, easing her out of his arms, his fingers on her shoulders as he urged her to her feet. "Gray Moon is waiting."

Lily was quickly overcome by jealousy, and not for a woman. It was for Strong Branch's strong, questionable alliance with Gray Moon. It was always Gray Moon that stood in the way of their togetherness—of their discussions of their future.

She looked bitterly at Strong Branch, this time determined not to allow him to leave. Now, she thought, was the time to tell Strong Branch about their child. It was time for him to take on the same responsibility as her—that this child that she was carrying was his! She would not allow him to leave tonight until he agreed on a wedding date. He knew the disgrace brought upon a woman if she gave birth to a child, unwed.

"I understand, Strong Branch," Lily said, forcing a smile. "I do not need much time to say what I have wanted to say so badly to you, the man who will be my husband." Her smile wavered. "You are still planning to marry me? Tell me, Strong Branch, that you are."

Strong Branch shaped his hands around the soft curves of her face, the sheer beauty of Lily causing the usual ache in his loins. Her pure white skin was touched tonight by a soft pink, which he had grown used to seeing when she was excited. Her hair was loose and billowing across her shoulders, the breeze causing it to shimmer down her back. Her eyes were soft and round, and fringed with thick, dark lashes.

Her lips, he marveled to himself, ah, her ruby lips, how they beckoned to him even now for a kiss—one that would surely delay his night's events if he gave in to the temptation.

"I have promised myself to you, have I not?" he

finally said, a touch of annoyance in his voice. "Why must I always be forced to tell you this over and over again?"

Stung by the sharpness of his voice, Lily took a step away from him. "Why must I always be reminding you?" she said, almost bursting into tears. "It is because you say that you love me, say that you will marry me, yet you do not! What am I to expect, Strong Branch? What? Do you expect me to wait forever?" She firmed her jaw and squared her shoulders. "If you do not tell me tonight a set date for our marriage, I absolutely refuse ever to speak to you again!"

Stunned by Lily's outburst, yet knowing that he shouldn't be, since she had done this more often than not lately, Strong Branch's eyes widened. But seeing the seriousness of the situation, and not wanting to lose these special, sensual moments with her just yet, he placed gentle hands on her shoulders and drew her into an embrace.

"My beautiful Lily," he murmured, gazing warmly into her eyes. "I do want you for my wife. But I want more time." He could feel her tense up again, so he hurried his words:

"But if it will make you happy, sweet Lily," he said, "let us say that we will be wed in seven sunrises. Does that please you, Lily? Is that soon enough?"

Happiness instantly seized Lily's heart. She began laughing and crying at the same time. She hugged Strong Branch tightly. "Seven sunrises is fine with me!" she said, her heart pounding.

"Then that is the way it will be," Strong Branch said. He placed his hands on her waist and eased her gently from his arms. "But promise me something, Lily?"

"Anything," she said, beaming.

"Let us not tell anyone just yet," he said, his brow furrowing.

Lily's face became shadowed with doubt again. "Why would you ask me not to tell?"

"It is something that we should do together," Strong Branch said. "Give me two sunrises. You secretly plan a celebration for when we make our announcement. Surprises are nice, do you not think so, Lily?"

He smiled weakly down at her, hoping that he was being convincing. What he truly needed was more time to make things right not for them, but solely for himself. He wanted this time to achieve the full power that he sought.

Most of all, he needed her silence to enable him to achieve this goal.

Things were finally going his way. Finally! He could not, would not, allow her to ruin it!

Looking at her, being near her, made a slow ache grow in his heart, for he did love her so much. Yet in truth, he did not plan to marry her at all.

"That is wonderful!" Lily said, clasping her hands, smiling again. "It will be much fun making plans!"

Then a thought came to her that saddened everything that she wanted to be wonderful and gay.

Her father was still missing. And her mother was so ill.

But she had to place such sadness from her heart. Because of this child growing within her, she had plans to make for her future. Her child's future, and she would not make them with a sad, burdensome heart.

She grabbed Strong Branch's hands and squeezed them. "My darling, I have the most wonderful news to share with you," she said, her voice lilting.

"And what might that be?" Strong Branch said,

filled with regret, knowing that this happiness that she was showing would soon be turned to remorse—and hate.

"My darling Strong Branch, I am with child!" Lily burst out, her eyes searching his face for shared joy over this wondrous news that she had held close to her heart for so long. Her smile wavered when she saw how shaken Strong Branch was by the news.

"Strong Branch?" she murmured, putting a hand on his cheek. "Are you not happy? Soon we will be married. We can then tell everyone that we are expecting a child! Our child. Is that not wonderful, Strong Branch?"

He forced a smile and drew her into his arms. "*Ay-uh*," he said flatly. "Wonderful."

He now felt his world slipping away. He felt completely trapped.

17

The early morning light was spiraling through the smoke hole in the ceiling. The fire in the fire pit had burned to shimmering orange embers.

Briana awakened, thrilled when she felt hands cupping her breasts through her dress and warm lips pressing into hers in a kiss savagely sweet and long.

All of her aches and pains of the prior night quickly faded into lethargic bliss as she twined her arms around Night Hawk's neck and returned the kiss. His hand crept up her skirt and found her wet and ready for him as he began caressing the core of her womanhood.

She sucked in a wild breath when he plunged several fingers inside her, thrusting heatedly, taking her to a world that knew no bounds of pleasure.

Night Hawk's lips slipped down her neck, then sucked her hard nipple through the cotton material of her blouse, until she felt faint with the pleasure he was arousing within her.

When he leaned away from her, she opened blissfully hazy eyes and beckoned with open arms for him not to leave her. She quickly saw that was not his intention at all. He was lowering his fringed breeches, his throbbing hardness springing forth as he dropped them to the floor.

He put his hand on himself, moving his fingers slowly over his hardness. She swallowed hard as he knelt down over her, soon straddling her. She lifted her skirt and opened herself to him, her lips parting when his mouth came on hers again, his tongue darting within. As his tongue danced within her mouth, he plunged his hardness within her and began his heated strokes.

Loosening Briana's blouse and lifting it away from the waistband of her skirt, Night Hawk slid his hand beneath it and cupped a breast, squeezing the nipple between a thumb and forefinger, drawing a heavy sigh from Briana.

She lifted her hips, twined her legs around his waist, and rode with him, thrust for thrust, stroke for stroke. Surges of warmth flooded through her body. Tremors cascaded down her back when he moved his lips to her breast and his tongue began circling the nipple, his teeth teasingly nipping it.

As he braced himself above her, his hands caught Briana's and held them slightly above her head against the soft pelts, his buttocks moving rhythmically, his strokes heating up within her.

Briana groaned throatily when he kissed her again, this time more hungrily, more demandingly. She knew that the passion was peaking, and that soon they would once again share the ultimate of wild rapture.

When his lips went to her breast again and he sucked a nipple between his lips, she drew in a sharp breath, and released a cry of sweet agony from the depths of her throat.

His hand then moved over her breasts, down her ribs, and across the soft, tremoring flesh of her belly.

He found her throbbing center again and caressed it as he continued his rhythmic strokes inside her.

Hardly able to bear the building ecstasy, Briana circled her arms around his neck and again drew Night Hawk's lips to hers, kissing him fiercely. When she felt his body stiffen, she knew that he was nearing that peak of pleasure that they both had been seeking. Their bodies jolted and quivered. For the moment they were the only two people in the universe.

Night Hawk pressed endlessly deeper. Briana clung to him, sculpting herself to his moist body, running her fingers along his tight buttocks, then clasping them as again she felt the pleasure grabbing her.

There was a great shuddering in Night Hawk's loins. Briana strained her hips up at him, crying out together at their shared fulfillment.

Sighing, wonderfully shaken by the experience, they lay exhausted together.

"This is a wonderful way to greet a new day," Briana said, giggling as Night Hawk, breathing hard, rolled away from her to stretch out on his back.

She then grew sober and stroked Night Hawk's perspiration-laced stomach. "But today there are more things to do than make love," she murmured. "You are going to see my uncle. You are going to search for your father. I shall fear for you until your return, my darling."

"My mother!" Night Hawk said, jumping to his feet. He drew on his breeches. "I must go and check on Mother. When she worries, her body weakens."

He brushed a kiss across Briana's brow. "I shall return soon," he said. He glanced down at the fire pit, then back up at Briana. "Upon my return I shall tend to the fire. I shall ask Lily to bring us food. And then, my love, I must leave."

He knelt before her and framed her face between

his hands. "Leaving you is not something I wish to do," he said. "Were we ever to have a full day for making love, I would not stop to eat or rest. I would make love to you until there was no breath left in me, or a beat left in my heart."

"That would be a bit drastic, wouldn't it?" Briana said, laughing softly. "My darling, when things are better, we will have a lifetime of sharing wonderful, blissful moments together. We would not have to use them all up in one day."

A frown creased Night Hawk's brow. "Sometimes I do not think life will ever become uncomplicated," he said, his voice drawn. "If it is not the interference of the white man or the Sioux, it is from the people of our own tribe of Chippewa! Greed causes many to become foreign to themselves."

"You are speaking of Strong Branch?" Briana said, stroking his broad back as she leaned up against his chest.

"*Ay-uh*, Strong Branch and Gray Moon," he growled. "They plot together for Strong Branch to be chief. It is becoming more and more evident that they would do anything to rid themselves of my father and myself. Perhaps they are in part responsible for my father's disappearance, and that saddens me."

He rose back to his feet, drawing on his fringed shirt. "My sister, Lily?" he grumbled. "She wishes to marry Strong Branch. Is not that the worst sort of complication?"

Briana nodded, then sat down beside the glowing embers of the fire and watched him leave, her heart heavy for him.

Night Hawk hurried to his mother's wigwam and found Lily sitting vigil at her side. When Lily lifted sorrowful eyes up at Night Hawk, he looked at their mother. Anger rose in his heart for those responsible for his father's disappearance, for this had caused his mother to worsen.

He knelt down beside Lily and drew her into his arms. "I see that Mother is worse," he said, stroking his sister's back. "And I will find the one responsible!"

"*Gee-mah-mah's* malaria has returned," Lily cried, clinging to him. "She is in the grip of a fever and melancholia over *gee-bah-bah*. Night Hawk, you must find Father! You must!"

Lily closed her eyes, trying to blot out everything ugly and unpleasant in the world, trying to concentrate solely on Strong Branch's promises that were fresh in her heart.

Night Hawk held her close, his eyes focused on his mother. Her breathing was shallow. The fever was almost consuming her.

He yanked away from his sister. "I must leave now," he said, more determined than ever to find his father. If not, he might lose his mother and father at the same time.

He clasped his sister's shoulders. "Briana is in my dwelling," he said softly. "Go to her. Lend her a hand with the fire. Take her food. I do not have time. I have someone to see and it cannot wait any longer."

"The white woman?" Lily said softly. "She is in your dwelling? I thought—"

"I found her and brought her home late last night," Night Hawk said. He looked over at his mother again. "Send for a Mide priest. See that he performs his magic over *gee-mah-mah*."

"*Ay-uh*, soon," Lily said, almost choking on a sob.

"Explain to Briana that I had to leave," Night Hawk said, then swung around and rushed from the wigwam.

Lily wiped tears from her eyes as she gazed down at her mother, guilt awash throughout her for having kept the secret of her child from her. What if her mother died, never knowing that she was going to be a grandmother?

She knelt down beside her mother and began saying a soft prayer, asking the Great Spirit for a way to find forgiveness within her mother's heart.

It was high noon. Blackie was on a podium near the capital building, hoping to draw a crowd of people as they came and went in their buggies and fancy carriages along the busy thoroughfare. He was making a speech to those who had already stopped and were standing around the platform, listening. His eyes wavered, realizing that his speech was lacking its usual spark. He couldn't get his mind off Briana, wondering what he would tell her parents if she didn't surface again; wondering where on earth she was.

But, of course, he suspected that she was in Night Hawk's village, having become his willing whore. And he could not do anything about it, because he could not draw any undue attention to himself that could lose him the election. He was too close to winning to worry about her whereabouts.

He had labored hard and long to make a name for himself. He would not let anything or anyone stand in his way.

At least he had succeeded in helping get the firearms moved to another hideout. Plus, he had made sure that Echohawk was still captive. He hoped that White Wolf would soon succeed at capturing Night Hawk again. That would be the icing on the cake. He would not only win an election with the white community, but also gain a firm hold on the Indian population as well.

Seeing that his speech was not going well, Blackie soon left the platform and stepped into his buggy. Snapping the reins, he sent his horse on through the crowded streets, needing the solace, the privacy of his house for the rest of the day.

Another successful raid behind them, Strong Branch and Gray Moon were riding together through the forest toward their village.

Gray Moon edged his horse closer to his chief's. "No matter what Wise Owl says, I feel that it is best that our band of Chippewa break completely away from Chief Echohawk's," he said stiffly. "Is now not a perfect time? Chief Echohawk is not there to interfere. I have thought long and hard about this, Strong Branch. This is truly the only way you will ever achieve any true peace as a leader."

Strong Branch had not been able to focus on much else besides his unborn child since Lily had broken the news. This changed everything, it seemed. He could not turn his back on a child. Because of his father's and mother's untimely deaths so long ago, he had been forced to be raised without parents, and he knew the emptiness that brought into one's life, especially a son's. He would not allow his child to live such a life. It seemed that he would have to marry Lily after all.

And if so, his plans to achieve the full powers of both bands of Chippewa would go awry. He could not go against his wife's very own people, could he?

Seeing that Strong Branch was not responding, Gray Moon sneered at him. "You allow a woman to shadow your vision of the future," he chided. "Our people's future! Not Lily's chieftain father's. Do you not realize that should Night Hawk be allowed to live, he will soon be chief—and he is part white, a lover of white skins. You should want no part of that band of Chippewa! You should want no part of Lily. White blood flows through her veins. Her skin is white. Her mother is white. What if she were to bear you white children? Could you live with such disgrace?"

A coldness grabbed Strong Branch in the pit of his stomach, having never even considered the possibility of his child having any skin coloring other than his own. But until last night he had not even considered having children by Lily. He had not planned to marry her.

He turned angrily to Gray Moon. "You have said enough," he shouted. "I need no one to tell me anything of my mind. I will make my own decisions, and that is final!"

Gray Moon quickly turned his eyes away, to hide the seething anger in their depths.

Concerned about Night Hawk, wondering why he had not yet returned, Briana went to the entrance flap and lifted it to look for him. But just as she did, Lily appeared with buckskin clothes draped over an arm and moccasins hanging from the fingers of her left hand.

"Night Hawk is gone," Lily said softly, seeing how Briana's eyes left her to again search the village. "My brother sent me to tell you that he had to leave. I am to help you with the lodge fire. I will soon bring you food." She held out the buckskin clothes, smiling. "I have brought you a change of clothes."

"That is kind of you," Briana said, trying to hide her disappointment at not seeing Night Hawk again, her heart pounding with worry for him.

She looked past Lily, and sighed, finding everything at the village so peaceful. It was hard to think that anything was amiss today.

"I can see in your eyes that you find my village pleasant," Lily said, stepping up to Briana's side, turning slowly to survey everything around her as well. "My village is noted for its sunny days and its cool nights, a paradise where children may gather pebbles in the beautiful river. It is the nesting place for many varieties of songbirds."

Lily uttered a sigh. "I love this valley filled with beautiful trees and clear, cool running rivers. It is a perfect place to raise children."

Smiling, her secret of soon having her own child held sweetly within her heart, Lily went on inside Night Hawk's wigwam. When Briana came and stood beside her, Lily placed the buckskin garments in her arms.

"These are mine, beaded and fringed by my own hand," Lily said softly. "Please enjoy them. They are now yours."

"Thank you," Briana murmured. "You are very kind."

As Lily worked with the fire and continued talking, Briana slipped out of her torn and soiled clothes, planning to bathe in the river as soon as she felt she could slip away. She put on deerskin leggings, tying them around her legs just under her knees. She slipped into a buckskin garment that displayed beads set in leaf and flower designs that came to her calves. The moccasins were soft and pleasant to her sore and tired feet.

"With our alert people, nothing is without purpose," Lily said, turning to face Briana. "The rattle of a rolling pebble or stone; the whirr of bird wings disturbed at their rest; or the warning snort of a horse—"

She paused in her chattering when Briana tried to smooth the tangles from her hair with her fingers.

"Allow me to make your hair pretty," she said. Briana smiled and silently nodded her approval.

Using her own personal hairbrush—the tail of a porcupine attached to a decorated handle—and instead of a comb, a hair parter—a slender painted stick, also with a decorated handle—Lily parted Briana's hair. She then carefully brushed and plaited it into two braids, tying the ends with strings of painted buckskin, called hair strings.

"Again I thank you," Briana said, drawing one of her braids around and admiring the hair string. It was a work of art, tipped with ball tassels of porcupine quills and fluffs of eagle feathers. "It is so very pretty, Lily."

"You look lovely," Lily said, stepping back and clasping her hands as she admired Briana.

"I feel lovely," Briana said, smiling. Then her smile faded when someone's chanting wafted into the wigwam.

"That is the Mide priest," Lily said solemnly, bowing her head. "My mother has worsened. The Mide is performing his magical cures over her."

Briana went to the entrance flap and lifted it, peering outside to see a crowd assembling around Echohawk's wigwam. A shiver coursed across her flesh. Now she felt a strange sort of doom hanging over the village, replacing what she had only moments ago thought was so beautiful, so serene.

She looked into the denseness of the forest, wishing Night Hawk were there, dreading what might happen to him while he was gone.

And, she wondered, where was Night Hawk's father?

Echohawk leaned against the cold, dank wall of the cave as he watched the renegades celebrating the victory of another night of raiding. He had also watched the firearms being brought into the cave, and the ammunition being stacked against the far wall.

It was apparent that they had found whiskey among the loot. Most were too drunk to stand now, many falling to the ground, having passed into a whiskey-induced sleep.

The night had been long and he could not tell even if it was now day. The cave was always dark, always cold and damp.

Moving to lie on his side on a blanket, he was starting to drift off to sleep himself when a body slid in behind him and arms circled around him. He could not find the courage to send Gentle Fawn away. He hoped that White Wolf would not awaken and find her there. She was White Wolf's woman, a possession to be used but not loved.

White Wolf was sitting in the shadows, watching drunkenly, a sly grin on his face. Letting Gentle Fawn warm up to Echohawk was just part of the misery he wished to create for Echohawk before he killed him. He could tell that the temptation was becoming too great for the old chief, even for a man who had a wife and two children.

Gentle Fawn's hands wandered slowly over Echohawk, until she could feel the arousal of his manhood. She had seen him watching and wanting her. She wanted him no less. He was a gentle, beautiful man. She had never been with such a man, and wanted him now as she had never before in her life wanted someone.

She began stroking his hardness through his buckskin breeches, but when his hand circled hers and eased it away, she knew that he was not the sort to be with another woman so easily when he had a woman of his own awaiting his return at his village.

She did not move away from him, in awe of White Wolf allowing her to stay. She snuggled closer, fitting her body into the curve of Echohawk's body from behind.

Having become aroused from watching Gentle Fawn try to pleasure Echohawk, White Wolf jerked her away and threw her to the cave floor. He yanked her dress up to her waist and plunged his throbbing tightness into her, his grunts of satisfaction reaching Echohawk like stab wounds to his heart.

Echohawk closed his eyes and tried not to hear, but how could he not when each of White Wolf's forceful thrusts inside Gentle Fawn made her cry out with pain? Echohawk gritted his teeth, vowing to get free somehow to see that White Wolf never touched the lovely woman again.

Echohawk knew that he shouldn't, that he was not free to, but he was falling in love with Gentle Fawn. He knew that this would have never happened had he and Mariah had the chance to share a healthy relationship these past years. But after having the sensual side of their marriage die when she had become weakened by her illnesses, he had ached many a night.

Now that he had been awakened anew with thoughts of desire, he knew that he could not deny himself the pleasure of it much longer.

Gentle Fawn. He wanted Gentle Fawn so badly. His whole soul cried out for her.

18

The moonlight of a perfect peace
Floods heart and brain.
—SHARP

Night Hawk waited in the shadows of the forest until
the moon had replaced the sun in the sky. Then he
ventured onto the streets of St. Paul until he reached
Blackie's mansion. Dismounting, he left his horse a
short distance away, then moved stealthily through the
darkness until he reached the protective shadows of a
towering elm tree. From that vantage point he
watched Blackie's house, trying to sort out which
room the politician was in by the splash of golden
lamplight in the windows. When he saw a light flicker
on in a room on the lower floor, he smiled, tapping
his fingers nervously against the pistol thrust into the
waistband of his fringed buckskin breeches.

He waited only a moment longer, giving himself
time to peer cautiously around the estate grounds,
watching for movements and seeing none.

Then springing forth like a panther, he ran across
the flat stretch of yard, up the steps to the wide veranda that reached around three sides of the house,
and then flattened his back against the house. He
edged himself along, hugging the wall with his back,
until he came to the window where he had seen the
lamplight flicker on.

Scarcely breathing, he leaned away from the wall,
only enough to be able to look in the window.

Through a thin gauze curtain he saw Blackie sitting at a massive oak desk, leisurely smoking a fat cigar, intently reading a book.

Night Hawk nodded, knowing that now was the time to make his move. Blackie was lost in another world—the one that "talking leaves," books, created within one's mind. Blackie would not hear the door open, or the approach of his enemy.

Going to the door, he slowly turned the knob, opened the door, then crept inside a dimly lit foyer. He stopped and stared down a long corridor, seeing the flood of light on the floor from only one room, and knew that was his destination. Night Hawk moved down the corridor, his moccasined feet silent. When he reached the study he burst into it, his pistol drawn, aimed at Blackie's heart.

Hearing the rush of movement, Blackie looked up quickly. When he saw Night Hawk standing there, a drawn pistol in his right hand, he gasped and dropped the book to the desk, the pages fluttering closed.

"What are you doing here?" Blackie asked, inching up from his chair. He moved behind it and fixed his fingers tightly on the back of the chair. "You crazy Injun, put that gun away."

"Tell me where my father is," Night Hawk said in a threatening snarl, his eyes having narrowed into two dark slits. "Tell me now, politician, or you'll soon be joining your ancestors in the land of the hereafter."

"I know nothing," Blackie said, his heart pounding as he looked down the barrel of the pistol, then slowly at Night Hawk's finger resting on the trigger. "Why can't you Injuns leave me alone? I'm—I'm a peace-loving, God-fearing man!"

"That is what you pretend in the public eye, but those who know you as you truly are know better," Night Hawk said gruffly.

He glanced to one side, seeing row after row of books along the side wall. Strange, he thought to himself, how a man of ill-breeding like Blackie Collins could have such a collection of "talking leaves." But that he did, Night Hawk decided, proved that Blackie must have acquired a love of them somewhere between being a gambler and politician.

Night Hawk stepped quickly and purposely to the front of the bookcase, and with his free hand he began knocking the books to the floor. His wounded hand pained him as he jerked each stack of books to the floor, yet he did not show his pain to his enemy.

He laughed when he heard Blackie gasping, obviously horror-stricken over his precious books being abused in such a way.

Keeping his aim steady on Blackie, Night Hawk chose a book, and with his one hand, let it fall open, then spat on the pages.

"Stop that," Blackie said, eyeing the soiled book with a bleeding heart, loving books almost as much as he had once enjoyed gambling. "Those are precious things. Leave them be." His face became suffused with color when Night Hawk dropped that book to the floor and took another one from the shelf, repeating the performance.

"You heathen," Blackie said, his teeth grinding together in his mounting anger. "You don't even know the importance of books. How can I expect you to realize what you are doing when you abuse them in such a way?"

"You speak of abuse?" Night Hawk said, kicking books aside as he stepped closer to the desk. "Did you not strike Briana? Did you not see the bruises—the blackness of her eye that was left as evidence of that abuse? You, who pretend to be a pillar of the community, are no better than a snake. I should force you on your stomach and make you slither down the streets of the city, so that the people who you wish to vote for you on election day could see you as you truly are!"

Blackie paled as Night Hawk inched himself even closer. "Stay away from me," he said, taking a step backward.

"Tell me where my father has been taken," Night Hawk said flatly. "I saw the explosion at the cave. Do you think that fooled me into believing that everything was destroyed—even my father?" He laughed. "For a moment, *ay-uh*, I was fooled. But then I realized it was a tactic to draw off my guard."

"What cave?" Blackie said, trying to be convincing. "What explosion? You crazy Injun, how would I know about either?"

"Because, just as you were in the past, you are again in cohoots with White Wolf," Night Hawk said, standing just on the other side of the desk from Blackie. "And don't tell me that you don't know anything of White Wolf's whereabouts now, or that I am wrong in assuming White Wolf is behind my father's abduction."

Night Hawk stepped quickly around the desk and aimed the pistol directly at Blackie's temple. "Do not tell me that you did not know of my abduction and that I was held captive in the cave," he said with another snarl. "I am sure it was you who ordered the abduction."

Paling, the pistol much too close for comfort, Blackie inched away from it. "You—you are wrong," he said, sweat pearling his brow. "Please don't do anything you'll be sorry for, Night Hawk. Leave. If you do, I promise I won't inform the authorities about your craziness tonight."

"Do you think I am concerned about the authorities?" Night Hawk said, laughing. "You could draw undue attention to yourself, and then your unscrupulous activities would be uncovered."

"I'm innocent," Blackie whined. "Innocent!"

Realizing that he would be unable to get answers from Blackie short of torturing him, and not wanting the coward's screams to attract any attention from passersby on the street, or the servants who were surely asleep in their quarters, Night Hawk began slowly taking steps away from him.

"I will find the answers," Night Hawk said. "Somehow. Then I will be back to finish what I started tonight."

Blackie sighed heavily and ran a finger around the tight white collar at his throat. "My niece," he blurted out before Night Hawk fled from the room. "You have been with her. Where is she?"

Night Hawk stopped and glared at Blackie. "You did not give me answers about my father, so I shall not give you answers about your niece," he said.

"I know you didn't abduct her because some of her personal belongings were gone," Blackie said, his voice drawn. "Did she come to you willingly?" He wanted to shout at Night Hawk and tell him that he knew that his niece had helped him escape from the cave—but that was a truth that he had to keep to himself, for it would condemn him for sure in the eyes of the Chippewa brave—and the entire community of St. Paul.

The mention of Briana's belongings brought something to Night Hawk's mind. Briana had pined over having left her beloved painting paraphernalia behind. He had promised to bring at least a portion of her painting equipment back with him. This was a promise that he was going to keep, for he wanted nothing to sadden her ever again.

"Where is Briana's room?" Night Hawk said, ignoring Blackie's question. "Take me to it."

"I told you that—that she isn't there," Blackie said, his words stumbling clumsily across his lips.

Night Hawk's lips formed a slow smile. "That is true," he said. "Now take me to her room."

"Why would you want to—to go there?" Blackie said, not having budged.

Night Hawk aimed his pistol at Blackie again. "Do as I say, politician," he threatened.

Blackie's knees trembled as he moved slowly from behind his chair, around the desk, and then past Night Hawk. Swallowing hard, he went out into the corridor, walked slowly to the spiral staircase, then began slowly walking up the plushly carpeted steps.

"What the hell are you up to now?" Blackie said, giving Night Hawk a glance over his shoulder, paling anew when he saw Night Hawk so close behind him, the pistol aimed at his head.

"Just do as you are told and ask me no more questions," Night Hawk said icily. "Take me to Briana's room."

"Then what?" Blackie asked, ignoring Night Hawk's demands to be quiet. He gasped when he suddenly felt the thrust of the barrel against his back.

Blackie said no more. He rushed up the steps and went to Briana's room, then stood back as Night Hawk moved stealthily and quickly around him and into the room.

Night Hawk's gaze roved slowly, feeling Briana's presence in the room, the aroma of the perfumes that he had become familiar with on her soft skin. He saw the painting paraphernalia that he had seen while in the forest with her.

"Get together Briana's paints, brushes, and everything that she needs to do her paintings," Night Hawk flatly ordered, giving Blackie a cold stare.

Blackie's eyes widened. "Why?" he asked, his voice faint. Then his lips parted in another gasp. "You're taking this to her, aren't you? Damn you, Injun, she is going to shack up with you, isn't she?"

"Do as you are told and say no more about Briana to me," Night Hawk said, smiling to himself as Blackie began scrambling around the room, getting everything into Briana's painting satchel that she used on her outings in the forest.

When this was done, Blackie set it down in the middle of the floor. "How many of her canvases do you want?" he grumbled.

"None," Night Hawk said. "She will paint on the canvas of the Chippewa—on stretched and bleached hides of animals."

"God," Blackie said, a shiver racing across his flesh. "She won't only be living like a heathen, she'll be acting like one."

Ignoring Blackie, Night Hawk backed toward the door. "Grab the satchel," he said, motioning with his head toward it. "Take it down the stairs and set it beside the door."

After Blackie did as he was told, he stepped aside. "Now what?" he said sarcastically.

"Allow me to leave without drawing attention to me, or you will die soon after," Night Hawk warned. "If I am not able to come and shoot the arrow into your heart, one of my most devoted braves will." He smiled darkly. "You will not know when or where it will happen. Only that it will."

Night Hawk picked up the satchel with his free hand, gave Blackie another threatening stare, then turned and fled into the night.

Briana's satchel secured at the side of his horse, Night Hawk rode away from the city, his heart heavy. How was he ever to find his father?

Echohawk gazed intently into Gentle Fawn's dark eyes. "The renegades are gone again," he said softly. "Help me escape. I shall take you with me. I will make all wrongs right for you."

Gentle Fawn rocked her child back and forth in her arms, tears pooling in the corners of her eyes. "I cannot do this thing you ask," she murmured. "Although I tended to your wound, I can do nothing else for you. I-I am too afraid of White Wolf. No matter how much you tell me that I will be safe with you, I cannot truly believe so. White Wolf would search until he found me. He would make me pay for disobeying him."

"I would kill him before he had a chance to get near you," Echohawk growled.

"I am sorry, Echohawk," Gentle Fawn said. "I am too familiar with White Wolf's cunning ways. I would die quickly, and also my child. I do everything now for my child!"

Seeing the futility in trying to talk Gentle Fawn into doing anything that frightened her so much, Echohawk settled back against the wall of the cave. "It is good to know at least that you are not here because you love the renegade," he said, sighing heavily. "You did not seem the sort to choose such a man for a husband."

"Nor did I choose this man for the father of my child," Gentle Fawn said sullenly, her eyes deepening in regret. "But he is. Moonstar is his, but also by force."

She unfolded the corners of the soft doeskin that was wrapped around her child and took the naked child from the blanket. She held her daughter out for Echohawk to see. "Although she is the renegade's child, she is beautiful and sweet."

Echohawk was immediately taken by the child, by her soft brown eyes, her tiny copper facial features, her tiny fingers and toes. He remembered when Night Hawk and Lily had been born. He doubted if White Wolf had given his child a second glance.

"She is most beautiful," Echohawk said, wondering where Night Hawk was, and if he was safe.

Pleased with Echohawk's response, Gentle Fawn placed her child's tiny hand on Echohawk's face. "Does she not have the softest skin?" she said. "Does she not smell so fresh and clean from her bath in the spring at the back of the cave?"

"She is both of these things, and even more," Echohawk said, relishing this time alone with Gentle Fawn and his acquaintance with Moonstar. "It is obvious that you have been a good *gee-mah-mah*."

Gentle Fawn smiled broadly as she wrapped Moonstar in the doeskin blanket again, then laid her aside on a pallet of furs.

Echohawk was stunned when Gentle Fawn crept to her knees before him and placed her soft hands on each of his cheeks, drawing his lips to hers in a sweet, wondrous kiss. Guilt splashed through him when he felt himself responding to the kiss.

He was even more stunned when she drew away from him and lowered her dress so that it rested around her waist. Soon her well-rounded, milk-filled breasts leaned against his bare chest, and then his lips.

"Kiss them," Gentle Fawn whispered. "Please?"

Echohawk sighed from the wondrous feel of her breasts, yet he could not help it when a mixture of sadness and shame engulfed him. Being with a woman, even in this small way, made him miss those carefree days of loving his No-din when she had not been ill, when she had wanted him as much.

His heart bled to see his wife, to touch her breasts! It had been too long since they had shared anything intimate. It had been many winters. And he needed a woman for these needs—for these hungers.

The guilt overwhelmed the pleasure he felt from the feel of a woman's breasts against his lips again, and he recoiled from Gentle Fawn.

"Do not do this thing," he said huskily, his heart pounding. "It is wrong!"

Gentle Fawn jumped with a start away from him. With lowered eyes she drew her dress back onto her shoulders. She lifted her baby and fled to the darker depths of the cave, leaving Echohawk alone, his thoughts troubled.

He lifted his eyes upward and silently pleaded with the Great Spirit to give him the strength required to have no feelings for this young, tempting woman.

He prayed that Night Hawk was all right, and that he would soon find this cave with many braves accompanying him. Many would be needed to fight off the bloodthirsty, greedy renegades. Echohawk found it hard to believe that they had allowed him to live this long, wondering what the purpose of this decision was.

He expected to die soon.

19

Now folds the lily all her sweetness up,
And slips into the bosom of the lake.
—TENNYSON

The sky was lightening overhead as Night Hawk rode into his village, having been forced to return home without any news of his father's whereabouts. His shoulders were slightly hunched, the regret heavy within his heart.

After placing his horse in the corral to graze with the others, he carried Briana's satchel to his mother's wigwam. He set it just outside the entrance flap and went inside. He found two maidens sitting vigil at his mother's side, both attentively awake as they took turns bathing Mariah's brow with soft, wet compresses. He knelt down beside one of the maidens, absorbing the sight of his mother as she slept fitfully, her breathing having taken on a rattle somewhere deep within her lungs.

"*Gee-mah-mah* has worsened," Night Hawk said, placing a hand on his mother's brow, feeling how fevered it was.

"*Ay-uh*, she has worsened," one of the maidens said. "We are doing all that we can. And the Mide priest? He has performed all of his magic over her. Now we must wait and see what Wenebojo has planned for your mother."

Night Hawk placed a kiss on his mother's cheek, then turned. "My *gee-bah-bah*?" he asked quietly. "Is there any news of him?"

"*Gah-ween*, none," the maiden said, her eyes revealing her sorrow.

Night Hawk nodded, then rose to his full height and left the wigwam, knowing that before he could gather many braves to search for his father again in the haunts of the forest, he had to rest—and he had to be with his Briana.

She knew ways to soften the pain in his heart.

He picked up Briana's satchel and went to his wigwam. Once inside, he placed the satchel on the mat-covered floor just inside the entrance flap.

He jerked off his fringed shirt, his moccasins, and his breeches, his gaze sweeping slowly around him. The fire in his fire pit had burned down to glowing coals, yet gave off enough light to see Briana. She was asleep on soft pelts, a blanket casually thrown aside, revealing the delicate curves of her shapely legs where her gown was hiked up past her knees.

Night Hawk's gaze worked higher, seeing the swell of Briana's breasts where her gown dipped low in front, then higher, seeing her sensually shaped lips parted slightly in her sleep, her eyelashes like golden veils where they lay spread thick and long above her delicate cheekbones.

Now naked, Night Hawk moved to his knees and crawled to Briana. He knelt down over her, resting himself with his knees on each side of her. He bent low, his hands framing her face between his hands, and drew her lips to his. He kissed her with passion, glad when she had awakened and began reciprocating with a fiery kiss, her arms twining around his neck.

Drawing one hand away, he swept it slowly down her curves, until he reached the hem of her gown, then slowly lifted it up past her thighs. He drew the gown over her head and eased it away from her.

Tossing it aside, he looked down at her with a fierce

need, his heart pounding as he let his gaze roam over her, his hands following the path of his eyes, touching, caressing.

Briana sucked in a wild breath as his hand moved between her thighs and found her swollen bud and began moving his fingers over it until it throbbed against his fingers.

"Night Hawk, when did you arrive home?" she finally found the sense to ask, yet breathlessly as the sensations began to burn within her like molten lava.

"Only moments ago," he said huskily, his other hand kneading her breast. He lowered his mouth to one of the breasts and teased the nipple with his teeth, then softly chewed on it.

"Your father?" Briana asked, removing his headband. She wove her fingers through his long, coarse, dark hair. "Did you find anything out about your father? Did—did my uncle cause you problems?"

"My father?" Night Hawk said, drawing away from her, turning his back on her, the magic spell that had been weaving between them momentarily broken. He hung his head in his hands. "No, no news of my father. And, no, no serious confrontation with your uncle." He turned glowering eyes to her. "Except that he lies over and over again. He said he knew nothing of my father."

"You don't believe him, do you?" Briana asked, running her fingers down his smooth copper back.

"Never," Night Hawk hissed. "But I could not get answers out of him, short of torturing him, and that is not a tactic I have practiced. I will have to find answers by other means."

"I'm sorry," she murmured. She rose to her knees and fitted herself behind him, pressing her breasts into his back.

She wove her arms around his chest, then moved

her fingers across its broadness, then down to his flat belly, stopping where she found his half-shrunken manhood resting against his thigh. She circled her fingers around it, realizing the pleasure it caused him when he emitted a low growl.

He allowed the caresses for only a moment. Then he turned around quickly and placed his fingers on her shoulders, urging her on her back onto the plush pelts. "Let us talk no more of sorrowful things," he said, his eyes filled with dark need. "Fill my heart and mind with only you, my darling. Make love to me, Briana. Let me enjoy being with you before I am forced to leave again."

Briana placed her hands on his shoulders and urged him to roll onto his back. She leaned over him, smiling, her hair trailing along the flesh of his stomach as she kissed her way down to that part of him that was now hard and erect.

She circled her fingers around him and moved them slowly up and down, then placed her lips to him. She asked for nothing, this time only giving. And when he gently shoved her away and the proof of his pleasure spilled within the palm of her hand, she was glad that she was there, the woman he could depend on for eternity.

They lay there, not saying anything, their bodies touching. In a few minutes he eased her down beneath him, revived and needing her again.

She saw the plea in his eyes and answered it. She spread her legs and slowly lifted them around his waist as he thrust his heavy shaft within her.

His lips were demanding as he kissed her hard and long, his hands all over her, teasing, caressing, touching, loving—all at once.

She clung to him, lifting her hips to receive him more fully within her. He moved in short, confident thrusts as her hands cradled his hips, pulling him deeper, deeper, deeper.

And then the peak of pleasure was met. The wondrous bliss that ensued caused them to cling together, not wanting to part.

Finally Briana caught sight of the satchel just inside the entrance flap. "Night Hawk," she gasped, causing him to roll away from her. "You brought my supplies!" She flung her arms around his neck. "Thank you! Thank you!"

She gave him a quick, wet kiss, then rushed to her feet excitedly and grabbed the satchel. She took it and sat down beside Night Hawk. She opened it and began bringing out that which was precious to her, when a sudden thought struck her.

She looked over at Night Hawk. "It is all so very wonderful," she murmured. "But, darling, how can I paint without my—my canvases?"

"You will paint on the canvases used by the Chippewa," Night Hawk said, reaching a hand to her hair, drawing his fingers through its softness.

"The hides that I have seen hanging outside the wigwam entrance flaps?" Briana said, eyes wide. She smiled and nodded. "Yes, that will do. I will stretch them between strips of wood. Yes, that will do just fine."

Night Hawk smiled at her sweet innocence, and was touched by how easy she was to please. He felt guilty, though, for this private moment with the woman he loved, while his father was—where could he be?

Having not slept the whole night through, Lily decided that it was futile to stay on her sleeping platform any longer. She had only moments ago seen Night Hawk come in to check on their mother. She had heard him say that he had not found their father.

This, and oh, so very much more, saddened Lily early this morning. All she had to do was look at her mother and her heart seemed to turn inside out. She had not told her about the child that she was carrying within her womb, and now perhaps she would never have that chance.

And Strong Branch.

Although he had promised that he would marry her soon, there was something in the way he had said it that made her uncomfortable.

Gray Moon. He was the thorn in her side that she could not shed. He would stop the wedding, she was sure.

Pulling a dress over her head, slipping into moccasins, and grabbing her fringed shawl, Lily smiled at the two maidens sitting vigil at her mother's bedside, then crept on around them and outside. She gazed up at the heavens, seeing the beautiful streaks of orange and pink suffusing the sky, a tiny sliver of the moon still evident in the far distance.

"I must go and commune with Wenebojo," she whispered, determinedly turning toward her secret trysting place. "I must get my mind settled, at least on one of my worries. Surely the Great Spirit will give me a small measure of comfort this morning."

She went through the tangled vines of the forest, over the damp leaves beneath the trees, and amid the stirrings of birds and animals awakening all around. Every once in a while she would stop and listen, when she heard something behind her that she did not think was made by the forest animals and birds.

When she would turn and search but find no one following her, she would shrug and go on her way, determined to find solace in her morning prayers.

When she was finally on the butte high above the farthest stretches of the forest, the river winding through the trees way down below her, she started to kneel but was stopped when someone suddenly came up from behind her and placed their fingers around her throat.

She grabbed at the fingers that were choking the life from her, but the strength of her attacker was twice her own. Choking and gagging, tears streaming from her eyes, the thing she thought of as she began to see a haze of black was her child. Her heart cried out for her child, a child that she would never hold!

And then she grew limp, the breath and heartbeat gone from her.

His heart beating soundly, torn with emotions over what he had just done, Gray Moon lifted Lily up into his arms. When he felt and saw her limpness, he held her for a moment, staring down at her lily white face, hating her for having interfered in his life so much. Because of her, Strong Branch had not moved ahead in making decisions for his people. Lust for this white woman born into the Chippewa tribe had blinded Strong Branch too much.

He had let his duties to his people take second place to Lily.

"But never again!" Gray Moon growled, carrying Lily to the edge of the bluff. He held her over it and then released her. He leaned over and watched her frail, limp body tumble over and over again in the air, then land with a thump on the rocks below, echoing back to his eager ears.

Smiling, wiping his hands on his fringed buckskin breeches, he started to turn but stopped abruptly when he heard someone approaching.

His heart skipping a beat, he dived into a thick stand of bushes and hid, his eyes narrowing as he discovered Strong Branch.

He watched his chief go to the edge of the butte

and begin pacing, kneading his brow thoughtfully all the while. Then he knelt and picked up several pebbles. Rising to his full height, he began tossing these over the side of the butte.

When he stepped closer to the edge, to watch the pebbles fall through the air, his sudden wails were so loud, it seemed as though the heavens might split open with the remorseful sound.

"He has seen her," Gray Moon whispered to himself, his lips forming a smug smile.

He waited a moment, then made a wide half circle so that he could approach Strong Branch from behind, to draw undue attention away from himself, and the possibilities of being accused of the crime.

"My friend!" Gray Moon shouted, rushing toward Strong Branch. He turned him to face him. "What is wrong? I was passing by. I heard your wails."

Strong Branch could not hold back the tears, not even to save face in front of his friend. Without turning to look again at his beloved, he pointed at the butte. "She—she fell to her death," he said, finding the words hard to say, since that made what he wanted to deny a reality. "Lily! She is dead! She lies down below, dead!"

"What a tragedy!" Gray Moon said, easing his hands from Strong Branch's shoulders. He went and peered down at Lily's body, then turned and gazed at Strong Branch again. "Lily has been here too often to lose her footing. She knows every inch of this butte. You know that, Strong Branch. You have been here with her often enough. Strong Branch, she must have been too distraught with life to carry on another day. She must have killed herself, Strong Branch."

Hearing Gray Moon be so matter-of-fact about his beloved's death, and seeing that the brave was even smug about it, Strong Branch recalled just how much

Gray Moon had always hated Lily. He had begged Strong Branch to forget his feelings for her.

A sickening thought came to him, making him dizzy with rage.

"You wanted her dead," he said, taking a slow step toward Gray Moon. "You are glad that she is dead."

Not having expected this reaction, Gray Moon stood frozen on the spot for a moment, then tried to circle around Strong Branch, away from the edge of the butte. He suddenly did not feel safe with his long-time friend. He seemed more the enemy at this moment, and perhaps had been for a long time, and Gray Moon had not recognized it.

"Strong Branch, stay away from me," Gray Moon said, his hand automatically reaching for the knife sheathed at his waist. "You—you have a wild look in your eyes. Why? I am not at fault here. It was Lily! She jumped to her death! Do you not see?" He stumbled backward. "Or she fell. That is it, Strong Branch. She stumbled and fell!"

"Lily did neither," Strong Branch snarled, moving closer to Gray Moon. "She did know this bluff like the back of her hand. And she would not kill herself. She had no reason to. She recently discovered that she was with child. We set our wedding date. She thought that we would be married soon."

"You told her you were going to marry her?" Gray Moon mumbled. "She was with child?"

"You fool," Strong Branch hissed. "From the very beginning I never planned to marry Lily. I just told her this to give myself more time to make adjustments for our people's future. Your people, Gray Moon, as well as mine! But murdering Lily was not in the plan! She was sweet and innocent! And—and I did love her, Gray Moon. I could have never loved another woman as much! I had changed my mind. I was going to marry her! For the unborn child she carried within her womb, I was going to marry her!"

"You are talking in circles!" Gray Moon said, his eyes wild. He yanked his knife from its sheath, brandishing it between himself and Strong Branch. "Is this the way you want it? That one of us dies today?"

"She died," Strong Branch said, moving stealthily around Gray Moon, avoiding the knife as Gray Moon started stabbing toward him. "And so shall you. You should not have killed her, Gray Moon."

"It had to be done," Gray Moon said, crouching, spinning around as Strong Branch spun around behind him, grabbing for his wrist. "She was in the way of our progress."

The actual confession was what set Strong Branch's emotions into a tailspin. He lunged for Gray Moon and began wrestling with him. The knife plunged into Gray Moon's chest, making him lose his balance. He toppled from the butte, clutching the knife and screaming.

Pale and shaken, Strong Branch looked downward and found Gray Moon lying beside Lily on the rocks, his eyes staring upward accusingly.

Turning away, holding his head in his hands, Strong Branch burst into tears, his whole body wracked with the hard crying.

After he was drained of tears, Strong Branch began walking slowly down the path that led to the forest below, where his horse was tethered. He looked at the gleam of the river through the trees and wanted to take the time to get Lily and take her back to her people for proper burial rites, but he knew there were dangers in that.

He could be accused of both deaths!

Tears flooded his eyes again, and he quickly mounted his horse, slapped his reins, and rode in the opposite direction. His whole body was empty over having lost Lily and Gray Moon, whom he had thought his best friend and adviser.

At this moment he was void of hopes and desires for his future—unless he could work it out, and he did not see how that was possible now.

He would try, though. Surely there was a way. And somehow he would find it. But now all that he could think about was escaping.

He must flee the wrath of Echohawk's family once Lily's body was found.

"I have lost everything today," he cried, hanging his head.

Wise Owl had seen both Strong Branch and Gray Moon leave the village on their horses, yet at different times. Earlier, he had seen Lily leave, and he had guessed then that she was going to her secret trysting place, which in truth was not a secret at all. Wise Owl had followed her there one night. He had witnessed the shameful lovemaking between Strong Branch and Lily, yet kept his silence.

Until now.

If Gray Moon was going to become involved also, it had to be stopped! Lily was becoming too strong a force to reckon with. And Wise Owl was going to put a stop to it, no matter how.

Hardly able to mount a horse anymore, his bones aching and swollen, he grunted and groaned.

Then finally comfortable enough in the saddle, he rode into the forest and dismounted next to the winding path that led up to the butte. He started to make the climb but decided first to quench his thirst. As he walked toward the river, he saw something strange on the rocks—then grew faint when he realized exactly what it was.

Shakily he rushed along the rocky shore. His eyes widened and he gasped when he saw Gray Moon, a knife still protruding from his chest, his body crushed from the fall.

He then gazed down at Lily, and turned cold inside when he saw the blood on her crushed body.

"Strong Branch! You did this!" he whispered, realizing that of late Strong Branch had become uncontrollable, even strange.

At first the shock was so intense, he could not think further than the fact that two murders had taken place. Then when his sense of logic began to reassert itself, he smiled. "Perhaps it is better this way," he said, strolling softly away from the bodies.

He nodded as he kneaded his chin contemplatively. "*Ay-uh*, it is better this way. I will become chief of my people. I am most deserving, because I am the eldest and wisest."

Somehow in time, he flatly decided, he would convince both villages of Chippewa that he was the wisest of them all.

20

She sleeps! My lady sleeps! Sleeps!
—LONGFELLOW

Sometime during the night, Mariah had heard a voice singing woefully and softly in the distance. Night Hawk had explained that this meant that sorrow was present.

The delicious aroma of steaming broth filled the wigwam. The two maidens had left Mariah's side to get their rest. Briana and Night Hawk were there, one on either side of Mariah's sleeping platform.

Briana's heart warmed at the sight of Night Hawk's devotion to his mother. He smoothed a damp cloth across her fevered brow, and she could tell that there was much between them that was good. She hoped that she could feel as close to a son, once one was born to her.

She smiled weakly at Night Hawk as he gave her a somber look. His time with his mother had to be short today, for he planned to leave soon with his many braves to search the forest for Echohawk once again. Briana had agreed to sit vigil at his mother's side for as long as it took for him to return.

Mariah's eyelashes fluttered against her pale cheek, and then rose slowly, revealing even paler eyes. She lifted a trembling hand to Night Hawk's copper cheek. "Echohawk, my darling," she murmured. "You have returned to me. You are safe."

A sob was wrenched from the depths of her being

when she just as quickly discovered her mistake. It was her son sitting there, not her beloved husband!

"*Gee-mah-mah*, it is I, Night Hawk," he said, his voice breaking. "Do you not recognize me?"

Mariah cleared her throat and wiped tears from her cheeks with her free hand. "My son, for a moment I thought you were Echohawk," she whispered. "But now I see that it is you." She patted his cheek. "I am always glad to see you, my son. Always."

Her eyes wavered and her hand crept down beneath the blanket again. "Your father?" she said, her voice quavering. "You did not return home with your father?"

It tore at Night Hawk's very being to have to deny his mother anything, especially good news about his father. Yet he had no choice. Even in her weakened state, she had to face reality.

"*Gah-ween*, no," he said, softly kissing her fevered cheek. "I am sorry. Father has not returned." He leaned away from her, glancing over at Briana, then back down. "But I am leaving soon with many braves. We will search the day through again. We will find Father!"

"I will stay with you until Night Hawk's return," Briana said, taking the damp cloth as Night Hawk handed it to her. She began bathing Mariah's brow. "I shall feed you some broth soon. You need your nourishment, as well as rest."

"Food doesn't sound good to me," Mariah said, her eyelids heavy as they closed again. "Sleep. All I want to do is sleep."

The sound of piercing wails outside the wigwam startled Briana and Night Hawk to their feet. Mariah's eyes opened wildly and she grabbed for Night Hawk's hand. "Go and see who wails, and why!" she cried.

Tears flooded her eyes. "Oh, Lord, what if someone has found your father—and he is dead?"

His heart pounding as the wails grew louder, Night Hawk pulled his hand from his mother's and stepped around the sleeping platform. Together he and Briana went outside, discovering Wise Owl standing in the center of the village, close to the great outdoor fire, his hands reaching to the heavens. His wails continued on and on as people gathered around him.

Night Hawk rushed to Wise Owl and stood square-shouldered beside him. "Wise Owl, why are you doing this thing in my village?" he asked, now scanning slowly around him, relieved when he did not see any bodies—especially his father's. Yet this made him even more confused by Wise Owl's actions.

Wise Owl turned his eyes into Night Hawk's. His lined face became even more furrowed as he frowned and placed a gentle hand on Night Hawk's arm. "I have brought disheartening news for you and your people, and then I must go and spread the same news to my village, for my people have lost one of their most valiant braves today," he said thickly. "Gray Moon. He is dead!"

"Gray Moon . . . is dead?" Night Hawk gasped. Then he tightened his jaw. "Who else is dead, Wise Owl? Who? And where are their bodies?"

Wise Owl lifted his chin and folded his arms across his narrow chest. "While going through the forest I stopped for a drink at the river," he said somberly. "I did not quench my thirst as planned. Something distracted me."

His patience running thin, Night Hawk took a step closer to Wise Owl and locked his fingers on the elderly man's bony shoulder. "Tell me what you found," he said flatly. "Now, old man. Now!" He swallowed hard, then said, "Did you find my father's body? Is that what you are taking so long to tell me?"

"Not your father's," Wise Owl said, a strange gleam in his eyes. "It was Lily. Your sister. She was lying beside Gray Moon on the rocks. They were surely shoved from the butte overhead." He narrowed his eyes and yanked himself free from Night Hawk's burning grasp. "Strong Branch must be responsible! He has disappeared. Does that not point to his guilt?"

Night Hawk's mind was swirling with what Wise Owl had said—Lily was dead? That Gray Moon had died with her?

And Wise Owl was accusing Strong Branch of murdering them. The chief that Wise Owl had always backed, even fought for, short of being banished from the tribe because of his strong viewpoints. Now Wise Owl was accusing Strong Branch of such a heinous crime?

To Night Hawk, it made no sense.

And then the full brunt of the news grabbed him at the core of his being—his beloved sister was dead.

Dead!

Dizziness overcame him and he would have fallen to his knees had not Briana caught him and supported him as he hung his head and fought back the tears that were battling to be set free.

Then Night Hawk regained his composure somewhat. "My sister," he said, gazing at Wise Owl. "You—you left her there, to be food for the bears?"

"I am an old man," Wise Owl said, pretending sadness as he lowered his eyes. "I could not lift her or Gray Moon to bring them to our villages."

Night Hawk erupted in snarls as he walked away from Wise Owl and headed for the corral. Briana ran after him, breathless. "Night Hawk, don't go alone," she cried. "Don't go at all. Send some braves. Night

Hawk, it won't . . . it will be such a terrible sight to see your sister like that."

Night Hawk stopped in mid-step and turned to Briana. He gazed down at her, then drew her into his embrace. "Help me to understand this," he whispered, holding her tightly to him. "She was so young, so vital. If Strong Branch did this, he will pay. He . . . will . . . pay."

"Night Hawk, darling," Briana said, easing from his arms. "Let someone else go for Lily. Right now you have your mother's welfare to consider. You have to tell her about Lily before she hears it from someone else. Hearing it from you will be easier—and you will be there to comfort her the instant she becomes grief-stricken."

Night Hawk sucked in a deep breath, then nodded. "You are right," he said, placing a gentle hand on her cheek. "You are always right."

He gave orders to several braves to go for his sister and Gray Moon, then he placed an arm around Briana's waist and drew her to his side. They walked together to his mother's wigwam. As they sat down beside Mariah, her eyes searched their faces for answers.

She discovered so much there that she turned away and began softly crying. "He is dead?" she murmured. "My darling husband is dead."

Night Hawk placed a finger under her chin and turned her head around, their eyes locking. *"Gah-ween, gee-mah-mah,"* he said, his voice breaking. "It was not Father."

Briana's hand crept beneath the blanket and circled around Mariah's and held on for dear life as Night Hawk told her the full story.

Mariah's screams filled the village, and then there

was an ensuing silence as she subsided again into a sad, deep slumber.

Briana flung herself into Night Hawk's arms, sobbing. "It is so sad," she cried. "Night Hawk, darling, I am so sorry. So very sorry!"

He held her for a moment, then rose to his feet. "I must prepare for my sister's burial," he said. He gazed down at Briana. "Please stay with my mother. Come to me if there is a change?"

Briana nodded, then turned back to Mariah as Night Hawk left the wigwam. A coldness seized her. Would she someday be forced to face such sadness about a husband? About a daughter? About a son?

The life of the Chippewa seemed one of constant trials and tribulations, continually wrought with losses.

Fairly bent over his saddle by the burden that he was carrying within his heart, Strong Branch drew his reins outside White Wolf's cave. Dismounting, he tethered his horse to a bush, then walked disconsolately toward the cave entrance. His head rose when he realized that he was no longer alone.

He made instant eye contact with White Wolf, who was leading his horse from the cave, ready to go on a morning hunt. Strong Branch remembered when life was sweeter, when every morning he had awakened with plans to ride with Night Hawk, to share their hunting adventures.

Back then, the rolling yellow plains had been checkered with herds of buffaloes. Along the banks of the streams that ran down from the mountains there had been many elk, which usually appeared in the morning and evening, and disappeared into the forest during the warmer part of the day.

Deer, too, had been plentiful, and the brooks had

been alive with trout. Here and there the streams had been dammed by industrious beavers.

In the interior of the forest there were lakes with many islands where moose, elk, deer, and bears were abundant. Waterfowl gathered in great numbers, among them the crane, swan, loon, and many of the smaller kinds.

If he listened now, he might hear the partridges drumming their loudest, while the whippoorwill sang with spirit and the hooting owl reigned at night.

This land of Minnesota was a paradise, he thought. Then, as now.

It had been shared with Night Hawk, a friend then, an enemy now.

"What has brought you here this time of day?" White Wolf said, walking toward Strong Branch. He stopped beside him, his eyes narrowing when he saw the pain etched onto the chief's face. "Gray Moon. Where is he?" he asked guardedly. "You usually ride together when you come to meet with White Wolf."

Rage filled Strong Branch at the thought of Gray Moon and what he had done. The camaraderie they had shared—the excitement of the raids, the thrill of taking the firearms and storing them in the cave for future use—had vanished. It was easy to banish the love he had had for Gray Moon, as though he had never even existed.

But never could he forget his feelings for Lily—and she had been taken from him because of Gray Moon's misguided jealousy.

"He is dead," Strong Branch hissed.

"Dead?" White Wolf said, forking an eyebrow. "And how did this happen?"

"My knife moved as though it had a mind of its own into the body of Gray Moon," Strong Branch said in a snarl. "He is dead—lying in the rocks along the river."

White Wolf's lips parted in a quiet gasp. His eyes widened. "Your voice and the look in your eyes tells me that you did this thing out of hate," he said, running his hand along the withers of his horse. "Why would you? You worked together to make life more tolerable for your tribe. Did he do something that did not suit you in your scheme of things? Is this why you killed him?"

"*Ay-uh*, he did something that did not suit me," Strong Branch cried. "He murdered my woman—my Lily."

"Chief Echohawk's daughter?" White Wolf said, glancing over his shoulder at the cave entrance, since Echohawk was still his prisoner.

"*Ay-uh*, Echohawk's daughter," Strong Branch said solemnly.

"She was an extraordinarily beautiful woman," White Wolf said, his eyes taking on the appearance of one in deep thought. "I saw her more than once. She was a half-breed, her skin as white as alabaster."

Then he regarded Strong Branch closely. "You say she was your woman," he said thickly. "You were going to marry her?"

"No . . . yes . . ." Strong Branch mumbled. "Now I am not sure! But still I loved her no less than if she have been my wife, the woman to warm my bed *ah-pah-nay*, forever."

And then another thought came to him, causing him to sway. When Lily had died, so had the child—his child. Keen sadness swept through him again, at the thought of having lost so much, so quickly.

"I had planned to kill Echohawk today, after my hunt," White Wolf said matter-of-factly. "Now I will delay his death. I will give him much time to live through his suffering once I tell him about the death of his daughter. He will wish he were dead."

He laughed and mounted his horse. "You can have the pleasure of telling him, if you wish," he said, gathering his reins into his hands.

"I do not wish to inflict that sort of pain on anyone, not even Echohawk," Strong Branch said. He looked up at White Wolf. "I have come today to tell you that I am surely going to be blamed for both deaths, Lily's and Gray Moon's. I feel that it is best for everyone— all of the Sioux renegades, White Wolf, and Strong Branch—to part ways. The soldiers are searching for you even now, and the forests soon will be filled with many Chippewa braves searching for Strong Branch. When things clear up, my friend, we can get together again."

"You go on your way, and yes, I will tell my comrades to scatter to the far hills for now, and you and I will meet again soon. But White Wolf does not flee like a coward," he growled. He dismounted and began leading his horse back into the cave. He smiled over his shoulder at Strong Branch. "It is time to begin Echohawk's true suffering."

Strong Branch swallowed hard, then mounted his horse again. Just as he started to ride away, he flinched as though he had been shot when Echohawk's wails pervaded the air with its agony.

Hanging his head, Strong Branch snapped his reins and urged his horse into a slow trot toward the darkness of the forest, not allowing himself to feel pity for Echohawk or to feel wrong about his association with the Sioux. White Wolf had been there for him, to assist him in getting ammunition and guns for an eventual battle with the white pony soldiers *and* Echohawk's village of Chippewa. All of this had been required for Strong Branch to gain eventual total control over this land of lakes. He craved total power.

And he would still have it.

He had vowed to himself long ago that he would be the voice of this land, over everyone else's. Still this would be true. But he knew that it would now be harder gained than ever before. The odds were slowly stacking against him.

21

We want each other so.
—ALFORD

Briana slipped from the sleeping platform and began
tiptoeing soundlessly toward the embers in the fire pit,
hoping to get the morning fire going before Night
Hawk awakened.

She glanced over her shoulder. He was still asleep,
the first time she had seen him sleeping this peacefully
since the death of his beloved sister. He had presided
over Lily's burial and had taken several days since to
sit vigil at his mother's bedside, to comfort her should
she awaken from her strange, drugged sleep. But she
had not awakened, not even when Briana succeeded
at getting some broth through her lips and down her
throat.

Today Night Hawk was going to end his period of
mourning. He was going to focus on his father again,
on the search that he had said would not end until
he had his father at his side, or answers about his
abduction.

Her cotton gown hardly enough this morning to
ward off the chill, since the month of August was
more than normally cool, Briana shivered and hugged
herself, then knelt down before the fire pit and began
laying twigs across the smoking, glowing embers. At
first they sent sparks into the air, then slowly began
to catch fire.

After they were burning substantially, Briana placed

several larger pieces of wood in the flames, then sat down and held her hands close to the fire, soaking up the warmth into her flesh.

And then she felt another warmth, this one more delicious than that caused by the flames. Hands crept around from behind her and cupped her breasts through her thin cotton nightgown. She shivered in delight when Night Hawk's breath became hot on her cheek as his mouth brushed against it.

"You leave my bed without awakening me with a kiss, or touches from your hands?" he said huskily, softly kneading her breasts. "My woman, every morning we should warm each other with our bodies, *then* worry about a fire in the fire pit. The fires created within our hearts should be enough, do you not think so?"

"I didn't want to disturb you," Briana whispered, moving in a slight twisting motion to help Night Hawk slide her gown down from her shoulders to around her waist. She sucked in a wild breath as his hands cupped her breasts, his thumbs circling the hardened nipples. "Darling, you needed your rest before . . . before leaving. Who is to say when you will be able to sleep again?"

"That is true," Night Hawk said, turning her to face him. He sat down and lifted her onto his lap, her legs wrapping around his waist. He looked at her, adoring her. "But being with you, loving you, is more important to me than sleep. Because of the recent sadnesses, it has been many nights now since we made love. It is important never to allow our lovemaking to become commonplace. We must nurture it, as though it were food for our body."

Briana's eyes closed with ecstasy. She flung her head back when he thrust his thick hardness within her. His hands enfolded her breasts again and he stroked them as he lifted her up with each of his thrusts.

She leaned toward him and clutched his shoulders and began moving her own body in fluid motions, while Night Hawk slowed his strokes and let her take charge.

Briana rode him, giving her all this morning to this man that she would die for. She rose up and down in rhythmic movements, his shaft impaling her over and over again—deeper and deeper. She leaned her mouth to his lips and sucked his tongue as he thrust it inside her mouth, their kiss deepening.

Night Hawk placed his hands on her waist and lifted her away from him. He lay her down on the mat-covered floor and rose over her. Nudging her legs apart, he positioned himself inside her again and began his strokes within her, his hands trailing over her, seeking, finding, and caressing her every secret place, causing her to whimper with pleasure.

His mouth closed over her lips again. They kissed wildly, their bodies on fire as they moved with an intense searching for that realm of mindless bliss that was close to erupting within them.

And then their bodies quaked together.

They clung and rocked against each other.

They rolled over and over again across the floor, their bodies still locked together, their passion unfolding within them in wondrous, repeated climaxes of sexual excitement.

Finally their bodies became calm, yet Night Hawk's strong arms still enfolded Briana within them, she on top, her breasts crushed against his chest.

She smiled down at him through eyes hazed over with the afterglow of rapture, loving the feel of his hands as they stroked the swell of her buttocks. "Everything you do to me, every time you touch me, causes me to melt inside, my darling," she whispered, brushing a kiss across his lips.

She inhaled a sudden breath when she felt his renewed male energy filling her again as he thrust upward into her.

She moved with him, biting her lower lip to stifle the cries of passion that were building within her. He filled her magnificently. As he bucked into her, she felt her whole body tremble with the pressure within her.

And his hands were everywhere, stroking, caressing. His teeth were teasing the lobes of her ears, nipping, his hot breath stirring her into a frenzy of pleasure.

And again, in one quick turn, she found herself below him. She wrapped her legs around his waist and rode with him, her hips responding to his every thrust within her. She closed her eyes in ecstasy as his tongue slithered down her neck and stopped at her breasts. She twined her fingers through his hair as he sucked on one nipple and then the other, his hands gently squeezing the breasts.

Before she reached that height of joy that she was drawing near, Night Hawk rose from her. With warm hands against her waist, he guided her into a different position that was foreign to her.

She did not question him when he asked her to move onto her hands and knees.

She did not question him when he moved behind her and she could feel him probing with his hardness, soon entering her, his thickness filling her and moving in rhythmic strokes within her again, his fingers locked on her buttocks.

She could hear his guttural moans, knowing that this new way of loving her was pleasuring him. She soon closed her eyes and became lost in her own wondrous pleasure, gritting her teeth so that she would not scream, the rapture was so wild and intense.

Soon she felt the peak of his desire as he thrust more wildly within her. She responded in kind, pushing back against him, receiving him more deeply, the bliss intense as it flooded through her, touching her every nerve ending with the ultimate of pleasure.

Night Hawk stayed on his knees a moment longer, shaken by the intensity of their lovemaking this morning, as his manhood ebbed within her. Then he eased away from her and and drew her down beside him.

Briana cuddled close, her eyes wide with questioning as she peered into his passion-dark eyes. "You never cease to amaze me," she murmured, smiling devilishly at him. "My darling, the way we just made love. It—it seemed so forbidden, yet I cannot deny the pleasure I found while doing it."

"It is not a forbidden way to make love," Night Hawk said, chuckling. He drew her lips close to his. "It is just because it was new to you. My sweet, innocent woman, the flower of my wigwam, nothing we choose to do together should ever be labeled forbidden. If our hearts lead us into it, then it is right, for we are as one, are we not? Soon we will seal that bond with a marriage ceremony."

Briana eased away from him and sat up, reaching for her buckskin dress. She had left it folded on the floor beside their sleeping platform, and she slid it over her head. "So many things keep us from what is most important to me," she murmured. "I feel so wanton sharing these sensual adventures with you since we are not married."

She wriggled the dress down the full length of her body. She turned to Night Hawk, whose nudity caused her heart to flutter anew, wanting him no less now than moments before. She was always filled with need for him!

Night Hawk took her hands and together they rose beside the slowly burning fire. "Before your God and my Great Spirit, we have been joined at the heart from the first moment we saw each other," he said softly. "So never feel wanton. Although no ceremony has been performed, we are man and wife. No love could be greater, or more sincere, than ours. That is what makes it right that we love one another as freely as we do. Never regret it. Regrets and doubts burn holes into one's soul."

She crept into his arms and snuggled close, her cheek resting on his muscular chest. "I do love you so," she murmured. "You are my soul, my darling."

"Keep that thought with you while I am gone," Night Hawk said.

He stepped away from her and began dressing. Briana watched him, admiring how his suit of fringed buckskin set off his splendid physique to advantage. When he lifted his rifle and stared down at her, she stifled a sob behind a hand, fearing that when he left this time, she might never see him again.

"Please be careful," she said, her voice breaking.

"I will not return this time unless my father is with me," Night Hawk said.

Briana locked her eyes with him, then turned quickly away and went to a buckskin bag that she had prepared for his trip—having filled it with an assortment of foods that would last for many days of travel.

"I wish you would stay long enough for us to share a warm breakfast," she said, handing him the heavy bag of food. "But I understand. You told your braves to be ready at sunup."

Night Hawk slung the bag over his shoulder, then with a bold sweep took her in his arms again, holding her tight against his hard body. "Do nothing foolish while I am gone, like leave this village unescorted," he said. "There are many things to fill your time. You can sit with my mother. Other times, you can paint. The children of the village would enjoy being taught your unique way with brushes and paints."

"It would delight me to show them how I paint," she said, beaming at the thought. "I shall paint a picture for each of them and give it to them to keep."

Night Hawk smiled warmly down at her. "Always you think of others," he said. "That is one of the many reasons I love you."

He crushed his mouth down upon her lips and kissed her with a savagery she had never known before, yet she understood why.

This might be their last good-bye.

The cave was dark and silent, the fire having burned down to glowing embers. Echohawk sat with his back resting against the cold wall. He had tried to lie down without success, aching with the want of sleep, not having been able to since he had received the news about his daughter. White Wolf had found the perfect sort of torture for his captive, for every breath was now torturous for Echohawk.

With each heartbeat he saw his lovely daughter: her dancing eyes, her soft white skin, her innocent smile, and the way she would duck her head when shyness overcame her. . . .

Hearing a slight stirring somewhere close by in the darkness, he stiffened, yet realized that he had not much to fear anymore. White Wolf's gang had disbanded, leaving White Wolf as his only threat. And White Wolf had not approached him much since he had given him the news that had shattered his heart into a million pieces.

But Echohawk expected White Wolf to grow tired of playing with him soon. Perhaps then Echohawk's miseries would be over, he thought bitterly to himself.

His daughter was dead!

His wife was lost to him, in many ways.

Ay-uh, perhaps it was time for Night Hawk to assume the duty of chief. It was for the better, it seemed.

Not far away, a torch flamed suddenly into view, drawing Echohawk quickly around. With a shallow-beating heart he watched White Wolf approach with Gentle Fawn. Lighting the renegade's face, the torch revealed a leering sort of smile. He kept one hand on Gentle Fawn's arm, forcing her to walk beside him.

When White Wolf shoved her to the floor on her back, he stood spread-legged over her. Echohawk's jaw tightened and he felt himself becoming filled with life and energy again as anger fused the wick that seemed to have died within him.

He wrestled with the ropes at his wrist, drawing blood as they bit into his flesh, his eyes wavering as he realized what White Wolf's intent was. He was going to torment Echohawk by forcing himself on Gentle Fawn—the woman that Echohawk now cared for. Although he knew the wrong of it, he had fallen in love with Gentle Fawn. Hopelessly in love.

And this was another reason why he had begun to feel that he did not care if he lived or died. He also loved Mariah and felt ashamed for having the needs that caused his heart to thunder within his chest every time Gentle Fawn came close to him.

When she touched him, everything within him cried out to kiss her. To hold her.

Dying a slow death inside, he watched the performance being acted out before him.

White Wolf lodged the torch into a hole in the

cave's wall. He slowly, teasingly lowered his breechcloth, revealing his swollen need at the juncture of his thighs. He kicked the breechcloth aside and knelt down over Gentle Fawn, thrusting his hardness within her, his mouth slobbering over her face and down to her breasts.

Gentle Fawn grimaced and sobbed, having to lie limply and be raped before the eyes of the man that she had grown to love.

Echohawk growled, his eyes two points of fire as he helplessly watched the sweet, innocent young thing be defiled, as though she were no better than an animal.

White Wolf bucked more wildly into her, and then his spasms subsided. He collapsed away from her, breathing hard, totally spent.

Gentle Fawn was allowed to rise. She gave Echohawk an ashamed, downcast glance, then fled to the darker depths of the cave, her sobs wafting through the air like softly falling rain, hurting Echohawk through and through.

White Wolf lay there awhile longer, panting, then moved slowly to his feet. Slipping his breechcloth back in place, he leered down at Echohawk. "She is very *o-nee-shee-shim*," he said, chuckling.

Then White Wolf grabbed the torch, extinguished it by covering it with a damp buckskin covering, and went back to his sleeping platform.

Echohawk breathed hard, hate seething inside him. He eased down onto the blanket on the cave floor, and with his teeth he drew another blanket over him. Chilled not so much from the cold, but from what he had just witnessed, he closed his eyes and tried to go to sleep. He tossed from one side to the other, trying to get comfortable, trying to forget so much that pained him. Then he stopped, his eyes flying open widely when he felt a slender body slip beneath the blankets with him.

He melted within when a soft hand touched his cheek.

"It is I, Gentle Fawn," she whispered. "White Wolf is asleep. I have come to you, my love. But not to make love. I have brought you something even more valuable tonight."

Echohawk's pulse raced maddeningly when Gentle Fawn's hand left his cheek and he felt her begin cutting through his ropes with a knife. He scarcely breathed, fearing that she would get caught, but sighed heavily with relief when his hands were finally free.

He took the knife and leaned over, and soon the ropes fell away from his ankles. He placed his hands on Gentle Fawn's arms. "Return to your child," he whispered harshly. "Stay with her. Do you hear?"

"I will get her," Gentle Fawn whispered back, her eyes wide and anxious. "Let us escape. Tonight! I am finally brave enough to do this that I have feared for so long. With you, I feel safe. Please! Let us escape now!"

"Nothing is ever as easy as it seems," Echohawk said. "Do you truly believe that White Wolf would allow you to steal the knife? It is a trap. Now return to your child. When he looks my way, I shall pretend that I am still tied up. Do you not know that he perhaps is waiting for us to try to escape? I am the wiser. I will fool him, pretending that I am still bound. When White Wolf approaches me in the morning, I will then take advantage of my unbound hands and feet."

"Echohawk, I am so afraid," Gentle Fawn said, her eyes frantic.

Echohawk framed her face between his hands and drew her lips close. He had ached for her for so long, yet was still unable to have her in the way his loins ached for. "My sweet one," he whispered. "Trust me. Tomorrow we both will be rid of this snake."

He wrapped her in his arms and kissed her, the intensity of his feelings for her stirring a memory of how it had felt when he was a young man. It had been too long since those needs had been fulfilled.

His life was a gamble, it seemed, always a gamble.

Gentle Fawn's lips quivered against his. Her fingers crept up inside his fringed shirt, slowly caressing his bare, muscular chest, then lower. She started to touch him through his breeches where he had risen in response to his feelings, but his hand clasped onto hers, stopping her.

"Go now," he whispered, his voice husky with passion. "*Wah-bungh*, tomorrow. Things will be different tomorrow."

Gentle Fawn gave him a final hard hug, then fled into the darkness.

Echohawk stretched out beneath the blanket again, his eyes open the rest of the night. When he heard footsteps approaching him, and the flare of a torch being held high as White Wolf came into view, a keen questioning in his eyes, Echohawk clasped the knife beneath the blanket and waited.

He closed his eyes and feigned sleep. First he sensed White Wolf standing over him. Then he felt the heat of the torch as White Wolf slowly knelt down beside him. Echohawk sprang up like a panther and knocked White Wolf to the cave floor, the torch rolling away from him.

White Wolf was as quick as Echohawk. He sprang to his feet and began to wrestle the chief, holding his wrist, trying to keep the knife away from him.

They fell to the floor. In what was supposed to be a death plunge, Echohawk brought the knife down, but White Wolf rolled out of the way. The knife grazed the flesh of his upper left thigh instead of his chest.

When Gentle Fawn came into view, the bundled child in her arms, Echohawk looked her way long enough for White Wolf to scramble to his feet and flee toward the cave entrance, where he had his horse tethered. Seeing the quick exit, Echohawk moved to his feet and started to run after him but stumbled, realizing that having been left bound for so long had taken away much strength in his legs.

He stopped, took a deep breath and steadied his legs, then ran onward. As he arrived at the cave entrance, he found that he was too late. Angrily, his hand doubled into a tight fist at his side, he watched White Wolf gallop away on his horse.

Gentle Fawn came up behind. "Echohawk," she murmured, clutching her wrapped baby to her bosom, "we are now safe? He is gone?"

Echohawk turned to her, forgetting White Wolf for the moment. He beckoned to her with opened arms and when she came to him, he hugged both mother and child to him. "It is going to be all right," he said. "I will take you to my village. There you will begin a new life—a life that will include much love and warmth."

"I will be your *ee-quay*, woman?" Gentle Fawn asked, gazing up at him with her dark, doeful eyes.

Echohawk's eyes wavered and he swallowed back a fast-growing lump in his throat.

He was torn between two loves. He could not give up one or the other. Somehow he would have to work it out so that neither were hurt.

"I have a wife," Echohawk said, his voice drawn. "But I will still care for you and your child." He stroked her delicate, soft face. "But I will not be there at night to warm your bed. You understand, though, that I will be there for you other times."

Gentle Fawn's eyes misted with tears. "I understand," she murmured. Then she lay her cheek on his chest, feeling his quickened heartbeat through the buckskin fabric of his shirt. "You are the first man I have ever loved. I shall never love another, Echohawk."

He inhaled a shaky, deep breath. He closed his eyes as he burrowed his nose into the depths of her silken hair. "I have loved two other women in my life before I met you," he said softly. "My first wife is dead, but my second wife awaits my return even now. I still love my No-din, yet I love you also, Gentle Fawn. My woman, it is hard—this loving two women with only one heart to give. I want you with all of my being, yet I must deny myself this want. I must be true to my wife. She is ill. She depends on me."

"You are an honorable man," Gentle Fawn said, smiling sweetly up at him. "That is admirable." She touched his cheek. "But, my beloved, when your hungers become too hard to bear, remember that I will be there to satisfy them."

Echohawk took her hand and kissed her palm, then turned and surveyed the cave around them, suddenly struck with the knowledge that although free, there were no horses to ride to freedom.

He turned back to Gentle Fawn. "Give me the child," he said. "It is a long walk to my village. Allow me to make your burden and walk easier. I will carry your child."

Gentle Fawn shook her head. "No, it is enough that you will be at my side," she said. "Your presence is all the strength from you that I need."

Echohawk saw the wisdom in this younger woman's logic, then stared into the darker depths of the cave, remembering the firearms. He must equip himself well. White Wolf could return and find them. Echohawk would be ready.

This time he would send a bullet through the renegade's heart.

22

Your mouth that I remember
With rush of sudden pain.
—RUSSELL

Downcast, with his braves following behind him on horseback, Night Hawk rode beneath an umbrella of elm trees, peering upward through their thick branches of leaves. He frowned. The sun was lowering in the sky, ending the day much too quickly for him. Although he had covered much territory, he still had not found any signs of White Wolf's new hideout or his father.

Night Hawk swallowed hard, beginning to doubt that he would ever see his father again. Perhaps, even, his father had died in the explosion at the cave and Night Hawk had just not wanted to accept it.

The ashes were cool now. If he went and sorted through them more carefully, would he find that which would wrench his heart from his chest?

He shook his head desperately back and forth, in an effort to loose his mind of such thoughts. He would find his father. Perhaps not today, but *wah-bungh*, tomorrow. If not then, the next day, for he had made a vow to himself that he would not return home again unless his father was riding at his side.

A shout stirred his thoughts back to the present. He turned to the brave at his right side, seeing an anxiousness in his dark eyes as he pointed to something up ahead.

Night Hawk turned and followed the path of the brave's vision, and his heart stopped when he caught sight of someone walking toward them, recognizing the proud stance of his father!

Then he saw someone else—a beautiful woman at his side, a bundled child clutched to her bosom. His throat went dry when he recalled the woman and child in the cave when he had been held captive. Could these be . . . ?

Too glad to have found his father, he brushed away any wonder about the woman and child and sank his heels into the flanks of his horse and rode on ahead at a gallop. When he reached Echohawk, he swung himself out of his saddle and flung himself in his father's strong embrace.

"Gee-bah-bah," he said, so humbled by his father's presence he was at this moment a child again. "I have finally found you, Father. I had begun to think that— that I never would. That you were dead."

Echohawk hugged Night Hawk to him, having had many fears about his son as well. "My *nin-gwis*, my son," he said hoarsely.

Night Hawk clung to his father a moment longer, then stepped away, resuming a dignified stance as he squared his shoulders in the presence of his braves that had followed him here to this place of an emotional reunion of son and father.

"Gee-bah-bah," he said, growing cold inside as his gaze settled on the rip on his father's shirt sleeve and the blood dried on it. "You were injured?"

"I was shot," Echohawk grumbled. "But the wound has healed adequately enough."

"You were shot?" Echohawk said, the very thought paining him, as though the bullet had entered his own flesh.

"It was only a flesh wound, my son," Echohawk

reassured him. "Nothing to concern yourself about."
He glanced down at Gentle Fawn, recalling her gentle
ways of bathing his wound, taking the heat from the
very core of it. He recalled the mixture of herbs that
she had concocted from the few she had found just
outside the entrance of the cave. Because of her, the
arm was almost healed.

"Then you are well otherwise?" Night Hawk asked.
"You were not tortured?"

"*Ay-uh*, I am well otherwise," Echohawk murmured. "Physically I was not tortured, but . . ." He
glanced down at Gentle Fawn again, remembrances
of having been forced to watch White Wolf rape her
filling him with renewed rage. Then he looked back to
Night Hawk. "But mentally I was tortured—in many
ways."

Night Hawk had seen his father glance down at the
beautiful woman more than once, then had noticed
something hidden in the depths of his eyes as he had
looked again at Night Hawk. "Father, when I was
held captive in the cave, I recall hearing a woman and
a child, but because I was blindfolded, I never saw
them," he said guardedly. "Is this them? Did she
allow you to rescue her? I tried. When I did, she did
not even show her face to me. She remained hidden
in the depths of the cave. I had to leave without her."

Echohawk possessively placed an arm about Gentle
Fawn's tiny waist and drew her close to him. "*Ay-uh*,
this is that woman and child," he said. "This is Gentle
Fawn and her daughter, Moonstar. While I was held
captive, she was not allowed to stay hidden. She was
forced to do many things in my presence." He swallowed hard, then gave her a soft look filled with gratitude. "But what she did for me was out of the pure
kindness of her heart. She saw to my wound. That is
why it is not festering now with infection."

Night Hawk's eyebrow arched when he saw the affection between his father and the woman. It was as though they held secrets within their hearts—perhaps those which would condemn his father in his son's eyes, since his father already had a wife.

He felt the dire need to change the subject from the woman, not wanting ever to resent his father. "Who besides White Wolf was responsible for your abduction?" he said, his eyes wavering as his father still did not release his hold on the woman at his side.

"Blackie," Echohawk said, his voice cold.

Night Hawk's jaw tightened. "So Blackie *was* responsible for all of this," he said through clenched teeth. "If I had resorted to his own tactics and forced the truth out of him, I would have found you sooner!"

Echohawk stepped away from Gentle Fawn and placed a gentle hand on Night Hawk's arm, urging him away from the others to talk in private. "My son, it was known that you were being held captive just before my own abduction," he said. "Gentle Fawn was forced to tell Blackie how you managed to escape. She said that a woman came for you. In Blackie's rage he said something about his niece having done it. Is that true, my son?"

"*Ay-uh*, that is so," Night Hawk said, nodding. "Briana. She awaits me even now at our village. My father, she and I will soon wed. And I know that you will be pleased with my choice."

Echohawk wanted to question his son at length about this woman—a woman of much courage. He wanted to ask how she had known where the cave was, and how Night Hawk had met her, and when he had become enamored of her. But another woman was now in his mind—his sweet wife, Mariah, his Nodin.

"Your *gee-mah-mah*?" Echohawk asked. "How is she, my son? How has she taken my absence?"

Night Hawk glanced over at Gentle Fawn, in his mind's eye still seeing his father's arm so possessive around her tiny waist.

He turned back to face his father, his eyes narrowing. "Mother has worsened in your absence," he grumbled. "She is suffering another bout of malaria, and she is filled with melancholia from worrying about you. We must tarry no longer, Father. We must return to our village. You must go to mother and show her that you are alive and well. This will give her a reason to smile again. Perhaps she then will recover from her latest bout of illness."

Echohawk lowered his eyes, his heart aching with mixed emotions. He was anxious to see his wife, hoping that she would soon recover again, yet he was torn with wanting to make everything right for Gentle Fawn. She had already suffered a lifetime of insults and humiliation. He had to make sure she suffered none of this at the hands of his people. Especially from his son, who would one day be her chief.

Night Hawk saw that his father was battling something within his heart, and suspected what, for he himself had noticed how sweet and lovely Gentle Fawn was, and he knew that his father had not had a wife that was a lover for many years now. So he placed all resentment of his father loving another woman from his heart and placed an arm around his shoulders.

"Father, whatever it is that is troubling you, I shall make it easier for you to cope with," Night Hawk said, squeezing his father's shoulder. "Have we not always shared our minds and hearts? It is no different now. I understand you, *gee-bah-bah*, as though we were of one heartbeat. That is the way of devoted sons to fathers. No matter what, Father. No matter what."

Echohawk turned to Night Hawk and embraced him. "You are a good son," he said, his voice breaking. "Thank you, Night Hawk. *Nee-gway-chee-wehn-dum*, thank you."

They remained in each other's embrace a moment longer, then swung away and started walking back toward the others. Suddenly, however, Night Hawk realized that he had news of someone else to relay to his father. Lily! His father had to be told about his daughter. And seeing his remorse would surely be the same as reliving her death all over again inside Night Hawk's heart.

Yet he had to tell his father now and allow the pain to lessen somewhat before he entered the village to go to his ailing wife. But Night Hawk feared that too many hurts at once might devastate his father, perhaps even age him many moons.

He placed a hand on his father's elbow and stopped him. He looked at him morosely, then knew that he could not hold in the terrible truth any longer. It was paining him as though someone were plunging a knife into his heart over and over again.

"*Gee-bah-bah*, there is something I must tell you that you will find hard to bear," he finally said.

"It is about your sister?" Echohawk said, gazing into his son's eyes.

"*Ay-uh*, it is about Lily," Night Hawk said. "How . . . could you know?"

"My son, I know that your sister is dead," Echohawk said, placing a gentle hand on his son's shoulder. "I grieved for her long and hard. But now I am looking forward to the welfare of those who are alive. So should you, my son. Life is short. So very, very short. It is for the living, to be lived."

"Father, how did you find out?" Echohawk asked softly.

"White Wolf," Echohawk grumbled. "It gave him much pleasure to tell me."

"But how did he know?" Night Hawk asked, his mind aswirl with wonder.

"*That* he did not share with me," Echohawk said, then dropped his hand from his son's shoulder and resumed walking toward those who were waiting. "That he told me was enough at the time. I could think of nothing else but my grief, my son. Nothing else."

When they reached the others, Night Hawk went to his horse while Echohawk went attentively to Gentle Fawn and placed a gentle arm around her waist, ushering her toward the mounted braves.

Echohawk smiled up at one of his most devoted braves. "Perhaps you could allow me the use of your horse today?" he said. "Perhaps you could ride with Blue Heron."

The brave looked questioningly at Gentle Fawn and his chief's attitude toward her, then nodded and slipped easily from the saddle.

Night Hawk stood back and watched the expressions of the many braves as Echohawk very gently took the child from Gentle Fawn's arms and held it to his bosom as she placed a foot in the stirrup and swung herself into the saddle. Night Hawk had many mixed emotions when he saw the sweet smile that Gentle Fawn gave his father as she reached for the child and took her into her arms. His gut wrenched when his father swung himself into the saddle behind her, again showing his possessiveness of her as he placed an arm around her waist to hold her against him as he prepared himself for the long trek through the forest for their return home.

Night Hawk sighed heavily, realizing now that for certain his father had found someone else to warm his bed at night, and prayed that his mother would never find out. If she did not already have enough that caused her life to be slowly ebbing away, this would perhaps cause her to take her last breath.

He mounted his own horse and rode up beside his father. His mouth parted in a quiet gasp as he watched Gentle Fawn lower a portion of her dress and offer her breast to the tiny lips awaiting it. He quickly looked away, this scene seeming to be much too intimate for him to witness, yet his father was behaving as though it were his own child now suckling at the nipple, for in his eyes there was much adoration.

Fighting back the urge to be jealous for himself and his mother, Night Hawk rode with a straight back and lifted chin beside his father. He had to remind himself that only a few short hours ago he had been losing hope of ever finding or seeing his father again. He had reason to rejoice now, for his father was riding at his side, scarcely harmed by his abduction.

And he knew his father well enough to realize that he would not do anything to hurt his mother. Even if he loved Gentle Fawn, he would not flaunt it. Nothing would make his father waver from being a devoted husband, especially now, when his wife needed him the most.

This made him more relaxed with the woman and child being held protectively close by his father. And Echohawk was known for his gentle ways. It would not be his nature to treat the woman and child any other way than with kindness.

Except that Night Hawk knew beyond a shadow of a doubt that his father's feelings for this woman reached much deeper than mere kindness. Hopefully he was the only one that would recognize it.

He glanced over at Gentle Fawn and saw the innocent beauty of her face; yet when Gentle Fawn turned his way, he recognized the look of one who had suffered much at the hands of her captors. Even when she smiled, there was a shadow of pain. He could see how his father had been moved to such protective feelings for the woman and child.

Night Hawk returned a soft smile to Gentle Fawn, wanting her to relax in his presence, as he would try to accept what she had become to his father. Deep down he wished that she had let *him* release her from captivity. Then she would have never met his father, perhaps avoiding much pain in the end, for Night Hawk knew that his father would never leave his wife for another woman. Not as long as his father's wife had an ounce of breath left within her weakened lungs.

Night Hawk looked straight ahead and urged his horse into a steady gallop, anxious to return to the woman *he* loved, finally able to have some semblance of peace within her arms before he and his father set out to avenge what her Uncle Blackie had done to them.

Their entrance into the village was met with much jubilation. Even though Echohawk carried a woman and child on his horse, people crowded around them, touching him, their eyes filled with much happiness and relief to see him again. He smiled down at them all, nodding a silent hello to those whom he favored— true friends of his since he had been a child.

He drew the reins before his wigwam. He dismounted, then helped Gentle Fawn from the horse.

Night Hawk acted quickly. He went to Gentle Fawn and took her by the elbow. "You will stay at my dwelling until my father makes arrangements for you and your child," he said. Hesitantly she glanced with desperate eyes over her shoulder at Echohawk.

"Do not fear me," Night Hawk urged, moving her onward, wanting to witness his mother's reaction to Echohawk's return. Hopefully, this would draw her from her self-induced sleep.

Quickly formulating explanations to offer Briana before rushing back to his father's wigwam, Night Hawk was surprised when he lifted the entrance flap and found that she was gone. He expected now to find her sitting vigil at his mother's bedside. She had done this willingly, not only out of the goodness of her heart, but because she was Night Hawk's mother, soon to be her mother-in-law.

He helped Gentle Fawn down on a soft cushion of pelts beside the low embers of the fire. "You must be tired, please rest," he said. He nodded toward a kettle of food that hung over the hot coals of the fire. "You must be hungry. Eat. Father or I will return later."

Gentle Fawn lifted her soft, doe eyes to him. "Thank you," she murmured. "You are a mirror of your father not only in appearance, but also in your behavior. Your kindness is most appreciated."

Night Hawk returned her smile, finding it hard to resent anyone as sweet and as vulnerable as this woman. He turned and fled the wigwam. He broke into a run, panting hard when he entered his father's dwelling. His gaze took in a sight that warmed him through and through. His woman was on one side of his mother's sleeping platform, his father on the other. His mother's eyes slowly opened as his father continued to speak of his love for her.

Night Hawk crept into the dwelling and sat down beside Briana. He reached for her hand and held it tightly as he watched his mother look adoringly up at Echohawk, trying to mouth her first words in many days.

"My . . . darl . . . ing . . ." Mariah finally managed to say, reaching for Echohawk's hand, clutching it weakly with her frail hand. "You—you . . . have come back to me."

Echohawk softly kissed her cheek. "No-din, my wife," he said, fighting back the urge to cry. His wife was hardly a trace of what she had been. The flesh of her face was drawn tautly across her bones. Her eyes were dark beneath, her breathing was shallow.

"Hold me, Echohawk," Mariah whispered, reaching out her free hand to him. "Please hold me."

Echohawk leaned over her and swept her frail body into his arms. He held her cheek close to his chest as he stroked her dry, lifeless hair. "You must get well," he whispered, choking back a sob. "My darling, you must get well!"

"I promise that I will," Mariah said, stroking his muscular back with her bony hands. "You shall see. I will be well soon. For you, my darling. For you."

Mariah drew away. Tears streamed down her cheeks as she gazed woefully into her husband's eyes. "Lily," she sobbed. "Our Lily is . . . dead . . ."

Echohawk choked back a sob. He took Mariah's hands and squeezed them softly. "I know," he murmured. "I know."

He then leaned over Mariah and enveloped her within his arms and held her, their tears mingling.

Filled with emotion, Night Hawk urged Briana to her feet and ushered her outside. He swept an arm around her waist and drew her to his side as he walked her toward their wigwam.

"That was so sad," Briana said softly.

"*Ay-uh,*" Night Hawk said, nodding.

"But I do believe Mariah is going to be all right," Briana said, giving him a reassuring smile. "And, dar-

ling, you are home safe, along with your father. I'm
so relieved and so . . . so happy."

Night Hawk tried to feel as content, yet the very
sight of his wigwam made him suddenly remember
who awaited inside. Gentle Fawn and her child. Right
now they were his responsibility, soon to be his father's! He had to explain to Briana before she entered
the wigwam.

He stepped in front of her. He placed his hands on
her waist and drew her against him, their eyes locked.
"There is something I must tell you," he said. "There
is a woman and child—"

He stopped abruptly when his father walked past
him and entered the wigwam. Wide-eyed, his jaw
slack, Night Hawk watched as his father soon emerged
from the wigwam, Gentle Fawn walking beside him,
her child clutched to her bosom.

Echohawk said nothing to his son. He took Gentle
Fawn to a nearby wigwam that had been vacated when
one of the elders of the village had died. Once inside,
with a comforting fire burning, he turned to Gentle
Fawn.

"You will be seen to," he said, his voice resonant
as he took one of her hands and held it. "But understand that I cannot come to you. My wife is quite ill.
She needs me."

Gentle Fawn lowered her eyes as tears rolled down
her cheeks.

Echohawk placed a finger under her chin and lifted
her eyes to his. "This is the only way it can be," he
said, his voice strained.

He turned from her and left the wigwam. His gut
twisted as he heard her soft weeping, his heart torn
between two women, both adored by him.

Briana and Night Hawk went on into their dwelling,
Briana questioning him with her wide eyes.

Night Hawk sat down beside the fire pit and drew his knees to his chest. "My father seems to have duties to two women now," he grumbled. "This I find hard to accept, for I do not believe in sharing my heart with but one woman. So should it be for my father."

Then he turned sadly to Briana. "Yet I can understand how he can be swayed by Gentle Fawn's sweet loveliness," he said, his voice breaking. "My mother has not been a wife for many years now. My father is a virile man who has denied himself the hungers of the flesh! Perhaps he has reached his limits of restraint. I must not judge him for this hunger, for I hunger just as much for what we share."

"Night Hawk, is she possibly the woman in the cave that you tried to encourage to come with us when I rescued you?" Briana asked, now recalling Night Hawk worrying about a woman and child.

"They are the same," Night Hawk said, nodding. "It seems she trusted my father more than she did me."

Briana eased into his arms. "I believe I am relieved that she did," she said, laughing softly. "If not, perhaps she would have cast her spell over you."

"*Gah-ween-wee-kah*, never," Night Hawk said huskily, easing her to the soft furs beside the fire pit. "You are my woman. Always and forever." He sealed that promise with an all-consuming kiss.

Then Night Hawk drew away from her and looked at her questioningly. "You have never told me how you knew about the cave on the day of my rescue," he said, placing a gentle hand to her cheek.

Briana smiled up at him and told him everything.

23

Out of a world of laughter,
Suddenly I am sad.
—RUSSELL

The Chippewa village was well into the mourning period for Mariah, who had died the very next morning after Echohawk's return to the village. In memory of Mariah, a tipi shrine had been especially erected at the far edge of the village on a slight knoll, where on a clear day the sun would always bathe it with its warmth.

A strand of Mariah's hair, symbolizing the living spirit of the buried dead, was the object of adoration. The hair had been wrapped in a bundle, the covering of which was made beautiful with paintings, porcupine quillwork design, and then hung on a tripod which had been painted red.

Just prior to the day of the memorial service, many gifts had been taken and tied to the tripod inside the tipi. The gifts had then been distributed among the people of the village on the day of the memorial service.

Briana was sitting beside her lodge fire, sewing beads on a new pair of moccasins for Night Hawk that she had fashioned from buckskin. She was deep in thought of the memorial service and how beautiful it had been. It had left her with the feeling that Mariah was at complete peace, and happy wherever she was— in Heaven or in the Chippewa's Land of the Hereafter.

Briana's thoughts shifted to Night Hawk and his dark mood ever since the burial. He and his father were carrying around too much blame—too much hatred toward her uncle, blaming him in part for having brought on Mariah's death so suddenly. They felt that if not for her uncle, she would still be alive.

And they vowed to find and kill White Wolf as well.

Briana stiffened when Night Hawk's and Echohawk's voices grew close outside as they walked toward the wigwam. Again they had been together, walking and communing with their Great Spirit in the forest, making plans that soon would be acted out once the mourning period for their loved one was over.

Briana cast Night Hawk a worried smile as he came into the wigwam, his father beside him. Night Hawk was so immersed in thought, his brow knitted into a frown, he did not even notice her sitting there. He went to the kettle of stew hanging over the lodge fire and dipped some out into two wooden bowls. He handed his father one of the bowls and a wooden spoon, then took a bowl of stew and a spoon himself and sat down close to the fire.

Briana was hurt that he did not even offer her a hello, but soon realized why. He and his father had just made plans that Night Hawk apparently did not believe she would understand or accept. And, surely, she concluded, because of this they did not include her in their further conversation about it.

Briana tried to relax, knowing that Night Hawk's decisions always came from the deepest recesses of his heart. Knowing that thus far he had been right in all of his decisions, Briana continued her beadwork, yet eavesdropped on the conversation anyway.

"Tomorrow we will place our mourning behind us,"

Echohawk said, then scooped another spoonful of stew into his mouth.

"*Ay-uh*, tomorrow," Night Hawk said, nodding his head in agreement. He also scooped a spoonful of stew into his mouth, chewing eagerly.

"We will bring him back to the village, Night Hawk, and let all of our people witness his punishment," Echohawk said, setting his empty bowl aside.

"*Ay-uh*, that is best," Night Hawk said, setting his own empty bowl aside. He wiped his mouth free of grease with the back of his hand and glowered over at Echohawk. "But, *gee-bah-bah*, I expect him to have taken flight, like a tiny sparrow trying to escape the claws of a mighty hawk. I doubt we will achieve our vengeance anytime soon because of his cowardice."

Echohawk managed a slight laugh, although his heart was still bleeding over the loss of his Mariah, his "Woman of the Wind." "If he is smart he will have become that sparrow," he said, stretching out a long, lean leg before him. "My son, we are the hawk, are we not? When we do find him, we will quickly and unmercifully snatch him up into our claws. He will only wish his death could come as swiftly as the sparrow whose neck is broken almost the moment it enters the claws of the hawk!"

"And how will we hand out his punishment, *gee-bah-bah*?" Night Hawk said, too matter-of-factly as far as Briana was concerned.

Whose punishment? she wanted to ask. What sort of punishments do you usually use?

Listening intently, growing more uneasy by the moment over what she was hearing, Briana gazed from father to son, suspecting that the only man they could be talking about was her Uncle Blackie, or perhaps White Wolf.

Nonetheless, it gave her a sense of foreboding, as

though a dark cloud was settling over this village of Chippewa as the conversation grew more dedicated to abduction and punishment.

"Perhaps we will let our people choose the punishment," Echohawk said, frowning over at Night Hawk. "Or do you think it should be the council's decision? What do you think, my son? You soon will be chief. Your voice in the matter is the most powerful of all the people who are linked with our band of Chippewa."

Night Hawk coldly turned toward Echohawk. "Until you appoint me chief of our people, you are still the voice of this band of Chippewa," he said. "And, *gee-bah-bah*, the choice of punishments for Blackie should be yours alone, for you have been the target of his hate for too long now."

"Blackie?" Briana said, finally voicing her feelings aloud.

She dropped her beadwork onto her lap, paling. Although she had suspected that her uncle was the subject of the conversation, she had held to the hope that somehow it was not so. Although she hated her uncle almost with a vengeance, she did not want to think that she had even the slightest part in harming him. What's more, if Night Hawk had a part in her uncle's death, surely the authorities would come and take him away. He could be hung, or shot by a firing squad. The thought sent spirals of dread through her.

"What you are saying, Night Hawk, about my Uncle Blackie?" she managed to say as two sets of dark, piercing eyes turned her way. "You can't mean that you are going to abduct him and drag him away into the night, and—and hold him hostage, and then kill him."

Night Hawk glowered at her. "Do you forget so easily what your uncle is responsible for?" he said, his teeth clenched. "Both my father and I were taken captive. My mother is dead because of this act of vengeance. It is the code of the Indian that it is an eye for an eye, a life for a life. Your uncle must die!"

Briana rushed to her feet and went to Night Hawk, kneeling down before him. She took his hands and held them tightly. "My darling, don't you see? Although it is true that I do not like to think of you killing anyone, even my dreaded uncle, it is not my uncle that I am concerned about," she said. "Think of the consequences, Night Hawk, should you manage to steal my uncle away and then kill him. The white community won't stand for it. They will come for both you and your father. You will be taken back to Fort Snelling. They will either put you before a firing squad, or they will place nooses around your necks!"

Night Hawk eased one of his hands from Briana's. "My woman, I know that what you are saying is from the heart," he said softly. "But, Briana, you are interfering where women should not. These decisions reached today were made between a chieftain father and son, and well thought out. Should the white pony soldiers come and investigate, no signs of your uncle will be found. Our scouts will have alerted us. So rest easy, my woman, that everything will be done that will bring no harm to me, my people, my father, or you."

With a nod he gestured toward the beadwork that had dropped to the floor when she scrambled to her feet. "Resume your beadwork," he said, more as an order than a suggestion.

Briana stared disbelievingly at him. She jerked away and plopped down by the fire, across from him and his father. "No, thank you," she said stubbornly, folding her arms across her chest. "I have lost interest tonight in my beading. And I may never do beadwork again! That is done to keep the fingers and minds of the women busy so that they do not interfere in the matters of the men! I am not a typical woman who sits obediently, voiceless and brainless, Night Hawk, to everything you expect of me. Perhaps—perhaps I will not even become your wife. I have freedoms, Night Hawk, that marriage to a Chippewa chief might cause to become stifled. I doubt if I can be stifled in any way, Night Hawk. I doubt that very much!"

Her gaze met his. "I have many passions, Night Hawk," she murmured. "Freedom of speech and movement is one of them!"

Her eyes slightly wavered. "Until tonight I had not minded sitting by, trusting your judgment in everything," she murmured. "But this, Night Hawk? The decision to bring my uncle here for punishment? I see it as perhaps bringing tragedy to your people, not vengeance. I chose to speak out tonight, Night Hawk, only because I fear for you and your people."

Not used to women speaking their mind so strongly, Night Hawk peered at her with a slack jaw. He turned his eyes from her and met an amusement in the depths of his father's.

He realized why. It was a well-known fact that his mother had been a stubborn, strong-willed person when she had been younger—a lady with a fiery spirit. His father was seeing this in Briana and enjoying it—and obviously accepting it, for he was not chiding her now for her outburst.

Night Hawk turned back to Briana. He went to her and knelt down before her. "Briana, you worry needlessly," he tried to reassure her. He placed a hand on her cheek. "Trust me. Trust my father. We are both known for seeking peace. No one will come looking for your uncle here."

Briana gazed into his eyes, wanting to believe what he said, yet doubts kept creeping into her mind.

Finally she realized what she must do. She had to warn her uncle.

She had to believe that he would flee the Indians' wrath instead of going to the authorities to stop the Chippewa. Knowing her uncle as she did, she expected him to take the quietest way out of this to keep from drawing attention to himself that could harm his chances in politics. A skirmish with Indians would make people ask why, and when they found out all of her uncle's dirty secrets, he would be ruined.

She wanted the worst for her uncle, yet she wanted to assure Night Hawk's safety more than she wanted to see her uncle finally pay.

Yes, she decided to herself, even now, while Night Hawk was looking into her eyes so trustingly, she knew that she had to sneak away from the Chippewa village and go to her uncle and encourage him to take flight—a flight that would take him far, far away from her, and the man she loved, and the beloved Chief Echohawk, hopefully forever.

"I understand," Briana said, keeping her unblinking eyes steady with his, the lie having slipped across her lips so easily. "Please go ahead and discuss what you must in my presence. I-I shall resume my beading. You will be very proud of your new moccasins, Night Hawk. They will keep your feet warm during the long winter days while hunting."

Night Hawk's eyebrow arched, finding her sudden change of heart hard to believe. Although she seemed to be accepting what was planned for her uncle, he doubted that she did. He did not want to believe that she was capable of lying, yet he suspected that she had—and he knew that he must keep a close watch on her.

"I will accept the new moccasins with a happy heart," he said, trying to keep the wariness from his voice. He turned to his father. "We have spoken enough today of our plans. Let us meet at sunrise tomorrow, *gee-bah-bah*, and finalize them."

Echohawk pushed himself up from the thickly matted floor. He swung an arm around Night Hawk's shoulder and gave him a warm hug, then went and lifted the entrance flap. "*Wah-bungh*, tomorrow, my son," he said somberly.

Night Hawk went to Echohawk and stopped him. "There is someone else we must now search for and make pay for wrongful deeds done to our family," he said sullenly. "It is time to search for Strong Branch. His absence this long is proof of his guilt. My thoughts were burdened by too much until now. But now my vision is clear and I see Strong Branch as guilty—and one who must pay!"

"If you are that positive of his guilt, I shall send many braves to search for him while you and I go in another direction to bring Blackie back for his punishment," Echohawk said, nodding. "*Ay-uh*, all those who have brought pain into our lives will pay, my son. And soon."

Night Hawk nodded, gave his father a warm embrace, and watched him walk away. He turned and went back to sit beside his lodge fire.

There was a strained silence in the wigwam after Echohawk's departure. Briana forced her fingers to string beads onto a long length of string, to store them for future use, knowing that to look at Night Hawk now might reveal that she had deceived him, even though thus far in intention only. She had never thought herself capable of deceiving the man she loved, even if it meant that what she had planned might ensure his safety.

She wanted him to trust her always, not have cause to doubt her during their lifetime together. But, she had already decided, if ensuring his safety meant losing him, so be it. His life was more important than having a lifetime with him. And hopefully, he would understand her motives and forgive her.

Night Hawk gazed with wonder down at Briana for a moment, her silence proof to him that she was either still angry at him, or she was trying to hide the truth from him—that she could not live with what he planned for her uncle. He hoped it was not the latter, yet he would not let down his guard. If she tried to flee to her uncle, he would make sure that she was stopped.

Thinking that there was any tension between them made a grievous ache circle Night Hawk's heart. He could hardly bear it.

He went to Briana. He took the string of beads from her fingers and lay them aside. Placing his hands in hers, he urged her to her feet, then led her to their sleeping platform, piled comfortably with warm pelts.

Without saying anything to her, he began slowly disrobing her. Within them rose a need that momentarily erased all sadness, doubt, and misunderstanding from their minds. All that mattered to them was their undying love for each other.

After her clothes were removed and she felt the warmth of the lodge fire caressing her flesh, Briana grabbed Night Hawk's fringed shirt and drew it over his head, revealing to her a copper chest all muscular and tight, the nipples on his breasts tautly erect.

She tossed the shirt aside, then placed her fingers on the waistband of his fringed breeches. Her eyes devoured his nudity as it was slowly revealed to her, his manhood springing free as she swept his breeches on down across his stomach, his thighs, and then dropped them to rest around his ankles.

Night Hawk drew in a wild breath and closed his

eyes as Briana circled his hardness with her fingers and started moving them around him, squeezing and fondling as she continued this up-and-down movement.

Night Hawk reciprocated by placing a hand at the juncture of her thighs and caressing the center of her passion. Briana closed her eyes. She sighed as the pressure of his fingers increased, sending her into a world that only knew pleasure—that only knew Night Hawk.

He then placed his hands on Briana's waist and eased her down onto her back on the sleeping platform. He kissed his way down her body. She was almost beside herself with pleasure. She twined her fingers through his glossy dark hair and urged him up.

As he stretched himself above her, his one hand guiding his shaft within her, a sensual shudder rocked Briana. She sighed and lifted her hips to take him more deeply inside her.

At first his strokes within her were gentle, but soon they became faster. Briana clung to his neck, his mouth seizing hers in a fiery kiss, his hands kneading her breasts.

The explosion of rapture came quickly. And after their passionate trembling had subsided, Night Hawk rolled away. She leaned on an elbow and watched him gather up his clothes and get into them. Never before had he left her so abruptly after having made love.

"Where are you going?" she murmured, drawing a fur robe around her shoulders.

"I feel as though I must go and be with my father for a while longer," Night Hawk said, not actually telling a lie. He did have to go to his father. He knew that he was torn. Echohawk wanted to go to Gentle Fawn and take comfort from her arms, yet had denied himself this pleasure until the mourning period was over for his beloved wife. Night Hawk had grown to accept his father's feelings for the young Chippewa, knowing that much of his feelings were because he felt her sadness that she still carried with her. She had been raped time and time again. Who could not pity her?

And she *was* lovely in features and personality. Who could not stop themselves from allowing her to find her way inside their hearts?

Ay-uh, Night Hawk could understand his father loving her. Night Hawk could have himself if he had not met Briana first.

Fully clothed, he went to Briana and kissed her. "I love you," he whispered. "You are a most beautiful flower for my wigwam."

He then turned and left. He did not go far. Instead of going to speak to his father, he went to the edges of the forest, positioning himself close to the grazing horses, where he could keep a close eye on his wigwam—and Briana.

If she fled into the night, he would be there to stop her. If she hated him for it, then her love for him had not been strong enough in the first place.

Knowing that this was the opportunity she needed to leave and warn her uncle, Briana scurried into her clothes. She was glad that it was growing dusky when she peered cautiously from the wigwam. That would make her escape much easier.

Slipping a fringed shawl around her shoulders, she left the wigwam, scarcely breathing. She stopped and looked guardedly around her, and when she saw that no one was noticing what she was doing, she broke into a mad run toward the fenced-in horses. When she reached them, she almost fainted. Night Hawk stepped out into plain view, his arms folded across his chest, his eyes narrowing angrily.

Briana then squared her shoulders. "Night Hawk,

let me pass," she said. "If you persist with this plan to abduct my uncle, I have no choice but to go and warn him. If a confrontation can be stopped, no lives will be taken. Yours especially, Night Hawk!"

"Briana, either you return with me to our dwelling peacefully, or I will take you by force," Night Hawk said flatly. "You cannot be allowed to warn your uncle. The evil man deserves what is planned for him."

Softening her stance, Briana began pleading with him. "Please, Night Hawk," she cried. "Tell me you won't go after my uncle. Everything we have planned could be lost! Is it worth it, Night Hawk, to seek vengeance when you are possibly jeopardizing everything we have together?"

"Do you return with me peacefully, or do I take you by force?" Night Hawk growled, refusing to listen to her pleas.

"You would actually force me?" Briana said, gasping.

"If it is required," Night Hawk said matter-of-factly.

Enraged by his cold indifference, Briana stared up at him for a moment longer, then turned and ran back to their wigwam. She tossed her shawl aside and threw herself down on the pelts before the fire and began crying.

When Night Hawk came to her and drew her into his arms, she jerked away.

"Just leave me alone," she said icily.

She stamped to the sleeping platform, placing her back to Night Hawk. When it came time for him to go to bed, he slept on the floor on the opposite side of the wigwam. Tears flooded her eyes, missing him, fearing what this meant for their future.

She, in truth, knew that she could not live without him.

24

I will have my revenge.
I will have it if I die the moment after.
—SPANISH CURATE

The fire was burning brightly, casting dancing shadows along the wall and the curved ceiling of the wigwam. The smoke was rising through the smoke hole, meeting the splash of morning sun as it rose upward into the sky.

Having lain stiffly silent as Night Hawk dressed for his journey of vengeance, Briana watched him slip on his war shirt, its breast containing a prayer for protection, and on the back the symbols of victory woven in beaded tapestry.

She shivered beneath her blankets when she noticed something else on the shirt—fringes of human hair— wondering . . . whose.

Briana pretended to be asleep as he finished preparing himself for the journey, and only when he finally left did she bolt from the sleeping platform, her own journey stretching before her.

Breathless from hurrying, knowing that she must ride hard to get to St. Paul ahead of Night Hawk, his father, and the many braves that she heard leave on horseback with them, she changed into fresh clothes.

She had one advantage today. Earlier in the morning, when Echohawk had come to Night Hawk's wigwam and they had stood outside talking in guarded whispers, she had crept to the wall and listened to what they were saying. She managed to hear Echo-hawk tell his son that before going to St. Paul, and before sending their braves out to search for Strong Branch, they should ride to the cave with their braves, and if the weapons were still lodged there, they would be confiscated.

Night Hawk had agreed, and Briana had just had enough time to rush back to her sleeping platform before he had come back into the wigwam to complete his wardrobe before leaving on his mission of revenge.

"Thank God Echohawk remembered the weapons in the cave," Briana whispered, slipping into soft moccasins beaded by her own hand. "That will give me the time I need to encourage Uncle Blackie to flee their wrath. Hopefully, that's what he will do—*not* go to the authorities."

Fear grew inside her heart at the thought of her uncle going to Fort Snelling and giving them the reason why he was pleading for their protection. Then her only hope would be that those at the fort would not believe him. They would ask for proof. There would be none, because she had to believe that Night Hawk's and Echohawk's vengeance would not lead them into such a foolish act as going on to Fort Snelling to achieve their vengeance.

Not only would their lives be in jeopardy, but also those in the village that depended on their leadership.

Her buckskin dress fit her like a glove. The fringes at the hem swayed as she went to the weapons leaning against the wall and chose a rifle. She quickly dropped a handful of bullets into the pocket of her dress. She lay the rifle on her sleeping platform and grabbed a fringed shawl and placed it around her shoulders, tying the ends together in front.

Taking up a narrow strip of leather from the floor, she gathered her hair together at the back and tied the thong about it, preventing her hair from constantly blowing in stinging wisps around her face while on horseback.

Swallowing hard, Briana eyed the entrance flap warily and reached with trembling fingers for the rifle. She knew what the consequences of her actions today could be. Night Hawk could turn his hatred of her uncle on to her. He could turn his back on her forever, even though what she was doing was to preserve his love—and his very own existence.

He would never understand. Never! He would see her as an interference.

And she knew that not only he, but no future Indian chief would tolerate such disobedience in a wife. She knew that it could make him lose face with his people, yet she had no choice but to do what she knew was best for everyone, except for herself.

Either way she would lose.

With a racing heart she took a determined step toward the entrance flap.

Echohawk drew his reins tautly. His horse came to a shimmying halt, Night Hawk drawing up beside him.

Night Hawk edged his horse closer to his father's. "Why do you stop?" he asked, seeing that their braves had also stopped behind them. "It is far to the cave. We must make haste. We must get that chore behind us, then hurry on to St. Paul. We want to arrive there just as it is turning dusk so that we can watch Blackie's movements before entering his house for the abduction."

"And that we will do," Echohawk said, nodding. His dark eyes narrowed. "I was wrong to encourage going to the cave before going to St. Paul. It was a foolish notion of mine to think that the weapons would be abandoned there, for the taking. As before,

White Wolf will have removed them. Along with the weapons, he will be our next target of vengeance. But later, my son. Later. Besides finding Strong Branch, it is imperative to get to Blackie before word reaches him that we are coming."

"And how would it, when only our trusted braves know of our plans?" Night Hawk said solemnly.

Echohawk put a steady hand on Night Hawk's shoulder. "My son, there is one among our people who I am not so sure can be trusted," he said, his voice drawn. "Did you not say that Briana tried to leave once to go to her uncle with a warning? Who is to say that she will not try again? She has torn loyalties, my son. I fear that the white blood running through her veins will guide her into that which could go against the Chippewa."

"*Gee-bah-bah*, please understand that what I say is not out of disobedience of a son to a father, but I believe I understand Briana's motives much more clearly than you," Night Hawk said in her defense. "In her heart, deep in her soul, she thinks that telling her uncle about the planned abduction is a way to protect the future of the Chippewa. She fears there will be a confrontation between the white man and the Chippewa if we succeed with our abduction. And, partly, Father, that is true. We are taking a risk. Yet a risk that must be taken. *Ay-uh*, we must achieve our vengeance, or live the *res* of our lives cowering in the shadow of that evil man and his evil ways that always go against the Chippewa."

"At least in that your thinking is clear," Echohawk said, his voice a low grumble. "And I hope, for your sake, the future chief of our people, that your thinking is clear about your woman's motives. If not . . ."

His words faded into the wind, since he did not want to speak of threats or foreboding this morning.

He wanted to think of hope and inspiration. Of a sought-after peace that only Blackie's and White Wolf's deaths might achieve for his people. And now also Strong Branch's death.

Echohawk turned to his braves and told them of the changed plans and urged them now to concentrate on finding Strong Branch.

He and his son then rode away from the braves, for the first time in their lives feeling a strain between them.

Briana lifted the entrance flap and peered outside, looking cautiously around her. When she saw the usual morning activity in the village, she sighed in relief. She had feared that perhaps Night Hawk had left one of his braves to stand guard outside their wigwam to stop her escape.

What she saw was innocent enough—the women taking wood from their piles inside their wigwams to get the cooking fires built, others going to the river for their early morning bath, despite the cool breezes of autumn that were on them. She gazed at the children, who were rowdy and playful as they chased one another or their dogs, causing them to yelp and howl if one or the other was caught by the tail.

She scarcely saw any braves at all wandering through the village, only the elders, who sat in clusters, smoking and chatting. Most of the young, virile braves who had not joined their chief and his son on their journey of vengeance had surely gone to strategic points in the forest to keep watch for any possible intruders during the absence of their chief and his heir. These braves were the worst threat to her escape from the village today. She would have to keep alert for them as she fled on horseback through the forest.

Not seeing anyone looking in her direction, Briana

stepped quickly from the wigwam, then froze in her path when a muscular brave stepped in front of her, peering down at her with his dark eyes, his jaw tight and his arms folded across his chest.

She had not thought that a brave would be hidden in the shadows of the wigwam.

"You cannot leave," the brave said flatly. He pointed at the closed entrance flap. "Go back inside. Night Hawk's orders!"

Briana paled and her eyes wavered. "He ordered you to stand guard?" she said, her voice breaking.

Her eyes became two points of fire as she gazed brazenly at the brave. "I don't care what he said, I'm leaving," she said, the strength returning to her voice.

She placed her free hand on her hip, her other hand clutching the rifle that she was almost determined to use if she did not get her way. "Step aside!" she said, lifting her chin stubbornly.

When the brave did not move and only stared angrily down at her, Briana started to lift the rifle, but was quickly shaken when the brave grabbed it from her hands and dropped it to the ground.

"Go inside," he said, nodding toward the wigwam. "Or I will take you there!"

Seeing that she had no choice, and frustrated that she was being held prisoner in Night Hawk's village, Briana turned around and stamped back inside the wigwam. She began to pace, growing angrier by the minute. She sighed heavily and plopped down beside the fire, gazing disconsolately into the flames. She truly couldn't blame Night Hawk for having her guarded. He felt as strongly about abducting her uncle as she felt against it.

They were at opposite ends of the spectrum this time, and it threatened to destroy everything that had blossomed between them so sweetly, so wonderfully.

Briana held her face in her hands. "Where is this going to end?" she said, unable to stop the tears from streaming from her eyes. "Where?"

She gazed around her, eyeing everything of Night Hawk's that was so familiar to her now. Strange how everything that she had known with him was so distant now, as though it had all been a dream. Yet there was his hunting gear, his breechclouts, his headbands, his bows and arrows, to remind her that it was real—she was here, and he had held her in his arms, professing his love for her time and time again.

"Now how will he feel after he hears that I tried to escape again to warn my uncle?" she whispered, panic seizing her, at the thought of him ever hating her.

As night fell over the Chippewa village, a lone figure ambled toward the council house. Wise Owl was seizing the opportunity to have council with the elders of both bands of Chippewa, to try again to convince them who their leader should be.

As Wise Owl entered the council house, the lodge fire was burning brightly in the center, lighting the faces of those who gazed up at him with questioning in their old, wisdom-filled eyes. He had called the meeting.

He felt lucky that they had complied with this request since Night Hawk and Echohawk were gone. Yet Wise Owl was acting chief on behalf of Strong Branch in his absence. It was only right that he should have a voice in the affairs of the two tribes. In fact, he hoped to convince the elders that he should have full control—the only chief over both villages.

He gathered the tail end of his long bearskin robe into his arms and settled himself down beside the fire where room had been left for him. All was silent as the calumet pipe was passed around to those in council, then all eyes were on Wise Owl again.

He nodded from brave to brave, then began his proposal in a monotone, his dark eyes almost hidden in the folds of his face. "It is good to be in council with you all again," he said. "It is important, this that I have to say, as an extension of what I have said before, yet I have never been filled with as much determination as tonight."

He did not cower before the frowning at his introductory comments. Instead he kept on talking, wanting to have his say before someone interrupted him, forbidding it. He knew the dangerous waters in which he was now treading. But he also knew that this was his best opportunity to convince the council that what he said was the best for everyone concerned.

Ay-uh, this was the best time to speak his mind—having purposely taken this opportunity while Echohawk and Night Hawk were away, the two who fought his every decision and suggestion, as though he were not present. Hopefully, when they returned to the village, they would see just how important he truly was.

"Elders of the council, Echohawk has proven his weakness as your leader by allowing himself to be abducted, and Night Hawk is no better," he began, his voice rising in pitch as each word was spoken. He lay the pipe aside. "He was also abducted. And he is a half-breed. White blood flows through his veins. Is this not a weakness in character in all Chippewa's eyes? I urge you to let Wise Owl be your leader. Wise Owl has never let you down. Never!"

Everyone seemed to rise at once, leaving Wise Owl sitting alone, his eyes wide, his mouth open as he gaped up at them. He flinched when one of the elders clasped his arm roughly and forced him to his feet. Then he led him from the council house, half dragging him to the center of the village, where the outdoor fire was burning brightly toward the dark heavens.

Against his will he was made to stand there until a crowd had gathered around to stare at him and listen as each of the councilmen began speeches that shamed Wise Owl for his disloyalty to the reigning chief and his son, causing everyone to scorn him and turn their backs to him as they went to their dwellings.

Wise Owl began backing away from the councilmen, his heart pounding.

"Leave and never return," one of the elders ordered. "Banishment is what you have earned tonight. Leave and do not look back. You are responsible for many ugly things among our people. These actions can no longer be tolerated. As is Strong Branch, who hides like a coward since the death of Lily and Gray Moon, you are no longer of our people. You are now destined to walk alone."

Wise Owl was trembling and his eyes were downcast as he turned to leave, not even allowed to take his personal belongings with him. As he walked solemnly into the dark shadows of the forest, he hung his head in shame, yet his heart was crying out for vengeance—and somehow he would have it!

25

Honor will honor meet.
—BRIDGES

When Night Hawk and his father ventured into the outskirts of St. Paul, the streets of the city were quiet. Only an occasional horse-drawn carriage clopped along the cobblestones, making an eerie sound as the hollowed clatter wafted into the night air.

The two tethered their horses in the trees at the far back of Blackie's estate grounds, and moved stealthily toward the house. The hour was late, yet a lone light remained shimmering golden in a window of the two-storied mansion.

Together, their breathing shallow, their movements hushed, Echohawk and Night Hawk rushed up the steps to the veranda that reached around three sides of the house. They moved stealthily to the window where they had seen the light and looked inside. Blackie was stretched out on a sofa before a roaring fire in the parlor, reading a book.

Father and son exchanged satisfied smiles, then crept to the door and tried the knob. Their smiles waned when they discovered that the door was locked.

Night Hawk needed no persuasion as to what he should do next. He went brazenly to the parlor window, took his pistol from the waistband of his fringed breeches, and crashed the butt of the firearm into the pane of the glass. Swiftly he cleaned the window of any glass as he moved his pistol all around it, scattering the glass in all directions.

Blackie bolted with alarm to his feet, dropping the book to the floor. He blanched, his face becoming ashen as he watched Night Hawk quickly climb through the window, his father following behind him.

"You . . . !" Blackie gasped, unable to back up, his back to the fireplace. "Night Hawk! Echohawk!"

He stared disbelievingly at the chief. "Echohawk, how did you get away from White Wolf?" he gasped.

"That I did is enough for you to know," Echohawk growled. "But I have come to you for answers, and if you are a wise man, you will give them to me."

"What . . . answers?" Blackie stammered.

Knowing that haste was needed to achieve their planned revenge without getting caught, Night Hawk slipped his pistol back at his waistband and grabbed a leather thong from his pocket. He hurried to Blackie and grabbed him by a wrist, twisting it as he turned him around.

"What are you doing?" Blackie managed to say between frightened breaths. His heart skipped several nervous beats, and he tried to get away when Night Hawk began binding his hands at his wrists with the leather thong, but found that escape was impossible.

A strangled sound came from the depths of his throat when Night Hawk just as quickly jerked a rope from his pocket and pulled it around Blackie's neck, tightening it, causing his eyes to bulge.

Echohawk went to Blackie and glowered at him, then nudged his chest with the barrel of his pistol. "You were easily found," he said. "But my son and I need assistance in finding White Wolf. He has become at large again. Tell me where he is. Now!"

"I don't know," Blackie breathed out anxiously, unable to move his head with the rope tightening around his throat. His eyes bulged even more and his tongue seemed drawn sideways inside his mouth.

"Please . . . have mercy," he said, his voice now barely a squeak. "Don't kill me."

"Perhaps not now," Night Hawk hissed. "But in time you will die, after you come to our village so that our people will be audience to your miseries!"

"God, no . . ." Blackie said, close to blacking out as the rope tightened even more snugly around his throat.

"If you tell us where White Wolf is hiding, I will loosen the rope around your neck," Night Hawk said, his fingers gripping the rope tightly. "Tell us. You will be spared some of the humiliation we have planned for you."

"I tell you, I don't know," Blackie whispered hoarsely. "He's gone his way . . . I've gone mine. My—my political career. Please let me go. I am so close to seeing my political aspirations fulfilled."

"You should have thought about that before siding with White Wolf," Echohawk said, leaning his face into Blackie's. "Those many years ago, when your life lay in balance on the riverboat, I should have ended it for you then. My wrong decision that day has been the cause for many hardships among not only the Chippewa community, but also the white! You have spread your evil far and wide. But now, it will finally stop. I will spare you nothing, Blackie. Nothing!"

"Oh, God . . ." Blackie shrieked as Night Hawk began dragging him across the floor, the rope cutting into the flesh of his throat. "Please . . . don't!"

Echohawk placed a gentle hand on his son's arm. "We must silence him before taking him from the house," he said, smiling at Blackie as he emitted a groan of fear.

Night Hawk nodded and watched matter-of-factly as his father raised the butt of his pistol and smacked Blackie on the head, rendering him unconscious.

Echohawk moved on ahead of Night Hawk, out into
the corridor, looking guardedly from side to side, then
peered up the spiral staircase, then down the dark
corridor. When he saw no signs of anyone having been
aroused, he nodded for Night Hawk to come ahead
and follow him from the house. . . .

Soon they had Blackie tied across the back of Night
Hawk's horse and were riding into the wind, the first
step of their planned revenge achieved.

Briana was brooding beside the fire, only half-
heartedly eating an apple. It seemed to be the only
food that she could tolerate this morning after having
been forced to stay in Night Hawk's village. The
braves had returned during the night, but without
Night Hawk and Echohawk—or her Uncle Blackie.
Nor had their search uncovered Strong Branch.

She stiffened and dropped the apple core into the
blazing fire pit when she heard horses arriving in the
village. Her heart beating loudly, she rose to her feet
and went to the entrance flap and lifted it. She grew
cold inside as she watched Night Hawk and Echohawk
arriving at the village, her Uncle Blackie tied across
Night Hawk's horse. His eyes grew wide with fright
as he noticed her standing there, watching him.

"No," Briana whispered, covering her mouth with
a hand. "They did abduct him. Oh, dear Lord, now
what are they going to do with him?"

She was thankful for one thing. It seemed they had
gotten away with the abduction, for no one had followed them—yet. She feared that this would be short-
lived. Her uncle was too well known in the community
for his absence to be ignored.

Yet, she realized, there would be no reason for his
absence to be blamed on the Chippewa. A man like
Blackie Collins surely had many enemies.

Briana pursed her lips tightly when Echohawk turned and caught sight of her standing there, his gaze momentarily burning into hers. He continued with his chore of loosening the ropes that had held Blackie into place during the long night journey from St. Paul.

It took all the willpower Briana could muster not to rush out to Night Hawk and pound his chest with her fists, to berate him for having imprisoned her—supposedly the woman he loved! But all thoughts of harshly scolding him were erased by astonishment as she watched a brave place a stake in the center of the village. Her uncle then was tied to the stake. Then a pile of tree limbs and split wood were stacked around her uncle and the stake. . . .

"Oh, my God," Briana gasped. "Surely neither Night Hawk nor his father will burn my uncle alive! That is the work of savages! They aren't savages!"

When torches were brought to the wood and sparks began lifting into the air as the flames began to spread around the stake, Briana felt nauseated and her knees were weak. Now she realized the seriousness of Night Hawk and Echohawk's decision to achieve their vengeance—to finalize it today.

"Tell us where White Wolf is and your life will be spared!" Echohawk said to Blackie as the Chippewa amassed around them.

"How can I when I don't even know myself?" Blackie cried, his eyes feverishly watching the flames eating away at the wood, drawing closer and closer to his boots.

He then looked past Echohawk, again locking eyes with his niece. "Briana! Don't allow them to do this to me," he pleaded. "We're blood kin! Doesn't that mean anything to you? What will your parents think when they find out that you allowed these savages to kill me in such a way? Please, Briana! Do what is right! Save me!"

Torn by his pleading, knowing that what he said was true, Briana choked back a sob. When she felt other eyes on her, as though hot brands were touching her flesh, she shifted her gaze and met the anger in Night Hawk's as he seemed to be daring her.

Then her whole body flinched when Blackie let out a scream of pain. She became faint when she saw that the fire was lapping at his boots. The smell of scorched leather was filling the air.

She gasped as she watched the fire reaching up toward the legs of his breeches, his screams seeming to split the heavens in half.

Seeing the utter savagery of what was happening to her uncle, Briana rushed from the wigwam and went to Night Hawk. She clutched his arm, looking wildly up at him. "Let him go!" she cried. "This is wrong, Night Hawk. Even though I know you feel you have cause to do this terrible thing, it is wrong! Please, darling. For me, let him go. I don't think I could live with the memory of my uncle dying such a horrible death, especially since you will be the one responsible for it!"

When Night Hawk did not respond, still staring angrily at her, she clutched his arm more feverishly. "Say something!" she cried. "Do something! Don't just stand there and allow this to continue!"

When he still did not respond in any way, Briana wrenched herself away and turned and looked pityingly up at her uncle. When she saw that his head was hung, that he had fainted clean away, his breeches smoldering, she realized that she had no choice but to defy the man she loved for a man she abhorred!

It was the humane thing to do. She must!

She ran toward the circle of flames and without

stopping began to run through them to get to her uncle and set him free. But almost immediately the lightweight fabric of the skirt of her buckskin dress caught fire. The intense heat against her calves alerted her to the danger. She looked down and a lightheadedness swept through her when she saw that her dress was on fire!

She tried to run on, to get to her uncle, her hands trying to beat out the fire on her dress, but felt suddenly trapped, seeing that she would burn long before her uncle would.

A muscular arm wrapped around her waist, and she felt herself being swept out of the fire. She was thrown onto the ground, Night Hawk covering her body with his to snuff out the fire on her dress.

Breathing hard, the flames at last extinguished, Briana gazed into Night Hawk's eyes as he leaned away from her. "Should I thank you?" she said sarcastically, then looked back at her uncle, panic rising within her.

He was now hidden behind the screen of billowing smoke!

She had no idea if he was burning, or if it was just the smoke causing this illusion.

She shoved at Night Hawk's chest. "I must go and save Uncle Blackie!" she cried, sobbing. "Please, Night Hawk. Please allow it!"

Night Hawk moved quickly to his feet and turned to his father. "Perhaps Blackie's punishment can be a less drastic one," he said, suddenly seeing that Blackie was important to Briana, yet not understanding why.

Father and son exchanged troubled glances, then Echohawk nodded to a brave. "Release him," he said.

They all jumped with alarm as a gunshot rang out, and as the smoke separated, they could see blood spiraling from a wound in Blackie's chest, where he'd been shot square in the heart.

Echohawk turned with a start and looked up at a butte overlooking the village. That was where the shot had to have come from, since no one in the village would have cause to shoot Blackie, or have even seen through the smoke to do it. Up high on the butte, though, someone would have a clear shot through the spirals of smoke.

Briana felt faint when she was able to see through the smoke and saw the blood and how limp her uncle hung from the ropes of the stake. She did not have to go any closer to know that he had died instantly from the bullet.

She turned away, tears flooding her eyes. The grief was not so much for her uncle, but for how it could have been between them if he had not been a heartless cad. His was a life wasted.

She spun around, eyes wide as she wiped them free of tears. "Who shot him?" she asked, peering up at Night Hawk, at least glad that he was not responsible for the crime.

Echohawk had already ordered several braves to go search for the killer, and their horses' hooves sounded like distant thunder as they galloped from the village.

"Hopefully, we will soon see," Night Hawk said, placing a gentle hand on her shoulder.

A brave stepped forward. "Perhaps it was Strong Branch," he cried. "We failed in our search to find him. Though I do not understand why he would kill Lily and Gray Moon, he must be guilty, for he is eluding us now with much trickery. Perhaps he has come now and killed the white man to prove his cunning again to us!"

Another brave stepped forward. "Perhaps it was Wise Owl," he said, clutching a rifle.

"Why would you say that?" Night Hawk said. "Why would Wise Owl kill Blackie?"

"His aim may not have been for Blackie," the brave said. "It may have been for you or your father."

"I do not understand," Night Hawk said, his voice edged with irritation.

The brave then explained about Wise Owl's banishment while Night Hawk and Echohawk had been gone. Night Hawk's jaw slackened as he looked quickly over at his father.

"The killer is more than likely White Wolf," Echohawk said. "Always the elusive renegade of the forests. I doubt if we will ever find him."

The fires around the stake were splashed out by buckets of water. Blackie was taken down and placed on the ground, a buckskin cape thrown over him.

Briana stood over him, silent for a moment, then she turned to Night Hawk. "I must return him to St. Paul for a proper burial. I must do this for my parents, who would expect no less from me," she said, her voice drawn. "And then, Night Hawk, I-I will prepare myself for a journey to France. I imagine that is the best for both of us."

And then a sudden panic seized her. "Lord," she said, gasping, "you will be blamed for my uncle's death."

And then she set her jaw firmly. "I won't allow that to happen," she murmured. "Although I was against you becoming involved in this abduction from the beginning, I cannot allow you to suffer because of it—for, in truth, my uncle was the one who carries the burden of his own death, because of the pain he caused you and your people. I shall tell a convincing lie, Night Hawk. I will tell the authorities that White Wolf abducted both me and my uncle and that—and that he killed my Uncle Arden. You think he did, anyway. Perhaps it will lessen the lie somewhat in my heart to think so."

"You would do that for me—for my people?" Night Hawk said. Then what she had said about a journey to France hit him like a blast of cold air. "And then you will leave for this place you call France? You will leave me forever, Briana?"

"I have no choice," Briana said, trying to keep her voice steady, to hide the trembling she was feeling inside to know that their final good-bye was so near. But she did not see how she could stay with him, for more than one reason. She had seen a savage side to the man she loved, and he had seen that she could defy him. Under these circumstances, she was not sure if they could ever feel the same about each other.

"You always have choices," Night Hawk said, drawing her closer, yet not completely into his arms. Many eyes were on them. Many ears had heard that she had said she was going to leave him. He had to protect his pride. Even if she were gone, he would have to face his people forever.

"Yes, I do," Briana said, gulping hard, trying to fight off the attraction that, as always, his mere presence aroused within her. "And I am doing what I feel is best."

She eased from his grip and looked regretfully down at her uncle's covered body. She went to the wigwam and began gathering up her things. When she felt a presence behind her, she stiffened, then turned and faced Night Hawk. When he took her into his arms and kissed her, she melted from the ecstasy that the kiss evoked, then wrenched herself free and continued getting her things together for leaving.

"I am leaving," she murmured. "Please prepare my uncle for the journey."

Night Hawk glared at her back, then spun around and left, his heart bleeding, his pride wounded. He knew that he had no choice but to let her go, but he would go for her again soon, and in private. When it was just the two of them, he would convince her to return with him.

She was too much a part of him to let go.

Strong Branch drew his reins tight and stopped his horse to rest beside the river once he was far enough from the scene of the shooting to feel safe. He patted the rifle sheathed on his horse, relieved that Blackie was dead. He had been the one who involved Strong Branch and Gray Moon in White Wolf's schemes in the first place.

Strong Branch realized now that Blackie, the evil man that he was, had deliberately stirred up this sort of Indian trouble to give himself a cover—if any of the people in the area possibly attacked him for hating the Indians, he would point out the reason why every-one should hate them. By doing this, he would be adding votes on election day, not taking them away.

Strong Branch held his head in his hands and sobbed, also knowing that he had had his own, selfish reasons for having joined with the Sioux. It seemed that Strong Branch's lust for power equaled Blackie's. He now realized the wrong he had done. And it was too late. He was no better than the renegade Sioux and the white politician. He himself was now branded with the ugly name "renegade."

Lifting his head and peering in all directions in the forest, he knew that, for his survival, he still had to depend on the likes of White Wolf. It was best to find him. He had to encourage him to get his men back together again.

In truth, no matter how much shame he felt, Strong Branch missed the excitement of the raids. The dar-ing. He must be a part of it again.

He also hoped that he would die amid such a raid,

and soon. He could not take his own life. He had been taught from childhood that a suicide never entered paradise.

He sank his moccasined heels into the flanks of his horse and rode onward, feeling the aloneness around him as though the world was closing in on him from all sides.

26

The morning sun was dappling the trees outside the window as Briana stood in the sun room of her mansion, gazing upon the peacefulness of the morning. Yet it bore no resemblance to the way she felt inside. It seemed an eternity since she had seen Night Hawk on that fateful day of her uncle's shooting, and as each day passed, she knew that she had made a mistake by leaving him.

But still she had not summoned the courage to go to him and confess to being wrong. She had hoped he would come to her.

She had concluded that although he had asked her not to leave him, he had more than likely decided that it was best—he could get on with his life as a proud Chippewa leader without the interference of a woman who had tried, in a sense, to betray him.

She turned and began strolling slowly around the room, touching things that, yes, were now hers. The white rattan sofa with its plush, flowered cushions. The tables and plant stands that were made from Chinese bamboo. Among the needlepoint pillows on the sofa were Indonesian batiks, all set against the languor of white canvas and linen.

Yes, surprising to her, on the day of the reading of her uncle's will, she had learned that all of his worldly possessions had become hers. She had been his sole beneficiary. She was now rich.

She settled into a plushly cushioned rattan chair and stared into the flames rolling like satin across the logs on the grate of the fireplace, realizing that being rich was not important to her.

She missed Night Hawk with all of her being!

She rose slowly to her feet again and went to a closed trunk beneath a window. She bent to her knees and opened it and began removing what she had placed there for her long journey to Paris. She had come as close to leaving as ordering her trunk carried to her private carriage—then had stopped the driver as he lifted it from the floor to carry it outside.

In a flash she realized that she could not run from her feelings. She would stay in St. Paul and battle them out within her heart.

Hopefully, Night Hawk would also be grappling with these same feelings, and somehow they would be drawn together again, in mutual love, mutual trust.

Until that day came, Briana had decided to put her other passion and this mansion that she had inherited to good use. She was going to transform the house into guest rooms. She was going to open a boarding-house for artists, hopefully attracting a generation of America's finest painters. She was going to turn this into a school for aspiring artists. She would hire the best teachers.

She had more than enough money to contribute to these studies. She would even offer scholarships for those who did not have the money to attend.

These thoughts made her remorse over losing Night Hawk somehow more bearable. She would throw herself into this project. It would make her come alive again, although not in the way that she felt while within Night Hawk's arms.

But it just might be the best substitute.

Hearing a movement behind her made Briana move

quickly to her feet and turn around. Her heart stopped when she found Night Hawk standing there in his full-fringed buckskin attire, his shoulder-length, raven black hair drawn back from his brow with a headband that she so vividly recalled having beaded for him. She looked quickly at his feet. He also wore the moccasins that she had sewn and beaded for him.

She looked up and melted inside when his gaze locked with hers. Within his dark eyes she saw such feelings of love, and yet also she could see the hurt in their depths—a hurt she had surely caused.

She bore the same pain in her eyes, the same longings within her heart.

Something compelled her to brush aside all doubts. She broke into a mad run and flung herself into his arms, so glad when he wrapped her in a tight embrace. She lifted her lips to his and closed her eyes as the kiss stole her breath and her senses away.

She clung to him as he picked her up and carried her toward the spiral staircase. She placed her cheek against the soft buckskin fabric of his shirt and could hear and feel the pounding of his heart against her flesh.

Tears of joy leapt into her eyes as once again his mouth found her lips. He stepped up to the second-floor landing and began carrying her down the corridor. She did not stop the wondrous kiss when they entered her bedroom and he placed her on a bed.

They wrenched their lips apart and he began to undress her, as she was undressing him.

He moved over her, their bodies meeting in a sweet reunion as he sculpted himself to her. When he looked down, their eyes met, locked in unspoken understanding, promising ecstasy. She twined her fingers through his hair and pulled his head down, and once again they kissed.

When he plunged into her, she arched and cried out, shuddering at the intense pleasure at how magnificently he filled her. Slipping her hands down to his buttocks, she gripped him tightly and strained into him, abandoning herself to the rush of feelings that were overwhelming her. Their naked flesh seemed to fuse, their bodies yearning for each other, their lips parting in a mutual sigh as the passion mounted.

It was as though they had never been separated. And she knew that nothing mattered now, except that they remain together for eternity. She would require no apologies for his long absence. She did not expect him to demand any from her. Today was the beginning of the rest of their lives. Neither one would allow any more interference.

Night Hawk pressed endlessly deeper within Briana. He buried his face into the sweet curve of her throat, inhaling the familiar scent of her. His tongue slid down her throat, to her breasts. She drew in a wild breath of pleasure as he locked his lips over one of her nipples and began flicking his tongue around its tautness.

He rolled away from her, his hands caressing their way down her body, his lips and tongue following their lead, finding and stroking her every pleasure point. Briana lay there and closed her eyes, enjoying these moments of sheer ecstasy again with the man she loved.

When his tongue found the bud of her desire, she arched her hips to give him more access to that sort of lovemaking that made her head swim with pleasure. As he stroked her with long sweeps of his tongue, she tossed her head and chewed her lower lip to keep from crying out.

Just as she felt that she was beyond coherent thought, he moved around, positioning himself so that she could reciprocate the same sort of pleasure. Moving to her knees, she leaned over him, her hair hanging over his thighs in silken waves, and placed her fingers around him. She ran her fingers slowly along his pulsing satin hardness as her lips began a soft pleasuring that caused him to groan and his body to stiffen with pleasure.

When she felt his body begin to tremble, she knew that it was time for them to join again so that the pleasure that had built up to such a peak of excitement could culminate in something even more wondrous, even more blissful.

He molded himself perfectly to the curved hollow of her hips. She locked her legs around him and moved with him as his thrusts became more determined, more maddening. She clutched him, pulling him closer and closer, and cried out as he made a last plunge. Their bodies quivered into the other, merging as though one mind, one heart, one soul.

Afterward, they lay still in each other's arms. Then Night Hawk rolled away, still gazing at her.

"I could not stay away," he said hoarsely, his hand moving across her body, stopping at a breast. He cupped it and drew its nipple between his lips, sucking it.

Briana's heart was pounding. She closed her eyes: the rapture was still so intense, it blocked out all rhyme and reason.

"I thought I had stayed away too long, that you might have left for that place you call France," Night Hawk continued, his hands now framing her face. As her eyes opened, he gazed into them with devotion and love. "But I took the chance that your love for me would be too strong for you to leave me forever. I felt that you needed time to sort everything out in your heart and mind. Now I see that you have."

He kissed the tip of her nose. "Your body relayed the message to me that you still love and want me," he murmured. "But I need to hear this also from your lips, my woman. I need to hear you say that you still wish to be my wife . . . that you will return to my dwelling and be the flower of my wigwam forever."

Briana took his hands and urged him into a sitting position. Smiling at him, she moved onto his lap, relishing the feel of his naked thighs against her body, and that part of him that always sent her into a tailspin of joyous bliss rising in its turgid strength again and touching the core of her womanhood with its renewed heat.

She placed her arms around his neck and leaned her lips close to his, her breasts just barely touching his chest. "Night Hawk, my beloved, I have never stopped wanting to be your wife," she whispered. "My darling, I need so much the quiet of your love. Oh, how I do love you."

"You will return with me to my village?" he asked, gently smoothing a lock of her hair from her eyes. "You will give up your world for mine?"

"Yes, except for . . ."

She paused and did not finish her sentence, leaving Night Hawk wondering why she hesitated at all. He lifted her from his lap and lay her beneath him, stretching out above her, the velvet tip of his shaft teasing her.

"You are not ready to commit fully to the man you love?" Night Hawk grumbled.

"No, that is not at all what I was going to say," Briana said, placing her hands at his neck, drawing his lips close to hers again. "My darling, this house is now mine. Uncle Blackie left everything to me. I-I don't want to give it up altogether."

Night Hawk eased his lips away from her, giving

him room to glare down at her. "Are you saying that you wish to live here instead of in my village, in a wigwam?" he said. "Is a wigwam too crude for you now? Before, you seemed to accept the way I live. Why have you changed your mind?"

Briana laughed softly. "I am not planning to stay here in my house," she said, smiling up at him. She placed a hand on his cheek. "I am going to live with you wherever you are, however you live."

"Then what are you saying about this house?" he asked, confused.

"You know my love of painting," she said softly. "My darling, I am going to share that *and* this house with others who have the same sort of passion. I am going to turn this house into a boardinghouse for budding artists. I am going to turn it into a school for artists. Doesn't that sound wonderful? It seems that Uncle Blackie's evil scheming came to some good, after all." She giggled. "I imagine he will turn over in his grave when he realizes what I have planned for his mansion. His interest in my painting was only for show, for everyone to see. In truth, he cared nothing at all for it."

A wave of melancholia swept through her. "But, Night Hawk, his having named me his sole beneficiary has proved that he did care for me," she said solemnly. "I truly never knew how much. He—he was not a demonstrative person in that way. Only when he was on a podium preaching politics."

"How could he not have cared for you?" Night Hawk said, brushing a soft kiss across her brow. "My woman, how could anyone not love you?"

His mouth covered hers in a warm kiss. She sighed as she received his lips, so glad that things had once more come together for them.

She could not think of anything that could postpone their happiness again.

Echohawk stood outside Gentle Fawn's wigwam for a while, contemplating life as it had been handed him. His first wife, Fawn, and their unborn child had been taken from him long ago. His beloved Mariah had been taken from him only a short while ago, and with these losses a portion of his heart.

Yet there was still so much of his heart that he was ready to share with Gentle Fawn now that the mourning period for his No-din was past. It was something ready to be left behind. He was eager to push such thoughts from his mind.

He had waited long enough to speak his mind to Gentle Fawn. He had waited long enough to hold her in his arms. He had not kissed her since before his wife had passed away. He hungered for her lips and the sweetness of her flesh.

She had made him feel young again, so very much a virile brave who had denied himself for too long the pleasures of being with a woman.

Not wanting to tarry any longer, he lifted the entrance flap. The mere sight of her sitting beside the lodge fire, the child sucking from the nipple of her abundantly filled breast, made his heart begin to pound like a young brave getting his first thrill from being near a girl of his desire. He went to her and sat down beside her.

Soon Gentle Fawn slipped the baby's mouth from her breast and laid the child aside on a thick layer of pelts. Moonstar's eyes were peacefully closed, her stomach comfortably filled.

Gentle Fawn then rose to her feet, and as her eyes met his, she slipped the dress down her body, stepping free of it as it fell around her ankles.

She beckoned to him with outstretched arms. Echo-hawk removed his clothes, then placed his hands on her shoulders and spread her out beneath him. With a rapid heartbeat, and desires that had been stifled for much too long now, he plunged inside her. His eyes closed with the pleasure and he groaned, her tightness squeezing his hardness as he stroked rhythmically within her.

His mouth covered her lips with a feverish kiss. His hands were exploring, touching and fondling her every secret point of pleasure. And just before his seed exploded into her, he drew his lips from her mouth and whispered something soft and endearing in her ear.

"Marry me," he said. "Marry me soon, Gentle Fawn. I want you every waking moment. Please allow it."

Tears streamed from her eyes. "*Ay-uh*, my love, I will allow it," she whispered back.

Their lips sealed the promise, their bodies responding as they swayed and rocked with the explosion of rapturous bliss.

27

I have thee by thy hands
And will not let thee go!
—BRIDGES

It was so cold the trees were crackling all about the wigwams like pistol shots. The day was now gone; the moon had risen; the cold had not lessened. The trunks of the trees were still snapping all around the council house where Briana sat with many of the village children, close to one of the four great lodge fires, showing them her types of canvases and how she applied her paints to them in wondrous designs of the forest, the sky, the rivers, and then a sketch of the village of which they were so proud.

She smiled at the children as they talked occasionally in mixed languages of English and Chippewa. They were excited as she allowed each one of them to take up a brush and apply some paint to the canvas, their eyes wide and bright as they made their own drawings of what pleased them.

A mischievous young brave sketched the moon with a face on it, evoking giggles from the others. A petite girl sketched a dog with several puppies trailing after it. Another lad sketched a young brave notching an arrow onto a bow.

All of this caused a serene contentment to wash through Briana, as well as what she had accomplished at her mansion in St. Paul.

It had taken some time, yet she had finally filled

the rooms with artists. She had found talented teachers who were eager to spread their lessons of art to those who were just as enthusiastic to learn.

She had hired a cook to keep food hot on the stove for those involved in this project. And she had also hired meticulous maids to be at the beck and call of all those who lived at the boardinghouse, all hours of the night and day. She had instructed the maids and the cook to do everything they could to please the students, for this would ensure their best work.

She smiled, realizing that she had perhaps gone to extremes in her plans, knowing that surely there was no other such boardinghouse or art school that could boast of having maids and a cook that only prepared meals that the budding artists requested.

A soft sigh escaped her lips when she thought of how soon her first art scholarship would be awarded to a young person who would not have the means to attend an art school otherwise. Being able to offer such a scholarship made her proud. Strange that it was her uncle's monies that made all of this possible, while all along she had regarded him as a selfish tyrant, always concerned for his best interests.

But of course, she thought further to herself, had he known how she would use her inheritance, he more than likely would have never named her his sole heir. And he had probably not had a chance to change his will after realizing that she loved an Indian. With his thoughts so filled with other things, it had probably not entered his mind to change the will.

She listened as the children conversed excitedly among themselves about how they had been taught to paint before Briana had introduced these sorts of new skills to them. They were talking about how their mothers had to dig in the earth for their paints and how they had always made their paintbrushes from the inner spongy portion of a socket bone of an animal.

They chattered on about how their mothers' paints were stored in bags instead of jars, and that the only artwork they had known before was the language of symbol and design that was employed in the decoration of wigwams, clothings, skin, and rawhide articles in flaps, banners, and tomtoms. This symbolism was rich and interrelated with legends, stories, songs, and ceremonies.

They each bragged about their mothers being talented decorators—their mothers' bags, purses, war bonnets, awl cases, and robes decorated in beautiful designs and colors.

They boasted of how their fathers decorated the outside of the wigwams—drawing figures of men and animals and objects of nature by which they told of historic events such as travels, battles, captures, and various other exploits.

A strong arm, suddenly thrust around Briana's waist, caused her attention to leave the children. Her insides became warm, knowing whose arm was claiming her.

She turned and looked up at Night Hawk. "The Chippewa children are quite talented on my canvases," she said, smiling up at him. "Do you see their sketches? I will enjoy working with them, to help them hone their skills. We will then display their paintings among those being painted by my students in St. Paul. Everyone will see their talent. I would say that many of the children could become well known for their paintings."

Night Hawk gazed past her, noting the impatience of the children as they waited for their turn to paint on this new sort of canvas. It was good to see not only that they were enjoying learning from Briana, but also that they had accepted her without question as the future wife of the next chief. He was as proud of their mothers and fathers who had also accepted Briana into their hearts.

"It is good to see this camaraderie that has formed between you and all of my people," he said, smiling at Briana. "Tomorrow our celebration of marriage will be one that will live within my people's minds and hearts for many moons."

Briana's gaze lowered, seeing how he was dressed— wrapped snugly in a buffalo robe, with the hair inside, a wide leather belt holding it in place about his loins. The winter winds were blowing and there was a smell of snow in the air. She had feared that the snows might come and ruin their wedding day. Many Chippewa braves had taken invitations of bundles of tobacco to the other Chippewa villages, requesting their presence at the wedding, and many acceptances had been sent back in similar fashion.

Briana raised her eyes to Night Hawk. "You have returned from taking the invitations to some of the neighboring Chippewa villages?" she said, gently smoothing a hand across his cheek, still rosy and cold from the blustery winds of November. "Did you bring with you many acceptances?"

"As many as I took to them," Night Hawk said. "Many will come early tomorrow and pitch their tipis along the edge of the forest, in groups, or semicircles, each band distinct from the others by the paintings on their temporary dwellings. My woman, your artistic talents will be seen by many Chippewa tomorrow. They will be in awe of not only your talents, but also your beauty. I will be the envy of every brave who looks upon you."

"Darling, please . . ." Briana said, laughing softly. She could not stop a blush that was suffusing her face with its heat, yet she was so happy that her fiancé was proud of how she had helped with the preparations for their wedding day. Just for him, over the entrance of their wigwam she had painted in red and yellow a picture of a pipe and, directly opposite this, the rising sun. He had explained to her that this painting was symbolic of welcome and goodwill to men in the full light of day.

She prayed that the sun would shine brightly tomorrow, and that the snows would be delayed at least until after the ceremony. She wanted nothing to stand in the way of this wondrous day. She had waited too long to be his wife.

"My father also feels your painting on his dwelling is something special," Night Hawk said.

Briana, seeing something akin to pain enter his expression at the mention of his father, asked, "Haven't you yet accepted the fact that your father and Gentle Fawn are going to be married along with us?" Her question was guarded, for she was unsure of whether or not Night Hawk would ever completely accept Gentle Fawn as his stepmother. He still carried the pain of his mother's death inside his heart.

Briana was not sure if he would be able to accept the thought of his father making love to anyone but his mother.

"It is what my father wants," Night Hawk said sullenly. "He deserves happiness, too. How can I, a mere son, speak up against it?"

His lips formed a smile. "*Ay-uh*, I do accept what is to be, as well as accepting Gentle Fawn as part of my family," he said. "She also deserves some happiness in her life. For so long she was a victim of abuse. My father has erased the ugly memories from her mind."

He placed a hand on Briana's cheek, his expression

sweet and caring. "And there is also Gentle Fawn's child," he murmured. "She deserves a chance at happiness also. My father will give her that chance. He already loves her as though she were his own."

Briana eased into Night Hawk's arms, placing her cheek against the warmth of the buffalo robe. "Just keep those happy thoughts, my darling," she murmured. "It is best for your father. He is happy."

Night Hawk stroked his fingers through her flowing hair. "But never will I call Gentle Fawn *gee-mah-mah*," he said. "Never."

Briana leaned away from him. "No one would expect you to call her Mother," she said softly.

She swung away from him and turned to watch the activity in the council house beyond where she and the children had positioned the canvases. "Everything is so exciting," she said, clasping her hands before her. "I can hardly believe it is truly going to happen, Night Hawk. We are finally going to be married."

"It has been too long in coming," Night Hawk said. "But there will be no more interferences."

"No," Briana murmured. "None."

She watched the women scurrying around, preparing for the great feast that would be shared by all on her wedding day. Hunters had brought fowl and fish and fresh meat from the hunt. The meat of wild game had been put aside with much care during the previous fall in anticipation of such a feast. There was wild rice and the choicest of dried venison, as well as turnips and berries that had been stored in holes that had been dug deeply into the ground.

Her attention was drawn elsewhere when a brave came into the council house carrying something that she was not familiar with. As he came and stood before Night Hawk, she curiously eyed the bundle of arrows tied tightly together.

"Night Hawk, instead of bringing back a gift in response to the invitations carried to our people, I bring you something ugly," the brave said, handing the bundle to Night Hawk.

A pained expression entered Night Hawk's eyes as he took the arrows and closely examined them. "Where did you get these?" he grumbled, turning his dark eyes up at the brave. "Who sent these in response to our invitation?"

"It is a strange thing," the brave said, scratching his head. "It was not given to me, actually, from anyone in particular. I found it hanging from my saddle after I paid a visit to one of your closest friends in the Chippewa community. When I took them to him and questioned him about it, he said he knew nothing of them, nor would any of his people, for they held only good feelings for you and your father within their hearts."

"Then how?" Night Hawk said, his jaw tightening. "Who?"

"No one saw it being placed on my horse," the brave said, his voice strained. "The person responsible must be as elusive as a ghostly vision one imagines while traveling the dark haunts of the forest. This person moved quickly, Night Hawk. First he is there. And then he is gone. Poof. Like a breath of wind!"

Determinedly, Night Hawk strolled in a dignified manner toward one of the roaring lodge fires. He broke the arrows over his knee, then dropped them into the fire and watched them being consumed by the flames. "White Wolf," he said tightly. "This is the work of White Wolf."

"Or it might be Strong Branch," the brave offered. "He has become just as elusive as White Wolf, and perhaps as deadly. Will we ever know, Night Hawk, what caused him to turn against his own people? Killing Lily and Gray Moon makes no sense to me at all."

"Nor to me," Night Hawk mumbled, never liking to be reminded of his sister's murder, or of the man who had killed her.

Briana paled. She went to Night Hawk and placed a hand on his arm. "White Wolf? Strong Branch?" she cried. "Do you truly think one of them did this? Is one of them planning to ruin our wedding day? Is he planning an attack on our village?"

Night Hawk looked down at her with fire-lit eyes, then took her hands and squeezed them reassuringly. "Nothing will ruin our wedding day," he said. "Nor will anyone attack our village during the celebration. I promise you that, my woman. With every beat of my heart, I vow to you that nothing will stand in the way of our marriage."

He turned to the brave. "It is a warning," he said. "Alert everyone. And send many sentries out. Tell them to place themselves at strategic points so that no one can get past them. Shoot anyone that looks suspicious. I am weary of such intrusions."

"But there will be many arriving for the celebration," the brave said, his brow creased with worry. "This will make it hard to keep watch for an attack."

"Not so," Night Hawk argued. "All of the braves of our village are aware of who is and who is not their enemy. It will be easy to choose who is to be shot, and who is to be allowed to come on into our village."

The brave nodded in agreement, then turned and hurried from the council house.

Briana looked up at Night Hawk. "You called the arrows a warning," she said, fear creeping into her heart. "In which way, Night Hawk?"

"When a bundle of tied arrows is found at one's doorstep, in Indian language this means 'war to the teeth,' " he said solemnly. "The only difference is, the recipient of this dark gift usually knows who has sent them. This time Night Hawk is forced to guess. And of course, my heart tells me it is White Wolf."

Briana tightened her hands into fists at her sides. "I wish that renegade would drop dead," she said, rage engulfing her at the thought of the Sioux renegade ruining the most beautiful day of her life.

"If given the opportunity, I will make that wish come true," Night Hawk said, chuckling at how beautiful she looked even while angry.

"Briana! Briana!" one of the young braves suddenly said from behind her. "Look what I have sketched on your canvas!"

Together, Briana and Night Hawk went and looked at the drawing. Briana was quickly taken by the artistic talent of the young man. She was looking at the most vivid colors of a rainbow arched across a sky that was half sun and half rain, and at the end of the rainbow he had sketched a young brave on his knees, reaching his hands to the heavens as he seemingly prayed to his Great Spirit.

It was a touching sight, and at this moment Night Hawk took it as an omen—of peace and happiness for the generation of young braves this painting seemed to represent.

He placed his arm around the young man's shoulders. "Two Stones, you speak well through your painting," he said. "I can hear the message as clearly as though you were speaking the words from your mouth. It is good, Two Stones, that you have such feelings within your heart that leads you to draw such a painting. Perhaps you will even learn the ways of a shaman, and when you reach adulthood you can be the shaman of our tribe. You can speak then, and teach the ways of the Great Spirit, if you wish, through such paintings. Does such a suggestion please you?"

Two Stones turned his wide, dark eyes up at Night Hawk. His lips were parted in awe of what Night Hawk had said. All he could do was nod his head anxiously. Then he ran from the council house. His shouts of happiness proved that his voice had soon returned to him.

Tears were shining in Briana's eyes as she turned to Night Hawk. "That was so lovely," she said, wiping a tear from her eye as it swam to the corner. "So very, very lovely."

"At this moment Two Stones gives me cause to hope again for our future generation of braves," Night Hawk said, taking her hands and holding them. "But the fear of someone planning to make war against my people takes so much of my hopes away. I fear true peace will never come. There is always someone whose heart is dark with greed and hate. Peace! If only it could be achieved and kept."

"I imagine as long as there is man on the earth, there will be war," Briana said, heaving a sigh.

Together they walked from the council house out into the chill of the night. Briana looked heavenward when she felt the softness of snowflakes on her face. Earlier in the day she had prayed that it wouldn't snow. Later, when she had heard wolves howling, whose cries always portended a snowstorm, she had known that her prayers had not been heard, and she had expected the worst.

But now?

She thought that it might delay any warring against Night Hawk and his lovely people. A deep snowfall would not stop the marriage, but perhaps it could stop the enemy's approach.

28

The winds of heaven mix forever,
With a sweet emotion.
—SHELLEY

The heavy snowfall failed to materialize, and the visiting bands of Chippewa were received with much enthusiasm. As soon as the visitors had arrived and begun putting up their tipis, the women and girls of Echohawk's village built fires close to the visitors' campsites and cooked great quantities of food.

They then carried the food over and spread the feast for the visitors, waiting upon them with every attention.

The council house was filled with Chippewa braves who had donned their finest belts of wampum and their finest feathers, and women who had put on their best beaded garments. Before the wedding ceremony there was much dancing, singing and hugging.

But there was total silence when the wedding vows were exchanged. The ceremony itself was as simple as the touching of the hands, a few words spoken, and gentle embraces.

As with Echohawk and Gentle Fawn, Briana read in Night Hawk's eyes, and he in hers, the plighting of their troth.

And then the feast was enjoyed by all. Assortments of meat were strung on a pole over the fire to cook. The food was served on wooden platters, and soup passed in horn spoons of different sizes, some of them capable of holding enough to fill a large bowl.

Before the food was served, a small portion was placed in the fire as a blessing for the meal.

The feast was followed by more dancing and singing. Briana giggled as though having consumed too much wine as she tried to mimic the dance that Gentle Fawn was trying to teach her.

Dressed in his finest beaded garment of white doeskin and fancy headdress of feathers, matching the attire worn by his father, Night Hawk stood back from Briana, watching her sway to the beat of the tomtoms. Her doeskin dress, beaded beautifully with seashells and porcupine quills, clung to her voluptuous figure, making him want to reach out and grab her up into his arms and carry her away to their wigwam.

Tonight he wanted to make love endlessly to her. Until the morning sky became flooded with the sunrise did he want to whisper in her ear how much he loved her.

Even then it would be hard to let her go, for she was now his. She made his heart take flight and soar like the *mee-gee-see*, eagle.

He glanced over at his father, whose eyes were as intent on his new bride. Only a twinge of bitterness came to Night Hawk today in realizing that his mother had been replaced in his father's heart. But this resentment he quickly placed behind him. It was good to see his father happy again, to see some life in his eyes, and to see the spring he once again had in his step.

And Night Hawk found it easier to accept Gentle Fawn as each day passed. Like his Briana, Gentle Fawn was sweet like the songbirds in the trees in the spring.

And it was good to see how Briana and Gentle Fawn had become friends so quickly. This had also helped ease the tension between father and son.

Night Hawk cast a troubled glance toward the entrance of the council house. He had not been able to relax and enjoy the day as much as he would have liked. He still feared an attack. Even though he had sentries posted all around the village, White Wolf could arrive with so many warriors that no amount of sentries would stop him and the devastation he could cause.

Although Night Hawk's heart was here in the council house, he still kept his ears alert to all sounds outside it.

He gazed back to Briana, seeing her as nothing less than exquisite today. As she laughed and danced, the wisps of her long, flowing hair whipping about her flushed face, her well-rounded breasts bouncing beneath the soft fabric of the doeskin, he could not help but go to her and take her in his arms.

He led her away from the dancers and sat her down on a soft pile of bear pelts beside one of the four lodge fires, while Gentle Fawn and Echohawk settled down across the fire from them.

"You exhaust yourself before going to bed with your husband on your wedding night?" Night Hawk teased, flicking a strand of her hair back from her eyes with a finger. "That is not wise, my woman. Not wise at all."

Briana threw her head back as she laughed softly, allowing her hair to hang in long waves down her back. She marveled to herself over this dress she wore today. After the tanning procedure, the skin of the dress was exquisitely white, richer in sheen than fine broadcloth, and softer than velvet. It had been beautifully painted by her own hands, and trimmed with fringe and quillwork and lovely seashells.

Then she gazed over at Night Hawk. "My darling, don't you ever worry about your wife not having enough energy for you," she said, scooting over close to him, reveling in the strength of his arm as he swept it around her shoulders and held her close. "Don't you know that I live for our private moments together? Even now I wait with bated breath for you to carry me to our love nest."

Night Hawk chuckled. "I see that I have taught you well," he murmured. He held her close as everyone left the floor and sat down in a large circle around the great lodge fire.

Young braves stripped to their breechclouts and painted bodies then rose and began dancing around the fire. The agile and graceful use of their bodies these young men made was a marvel to see. They danced in quick-paced, flashy steps, their intent to keep pace with the drum while using a wide variety of hand, arm, leg, and body movements. This dance reflected the athletic ability of the dancers as they attempted to distinguish themselves from the other dancers that had already performed.

When these young braves concluded their performance, one by one several partially clad braves came into view and leapt into a circle, amid the larger circle of viewers, chanting songs and dancing to the beat of the tomtoms. Their breechcloths bounced, their headbands of feathers seemed to take flight, as they shook their bodies and bobbed their heads, their chants becoming louder, their dance becoming more frenzied.

Wild sage, the symbol of cleanliness and purity, was wrapped around the ankles and wrists of the dancers. Small sprigs of wild sage were also tied to the eagle-bone whistles next to the mouthpieces of some dancers, and when they began to feel thirsty, they bit off small pieces of the sage and chewed on it.

Briana noticed that all of the children were shuffled from the council house as several scantily clad maidens entered the circle of dancers and joined the dance. Their breasts swelled almost free of the band of fur wrapped around them, bouncing, it seemed, in time with the music. They wore a scant strip of fur around their lower abdomen, reaching down only far enough to cover their uppermost thighs.

Briana watched as the rhythm of the women dancers became more frenzied, soon joined by several braves who had only moments ago been observers. She watched as these braves joined the women in the frenzied movements.

Briana drew in a shaky breath when Night Hawk jumped to his feet and motioned for her to come with his outstretched hands.

She blushed and timidly shook her head, but that did not dissuade him. He reached down and grabbed both of her hands, pulling her to her feet before him.

Out of the corner of her eye Briana saw Gentle Fawn and Echohawk joining the dancers, their bodies almost locked as they swayed in rhythm with the tom-toms and chanting.

Soon Briana also felt her body responding to the drumbeat. She drifted toward Night Hawk, and soon moved into her husband's arms without any more coaxing. She twined her arms around his neck and pressed her breasts against him, finding it easy to forget her bashfulness while becoming entranced by the magic of the dance and the eyes of her beloved. She felt his thick arousal pressing against her stomach through their clothes and slid in a gyration of movements against him.

Becoming consumed herself with wild rapture, she closed her eyes and held her head back, his lips hot as he kissed the hollow of her throat.

Then when she felt that she was too close to that realm of pleasure that she wanted to enjoy only in the privacy of her bed, she stepped back from Night Hawk and reached a hand out to him, in her eyes a pleading that he understood.

He lifted her fully up into his arms and carried her away from the council house.

When they were inside their wigwam, and all was quiet except for their heavy breathing, they quickly disrobed each other.

They both groaned as their bodies met hurriedly. Briana gasped with pleasure as he drove his thickness deeply within her and began his heated strokes, which began lifting her up above herself, it seemed, as though she were floating.

Briana's nipples became taut and pleasure flowed through her as Night Hawk ran his fingers over the creamy curves of her flesh. She moaned against his chest as she placed her lips against his flesh. Night Hawk's hands slipped farther down her body and furled the hair at the juncture of her thighs, touching her swollen bud of desire, caressing it as he continued to move rhythmically within her.

Briana reciprocated by strolling her fingers across his muscular body, across his deep chest and straight shoulders; along his hard stomach and large and powerful thighs; and to that wonderful place between his legs. She splayed her fingers out between her thighs and where he was moving himself in and out of her, reveling even a moment's touch of that part of him that always set her body aflame.

She then moved her hands around him and locked her fingers into the flesh of his buttocks, urging his hips to press harder into her loins, the full length of him buried within her, yet wanting him to fill her even more deeply.

His strokes were strong and long, his face pressed

within the soft pillows of her breasts, his breathing raspy.

Briana closed her eyes and let the euphoria claim her. As his body tightened and hardened, she arched and cried out, and together they shared the explosion of ecstasy.

Echohawk carried Gentle Fawn into his wigwam. Before placing her on a pallet of furs on the floor beside the fire pit, he gave her a kiss, finding it sweet and wonderful.

He lay her on the furs, and as she smiled up at him, he removed her clothes. Then he bent down over her as she removed his garments.

When both were naked, Echohawk drew her up onto his lap, easing her legs around him and thrusting his thick shaft into her. As she clung to him around his neck, he ran his fingers over her smooth copper body, stopping at her abundant, milk-filled breasts.

She closed her eyes and sighed as he kneaded them, then lowered his mouth over one, flicking his tongue around the nipple. Then Echohawk lifted her away from him and lay her down on her back and knelt beside her, his tongue and lips paying homage to her every secret place.

She placed a hand on his head and urged him away. She moved to her knees beside him, pleasuring him in the same way, smiling up at him when the flick of her tongue drew a guttural sigh of pleasure from the depths of his throat.

Finding himself too close to that brink of bliss that he wanted only while deeply imbedded in her, Echohawk lifted her again away from him and lay her down beneath him, soon thrusting his hardness deeply within her again. Their bodies strained together and their lips burned from their heated kisses.

Soon they went over the edge into total ecstasy. They laid together, clinging, their bodies still tingling from their joyous moment—their first sexual joining as man and wife.

"You make Gentle Fawn so very happy," she murmured, kissing Echohawk gently on the cheek. "You are so good to me. Gentle Fawn will forever be grateful."

"You are my wife now," Echohawk said huskily. "I am the one who is grateful."

Gentle Fawn smiled sweetly and snuggled against him again.

Wrapped warmly in buffalo robes, Briana and Night Hawk sat beside the fire, feeding each other pieces of sliced apple. "Can this truly be happening?" Briana said, beaming with the bliss of being married after having thought she might never see Night Hawk again. "Are we truly husband and wife?"

"Although the ceremony was a simple one, *ay-uh*, we are married," Night Hawk said, chuckling. He reached his hand inside Briana's robe and brought one of her breasts within his fingers, drawing an ecstatic sigh.

"You had better remove your hand, or my darling, you will have to give me more of what such caresses promise," Briana said, daring him with a flashing smile.

She leaned into his hand as he moved it from her breast, smoothing it along her ribs, down the flat plane of her stomach, and then between her thighs, where she was still tender from their previous lovemaking.

She gasped as he pushed his finger up inside her and began thrusting it gently, over and over again.

"My darling, please . . ." Briana whispered, her face becoming flushed from rising passion.

She laughed throatily when he suddenly clasped his hands on her shoulders and half threw her on the pallet of furs, casting off her robes and his gaze feasted on her velveteen softness. She tossed the apple aside and closed her eyes, trembling with pleasure as again Night Hawk began kissing his way down her body. Her eyes suddenly flew open with alarm when a gunshot broke the reverie, and the sounds of the celebration at the council house stopped.

Night Hawk bolted to his feet and pulled on his breeches. He hurried into his moccasins and shirt and grabbed a fur robe around his shoulders before stepping out into the chill night wind.

Briana hurried into her own clothes and raced after him, stopping when one of the village braves came into the light of the great outdoor fire, carrying a limp body in his arms.

"Wise Owl," Night Hawk said, gasping as he recognized the old Indian.

Echohawk stepped up beside Night Hawk, his gaze locked on Wise Owl's death stare. "Wise Owl," he said, his voice drawn.

With a nod of his head Night Hawk motioned to the brave to place Wise Owl on the ground.

"He was moving stealthily toward our village with a loaded rifle," the brave explained. "When I yelled at him to ask him why he was there, since everyone knows of his banishment from our tribe, he turned his rifle on me. But before he got the chance to shoot me, I shot him first."

"And so *he* is the one responsible for the gift of bound arrows," Echohawk said, his jaw tight. "He hated us so much that he returned to kill his own kind."

"*Ay-uh*, it is sad. Yet I am much relieved to know that only he was the threat. Everyone can sleep in peace tonight," Night Hawk said, trying to find something good about the unfortunate circumstances of someone who was once a beloved brave of the Chippewa.

"Finally the old man has found a semblance of peace, even if death was the only way he could achieve it," Echohawk grumbled. He nodded toward the brave. "Take him away. See to his burial."

Echohawk turned to another brave. "Send word to the sentries they can be relieved of their posts and return to the village," he said. "It is safe now for everyone to resume their normal activities."

Echohawk returned to Gentle Fawn and held her close as he fought back tears of regret over Wise Owl and how he had become someone unknown to him.

Night Hawk walked with Briana back to their wigwam, and clung to her beside their lodge fire, fighting back his own tears.

The gunshot in the distance had sounded like a lone clap of thunder echoing through the forest. White Wolf and Strong Branch hovered over a camp fire. "Today dual marriages were performed in Echohawk's village," White Wolf said, squinting over at Strong Branch. "To get them off guard, I allowed it. Tomorrow we will arrive at sunup at their village, when they least expect it. They will then know who sent them the gift of arrows."

White Wolf laughed boisterously, his breath like white silver against the dark shawl of the night.

Then he grew serious as he glanced over his shoulder at the many renegades that he had managed to round up for the attack. He gazed intently into Strong Branch's eyes. "When you found Wise Owl wandering in the forest, it was clever of you to give him a rifle, suggesting he use it to achieve his vengeance," he said, smiling crookedly. "This drew the attention away from us, the true danger. And you knew he'd get shot before he got anywhere near the village. Yes, Strong Branch, that was clever."

Strong Branch offered no response, in his eyes a strange, haunting sadness.

29

I saw the arrow from the bow-string part;
I heard the hoarse, blood-freezing war-whoop well;
I heard the victor shout—the dying yell.
—ANONYMOUS

Night Hawk awakened with a start, sweat pearling his brow. Briana leaned up on an elbow, eyes wide, the morning light spiraling down from the smoke hole in the ceiling, giving enough light for her to see the fear etched onto her husband's face.

"Good Lord, what is it?" she gasped, reaching a hand to his brow and smoothing the perspiration from his flesh with her fingers. "You awakened as though you were shot."

Night Hawk turned troubled eyes to Briana. "In my dream I was," he said. "And also my father." He clasped her and drew her into his embrace. "Also you, my love."

Placing her cheek on his bare chest, Briana clung to him, feeling his rapid heartbeat thudding. "I'm sure you dreamed that because of Wise Owl's death," she murmured. "Please forget it, darling. We've so much to be happy about. Let us enjoy it."

"*Ay-uh*, I am sure you are right," Night Hawk said, easing her out of his arms. He urged her back down onto the pelts which covered their sleeping platform. He swept the covering of pelts away from her, his gaze warming her flesh where his eyes touched her with a caress.

"I never get enough of you," he said, smoothing his

hands across her stomach, eliciting a low moan from deep within her. "Perhaps we shall spend the day making love. We would not be missed among our people. Not today, the second day of our marriage."

Although every nerve ending in her body cried out for his tender caresses, and feeling as though she would be neglecting him by refusing to stay with him for a day of lovemaking, Briana crept away from him and rose from the sleeping platform. She sighed with regret for the plans that she had made for early this morning when he gazed up at her with keen disappointment and puzzlement in his eyes.

"Why do you say no to Night Hawk, your new husband?" he said, reaching toward her, beckoning for her to return. "It is not what I would expect of you the second day of our marriage."

"And I am sorry," Briana said, moving back onto the platform, kneeling beside him. She kissed him sweetly on the lips, then took his hands and held them. "I promise never to let this happen again. Every morning from now on will be yours. But today I can't. Yesterday, while painting with the children of our village, somehow I got drawn into agreeing to take many of them into the forest with canvases today, to paint the wondrous scenes of winter. When they asked, even begged, how could I say no?"

"There is not enough of you to share," Night Hawk teased, laughing softly. Then he nodded. "*Ay-uh*, today is the children's. Tonight and tomorrow are mine."

Briana threw her arms around his neck and gave him another kiss, then bounced from the sleeping platform. She went to a peg on the wall on which hung her buckskin dresses and chose one with long sleeves and also warm leggings to wear beneath them.

Night Hawk rose from the platform, yawning and

stretching his arms over his head, then grabbed a pair of fringed leggings and jerked them up his muscular legs. "If my life were guided by my dreams I would not allow you or the children to go into the forest today," he said, giving her a troubled glance as he reached for his long-sleeved buckskin shirt. He also yanked this on, soon positioning his headband around his brow. "But as it was only a dream, it would be foolish to deny the children their day in the forest with you. Wise Owl sent the bundled arrows. And he is now dead."

"But have you so easily forgotten White Wolf?" Briana asked, drawing her hairbrush through her long hair. "Where do you think he has made his new hide-out, Night Hawk? Perhaps he has even fled to Canada. You may never have him to worry about again."

"The Chippewa never forget any Sioux that have been a threat to them in the past," Night Hawk said, slipping into his moccasins, then squatting on his haunches beside the glimmering coals in the fire pit. He began stirring them and placing fresh wood on. He fanned them with his hands as they began to smoke and sputter.

"The Sioux never forget their enemy the Chippewa," he said. "Especially the Sioux renegade White Wolf. He hates all Chippewa, especially those with the names Echohawk and Night Hawk. He will come one day and prove how deeply this hatred is imbedded in his heart. He will come to kill and maim our innocent people. My father and I will not truly rest in this lifetime until White Wolf is dead."

"But, darling, I was told that White Wolf caused your people no problems for many years," Briana said, trying to ease his doubts. "Perhaps it will be the same again. Perhaps he is gone again until, let's say—maybe another twenty or so years?"

"He does not have enough years left," Night Hawk hissed. "Although my father's heart seems younger today because he is bedding a young wife, he is a man of sixty winters—and so is White Wolf. If he waited twenty winters to achieve his vengeance, he might be too old even to lift his bow and arrow against his arch enemies."

He rose to his full height and turned to Briana, whose hair was now free of tangles and hanging lustrously glossy and long down her back. He placed his hands on her waist and drew her against his hard body. "My woman, no matter when he comes to face his enemy, I will be here to protect you," he said, brushing a kiss across her lips. "Also the children that seek teaching from you, like they are your own children, for they are the future of our people."

"Night Hawk," Briana said, gazing unblinkingly up at him. "You speak of children with so much affection. I hope to become with child soon. That will complete my happiness, my darling."

"A child would please me very much," Night Hawk said, then jerked away from her, his eyes wide with alarm.

"What is it?" Briana asked, his alarm causing icy chills to run up and down her spine.

"Listen!" Night Hawk said, his jaw tight. "Do you not hear the hoot of an owl? I hear it sometimes in my sleep, for my father taught me long ago that it is deemed wise to impress the sound of an owl early upon the mind of a child."

"But why?" Briana whispered, stepping closer to him, flinching when she herself heard the distinct sound coming from somewhere in the nearby forest.

"The hoot of an owl is commonly imitated by Indian scouts on a warpath," he said, grabbing his rifle. "So often in the past with the Chippewa, a dreadful massacre immediately followed the call."

Concerned, he turned back to Briana. He thrust the rifle into her hand. "You stay in our dwelling and if the enemy somehow gets past me, kill him," he flatly ordered.

Briana swallowed back a lump of fear that had lodged in her throat. She nodded anxiously, then watched as he grabbed another rifle, then rushed from the wigwam.

Briana felt faint when war whoops suddenly filled the air, followed by much gunfire and cries of pain. She could not stand to stay inside the wigwam, like a coward, when she heard some of the Chippewa screaming, so many silenced, surely by either arrows or bullets as the massacre became widespread throughout the village.

Briana did not stop to pull on a robe to ward off the cold of the day. She knew that her gunpower was needed. And as she stepped outside, what she saw caused a keen lightheadedness to sweep through her. Many innocent Chippewa had been killed, both women and children. Some braves were lying wounded on the ground.

Desperately, Briana looked around to see if Night Hawk was all right, and also Echohawk. But she saw neither in the confusion of the fighting.

Her gaze was wrenched to a scene that made her almost faint dead away. Somehow she found the strength to lift the rifle, aim, and shoot a Sioux renegade in the back just after he had scalped a woman and leaped away with a whoop, her bloody scalp held tightly in his hand.

Briana watched the Sioux renegade's body lurch with the impact of her bullet. She was glad when he finally fell forward, his face hidden from her view as it went straightforward onto the ground.

Other high-pitched war cries split the air.

Torches sputtered and flared to life.

A horde of screaming Sioux renegades began running through the village, tossing the torches onto the wigwams. Others sent their bullets crashing through the smoke flaps and pole tips of the painted lodges, toppling buffalo hide walls into the cooking fires.

Although shaken by the experience, filled with a keen sadness for those people that only last night had celebrated her marriage to Night Hawk, Briana aimed over and over again at the warring renegades, smiling triumphantly when she hit her target and was able to stop at least some of the vengeful acts of the Sioux.

She took a step back, gasping, when only a few feet away from her a woman staggered. She caught herself momentarily to stand tall and unafraid beside her husband as he then was also shot.

Briana sobbed as both victims crumpled to the ground, and her heart ached as she watched their hands seek each other's. Just as their hands became tightly clasped, both convulsed, their eyes staring blankly into each other's.

Briana lowered her rifle and covered her ears with her hands. She closed her eyes as the deadly hail of gunfire screeched all about her. She could not help it when she began screaming, for the infernal tumult was now too much for her to bear.

A strong arm around her waist drew her back into herself as her eyes opened widely and found Night Hawk there, drawing her protectively behind him.

"You were told to stay in the dwelling!" he shouted, standing in front of her, aiming and firing. "Do you not see the women and children? The Sioux have no pity! They have come to totally annihilate the Chippewa!"

"Your father! Gentle Fawn and Moonstar!" Briana cried. "Have they been killed?"

"My father led Gentle Fawn and Moonstar into the forest for safety and then returned. Until now he stood beside me, father and son, fighting the Sioux as though one heartbeat," he shouted, then began smiling as he watched some of the Sioux retreating.

"My father is fine!" Night Hawk added. "He will not allow death to claim him so soon after becoming alive again with a new wife!"

He proudly watched as the Chippewa braves went after the Sioux renegades, not allowing them to advance farther than the edges of their village without first becoming the recipient of a poisoned arrow.

Then his smile faded when he caught his first sight of White Wolf among those who remained in the village alive. In the fierceness of the beginning battle, Night Hawk had not seen any recognizable faces. To him the enemy was the enemy. To him, as he fired his rifle, they were nameless. They were faceless.

But now he was focusing on the face. White Wolf was approaching Echohawk from behind! His tomahawk was raised. . . .

Briana caught the terrifying sight almost at the same instant as Night Hawk. Quickly, as though some hidden spirit had drawn her there, Briana stepped around Night Hawk, lifted her rifle, and fired. She missed White Wolf's body, but instead shot the tomahawk from his hand.

His hand bleeding, White Wolf whipped around and stared disbelievingly at Briana, who still stood poised with the rifle, frozen at what she had achieved!

Night Hawk smiled down at her, then ran to White

Wolf and knocked him to the ground, placing a moccasined foot on his chest, to hold him there.

Briana noticed an abrupt silence around her. She glanced on all sides, seeing that no more Sioux remained alive in the village. They were dead—the recipients of poisoned arrows and gunshot wounds. But she noticed that unlike the Sioux who had viciously removed many scalps today, none of the Chippewa had scalped their enemies.

Suddenly she spotted one of the injured renegades moving. She watched as this person reached for a rifle, leaned up on one elbow, and aimed at Night Hawk.

Briana was too stunned this time to react with her firearm. She began screaming. "Night Hawk!" she cried. "Fall to the ground, Night Hawk!"

Echohawk scanned quickly around him. Catching sight of the renegade whose aim was on his son, he lifted his rifle, aimed, and fired.

Night Hawk turned with a start and saw the renegade's rifle fall limply from his hand. Then he recognized the face as the Indian gazed up at him with wide eyes and blood curling from his nose and lips.

"Strong Branch!" Night Hawk gasped, allowing his grip on White Wolf to loosen.

Before he realized what was happening, White Wolf had grabbed his leg and yanked him to the ground, soon straddling and choking him.

Night Hawk grabbed a knife from its sheath at White Wolf's waist and lunged upward, thrusting it deeply into White Wolf's groin. At almost the same time two gunshots rang out, the bullets lodging in White Wolf's back.

Echohawk and Briana exchanged knowing glances as their rifles smoked in the early morning air.

Night Hawk brushed White Wolf's limp body away from him and rose nobly to his feet. He went to

Strong Branch, who was gasping for breath and clutching his chest. He knelt down beside the fallen young chief and lifted his head from the ground.

"First Wise Owl betrays his people, and now you? You hated your people so much you would bring such disaster to them?" Night Hawk cried. "Strong Branch, as children we were friends. When did you decide to be not only my enemy but also our people's? You even killed my sister, the woman who you were to marry. Why, Strong Branch? Your actions became that of a madman, not someone who once was my devoted friend."

Strong Branch coughed fitfully, spewing blood from his mouth, then gazed sadly up at Night Hawk. "Strong Branch did not become your enemy because of hatred," he said breathlessly. "But out of love of power instead." Through a broken speech he admitted many truths to Night Hawk: about Gray Moon killing Lily, that she had been with child; about his having killed Gray Moon, and about his and Gray Moon's roles in the raids, and why he had done these things against the Chippewa.

Strong Branch reached for Night Hawk and clasped his shoulder. "From . . . the . . . depths of my heart, I am sorry," he rasped. "Today I became witness to what my drive for power caused. I became . . . a part of something that will keep . . . me . . . from entering paradise."

Strong Branch clutched desperately at Night Hawk's shoulder as his tear-filled eyes became locked in a death stare.

Briana stifled a horrified gasp behind her hand, then slowly turned and gazed at the death and destruction in the village.

A sudden thought seized her—that she was, in part, responsible. Had she not defied her uncle by coming to live with Night Hawk, perhaps none of this would have happened. Blackie had planted the seed of the Chippewa's destruction inside not only White Wolf's heart but also Strong Branch's. She could not help but think that had she never allowed herself to become involved with Night Hawk, none of this would have happened. For many years White Wolf had kept his distance from Echohawk's people. There had to have been a cause for his changed mind, to wreak havoc on their lives.

"I am that cause," she whispered to herself. Tears rushing from her eyes, she turned and ran blindly away from the death scene. Panting hard, unaware of the harshness of the cold penetrating her thin buckskin attire, she ran into the fringes of the forest.

When a hand gripped her arm, stopping her, she turned weeping eyes up at Night Hawk as he spun her around to face him.

"Let me go!" she cried, trying to wrench herself free. "I have brought nothing but heartache to your people. Everything is my fault! Everything! I should've never allowed feelings to develop between us. Especially—especially after seeing how my uncle felt about you. I should have known that he would do everything within his power to cause problems for you because of your feelings for me."

She lowered her eyes. "Let me go, Night Hawk," she softly pleaded. "I wish to go to Paris, to be with my parents. I should've never come to Minnesota in the first place."

Night Hawk gave her a soft shake, causing her to look quickly up at him again. "What you are saying are words your uncle would want you to say," he murmured. "If you leave me, that is what he would want you to do. Are you going to allow him, even in death, to tear us apart?"

"I don't want to," Briana said, her voice breaking. "But—"

"I will not hear any more about it," Night Hawk said flatly. "Nor will I allow you ever to speak of blaming yourself again. Everything you have done has been in the best interests of your husband and his people. They know this. I know this. And so shall you, my woman, for I will not allow you to think otherwise."

Gentle Fawn stepped into view, snug in a buffalo robe, her bundled child pressed to her bosom. Her eyes were filled with fear as she moved slowly toward Night Hawk and Briana.

"My husband?" Gentle Fawn whispered. "Is he alive?"

Seeing the fear etched onto Gentle Fawn's tiny face made Briana quit thinking of herself. She knew that the young Chippewa maiden was again experiencing the terror that Echohawk had hoped he had saved her from.

Briana went to her and placed a comforting arm around her waist. "Echohawk is just fine," she murmured, casting Night Hawk a nervous glance as she recalled the bloody remains that lay strewn across the ground at the village. "But, Gentle Fawn, I don't think you want to go to the village. What you would see is not a pleasant sight."

"Gentle Fawn is strong," she said, determinedly walking straight ahead. "In my lifetime I have seen much death. I want my husband. I want to see my husband!"

"Let her go," Night Hawk said, stepping back to stand beside Briana. She turned to him and accepted the warmth of his embrace as he held her close to him. "Today will live within my mind forever," she whispered, shuddering.

"I shall help erase the memory, my love," Night Hawk whispered back.

Then he held her away from him, realizing that she was not wearing proper clothing to protect her from the cold. He picked her up in his arms and began running back toward the village with her.

Once there, he took her to their wigwam—one of the few that had not been destroyed by the enemy. He lay her close to the fire and covered her with several pelts. Her chills reached clean into his soul as he watched her shivering. "You stay here while I go and help see to the wounded and dead," he said. "I do not want to add your body to the burial grounds also."

Briana nodded anxiously, glad to be able to escape the gruesome sights. She relished the warmth of his lips as he kissed her, then turned toward the fire, shuddering anew when within the leaping flames she saw a reenactment of the grueling, bloody battle.

She pressed her eyes tightly closed, her sobs filling the awkward silence of her home.

30

Sing me a sweet, low song of night
Before the moon is rising.
—HAWTHORNE

The rebuilt Chippewa village basked in the heat of July. Wild rice was growing in abundance in the river beds, and the crops were knee high in the garden patches.

Briana and Gentle Fawn waddled toward the council house, their shadows on the ground beside them revealing their swollen abdomens. Both were now eight months heavy with child.

Briana wheezed and wiped beads of sweat from her brow, each heavy footstep an effort. She placed her hands at the small of her back, laughing lightly when she saw Gentle Fawn follow her lead, her own discomfort matching Briana's.

"I wish I hadn't gained so much weight," Briana said, groaning.

"I gained even more weight with my first child," Gentle Fawn said, giggling as she peered over at Briana with her dark eyes. "And then I thought I was so miserable. Perhaps this time I will have a boy child, do you think, Briana?"

Briana turned her gaze to sweet Moonstar as the child walked in short, awkward steps beside her mother, clinging trustingly to her hand. She was touched deeply by Moonstar, having become as close to the child as if she were her own. "I don't think you would be all that disappointed if you had another girl, would you?" she said, smiling as the tiny, delicate thing smiled widely up at her. "Moonstar is so sweet. Surely boys aren't as sweet or adorable."

Gentle Fawn laughed softly. "Boy children are not supposed to be sweet and adorable," she said. "They must be taught ways of men from the beginning—to be strong, brave, and noble. Boys would not want to be cuddled, for that would make them feel as though the elders would look at them as no more than a girl."

Briana's smile wavered, hardly able to imagine any child of hers not being cuddled. She could remember her father singing her lullabys. Her mother had taught her nursery rhymes while she had cozied on her lap. She would want no less attention for her child, even if he were a son.

"I see your smile is not as bright at my mention of a boy child," Gentle Fawn said. "Do not worry so about what is expected of them. They learn by watching, listening, and imitating their fathers, by observing ways of their fathers, imitating examples placed before them. Slowly and naturally the faculties of observation and memory become highly trained in the manners, lore, and customs of our people without a strained, conscious effort. Body and mind grow together."

"That is such a lovely explanation," Briana said, smiling again at Gentle Fawn. "A son born to me and Night Hawk would surely be very wise and self-confident, for his father is filled with much wisdom and patience to teach it."

"The world of the Indian boy child teems with life and wisdom," Gentle Fawn explained. "From childhood their life is filled with a great desire to do, to be, and to grow. They all yearn for wisdom. They feel if they grow wise, their people will honor them. If they become very brave, they should be like their father; and if they become a good hunter, it would please their mother."

"I hope one day I will be as knowledgeable of children, and of what is expected of me, the mother," Briana said softly.

"Always remember that just as tiny roots of a plant silently absorb the earth food, so does the consciousness of the child absorb the influences which surround them," Gentle Fawn said. "Also, Briana, you will learn the ways of Chippewa mothers by watching and listening to those who already hold the proud title of *gee-mah-mah*."

As they approached the entrance to the council house, all talk of children ceased. Chippewa men and women were entering the large dwelling, their faces solemn. Although several months had passed since the massacre, this was the first meeting of the Chippewa to discuss their future. Until now, everyone had concentrated on mourning their loved ones and rebuilding the village. And now that both were done, Echohawk had called his people together so that they could put their hearts and minds together and gain hope for their future from one another.

If they could forget that tragic day, they would now get a sense of sweetness and peace in the joined villages. But these were times of false fronts, everyone pretending that all was well in their worlds, while deep within their souls they were crying for all that had been taken from them.

Briana waited for Gentle Fawn to grab Moonstar up into her arms, and then they went together into the large council house, where no fires had been lit in the fire pits due to the sweltering heat that hung over everyone as though the fires of hell had been set loose around them.

The lighting for the dwelling was from the opened

holes in the ceiling where the smoke usually escaped. These holes had been widened to allow more light and air into the spacious room. Briana soon spotted Night Hawk and his father, who sat together on a platform high above everyone.

As Briana sat down beside Gentle Fawn, she could hardly take her eyes off her husband. He was sitting with his legs crossed and his arms folded across his muscular copper chest, his raven black hair held back with a headband that she had just finished beading for him that day. Breechcloths were his and his father's only other attire.

Even though she was a very married and pregnant woman, the mere sight of Night Hawk could send her heart into a tailspin of passion, her pulse racing as proof of her feelings for him. Oh, how she was physically attracted to him! It would be an easy task to have many children with him. She could hardly imagine a night without showing him just how much she loved and adored him.

Briana was aware of the total silence around her. By now everyone was in the council house, each one sitting on mats on the floor.

A long-stemmed calumet pipe was passed from man to man, a tangible link that joined man to Wenebojo, every puff of smoke that ascended in prayer unfailingly reaching his presence. With the pipe, faith was upheld, ceremony sanctified, and the being consecrated. It signified brotherhood, peace its greatest significance of all.

As the last man smoked from the pipe, then laid it aside, Briana looked slowly around her and saw the intensity with which everyone stared up at Night Hawk and Echohawk, trusting that they were going to lead them into a brighter future that hopefully would no longer involve surprise attacks from their enemies.

Echohawk rose tall and erect over his people, looking slowly around the room, from man to man, woman to woman, and child to child, his eyes lingering a moment longer on his wife.

Then, as he again gazed around the room, he began speaking softly and eloquently, as though his words were touching them in a caress. "My beloved Chippewa," he said, "it is with sadness that I have witnessed these past months of mourning brought upon you by those who were our enemy. But the time of mourning is now past, and it is time to rebuild faith and hope within our hearts. You are a strong, compassionate people. You have endured everything with squared shoulders and straight backs. And so will you endure whatever else befalls you, be it good or bad. But, my beloved Chippewa, we must think with a smile, and know that what lies before us is good. There are among you women blossoming with children within their wombs; my wife and my son's wife are also sweet with child. These children will be born into a kinder world and will carry on the peace-loving name of the Chippewa even after we, the parents and grandparents, are walking the roads of the hereafter."

He turned toward Night Hawk and placed a hand on his shoulder. "Rise, my son," he said. "I have something else to say that our people must be witness to."

With much grace and ease Night Hawk rose to stand beside his father. When their eyes met and held, Night Hawk saw such wisdom in the depths of his father's, yet something else—a soft gleam, as though something wonderful was just about to be released from the depths of his soul.

"My son, it is now time for me to step down from

my duties as chief of our joined villages and proclaim
you chief," Echohawk said, his voice steady. "I do
this with much pride, for in you there is much compassion and wisdom that has been carried down through
the generations of Chippewa before you, through
blood ties of your forefathers. In your hands now lie
the future and hopes of our people. I see this as no
risk at all."

Touched deeply by what she was witnessing, Briana
wiped tears of joy from her eyes. She smiled over at
Gentle Fawn as she glanced her way, realizing that in
part Echohawk's decision at this time was because of
her. He wanted to spend more time with his young
wife. His time with Gentle Fawn was surely more precious because of his age. His time with his children
was also more precious.

When Night Hawk began to talk, Briana turned her
head and gazed at him, at this moment idolizing him
as never before.

"I accept the title of chief with a warm heart and
much gratitude," Night Hawk said, reaching a hand
to his father's shoulder. "I will carry the title with a
lifted chin and squared shoulders. I will never give
you cause to regret having lent me the title you have
carried so graciously for so long. Like your father before you, you are cherished by everyone. I hope that
at my age of sixty winters, I will be as cherished."

"And that you will, my son," Echohawk said, drawing Night Hawk into his embrace and giving him an
earnest hug.

Echohawk whispered into Night Hawk's ear, "My
son, one more thing. You must endeavor to equal
your father and grandfather as peacemakers."

Night Hawk returned his promise in a whisper.
"You have my word," he said, then they broke away
from each other, standing arm in arm as everyone

stood and broke into loud chants, proclaiming their acceptance of what Echohawk had chosen to do that day.

They stepped down from the platform side by side and received the warm hugs and kisses from their people. When the council was over, and the people had gone to their own corners of their private worlds, Briana and Night Hawk stood with Echohawk and Gentle Fawn. The former chief was holding Moonstar in his arms, his child in almost every sense of the word.

"It is done," Echohawk said, smiling over at Night Hawk. "My son, it has been good to watch you grow into a man. It will be good to watch you preside as chief over our people. I saw no need in delaying the process of son following father into chieftainship until I was on my journey to the hereafter. Now I have the opportunity to witness firsthand how you choose to use my teachings. *Ay-uh*, you will have your own views on things in council that will bring changes to our village, and the lives of our people. But that is how it should be. You are of a young mind and heart. Youthful thoughts and ideas will be welcomed."

He grew solemn for a moment as he looked into Night Hawk's dark eyes. "It is true that Strong Branch wanted to bring young ideas to the council, but his were twisted, as was his loyalty, it seems," he said, his voice drawn. "And of course we know who we must blame for this. Wise Owl. He was Strong Branch's adviser long before he began to seek ways to oust me from power. Wise Owl placed hatred and greed inside Strong Branch's heart, I am sure, as early as when he took his first step in this world. Had Nee-kah lived, she would have never allowed Wise Owl's interference in her young son's life."

"Nee-kah?" Briana said, raising an eyebrow. "Who is Nee-kah?"

"Nee-kah was Strong Branch's mother, and Mariah's best friend after she came to live as my wife among the Chippewa," Echohawk said, giving Gentle Fawn a troubled glance, relieved that she did not show any signs of resentment over him speaking about his second wife. Yet he knew that she was not the sort to be jealous. Her sweetness was genuine.

"And she died young?" Briana asked, slipping an arm through Night Hawk's, at this moment so enjoying this time of camaraderie with her husband's father, this moment seeming to draw them closer, yes, into a true family.

"*Ay-uh*, she left this earth much too soon," Echohawk grumbled. "It was a strange death. One day she was well. The next she was dead." He tightened his jaw and anger filled his eyes. "I suspect she was poisoned."

"Poisoned?" Night Hawk said, shock registering in his eyes. "You have never spoken of that theory to me before, *gee-bah-bah*."

"My son, never had I thought of it before," Echohawk said, his voice shallow. "But now it all fits together as though one fits pieces together of a puzzle. Wise Owl never approved of Nee-kah as Silver Wing's wife. She was headstrong. Wise Owl accused her of being a woman of defiance. Then when Strong Branch was born, and Silver Wing was dead, Wise Owl wanted full control of Strong Branch. As long as Nee-kah was alive, she would not allow it—even though Wise Owl was the wisest of Strong Branch's tribe and a close adviser of Chief Silver Wing. Nee-kah became wary of Wise Owl's intentions. Wise Owl saw her as a threat. I am sure he placed poison into her food."

Echohawk hung his head. "And what a loss it was," he said softly.

Moonstar started to wail, bringing everyone out of

their saddened reverie. Echohawk was jolted somewhat by the sudden blast of lungs, then laughed and
gazed down. He touched Moonstar's cheek gently as
he looked into her beautiful eyes fringed with thick,
dark lashes gazing up at him, not even tears spoiling
their loveliness.

"And so you are always hungry, it seems," Echohawk said, placing a gentle kiss on Moonstar's brow.
"I think you need your mother for that, not your *gee-
bah-bah*."

He handed the child to Gentle Fawn, and although
Moonstar was now past her first birthday, Gentle
Fawn slipped a corner of her dress down and let the
child's tiny hands clutch the proffered milk-swollen
breast, her perfectly shaped lips already sucking on
the taut nipple.

"Her supper is always available," Night Hawk said,
chuckling as he watched the child. He placed an arm
around Briana's waist and leaned down into her face.
"Soon we will be an audience to our own child feeding
from its mother. What a joyous sight that will be!"

"My darling, I want to keep a child suckling at my
breast forever," Briana said, smiling up at him. "We
shall have to build a monstrous wigwam to make space
for all of the children I will have for you."

Night Hawk chuckled again, realizing that, of course,
she was speaking out of inexperience. Perhaps two
children would do for her once she realized the re-
sponsibilities involved in raising a child.

She needed time for her other passion—her painting. And he was going to see that she had it. He did
not need a brood of children to prove his virility. Having Briana as his woman was proof enough, for what
man would not give his right arm to have such a
woman for a wife?

Night Hawk and Briana bid Echohawk and Gentle

Fawn a pleasant good-bye, then took a long, leisurely stroll through the forest. Evening was nigh. The air had cooled to a tolerable level. The breeze was sweet and filled with the fragrance of the blossoms of a wild crabtree and lilacs, which grew heavy in bloom on many bushes throughout the forest.

The birds overhead were making a racket as they settled into their nests for the night. A squirrel scampered from tree limb to tree limb, taking flight, it seemed as though it had wings.

"I so love the forest," Briana said, taking small steps, all that her large belly would allow. "It is as though I were born here, myself, a part of it. It touches my very soul with its loveliness." She closed her eyes and inhaled deeply. "The fragrances are so sweet, as though someone has opened many large bottles of French perfume and sprayed fine mists into the air."

Her eyes opened quickly as she felt Night Hawk's hands on her waist, stopping her from going any farther. She smiled up at him. "My darling, in your eyes I see something quite familiar," she murmured. She placed a hand to his cheek. "It is the look you get when you desire me."

"Flower of my wigwam, I desire you always," Night Hawk said huskily, leaning down to flick his tongue across her soft lips. He drew her as close as her tummy would allow and kissed her, touching her tongue through her parted lips.

Briana knew that soon she would not be able to make love with Night Hawk until after the birth of their child, but that time was not yet upon her. So she welcomed his arms as he lowered her slowly to the ground on a soft cushion of leaves.

As though in a gesture of worship, Night Hawk knelt over her and smoothed her dress up, past her stomach, then framed the large, tight ball between his hands. Bending lower over her, he kissed her stomach, then placed a cheek against her flesh as she twined her fingers through his hair.

"Do you feel our child's moving within me?" Briana murmured, herself feeling the slight kicking movements. Some days they were more energetic than others. Today, the child seemed to sense the peace within her heart, for its movements were soft and sweet inside her womb.

Night Hawk pressed an ear against her abdomen. His eyes widened as his lips spread into a smile. "I hear so many strange sorts of sounds," he said. "Our child is eager to begin its journey of life with its *gee-mah-mah* and *gee-bah-bah*."

"And it will soon," Briana whispered, placing her hands to Night Hawk's cheeks, urging his lips to hers. "Kiss me, my darling chief. Hold me. I love you so much."

As Night Hawk kissed her, he managed to remove his breeches, then he felt her breath catch as he very gently shifted the strength of his arousal within her. In a shared, spiraling need, their bodies moved rhythmically together.

Soon they joined on another flight of bliss, as though once again on the widespread wings of an eagle, soaring high into the heavens, reaching the moon, the stars.

Afterward, Night Hawk lay beside Briana, cuddling her close. The stars were fresh in the sky, the Milky Way creating a wave of light above them. "My woman, you are everything to me," he said, caressing her swollen abdomen, again feeling the movements of his child within it. "And soon we will be a family."

Briana snuggled closer. "I am so proud of you," she whispered. She smiled up at him. "And I have been remiss in saying something to you that needs saying."

"Oh, and what is that?" Night Hawk said, turning to face her, his hands cupping her heavy-laden breasts as he reached higher up inside her dress.

"Congratulations, my darling," she whispered, leaning up to kiss his cheek. "You are now the chief of your people. My sweet chieftain husband, congratulations."

"It means much more to me now that I have you at my side," Night Hawk said, smoothing her dress down to ward off the chill of the night.

Night Hawk offered her a hand and helped her up from the ground. "Come," he said softly. "Let us return to our dwelling. Let us lie down together. Let me hold you the whole night through, Briana. I remember a time when I hungered for just that and it was not possible. Now it is. Everything is possible for us now, my love."

Briana leaned against him as they walked with wondrous peace through the forest, toward the beckoning outdoor fires of their village. She hoped that now that peace had been won among Night Hawk's people, it would always be as it was at this moment—forever paradise.

31

Love? I will tell thee what it is to love!
It is to build with human thoughts a shrine,
Where Hope sits brooding like a beauteous dove;
Where Time seems young, and Life a thing divine!
—SWAIN

Like golden waterfalls, lemonade was pouring from
pitchers into many crystal goblets. Finger foods,
cakes, and cookies were heaped on huge platters on
the oak dining table of Briana's artists' boardinghouse.
At least a hundred candles burned from a crystal chan-
delier above the proffered delicacies.

Her cheeks rosy, her eyes shining in her moment of
triumph, Briana stood back and watched the flurry of
those who had participated these past three years in
her dream of seeing her boardinghouse and art school
become a success.

And to her delight, it had.

Aspiring artists of all ages and from all corners of
the world had come to the state of Minnesota, where
today they were chatting among themselves in Briana's mansion about this artists' "colony," as it had
come to be known. She had created a haven for those
who were scorned in the more public schools and col-
leges. Their interest in painting was called trivial;
those who cried loudest against artists called them too
lazy to make an honest living.

"The pride shows in your eyes," Night Hawk said
as he came to stand beside her. "And you have cause
to be proud. You wanted a dream, and now you have

it. I feel the excitement. I see it. It was right, Briana, what you have done for these people who share your passion of painting."

Several squealing children running past them drew Briana's and Night Hawk's attention. "Our children are enjoying the day as well," Briana said, watching their twins, Spotted Eagle and Precious Dawn, and Echohawk and Gentle Fawn's twins, Yellow Bird and Dancing Star, running past them, then out the opened French doors at the far end of the room to romp in the large yard.

On the morning of the birth of their twins, Night Hawk had shouted the news to the village and given away two horses. He then had explained to Briana that twins were special among his people—they were regarded as mysterious beings who had lived with the tribe at some past time and had come back again to live life over.

He had further explained that the spirits of little twins would hover above a wigwam, lifting up the entrance flap and peeking in. They were looking for a place in which to be reborn. They were visible only to certain people, and when the person who saw them shouted or called for someone else to look, the twins disappeared. These little twin spirits always appeared about the wigwam tied together with a rope.

Last, he had explained that twins had habits boys and girls born singly did not have. Though it was forbidden for brothers and sisters to speak freely with each other, twins were closest of companions—ties that did not exist between other brothers and sisters.

Since the twins' births, Briana had seen how proud Night Hawk was of them both. Often she had watched her husband lie on the ground on his back, and with his legs crossed, he tossed first one child, and then the other, up and down on his foot. It was the children's delight, and Night Hawk's, to play horse in that manner.

Briana had listened to him sing warrior songs to his children so that they would grow up loving the songs of his people. She had listened to him teaching his children of his ways, telling them there was no such thing as emptiness in the world, and that even in the sky there were no vacant places. Everywhere there was life, visible and invisible, and every object possessed something that would be good for the Chippewa to have—even to the very stones. This gave a great interest to life.

It was his firm belief that one was never alone.

"Does it disappoint you that as yet our son and daughter have not one serious bone in their body?" Night Hawk said, laughing softly as he placed his arm around Briana's waist. "They rarely stop long enough to take up a brush to paint on the canvases that you leave out for them in hopes that will stir them into painting."

"No, I'm not disappointed," Briana said, sighing deeply. "They have plenty of time to realize their dreams for the future. That they are strong and healthy, both our daughter and son, is enough for me right now."

Night Hawk leaned close to her ear. "Are you ready to fill the wigwam with more children?" he teased.

Briana rolled her eyes skyward. "Heaven forbid!" she said. The twins kept her hopping from morning till night!

"Briana, look in the next room," Night Hawk softly encouraged. "Look at Moonstar."

Arm in arm, husband and wife strolled into the adjoining room, where many paintings were on display. Briana felt warm through and through when she found

Moonstar studying the paintings closely, her mother and father following close behind her. In her right hand Moonstar held several paintbrushes, gifts from some of the teenage artists who were taken by her interest in their work, revealing her own deep passion for painting.

"When I look at her, I see myself as a four-year-old," Briana murmured. "She has already found her dream, Night Hawk. I will build on that dream for her, and see that she has all of the advantages that I had. Perhaps I shall even take her to Paris!"

Night Hawk swept her out of the room and led her up the grand spiral staircase to the second floor, where she kept a room for herself and her family on their visits to the boardinghouse. Night Hawk walked her to it.

After entering, he turned and locked the door, then swept Briana into his arms and gave her a heated kiss.

Together they moved to the bed and stretched out on it. Slowly, almost meditatively, they removed each other's clothes. Briana then moved her body sinuously against his as he thrust himself inside her.

"Let me hear no more talk about Paris," Night Hawk whispered huskily against her lips. "It is not a part of our world." He moved gently within her. "This is."

She felt no need to complain. This wild rapture that was always there waiting for her within her husband's arms was more grand, more wonderful, than a place called Paris.

Briana nestled close to Night Hawk, their bodies rocking and swaying together in their building passion, truly never wanting more than what her Chippewa chieftain husband's embraces promised.

Briana was fulfilled, and oh, so gloriously happy.

Night Hawk had told her often how content he was in his world that forever included her. The peace, the ideal which man sometimes reaches, was always there for him while he had her.

Dear Reader:

I hope you enjoyed reading *Savage Touch*. It was originally *Wild Rapture* and published as a part of my Signet Wild series. All nine books of the Wild series are being reprinted by Leisure and added to my Savage series.

I would love to hear from you and will respond to your letter with my personal newsletter, backlist of books, autographed bookmark, and fan club information. Please include a self-addressed stamped envelope with your letter.

Send to:

Cassie Edwards
6709 N. Country Club Road
Mattoon, IL 61938

Many of my readers are collecting the Savage series. I hope you will join the challenge to find each and every title and begin collecting them, too!

Thanks!

Cassie Edwards